**Also available from Suleena Bibra
and Carina Press**

Stay tuned for the next book in the series,
Sonia's story, coming soon!

TWO HOUSES

—

Suleena Bibra

carina
press

Recycling programs
for this product may
not exist in your area.

carina
press®

ISBN-13: 978-1-335-98487-6

Two Houses

For questions and comments about the quality of this book,
please contact us at CustomerService@Harlequin.com.

Carina Press
22 Adelaide St. West, 41st Floor
Toronto, Ontario M5H 4E3, Canada
www.CarinaPress.com

Printed in U.S.A.

To Mom and Dad.
But please don't read this.
If you do, maybe someone kidnapped
my manuscript and wrote all those spicy bits
and curse words and I have no idea
how they got there?

To Rod and Oliver. I love you.

TWO HOUSES

Two houses, both alike in dignity,
In fair New York City, where we lay our scene,
From ancient grudge break to new mutiny,
Where civil blood makes civil hands unclean.

Chapter One

Gavin Carlyle is here. Because of course he is.

Tension snaps my back ramrod straight and my fists clench at the sight of him, my body getting ready for a fight.

I've got too much to do today, and I can't deal with my mortal enemy since preschool. It takes a lot of energy to hate the same person for so long, but my natural pettiness really helps.

Character faults aside, I don't need him here now, when I'm trying to devote all my energy to wooing this client at a Four Seasons power lunch. Gavin looks busy (and annoyingly sexy in his suit) at his own table, so hopefully he'll stay away.

Or maybe a very specific, very small sinkhole will open up under his chair and swallow him into the earth, quickly closing before anyone else's day can be disturbed.

I subtly shift my chair and hunch down so I can't see Gavin, and force myself to relax. I turn my attention back to Harrison Richmond. The white man in front of me exudes power and money from his expensive suit to his flashy watch to the shoes on his feet. Shiny, well-made accessories and not a hair out of place to let us all know we couldn't measure up.

"How's your daughter doing?" I ask. We've been at lunch for about forty-five minutes now, and even though I just want to ask him about his art pieces, I've got at least another fifteen minutes of small talk to go. I'm timing it.

But subtly.

So far, I've gushed over his company's new ad campaign and his wife's latest charity ball. Which legitimately was fun. And for a good cause.

"She's doing great. She's doing a study abroad in England right now, and I don't know if she's going to come back home when it's over."

I laugh. "I did four years of college in England, and I threatened the same thing. I did come back though."

Harrison toasts me. "Good news then."

"The hardest part was definitely leaving the art and architecture behind. But I'm lucky that I get to work with some amazing pieces here." At last! A transition to the business we're here for.

Harrison has family money from some robber baron ancestor who was big in railroads, and he took that money and made even more investing in renewable energy. After he set his company up, he turned his attention to increasing his family's art collection, buying and selling some of the most beautiful pieces I've ever seen. Gossip says he's looking to sell a large chunk of his collection, so he can make room for pieces more to his current tastes.

I want to be the auctioneer who sells that collection.

"Loot is a fantastic house, but Kabir hasn't had much

experience outside Indian art and antiquities." He brings up Loot's biggest weakness.

But I know it is too, and I'm ready. "Dad doesn't have that experience," I say, throwing Dad under the bus. He's as cutthroat as I am; he'll understand. "But I studied Art History at Cambridge, and I've been working on more and more diverse sales since I started at Loot six years ago. I hope you consider us if you want to auction any of your pieces. I've been coveting your collection since I was a kid, and I've imagined a hundred different ways I could present your works."

And with a collection on this level, we can show the market that Loot is a serious contender in all types of art, not just Indian art.

My shoulders relax a little as business is finally introduced. It's a delicate balance between not wanting to scare the millionaires by discussing crass commercial concerns and needing to get that sale. But it's where I'm comfortable.

"Since you were a kid? You're making me feel old."

"Never. You get younger every year, Dorian Gray. But I have been around this business for a while."

Harrison smiles. "All right, how would you sell my work? On the off chance I want to sell."

The familiar electricity rushes through my veins, all my preparation focused on this moment.

"In this particular case, I would try to keep as much of the collection as possible together. I want to sell the Richmond experience. You come from an old family, and there are plenty of buyers who want to capture that connection. If possible, we could do the sale at your home in Long Island. And it would be minimum fuss for you; we'd rent a tent for the sale and make sure no one wandered around your estate."

I get out my iPad, bringing up a picture of some past house sales I've done to show him how much grandeur we can put in a tent, pointing out specific pieces he owns that could be the highlights.

"You've done your research on my art." He sounds impressed, and I mentally pat myself on the back. First step complete.

"It's never work to look at your pieces—"

"Priya Gupta," says a voice behind me, causing every muscle in my body to clench in anticipation for a hit. Not a physical one, but we can't be near each other without throwing verbal punches back and forth.

"Gavin Carlyle, what a *pleasant* surprise," I say through clenched teeth, turning to look at him so Harrison can't see the smile that's more of a snarl. I really want to add that it's a surprise that he was able to drag himself out of bed before noon, but I can't do that in front of the client. Because then *I'm* the unprofessional one.

"And, Harrison, good to see you again, so soon after the last time." He extends his hand to shake Harrison's.

Let the games begin. Because if they recently met, Gavin's heard the rumors and he's trying to get Harrison's collection for *his* family's auction house, Carlyle's.

We grew up as children of competing auction houses, and so I've never been entirely comfortable around Gavin. I fell into the pattern of competing with him academically like our parents were competing in the art market. Made more difficult around the eighth grade, when I realized how distractingly, and therefore distressingly, attractive he was.

The grudge pushed me to spend extra time studying so I got better grades than him, made me make that voodoo doll, and, of course, made me check Facebook religiously when we were in college to make sure he didn't win a Nobel Prize or start a company when I was studying out of the country.

Before Harrison can respond, something catches his eye behind me. Whatever it is must be important, because he gets up, throwing his napkin on the table. "If you'll both excuse me for a second, I see someone I have to talk to about a missing contract signature."

Harrison walks across the room, leaving us alone at the table.

"You're trying for Harrison's collection? Your auction house doesn't even do non-Indian art." Gavin glides into the seat across me. Vintage Gavin—feeling entitled to any space he sees.

"Loot might not, but I do. Which you already knew."

Because there's no way Gavin doesn't know what the competition is doing. He's too smart for that. And while it's true Loot has specialized in Indian art since Mom and Dad opened the first US office in New York, after I started working there, I slowly introduced non-Indian art to our sales. Because a bigger market means more profit.

Gavin shrugs. "I may have heard a rumor or two."

I contemplate throwing my roll at his head, but getting banned from the Four Seasons restaurant will stop all the business lunches I do here so I restrain myself.

I clasp my hands together in my lap under the table just in case they get any rogue ideas about that roll. "Everyone must be talking about it to reach you on a yacht in Croatia. Or was it driving along the southern coast of France last week?"

Gavin's a jetsetter auctioneer who takes a little too much pleasure in the jetsetting aspect. He flaunts that part of the job all over social media. Gavin with a tan, blond hair blowing in the breeze on a yacht in the Mediterranean. Gavin filling out a tux better than anyone has a right to at a charity event in Rome. Gavin going hiking in Peru, meeting adorable llamas and looking good with dirt artfully smudged on his stupid, perfect face.

And yes, I do follow his social media, through an anonymous account of course. I need to keep an eye out on the competition. And if that means also keeping an eye on those pecs, it's just a sacrifice I'll have to live with.

"Some of us know how to enjoy this job, and all the perks that come with it."

"Some of us just take joy in *doing* the job."

Gavin recoils in horror, hand to his heart to sell the emotion. "And let the supermodels sip champagne by themselves? I'm not a monster."

"Why don't you go back to those parched, lonely supermodels?" I snarl, immediately changing my face at the last word when I catch Harrison coming back to the table in my peripheral vision.

I turn a professional smile to Harrison, as Gavin scrambles up from his seat. "I hope your business was successful."

"It will be." Harrison smiles, confidence and satisfaction radiating from him.

"Good." I turn to Gavin. "Well, we can't keep you from your lunch." *So go away.* I motion back to his table, and the stunning, chicly dressed woman waiting for him.

Probably one of the supermodels from the yacht.

"Always a pleasure." Gavin extends his hand, and I don't know how to refuse without looking ungracious. I take it in a brief handshake, and immediately let it go like it's covered in bird poo.

I ignore how firm his handshake is, the same way I always do on the few occasions that we've made physical contact over the years. Because it's just not fair that someone this annoying feels this good.

Without my permission, my eyes track his trip back to his table. He saunters away, taking his time moving in the crowd that shifts to accommodate him.

Everything he does is effortless, from that walk, to his adorable I-just-got-out-of-bed tousled blond hair, to his bright blue eyes and lips that are always quirked in a smile. Of course he's happy; he's the heir apparent to his parents' successful auction house. With all obstacles bribed, bulldozed or bartered out of his way by his parents.

In contrast, everything I do takes effort. Every show I want at Loot, I have to work to get, since my dad wants to give them all to Ajay, my younger twin. Every collector I go after I have to convince we're a legitimate auction house, even though we've been in the States for over thirty years, since before I was born.

I'm tired.

But I love watching a show come together, listening to the prices get higher and higher for a piece that I know is going to cause a bidding frenzy. Or walking into one of our exhibits before the auction, seeing the museum-quality way we display the art.

It's worth it.

With Gavin safely back at his table, I turn my attention to Harrison. I wake up my iPad and show him some more of my highlights. I'm proud when I scroll through them. My entire life in artfully staged exhibitions and happy buyers. "And if you want, I can do a mock catalog for the sale we would do for you."

Usually I would have done the catalog before meeting with a potential seller, but I didn't want to be too presumptuous, since Harrison hasn't actually told anyone he wants to sell yet.

He flips through my iPad photos himself, nodding along here and there. The waitress comes with our tea, and I add milk and sugar to distract myself from the anxiety of watching him judge my life's work.

"This is great work, as always," Harrison says.

I smile at him, hoping this is a prelude to him giving us his collection. This sale wouldn't just make the market take us seriously; it would make Dad take me seriously.

Harrison leans in closer, lowering his voice. "And I am selling off a large part of the old collection. Make the catalog and I'll decide who to go with."

I'll take it! "When do you want the catalog by?" My mind is already spinning, going through different ways I can present the collection.

"A week, if that's not too little time? Now that I've decided to sell, I want to move quickly."

"No problem at all." *High-maintenance man, you just took away my sleep for the next week.* "If you wouldn't mind sending a list of the items you're thinking about including in the sale, I can make a theme, exhibition layout and catalog for them."

"I'll email you a list."

"Perfect. I look forward to showing you the finished product."

"I look forward to seeing it. But I still have meetings with other auction houses."

"Of course. I wouldn't have it any other way."

And then it'll be that much sweeter when I beat Gavin Carlyle.

Chapter Two

"Sonia! I neeeeeed you," I yell when I get into my office, toeing off my very high heels the second I get in the door, pausing for a second to dig my toes in the plush carpet.

I love my office. I don't remember exactly what the walls look like, since all the vertical space is now covered with bookshelves, all overflowing with catalogs from our sales and our competitors', and books on art history. With the occasional antique vase or small statue.

There's a comfortable leather couch to one side, that I might have used as a bed after one or two or a hundred and fifty late nights at the office.

But the desk is my favorite part of the office. It's two separate oak pieces made in 1870 from England, with elegant curved legs ending in lion paws. I put the two desks together to make a modern L-shaped desk out of the beautiful older pieces. On top of them is a slightly newer desktop computer, with a laptop next to it.

Just behind the desk, my windows look out over Central Park, a lake of green resting peacefully between metal and glass shores. It's one of the best views in Manhattan, and I love looking out over my city.

Plus, if I get the angle right, I can creep on my neighbors. And they live *very* dramatic lives.

Moment of admiring my own office over, it's time to get back to being a titan of industry. I collapse at my desk and wake up my computer. Fifty-seven new emails…in the last hour. And at lunch, no less. So much glamour, these auction houses.

"Sonia!" Sonia's my cousin, and also my right hand. And my best friend. She wears a lot of hats.

When I came back from college, Dad gave me a vanity title, executive vice president of special events, but he forgot to actually give me any special events to lead. I carved out a space, pilfering duties and creating shows where I could until I made the job into something I wanted to do. Sonia was one of the first people I stole for my fake department, and I couldn't imagine doing this with anyone other than her.

We grew up close, since she was born only a few months after Ajay and me. Her parents came with Mom and Dad when they moved to New York to set up this international office. But five years in, they left the States to run Loot headquarters back in India because of some emergency no one remembers now. They decided Sonia should stay in the States with us, because of the opportunities she could get here.

Sonia wasn't happy about her parents' decision, so one day I grabbed her pillow, Minnie Mouse suitcase full of books, and a change of shoes, and moved them into my room.

But Sonia was really hurt when her parents left, and at first she was in no mood for my attempts at bonding. After numerous s'mores in our pillow forts, she warmed up to me. Or she wanted the s'mores train to keep on coming to the station and faked liking me.

And then we became inseparable.

We all spent so much time together, family and friends called Sonia, Ajay and me the triplets. It didn't hurt that Sonia looks more like my twin than Ajay, from our long, thick wavy black hair to the shape of our noses, to our chocolate brown eyes.

"You rang, your annoyance?" Sonia walks into my office, notebook in hand. She closes the door behind her and jumps on my couch, said notebook at the ready. She's been in the office all morning, so her heels are long gone.

"Aren't you going to ask how my meeting went?" I ask her.

Sonia puts on a terrible English accent. "I would never presume to be so presumptuous as to *ask* for information. If my most noble liege wants me to know, she would tell me."

"You've been watching *The Tudors* again, haven't you?"

"It's not outside the realm of possibility, mi'lady."

I roll my eyes. Sonia has a flare for the dramatic, and I can't fire her because Mom told me so. And because I love her and she's as good at this as I am. But I'm not letting her know that, because then she'll demand a raise.

Because she's also as mercenary as me.

"My meeting went great. Harrison's letting us have a go at making a mock catalog, so I'm going to email you some of the work for the other shows we have going on." I start going through my emails and forwarding the more boring ones to her. The perks of being the boss.

"Are we sure Chacha's going to give the show to you and not Ajay?" She knows her uncle too well. But I don't have to like it, even when she tells me the truth.

"You know, I think there's a kindly old woman in the middle of Montana who has a few pieces she wants appraised. Maybe you need to go see them in person." I add the trip to her calendar.

"Noooo! I'm sorry. I love you and you're clearly the best for the job, and Chacha is blind to not see that."

"Thank you. But you're still going to Montana. I hear it's very pretty, from a nature standpoint."

"But the cell reception…"

The rest of Sonia's complaints are drowned out by my door bursting open. "Guess what I saw today?"

"Hello, Ajay. Nice to see you, Ajay. Please come in, Ajay." I keep going through my emails. There's only a .5 percent chance that this will be work related, so I feel comfortable only giving him one fourth of my attention and getting back to what I need to do.

Ajay lifts Sonia's legs to make space for himself on the couch, setting her legs back in his lap when he sits down. "Guess what I saw on Twitter, Sonia?"

"Ohhh…what?"

I ignore both of them. This working with family thing makes everyone far too comfortable with each other. It's gotten to the point where I have fantasies about coming to work and having tepid, impersonal conversations with coworkers, and not really knowing anything about them. Just complaints about having a case of the Mondays and how cold the office is.

"Guess who was at the same restaurant as Priya?" Ajay asks.

"Mindy Kaling?"

"No."

"Roxane Gay?"

"No."

"Andy Cohen?"

"God, can you just tell her before she goes through all of her role models?" I ask. But I'm curious who he's talking about. The Four Seasons is a popular spot for the art world, and business lunches, but I didn't see anyone who would get my cousin excited.

"Priya's *boyfrand* Gavin!"

"He is not my boyfriend!" If I didn't love the art world as much as I did, I would be out of this office so fast. No one should be forced to endure their twin while trying to work. Maybe I can join a paper company. From the multiple television shows about them, it seems like less aggravation than my life.

"What? Why didn't you tell me you ran into the competition?" Sonia perks up.

"Because it's not important. How do you know anyway?" I've gotten through ten emails while they cackle over my strife.

"He was there with his latest flame, a hot new contemporary artist I follow on the 'Gram," Ajay responds.

I don't know if Ajay means hot as in attractive or hot as in popular, but knowing Ajay it could be either or both. He keeps a close watch on contemporary artists because he wants to be the next big artist, despite the fact that Dad wants him to take over the company.

"And did he look delicious as always?" Sonia asks.

Yes. "He's not a cheesecake," I mumble, bad tempered at having to spend more of my day thinking about Gavin.

"That's not an answer."

Because I don't want to give one. Because despite all the healthy competition and less-healthy anger, I'm *really* attracted to Gavin Carlyle. He's got the strong jaw and broad shoulders of Adam in Michelangelo's *Birth of Adam* and somehow also has the confidence and power of God in that same scene.

And those facts make me really angry that the bottom half of me (strongly in favor of his face and body) can't get on track with the top half of me (strongly opposed to the rest of him, all smarmy charm and arrogance).

"Priya's not going to admit to something as pedestrian as lust. Even with someone as solid as Gavin," Ajay says.

I curl my lips in distaste. Ajay and Sonia were in the same classes with Gavin and me in school, but they never felt the same competition with him that I did. Probably because they aren't as consumed with the company as I am. Sonia is more supportive of my tiny war with the man, but I once saw a social media post of Gavin and Ajay getting drinks together.

I didn't talk to Ajay for two entire weeks after that.

Five more emails down while I try to ignore the ruckus in my workspace. "You two both have work to do." Out of spite, I forward them more emails to handle so I can focus on this mock catalog.

Sonia takes out her phone when it beeps, looking at the screen. She just got all the emails I'm sending. "Damn it, boss lady."

"Get to it, peon!"

She reluctantly heaves herself off the couch and sighs deeply, puppy-eyes pleading at me to help. I'd feel worse for her if I didn't sign her checks every two weeks and know how well she's getting paid.

Sonia leaves my office, and I get the email from Harrison, outlining the pieces he's considering selling. I open the list on my tablet and walk to my bookshelves, picking relevant books for research.

Ajay clears his throat behind me.

"You're still here?" I ask, the pile of books in my arms getting larger.

"Here, let me help you." He reaches for the books.

I pull them out of his reach. "I can get it."

Undeterred, he takes them from me. "Stop being so stubborn and accept help."

"Fine. What's going on?" I let go of the books and keep loading him up with more, getting use out of him if he's going to stay. I don't feel bad because every time Ajay wants to linger and chat, it's because he needs something.

"Dad wants me to work on this upcoming nineteenth-century furniture show, but with all my other work and with painting, I'm not going to have time to do it all…"

There it is. I shouldn't be surprised. Ajay is a great artist, and he doesn't want any part of the plans Dad has for him. He comes to work, sometimes does the bare minimum (and sometimes gives the bare minimum to me) and leaves as soon as he can make an excuse to paint more. He's good at the job itself, he just doesn't like putting in the time and effort to do the actual work.

And I let him dump the work on me because I'm supposed to protect him. I'm the older twin, the one who was always better at school, and then better at auctioneering. I'm the one who actually *wants* this auction house.

This is hard work, but it makes me happy. I want my baby brother to feel the same contentment I do. And if there's something I can do to help him with that, I want to do it.

But I just can't take his work on right now.

"I can't keep doing your work, especially not with part of the Richmond Collection up for grabs. I have a week to think about a theme, get this catalog written up for over a hundred pieces, and design an exhibit. This sale will be huge for us, if we get it. And then I have to do all my regular work for my ongoing shows." My heart starts racing when I verbalize all the tasks I have to complete.

"But a gallery is interested in showing my work. If I can put together an impressive catalog, this could be my break into painting."

"I get it." If he feels as strongly for painting as I do for selling paintings, then I can understand the need he feels to follow his passion. "But I can't keep doing both of our jobs. There aren't enough hours in the day."

"He should just give the title to you."

Ajay is an executive vice president, but he's also the managing director of North American sales. A position I would have loved on my way to president and CEO, Dad's position.

"Yeah." We work in silence as I resume putting books in his arms and then direct him over to my desk where I want them.

I sigh, mentally shifting tasks around to add the work to my schedule. "*Fine.* Tell your team I'll be giving out their assignments for the show, and they need to send their work to me for review."

Ajay puts my books on my desk and gives me a tight hug. "On it. I love you, didi." Ajay busts out the Hindi to call me sister, a sure sign he's still buttering me up even though I've already agreed.

"I love you too. But you didn't let me finish." Ajay looks nervous. Good. He deserves it for how busy I'll be in the next week. "I'll only do it if you talk to Dad about stepping back if you get in the gallery. Step back and spend more time painting and getting where you need to be as an artist. Then Dad can hire someone else, and Sonia and I won't have to take on a double load of work. And whatever happens with Dad, you know I'll support you."

Ajay rocks back on his heels, thinking out the deal for a solid minute. I'm about to tell him he can think this over in his own office and email me his decision, because I need to work, when he speaks. "Okay. Yeah. It's probably time."

Ajay looks more subdued than I've ever seen my twin, but he looks hopeful too, with a ghost of a smile on his face.

"Jao." I tell him to go, giving him a push toward my door. "I just sent you emails to handle, but you can send them back to me." This will all be mine one day anyway, better not let it fail before I get to the top.

Ajay waves at me as he leaves my office.

I look out of my window from the Fifty-Seventh Street skyscraper our offices are in. The view is as stunning as it was fifteen minutes ago, and this time I look down at the bustling city at my feet. So many people, with their own lives, their own problems, and their own dreams. All living together in one of the most vibrant cities in the world.

Refueled with energy from my home, I turn back to my computer, getting back to doing my job, as well as Ajay's.

"I don't have time for this," I tell Sonia, putting my cell-phone, wallet and tinted lip balm in a clutch.

"Chacha wants you there." Sonia puts her own clutch together in my condo bathroom.

"But I have so much work to do." I'm not dignified about the change in my plans. I had gotten home with my books, ready to spend the night with wine, my lap-top, and Netflix, making a mock-up catalog for Harrison.

Then Sonia barged in, telling me Dad wanted us to go to a Sotheby's auction of Old Master paintings to check out the competition.

It's hard to argue with a man who's not even there, so I give in, telling myself it is important to see what the competition is doing. And then I'll get some more work done when I get back.

I squeeze myself into a simple black sheath and shove my feet back in black stilettos, my uniform of choice.

We call a car and it takes us to the Sotheby's office. Sotheby's was one of the first auction houses to make their sales into the extravagant events they are now, and they're continuing the tradition tonight. Employees in suits and white gloves seamlessly manage the event while guests arrive and find their seats.

We settle in and I idly flip through the guide for the sale. They're going to make some serious money tonight. I squelch the flare of jealously that rises up.

Loot's been doing very well but there's still a long way to go until we're a household name and can have blockbuster show after blockbuster show.

Getting the Harrison Richmond collection will be a large step in that direction.

"Twice in one day. Are you stalking me?" The voice next to me jerks me from relaxed to whole body tense and prepared for battle in point two seconds flat.

Like it always does.

Shit, not again.

Chapter Three

Gavin drops his suit-clad form into the empty seat next to me. Like a giant male lion, powerful and graceful and lazy, all at the same time.

I still resent when he stole the first client I was wooing away from me. I had just graduated college and moved back to the States from England, when Dad gave me that meaningless title.

So I decided to put together my own show. Dad was focused on Indian art of all periods, and I wanted to expand that. I decided to put on a show that would sell Indian pieces, Western pieces inspired by Indian art, and some that mixed the two traditions. It was Loot's first time selling non-Indian pieces.

I just needed a painting of Queen Victoria at the Indian Pavilion of the Great Exhibition. The collector who owned it wanted to sell, and we had four meetings to discuss the show and me selling the piece.

Then Gavin showed up and persuaded the collector to sell with Carlyle's. He offered them a higher guarantee for selling the piece, and a smaller seller's commission. The piece wasn't even that valuable, so I know the little prat just did it to screw me and my show over.

I got him back the next time by putting a modest

dose of ex-lax in his food at an industry dinner. He was rushing to the bathroom so often that I took over talking to the collector he was sitting next to. By the end of the dinner, Gavin looked unstable because of all the tummy troubles, and the collector went with Loot.

That was on him for having such a weak stomach.

Back in the present, I try to avert my eyes to avoid how good he looks in his tailored suit. The slim lines emphasize his broad chest and slim waist, making me get what all those models in the south of France found so appealing about him.

When does he even have time to work out? We both have the same, sedentary job that takes up the entire day, leaving no time for things like going to the gym.

"I was sitting here first," I say. "So I think it would be hard for *me* to stalk *you*."

"What better way to throw someone off the scent than by getting to places before your prey? We all know you're smart." He smirks at me.

A compliment from a rival? No. Must not be distracted by him and his appealing smirk. "How would I even do that? Have psychic powers?"

"Or call my assistant and find out where I am at any given moment. That's how much you need to be near me."

I make gagging motions. "As if."

"'The lady doth protest too much, methinks.'"

"The twat doth dream too much, methinks." I'm fired up by the exchange and really getting into it, to the exclusion of everything around me.

"Um, hello," says a woman from the other side of Gavin.

I lean over to find the woman from lunch earlier.

Apparently, I'm not the only one he's seeing twice in one day.

"I'm Stella." The strawberry-blonde goddess extends her hand. She looks like the literal goddess from Sandro Botticelli's *The Birth of Venus*. I'm shocked she's not rising out of a shell, surrounded by a crowd of adoring wind god attendants.

And that is not jealously talking. Even though she looks thinner than Botticelli's Venus, and maybe with better skin.

"Hi. I'm Priya." I take her hand.

"Sonia." My cousin also shakes Stella's hand.

"They're from the competition, Loot," Gavin explains to Stella. Then to us, he says, "Stella's my latest contemporary artist. She agreed to sell exclusively with Carlyle's." His tone suggests that's not all they're doing together.

"Oh, Stella Martin? That Stella?" I look at her with renewed interest. She makes fascinating art about gender inequity by overlaying scenes from the past and the present.

"Yes, that's me." She holds her hand up adorably.

"I love your work! Every piece at your last show made me relate so hard with dating in New York."

"I'm glad it resonated."

"And she's exclusive with Carlyle's now," Gavin adds again.

"So you've said." That's a good get for them. Stella's work is just going to keep getting more and more popular. I wonder *how* committed she is to them…

The show starts, cutting off any further conversation. Despite me not wanting it to, my body is ridiculously aware of Gavin next to me. How his arm brushes mine when he shifts, how often he leans over to whisper into Stella's ear.

I don't remember a time I wasn't aware of him whenever we were in the same room together. It started out as intense irritation over being children of rival businesses, but at some point, around puberty, I noticed how good-looking he was. Which irritated me even more.

And then as adults, he had the nerve to be just as good as me at auctioneering, only he did it with an easy charm instead of my dogged stubbornness. Which irritated me the most.

Halfway through the show, Stella excuses herself to go to the bathroom, and my bladder acts up in solidarity, pushing me out of my seat to follow her.

"Oh shit, my dress is sagging at the straps," Stella says, looking at herself in the mirror after washing her hands.

"Oh, I've got a safety pin." I rummage through my purse, pushing aside my emergency supplies: tampon, ibuprofen, pen and, eureka! Safety pin.

"Here you go." I extend it to her with a smile.

"You're a lifesaver." Stella starts trying to reach her back strap, struggling with the task. "Actually, could I ask for some more help?"

"Of course." I take back the pin and stand behind the woman, gathering her strap and the back of her dress. "I'm obsessed with being prepared so it physically pains me to trim down to a clutch, but my cousin told me my Mary Poppins bag doesn't match this outfit. But if I *had* brought my purse, I could have given you thread and needles to fix the dress."

I step away from her to make sure both sides are even. "To be fair, I probably wouldn't be much help doing the actual sewing, but I could provide the raw materials for the job."

"Yes! I feel naked without my sketchbook and a set of oils tonight."

I laugh with her, and an idea forms. A cutthroat idea.

"You know, I actually looked at your work for one of my upcoming sales. Before I found out you were exclusive." I hold my hands up.

It piques her curiosity, as I hoped. "Oh? What kind of sale?"

"It's called *The Female Gaze*, and I want to center women artists and a woman's perspective that gets ignored in traditional art history canon. From antiquity to contemporary."

"That sounds really interesting, actually."

"Yeah. Don't get me wrong, who doesn't enjoy naked Venuses? But I thought it would be nice to see something different."

"That sounds amazing."

"Well, I don't want to step on any toes." *Lies.* I want to stomp on Gavin Carlyle's toes in wooden clogs, with Legos attached to the bottoms. "But if you want to be in the sale, Loot would love to have you. And we could help with any contract you may have signed with Carlyle's as well."

"Let me think about it."

I rummage around in the clutch again. "Here's my card. And whatever happens, if you want to meet for coffee and discuss the market or whatever, let me know."

Stella takes it and tucks it into her own clutch with a smile. "I'll do that."

We walk back to the seats, and I can barely control my giddiness. Not only because if this does work, I'd have another great piece for one of my shows, but also because it would make Gavin sad.

Even one of those is enough to make a happy day, but if both of them occur…it'll be like Christmas and my birthday and Thanksgiving all rolled into one.

The rest of the show makes a big night for Sotheby's. I love the Old Masters shows, but they're getting rarer as the supply gets bought up and more works find themselves in museums. Don't get me wrong, I love pieces going to museums; I just want to be the one to sell them to those museums.

After the show, with a sincerely warm goodbye to Stella and a much colder stiff nod to Gavin, we leave.

Sonia comes with me to my condo, orders some food and helps me get started on the Harrison catalog.

Well, she says she's helping, if helping is sitting on my couch, watching *Vanderpump Rules* and eating takeout while I make a spreadsheet of the paintings and try to find a good way to organize them.

At 1:00 a.m. I decide I really need to get to sleep or I'll be useless tomorrow. Sonia's long asleep, so I cover her with a blanket and turn the lights off.

Six more days to finish something that should take months.

Just another Monday at Loot.

I need a kettle in my office. That's apparent as I jerk awake for the fourth time at my computer. I've got research open on my laptop and iPad, and I've already got one description written for a painting on my desktop.

I've also already drunk three cups of coffee and one of tea, and it's only 11:00 a.m. I need another cup of something but I can't go to the kitchen to get it—Sonia will judge, since her office is right by the kitchen.

Usually her location helps me, because she passes on all the gossip she overhears in the break room, but it's a double-edged sword because she also keeps track of how many times I get snacks and caffeine. And then tattles to Mom about my caffeine and sugar intake, because family.

Hence the need for the personal kettle.

I'm building up the fortitude to refill my Starbucks London souvenir mug when Sonia bursts through my door.

"I tried, Priya," Sonia says, looking over her shoulder. The words are apologetic, but she looks a little amused.

"Tried what?"

Before she can answer, my slowly closing door is thrown open again. This time by one very arrogant, very irate looking Gavin Carlyle.

"You're stealing my girlfriend?" he growls at me.

Chapter Four

Gavin tosses a mini sketchbook and a set of travel paint on my desk. The side where I attached a note to the paint tin saying "For the next time an emergency comes up" faces me. It was the first thing I did this morning.

"It's fine, Sonia," I say. She looks like she wants to stay and watch the drama, but my eyes cut to the door meaningfully and she leaves.

"Did you snoop through her mail?" I begin. "I think that's a federal offense."

"I was with her when she got it."

Ewwww. I scrunch up my nose. He means coitusing her. I don't like the image of those two attractive people making the beast with two backs.

I decline to examine why I don't like that.

Maybe it's because now I can't stop imagining how Gavin has sex. It starts out as a parody, him announcing to his partner he's going to come using his fast-talking auctioneer voice: "I'm gonna come."

"Can I get five more seconds?"

"Yes, I have five more seconds."

"Can I get ten more seconds?"

"Excellent. Can I get another five?"

But then it gets a lot more intimate, fast, and I genuinely start imagining what he would look like naked, sweaty, and slowly kissing his way up my body while I mentally auctioneer with myself to hold out a little longer.

Ugh, I'm angry at how much I want him. How much I always want him.

"As lovely as Stella is, I'm not trying to steal your girlfriend." I lean back in my seat. He opens his mouth to contradict me, and I cut him off. "I am *going* to steal your *artist* though."

"It's the same thing," he says, anger still in his voice.

"I don't know how you do business over there at your establishment, but I can promise you, you don't have to sleep with all of your sellers."

"You've gone too far this time, Gupta." He paces in front of me.

"You've stolen enough sellers *and* buyers from me in the past. The Annunciation painting, then the Rembrandt, then the Striker Collection. It's the nature of the business." I shrug. Never mind that I reacted the same every time he stole one of my clients. Even worse really. Hence the voodoo doll.

He doesn't answer, pacing himself into quite the state.

I can't help twisting the knife a little more. "But, you know, if you were treating her right, she wouldn't be open to other auctioneers."

Gavin barks out an incredulous laugh before he can stop it. "Seriously, Riya?"

God I hate it when he calls me that. A nickname makes our relationship feel intimate, even though it's really about hoping the other person fails, spectacularly and publicly and often irrevocably, ruining their reputation so the other one can win bigger.

"Yup. I can make her happier than you can."

"Apparently, Mr. Steal Your Girl."

"It's Ms. Steal Your Girl, please."

He inclines his head. He looks calmer than when he walked in, and even takes a seat in one of the leather chairs in front of my desk.

It's kind of anticlimactic, really.

"Okay. I can acknowledge that was well played," he concedes.

I ruthlessly squelch the surge of pride that rises at the praise. I don't need praise from him. "Does she want to be in my sale then?"

"She told me this morning she wants to break the exclusivity clause in her sale contract, so yeah. She'll probably be calling you soon to let you know."

I try not to gloat, satisfying myself with a nod at the admission. And make a mental note I need to resend the sketchbook and paints. Have to keep my clients happy.

"How did you even… *When* did you even…"

"Bathroom," I answer simply. That should be all the answer he needs.

"What?"

Guess that's not all the answer he needs. Trust a man to not understand the level of camaraderie that occurs in a women's public restroom.

"It's all right, anyway," he says. "This way I won't feel bad when I get the Richmond Collection."

"Ha! Did you hit your head when you barged through my door?" I glance down at my computer quickly, minimizing the windows with work for Harrison. So everything.

"We'll see who's out of their mind when I'm on the rostrum, selling all of his pretty art."

I swallow. I've seen him lead auctions from the raised platform of the auction room, and his command of the room is impressive. All eyes are on him, and not just because he's in the front of the room, but because he's in turn charming, funny, and aggressive in leading the sale and driving the prices up.

I love the rush of the rostrum myself. All the work of setting up a sale, putting together the exhibition and the catalog, for that one moment. That one moment where the energy of the crowd depends on how excited I can get them. There's nothing better than hearing bid after bid, surpassing the reserve, a minimum price required before a piece can be sold. And if it surpasses our internal estimate, it's a very good day. The frenzy (and hopefully it's a frenzy and not just me talking to myself) culminates in a sale, the point of my job. Months of work for a few minutes of action per item.

"I'll make sure to save you a front row seat, when *I'm* on the rostrum, so you can see how it's done," I say sweetly.

"We'll see."

"We will." I expect him to leave after that. But he doesn't. "Did you want something else?" I ask, tone making it clear he better not want anything else.

"Do you want to know if I'm still with Stella?"

Yes. "No." Please let me sound convincing.

Gavin answers anyway. "I'm not. My fragile male ego couldn't handle the business rejection."

"Surprising no one," I mumble under my breath, ruthlessly squeezing down the quick burst of happiness the news brings.

Gavin ignores that but does get up. "Do you want to make this interesting?"

"Will it make you go away faster?"

"Probably."

"Then what do you want to make interesting? Nineteenth-century American cabinet trends? Hah." I laugh at my own joke. "Like you could. They're already a hoot."

Gavin ignores me, putting both hands on my desk and leaning over it. "If I get Harrison, you have to go out with me."

That makes me snap to attention. Possibly the only thing that fully got my attention since Harrison said he would consider Loot for his sale.

"Like a date?" I ask for clarification.

"With food. And adult beverages, if you want."

"I'm not fucking you over a bet."

Gavin stares at me, one perfect brow raised but his expression otherwise neutral. I shift in my chair, suppressing even more thoughts of an amorous Gavin, and disliking how easily he can get me to think about us and sex. Us having sex.

Then he saves me from the silence with a smile. "I wasn't asking you to, despite how quickly you went there. But it's telling you don't think you'll win."

"We both know there's no accounting for taste. I'm not going to bet my virtue on the whims of a rich collector. They buy and sell the same art constantly."

"Just dinner," Gavin confirms.

"Why? Are you going to mess with my food?" Like I already did to him.

Gavin crinkles his nose. "No."

"Are you going to steal my phone and smartwatch and abandon me in the woods?"

"Why are you like this?"

"Because of the time you set my ringtone to sex

moans and it went off in the middle of my own auction." Good thing I'm talented and made everyone laugh it off. It actually loosened everyone up and made them willing to spend more, in the end.

"And in retaliation you hired a woman to barge into my auction and accuse me of fathering her child."

"I *allegedly* hired that woman. It was never proven." There, this is where I'm more comfortable. Back in this rivalry. Not thinking about us having sex.

"Dinner. No sex." Gavin tries to bring the conversation back to the original point.

"Why though?"

"Because you're hot. Frighteningly intense. But hot." His face is serious. Not even his ever-present smirk is here now, a first that I've seen. But he doesn't look happy with the fact that he finds me hot.

I'm not happy about the unexpected turn either.

It's *Gavin*. In college I begrudgingly accepted that I found him attractive, when I realized I couldn't change how I saw him. But I never imagined that he would feel anything similar toward me. He was just dating a Renaissance goddess, who is as far away as she can be from me in the looks arena.

Finding out he does find me attractive is shocking me into silence. When the silence stretches out for longer than is comfortable, I clear my throat and try to get back to confident, take-no-prisoners Priya. By changing the subject. "What do I get if I win?"

There. My voice isn't as strong as I want it to be, but it's getting there.

"What do you want?"

"Five million dollars," I throw out, brain still not

functioning at 100 percent, since a large percentage of it is stuck on Gavin's new revelations.

"I'm not giving you five million dollars on a bet."

"Okay. Now who doesn't believe in himself?"

"What do you want *within reason*?"

"Chicken." I lean back in my chair, a bit more comfortable now that Gavin is looking annoyed. Better than his intensity when he was talking about finding me attractive. "I want...you...to..." I drag it out. Let him suffer some.

"Don't keep me in suspense, Gupta." He motions me to get on with it.

"I wasn't keeping you in suspense. I don't want anything from you, so this is kind of hard to think of." Maybe make him do an auction in his underwear? But then I might be a little affected by that image.

No, that would backfire too much on me.

"You've got me in the palm of your hand."

Fat chance of that being true, with how contrary Gavin can be. But an idea does come. "Oh, you have to potty train my dog!" I smile to myself.

"You have a dog?"

"No. Because I don't want it to pee on my carpets. So when I win, I'm going to get an English bulldog. And you're going to potty train them."

"That's seriously what you want? Unlike you, I'm fine with being naked at your beck and call."

Oh no. That echoes my first instinct a little too close for comfort. And how can he go from talking about a peeing dog to him naked and doing things to me? I fight the urge to tug at my collar.

"The point of this bet isn't to give you something you'd enjoy. And you would enjoy that." I give him a level look, faking the confidence that statement needs, and enjoy the flash of triumph that rises when he's the one affected this time, if the clearing of his throat is any indication.

"You better go prepare your apartment for my future leaky baby." I turn my attention back to my computer, so I don't have to think about Gavin Carlyle asking me out. I do a quick search for bulldog puppies and keep the image result page open next to my Word document. For inspiration. And distraction.

The picture of the future Baby Gupta is set up, but Gavin's still here. "You should go. You'll need the extra time to prepare."

Gavin rolls his eyes and leaves without saying anything else. I let myself enjoy the sight of him walking out of the door. Why are his pants so tight in the butt area? It's a hazard for my concentration and I don't like it, because I like it too much.

Seeing the man three times in twenty-four hours is clearly messing with my brain. And him telling me he thinks I'm attractive and asking me out isn't helping the situation at all. It takes me an entire three minutes to get focused on work again after Gavin leaves the room, which is unacceptable.

The next time I see him, I resolve to throw myself in the closest landscaping feature or under the nearest desk to avoid having to interact with the man.

When all the words on my computer start blurring together, it might be time to give it all up and live as a squatter in an empty mansion in Long Island.

But the amount of work it would take to move all my shit makes me pause. However, I can put my head down *just for a second* to rest my eyes.

Then that second grows to a few minutes, and I start imagining how I would decorate a Gilded Age Mansion on Fifth Avenue, if I could have gotten one before most were demolished. I liberally steal pieces from Loot, Carlyle's, and all the museums I've been to, a wistful smile on my face.

When I'm filling the second library, Sonia barges into my office. "You won't *believe* the gossip I just heard."

"No! The red damask wallpaper will clash with the pink Louis XV chairs." I jerk upright.

Sonia reels back. "What happens in your brain?"

I'm still groggy from the nap I was torn from, so I don't dignify that with a response. "What did you want to tell me?"

Sonia leans over without missing a beat and wipes the corner of my mouth with a tissue she pilfered from my desk. "Carlyle's is trying to do a female artists throughout the ages kind of thing, before yours comes out."

"What?" My voice rises two octaves in disbelief. "Female artists? Throughout the ages? That's my thing. I'm doing it." I stole Stella for it.

"Yes. But so are they, apparently."

"What pieces do they have?" I run through the list of the items I already have, the ones I'm sure I'm getting, and the pieces I'm reaching for.

I've been ignoring the show a little for Harrison's last-minute project, but I frantically find and scan through the spreadsheet now.

"I don't know. How would I know until I see a catalog?" Sonia comes to my side of the desk and looks over my shoulder.

"I need to see what items they have."

"How are you planning on doing that? They're locked up in a storage room, hidden away from the prying eyes of the enemies." She gives me a meaningful look, in case I was wondering who those rivals were.

Then there's only one way to see them. "Well. If the mountain won't come to me, I'll go to the mountain."

"What does that— Oh no! Priya, no." She looks horrified. Which is a tad overdramatic, since it's not like I want to steal firemen's pensions or whatever CEOs are doing now.

It is nice that my right hand knows what I want to do without me having to incriminate myself. Just a little light entering, and hopefully no breaking.

A little sneaking. Right into the Carlyle's storeroom.

"But what's the worst that could happen?" I ask. "Really?"

"Jail. Death by falling out of a tall window if surprised. Death by falling down some stairs when fleeing. Death by severe embarrassment when people find us." She counts off all the possibilities on her fingers as she lists them.

"That's why we gotta be really sneaky." I lower my voice as an example of the primo sneaking she can expect on this caper.

"No," she firmly says.

I do a pouty face, quivering my bottom lip for maximum begging. We have a staring contest for another thirty seconds.

She relents first, because she knows my deep well of stubbornness can't be defeated. "Okay. Ground rules. I'm going to be lookout, in public spaces only. We'll get some earpieces and I'll order something shaken not stirred and keep an eye out on whatever door you tell me to. I won't be doing any actual trespassing."

I think about the compromise. "And getaway driver? And diversion if needed?"

"Unless the police come and it all gets too hot. Then the only person I'm driving is myself. As far away from you and as fast as I can. And you have to wear matching jammies with me for Christmas and make Ajay do it too."

Christmas-obsessed cousin. But I nod. "I accept these terms. Want to come over later and seal the deal by eating all my pizza and watching all my Netflix?"

"Is this your sad attempt to get me to hang out?"

"You can hang out while I work on this catalog." I hold up my iPad.

"You need more friends."

Friends? How does one get those? All the people I knew in high school are spread across the US, my friends from college are all in England, and I haven't had time to meet new people since I started working seventy-hour weeks. Meeting new people sounds exhausting.

Eh, I'll just keep making my family hang out with me.

"Do you want to come over at like six, or seven?"

"At six. Do I need to order the pizza?"

"Yes, please. Love you. Thanks, byyyyyyyyye."

Sonia leaves my office without saying anything, and I assume that means she's ordering the pizza, because otherwise we're having ketchup, tea and whisky for dinner. Maybe a microwave dinner. Whatever I can find in my kitchen.

My computer dings, the calendar letting me know I have a reminder.

Weekly meeting with the king.

Damn it, it's that time already?

Chapter Five

I get a notebook and pen, and walk out of my office. Then I realize I probably need my phone, so I rush back in to get that. Then when I'm outside again I realize I could use my tablet, so I rush back in. But what if I get thirsty? That'd be terrible. I come back inside and get my water bottle.

Then I run out of things to get and have to acknowledge that I just don't want to go to the meeting.

Dad makes me and Ajay come in every week to sit down and go over what's been happening, and what's coming up. His meeting of the "inner circle," like we're an ancient secret society for preppy college boys on an Ivy League campus.

I don't know why I'm there, because Dad spends all his time talking about Ajay's projects. But it's better to be in the loop than wonder what they're doing here, so I keep going. I try to get Sonia to come, but she says she doesn't want to deal with the bureaucratic crap, the same reason she gives for her continual refusal to be promoted to getting her own department.

I get in the elevator to go up one floor, not necessarily trusting myself to go all the way if I had to walk there. Plus heels.

A predictably short elevator ride later, the door opens to the penthouse of our office building. I have to stop my hand from pushing the button for the ground floor and taking a nice walk through Central Park. Or maybe the Met. That could be research for the catalog, legitimately.

An employee heads for the elevator I've taken over, so I force myself to do the adult thing and leave the space.

The first thing I hear when I walk into Dad's office is laughter. Dad and Ajay are having a great time, apparently. Against my will, I'm ten again, getting dressed up to go to the office with Dad only to have Mom tell me that he already left with Ajay.

But that's supposed to be over now. I'm here. I've got a damn seat at the table. So why do I still feel like I'm still on the outside?

"Did you start the meeting without me?" I saunter to the table, projecting confidence until I actually feel it. I set my iPad up, opening my notes in an effort to avoid eye contact, just in case the insecurity is visible there.

"Just talking, beta."

I hate it when Dad calls me child. I'm not a child; I'm a grown ass professional woman, at my place of work. Maybe he needs to be reminded of that. "Okay. Well, I'm working on Harrison Richmond to sell his pieces in a house sale, and I'm getting more and more pieces for my *Female Gaze* show." I look up expectantly, waiting for the hit.

And he doesn't disappoint.

"Harrison Richmond has a big Western art collection. It's not what we do." Dad gentles his voice, as if it was tone that I would object to and not the fact he wants to stop me from building my empire.

"It would be a great opportunity for Loot to expand," I say. I refrain from telling him my *Female Gaze* show is also a mix of cultures, with a lot of Western art represented.

"It's not what we do. We made a strong name for ourselves here specializing in Indian art. Why change that?"

"Because we could make a name for ourselves. Bigger clients, bigger sales. Bigger profit." I recite the lines I've said to him countless times before.

"Bigger failure when we can't pull it off. And bigger damage to the business we do when people find out about the failure."

"But we can pull it off." I have been pulling it off, on a smaller scale.

"I've let you have a lot of freedom in your sales, but we can't put that many resources into a collection we aren't ready for, damaging our reputation in the process."

"Just let me do this and you'll see that Loot can do something other than Indian art, and we can do it well. And you can see the increased profits that come with it."

Dad sighs and looks through something on his own tablet. Just when I think he's chosen to not respond to me, he speaks. "Okay. You want this? You can try it. But if you don't get this in the next two weeks, we move on. And you move on completely from this idea and focus on our staples. I don't want to hear about it again."

"I'll take it," I say immediately. I'll take two weeks of Dad off my back and hope and pray that Harrison makes his mind up before then.

This has to work. Because while I love the Indian art I grew up around, I don't want to be limited to it until Dad retires. There's a whole wide world of art out there.

"Good." That settled, he turns to the golden child. "How is the nineteenth-century furniture show going?"

I'm curious to see how Ajay's going to answer that. Since all his people are emailing me about questions and progress, I'd *love* to see what he knows about it.

"It's all on track." Ajay lies awkwardly.

How can Dad not realize how much Ajay hates the business side of this? Because he lies *so* badly. Maybe Dad wants Ajay to be the heir so badly he ignores it, or he has a giant blind spot where Ajay is concerned.

If I didn't love Ajay so much, I would be mad at him for the favoritism he gets. But the little snot obviously isn't happy having that much of Dad's attention, which just means I feel bad for both of us.

"Have all the pieces come in?" Dad asks.

"Yee…" Ajay trails off when he sees me lightly shaking my head. "No."

"What's holding the pieces up?" Dad scans his phone while we're talking. It's scary and impressive how well the man can multitask. Even if I might have picked up some of that bad habit, I'm still not as bad as him.

Ajay looks at me, eyes beseeching me for help. I should let him suffer, because I've cc'd him on all the emails to and from his team, so he should already know this information.

I meaningfully look down at my iPad and do a quick search to find the email we need.

"Well, the issue is…" Ajay drags his words out while he looks at his own screen.

I forward him the email, *again*, and his eyes light up in relief.

"The seller made it a condition that he wanted to keep the piece as long as he could." Ajay reads off the email. "They had to sell because of some debts, but they're reliable, so we let them hold on to it till the last minute as a favor," he finishes, head up in pride.

I mean, I felt pride when I negotiated the deal itself, but okay, he can feel pride for reading an email.

We both breathe a sigh of relief when Dad moves on without questioning it.

I text Ajay: You're. Telling. Dad. Soon.

Ajay looks up at me and nods, and texts back. I love you.

The meeting ends without Dad giving Ajay any of my work, so it's basically an unqualified success.

Ajay walks with me to the elevator. "We're getting so good at those."

"Too bad we won't need that skill when you come clean about wanting to spend more time painting."

Ajay sighs deeply. "I know, I will. But, Priya, you have to see this amazing piece, it's about—"

Before he can launch into an hour-long speech on the meaning behind his art, I cut him off. I love him, but I have work to do. And his work to do, actually. "Don't tell me until I see it. I want to take it all in at once." I try to soften the blow.

"Sure, sis. Bye."

I get out of the elevator and take a few steps down the hall before I realize he's not with me. But his office is on the same level as mine. When I turn to give him a questioning look, he looks sheepish.

"I'm just going to take a long lunch and get some painting done," he says in a rush.

The elevator doors close in front of me before I can give him a lecture on how irresponsible he's being.

He's heard the speech before, so I don't beat myself up for not making sure he gets it one more time.

Plus, I have a caper to plan.

"Ta-da!" I hold up two pairs of coveralls, showing Sonia what I came up with after lunch today.

"Why am I looking at a Rosie the Riveter costume? It's not October."

"We're using it tonight, to find out what Carlyle's is up to." I shake the coveralls.

"And how exactly will this Halloween costume do that?" She sounds doubtful of my plan, which is frankly hurtful.

"Have some imagination. We're going to dress up as building maintenance and infiltrate the Carlyle's storage room."

She still looks doubtful. "I'm lookout. So I'll be the opposite of where you'll be. Somewhere safe. Dressed not in that."

"Fine, wimp. You can pretend to be a guest at the exhibition tonight and I'll sneak in to the storeroom and check out what they're working with." I have been hoping to get her to join me in the storeroom, but if this is the best I can get, I'll take it.

"Why do I agree to your shenanigans?" she asks me.

"Because we pay so well?" I ask her, already stepping into my disguise for the night. "I also got you some super sweet spy tech, to go along with the martini you're going to order." I finish zipping up the adult onesie.

This is exceptionally comfortable. I think I want to wear it forever. And it has pockets! If I have to change careers and be a mechanic or a military pilot to wear this more, I'll do it.

I pull an earpiece out of my purse and hold it out to her. "So you can have me in your brain." I hold it out to her.

"That's terrifying." But she takes it. "Where did you get this, again?"

"Well, when you have the best assistant in the world, you can get things done." Our department assistant Roshni had looked at me in fear, but she'd done it. Without asking any questions. She's getting an excellent annual review.

We get ready with a minimum of sass from Sonia. As a finishing touch, I put my hair up in a bun and cover it with a hat. There, I just need to look down a lot so people can't get a good look at my face.

Sonia walks the short distance to Carlyle's with me, passing our office on the way. I live near the office, which I acknowledge is sad, but also very convenient when I want to sleep in for a few extra minutes in the morning. And it's cut down on me sleeping on my office couch.

In fact, my apartment, Loot and Carlyle's are all on the same street, and it doesn't escape my notice that as bitter enemies, we could probably get a trebuchet and some archers and conduct medieval sieges against each other. Or whatever normal, modern people do to their competition.

Sonia leaves me a block away from Carlyle's, so the rich auction-goer and the maintenance worker aren't seen coming in together, raising questions.

I walk around the back and notice a service entrance to the side of the tall New York skyscraper. Before I go in, I remind myself that I regularly face down the scariest man in the auction world: my dad. And if I can do that, I can handle anyone and anything.

Getting in turns out to be easier than I thought it would be. I spent all afternoon making up plausible reasons to be in behind-the-scene spaces of Carlyle's, but no one asks me why I'm there, mostly ignoring my presence.

Thanks, uniform.

After some wandering, I admit that Carlyle's might be a bit bigger than Loot. But the one person I asked was helpful since I look the part, and soon I'm in front of the storeroom for the women artists show.

With no word of warning from Sonia, I go into the room.

I open the door and close it quietly behind me, waiting a few seconds to listen for any incoming footsteps. Hearing nothing, I turn into the room and get my phone out, ready to document the competition. I turn on the flashlight, pointing it to the ground to give me a little light without turning on the lights and getting any extra attention.

Shit. There are some really nice pieces here. This can't be a coincidence…they probably heard from sellers I'm contacting about the show, and decided they're doing their own. And it *might* be better than mine. Until I get more pieces, at least.

To actually copy my show is so low. A very Carlyle move.

"I don't know how much you thought this through,

but I can't see where you are for the lookout part of my job," Sonia says into my ear.

I jump and clutch my wildly beating heart. I'd forgotten I'd put the earpiece in, and that Sonia would be talking to me.

I answer after a pause when I get my breathing under control. "I figured. I need you to focus more on being a distraction if I need it, but so far everything's okay."

I move from piece to piece, taking pictures as I go. Damn it, they have an Artemisia Gentileschi. And a good one too, one of her depictions of Judith and her maidservant after they cut off Holofernes's head.

I'm so disappointed by the excellent collection they have, I don't hear the sound of footsteps outside the door or any other indication that I'm going to be found out, until I hear the door itself open. My heart ratchets up again at the thought of being caught, so all I can hear is the pounding of my own heartbeat in my ears.

Shit balls tits! I run, as quietly and quickly as I can, to hide behind an antique couch.

I don't want to go to jail. There are no sales for me to run in jail. Or any Shake Shack.

"Priya?" a man asks from the door.

Chapter Six

"Gavin. Heeeey." I pop up from the couch that I had barely hidden behind.

"Do you need me?" a panicked Sonia screams in my ear.

"No," I whisper, and then cough to try to cover it up. It's Gavin; I can handle him.

"What are you doing here?" He has a notebook in his hands, and he looks back and forth from the door to me.

"What? Isn't this the bathroom?"

Gavin takes in my outfit and the phone in my hand, still open to the camera app, the flashlight on. I rush to turn everything off, but not before he sees the damning evidence.

"You came to the sale in a maintenance uniform? That's what you're going with?" He crosses his arms across his massive chest, turning me on and expressing his disbelief all at the same time.

"Hmm-huh." I smile, trying a different route with the man. Charm.

"Did you just break into Carlyle's to be closer to me?" Gavin smiles back, comfortable now that he's over his initial confusion.

"No." I throw out instantly, then think better of it. I am trespassing. "I mean, yes?"

"Why are you here?" he asks again, sitting on one of the antique chairs, languidly crossing one ankle over his knee and leaning back.

I refrain from pointing out that he shouldn't sit on the antique furniture, since I'm the criminal in this situation. Allegedly.

"Priya, what are you doing here?"

We're still on that? "I heard there was a nefarious plot to steal your items, and I didn't think you would believe me, so I came to save your art."

He doesn't respond, but quirks his eyebrows up, silently offering me another chance.

"Would you believe I'm sleepwalking?"

The eyebrow quirks higher.

"Right. Would you believe I'm drunk and also high on all the drugs, and I'm looking for a children's bounce house?"

The eyebrows draw together for that one. "Do you even know how to do *any* of the drugs?"

"I think people can smoke them? And maybe snort them? Oh, don't some come in like rock candy form and you can eat it?"

"You've never done any drugs before," he says with certainty.

"Well, thank you. I guess."

"So what are you doing here?" he asks for the fourth time.

I sigh, knowing the jig is up but not wanting to go down with grace. "I heard you guys were doing a sale with women artists and I wanted to see how it would compare to the one I'm doing."

"Now that does seem plausible."

"Are you going to call the police on me?"

"No."

But if he's not going to call the police on me, what *is* he going to do? He hasn't moved from his relaxed position on the chair, like he's watching TV and not watching the law be broken.

"Then I should get going…" I walk to the door backward and slowly, keeping my eyes on him like he's a feral cat I'm afraid to turn my back on.

"You can go if you want. Or you can stay and look at some art with me."

I stop, certain this is a trap but not able to figure out how.

"Without your phone." He sends a meaningful look at my spy equipment.

"That's excessively fair." I put the phone in the pocket of my coveralls and look at him warily.

"So, why this show?" he asks, getting up off the damask chair.

"Why this show what?"

"You've never tried to break into our offices and see the art before. What's special about this show?"

"I heard you guys were ripping me off on an upcoming show, and I wanted to see if the rumors were true."

He turns away from the art and back to me. "You think we're copying you? Doing a show on women artists? You know there're only so many options. More than two, but still, it's limiting."

"Obviously I know it's not the most original topic, but the timing is suspicious, and it's meant to steal my thunder." Although when he puts it like that, it does sound ridiculous.

"Right, Riya, I'm going to vote for this being a co-incidence," he says gently.

Well, I probably would too. Now. It felt much different this morning, still fresh from an argument with Gavin and a meeting with Dad.

"You do have nice pieces." I concede the point to change the subject. If the words are pushed out through my clenched teeth, it's because I'm still used to seeing him as an adversary.

"That's because we're a top-rate auction house." After a pause he continues, in a tone as begrudging as mine. "I'm sure you've got nice pieces too, since you guys are almost as good as we are."

Huh. That's two compliments to each other in a row. Are we becoming tolerant of each other?

"I mean, you guys don't usually have as many pieces, but I'm sure the few pieces you get will be very nice."

And there we go, back to sniping at each other, any camaraderie ruined. This I can handle; this I prefer. "We would rather hold out for quality pieces, so our clients know they're getting the best stuff."

"I think our clients, like Harrison Richardson, think our pieces are pretty good."

"He's not your client yet." A piece catches my eye. "What do you guys have over here?" I walk to it, brushing past Gavin on my way to the treasure. He moves out of the way, but not before I feel his arm against mine. Even through the layers of clothing separating us, I can feel the strength in his arm, like brushing against a mountain of stone.

It feels intriguing. But I'm glad the touch is only momentary, because even the quickest touch scrambles my brain a little.

I clear my throat. "Is this a Vigée Le Brun?"

"Great eye."

"It's Lady Hamilton," I say, impressed and jealous. "The woman who worked her way out of poverty and into the arms of Admiral Nelson. Resourceful lady, making opportunities for herself in a place there weren't many. And then painted by a woman when not many could become artists."

I try to leech as much of Vigée Le Brun and Lady Hamilton's combined lady badassery as I can, hoping it'll help dealing with Dad and the business.

"Who's doing this show anyway?" I ask without looking at Gavin.

"I am."

"*You're* doing a women artists show?" I scoff. "Figures."

"It's a good financial decision. I can draw people to the show."

I give him a blank look. He's not wrong; he's a big name. But a woman not doing it—kind of the point I'm trying to make. Too many men in all parts of this industry; not enough women to do their own damn shows.

I keep walking slowly around the room and move on to the next few pieces. They've got paintings from the Baroque period and the nineteenth century. I need to step up my game.

"How does your dad feel about the Richmond Collection?" Gavin asks.

A sad smile flits across my face. My father's reputation is pretty well known in the art world: he's reluctant to change, even though he was the one who wanted to expand the auction house to the Western market. I think he was hoping he could just start a copy of Loot in New

York and that would be the end of it, but we can be so much bigger if we expand.

Gavin is surprisingly gentle when he asks. Like we're friends and he cares about what's going on in my life. It's weird and I'm shocked, which might be why I respond with uncharacteristic honesty.

"He doesn't understand." I shrug. "If I had my way, we would have done a show like this years ago. But I've only recently been able to convince him."

Maybe it's the ambiance of the room that lowered my defenses. Gavin left the door open when he walked in, so the room is bathed in soft light from the hall. We're surrounded by beautiful paintings, sculpture and furniture. This is a general storeroom, not just for the women artists show, and there's art everywhere: on the walls, piled up, and crammed in next to each other. It's seductive.

For an auctioneer, at any rate.

"I get it. My dad's been open about letting me pursue what I want, but if a sale doesn't meet his inflated standards, he doesn't hold back in telling me how much I fall short. With no sugarcoating."

"What happens when he criticizes your show?" I'm genuinely interested in this newly uncovered facet of Gavin.

"I give in, usually." Gavin looks unusually serious when he gives me the answer. "He's the one who's been in the industry forever and has the best advice that everyone should listen to...just ask him."

I'm startled enough at the similarities of our dads to distract me from the beautiful art in front of me. Gavin is always so charming and effortless in person;

I would have never thought that he was getting shit from his father too.

I'm not entirely sure I know how to react to that, so I make a sound of agreement and hope that'll be enough.

We finish a big circle around the room and then we're back to the door.

"Thanks for being cool about the alleged trespassing," I mumble, not liking having to thank the scourge of my professional and personal life but acknowledging that he could have made this a lot worse for me.

"Oh, Priya." At the pitying note in his voice, my head snaps up. "Did you think I was going to let you off that easy?"

Chapter Seven

"What do you want?" Not that I expected the kind sharing to last. Not that I *wanted* the kind sharing to last. "And before you say anything, I will not do anything illegal or immoral."

"That does strike a few options off of my list," he says, eyes twinkling now that he has the upper hand.

I reach into my pocket. "I've got...three dollars and a half-used fifty-dollar lipstick."

"Fifty dollars for lipstick?" He sounds shocked. He may be rich, but he clearly doesn't pay attention to what his girlfriends spend on beauty products.

"Beauty is expensive. Now out with it. What do you want?"

"Hold on, I'm savoring the moment."

"Savor it faster, I have work to do." I clasp my hands behind my back, and make sure my phone is positioned camera out.

"Can you go back to looking that adorable mix of scared and pleading? It was doing wonders for me."

I glare at him and try to take subtle pictures of the room from behind my back. Just because he's a jerk and deserves the treachery.

After I think I have a few shots I cross my arms

across my front, catching a split-second look at my phone and confirming I do have some photos of their art. They're probably blurry but I have something.

Since Gavin has the attention span of a Labrador in a peanut butter store, he breaks first. "I need to go to a charity banquet for a client who wants to sell a classic car collection. And I need a date."

I stop trying to take pictures, corporate espionage forgotten. "Why do you keep blackmailing me to go out with you?" I ask, flustered despite myself at his persistence. "It's desperate."

"Because it'll make you unhappy. And that would be enjoyable."

"But then I'll just make you unhappy back. I'm good at it."

He already looks uncomfortable, proving to both of us that I can make the man squirm.

"Plus, I'll just steal your clients and put on a better show. We know I'm good at that too."

"Loot doesn't sell cars."

I tilt my chin in challenge. "Yet."

"You would hate having to learn about cars."

Ugh, it would be the worst. Something something crankshaft? Dipsticks? Lube? If only those car words were half as interesting as they sounded.

Not that I need to think any of those words around Gavin. It'll just make me think about sex with Gavin, and I don't want that.

"I might not enjoy the effort of learning about cars, but I would like the mental image of you crying yourself to sleep every night because I won."

"All right. You can do your best to steal the client. But you have to come with me to this dinner. I hate

going to those things alone and you stole my girlfriend."
He not so subtly reminds me of my most recent victory,
mistakenly thinking that would guilt me into anything.

"That's bullshit. You could get anyone to come with
you if you just needed someone on your arm. Why do
you want *me* to go with you?"

"Maybe I want to win one and rub it into your face."
But he sounds too glib.

"Nope. I can read you better than that." The hazards
of knowing someone since they were a toddler—and
competing with them since that long. For the record, I
had the better finger paintings. "Tell me why, for real,
and I'll go."

What the hell? Banquets usually mean good food
and lots of drinks.

A struggle passes over his face, his mouth opening
and closing multiple times in succession. Then it clears.

"Because I'm sick of the best part of my day being
sparring with you. Sick of being at work and thinking
about how you'd react to something I did, if you'd be
annoyed, or impressed. When you stole my girlfriend,
my first thought was admiration. Not anger. In fact,
I was mad that I wasn't mad, which is why I stormed
into your office. That's when I realized how much time
I actually spend thinking about you in a day. And we
haven't even slept together."

I can't see my own face, but I'd put money down
that I'm doing a good impression of a fish: eyes wide
and mouth gaping.

But he's not done. "So let's go out. I've probably
built it up because we're always competing and there's
all this energy." He moves his hands between us. "But

then we'll go out and it'll be shit and I can get back to normal."

I try to bring up arguments for why he's 100 percent wrong, but they don't come. I do think about the bastard all the time. Or as much as I think about anyone. I thought I just wanted to prove to my dad I could do this job, but every time I accomplish something, my first thought is rubbing it in *both* of their faces.

Oh god.

I feel my stomach drop like I made a terrible choice and got on a roller coaster. Because I do want him to see my victories. I think his opinion matters to me. I think it's mattered for a while.

But I can't really like him. Because on the list of things that I've known since elementary school is: I'm going to run Loot, I'm going to have a puppy at some point, and I hate Gavin Carlyle.

He makes my blood boil…in anger, nothing else.

But if he's showing weakness, I need to get my stomach in order and take advantage. The lion doesn't call an Uber to take the wounded gazelle to the hospital— she takes him down.

"I don't promise I won't steal all your clients, but if you can accept that, then I suppose I'll go." I concede with all the grace of the queen allowing Parliament to make laws. Graciously giving permission even though I don't really have a choice.

Gavin shakes his head. "You're something, Riya."

"You can pick me up at six."

"It starts at five thirty."

"Like I said, you can pick me up at five from the office."

I gather what little dignity I have after being caught

red-handed in subterfuge and flee. I don't slow down until I burst out of the building to the sweet, cool air of freedom. I turn the corner into an alley and lean against the wall to catch my breath, hand on my heart. Trying to figure out what just happened is worse than trying to figure out which purse to use when I go out.

I hear the sound of footsteps around the corner and my body tenses for flight or fight. While I'm still stuck on freeze, Sonia rounds the corner.

"Priya and Gavin, sitting in a tree," she starts to sing.

"Shut up." I shoot out my hand to grab her arm and pull her in the alley with me. "Why didn't you help me?"

"You were fine. Your virtue might have been at risk, but I know you haven't had that since your first year at Cambridge."

"Okay. Super harsh."

"I was at the ready when he barged in on you. I was preparing my best swoon. I even started commenting on how hot it was and fanning myself with my clutch to make it believable. But then he started showing you art and asking you out, so I figured you were in good hands."

Strong, attractive hands. Hands I've seen show the utmost care in handling some of the most beautiful works of art in history. The contrast of his strong hands and the delicate materials never fails to make my nether regions perk up and take notice.

Focus. I mentally snap my own fingers in front of my face. Where were we?

Right, yelling at our disloyal family.

"Now he's holding me hostage at some charity event."

"No one believes you're a hostage. You'll probably

get a new client out of it, and you'll be able to do it in front of Gavin."

I open my mouth to explain that I'll have to make small talk with the devil, when she cuts me off.

"And it could be worse. You could be in prison. Do you know where the bathroom in prison is? In the middle of the room, that's where."

In a rare moment for me, I'm speechless. A forced date with Gavin isn't as bad as prison, if she's forcing me to acknowledge reality.

"Can't you even let me have my moment?" Body finally relaxed after the excitement of the last thirty minutes, I slip my arm in the crook of Sonia's arm and drag her toward my apartment.

"Not when you're bringing unnecessary drama to the situation."

We look at each other and laugh. Because it's a truth universally acknowledged that a Gupta brings the drama. In the tradition of the best Indian soap operas.

Chapter Eight

"What does one wear to a blackmailed event?" I ask Ajay in front of my mirror, imagining different outfits. "Should I make him eat his heart out in something tight and short, or embarrass him by going for comfort in yoga pants and an old Margaritaville shirt?"

Ajay puts off answering by eating all the snacks in my office. I don't know when he got my bag of mini brownies, but it's a lot lighter than it was when he came in.

"I think you should stop asking me questions that we all agreed were Sonia questions."

"*You* walked into *my* office. If you don't want to participate in what's happening here, you can leave."

All day, the charity banquet loomed in the back of my mind. It wasn't enough of a distraction to stop me from getting work done on the Harrison catalog and other assignments, but it was enough to make everything take longer.

It's also enough to make me annoyed, which doesn't seem like the best head space for a charity event.

Ajay takes my words to heart and gets up to leave.

"Wait, you still have to answer the question. I invoke twin bond."

"Oh, didi. That's not a thing." He walks out, hardening his heart against my pleas.

"At least send Sonia in then," I yell after him. "Useless," I mutter to myself.

"You bellowed for me?" Sonia magically appears.

"No." Honesty compels me to add, "I bellowed for Ajay to bellow for you. You just heard because you're a stalker, like a CIA operative loitering around my office hoping I'll give up state secrets."

"No, I'm not. And make him eat his heart out with the good shit," she says, proving she was listening like the aforementioned CIA operative. "Now can we discuss some emails from Ajay's team that we apparently need to handle?"

Sonia doesn't say how frustrated she is with that, but her tone is doing a lot of heavy lifting to let me know her feelings on the subject.

"He's going to talk to Dad after this upcoming gallery show. He promised." I defend my baby brother, feeling the knee-jerk reaction to protect him.

"I hope he does." Sonia doesn't sound convinced.

I sigh, looking at the amount of work we have with Ajay's show. I take a moment to imagine myself in the president and CEO's office. Goal firmly in mind, I put out small fires with Sonia for the next few hours.

"It's quarter to five!" Sonia bursts into my office.

I jerk my head up from my computer screens, fingers still typing. "No. No, it can't be. I still have work to do."

"I'll make a note to learn how to stop time, but in the meantime, I'm going to need you to obey the laws of time." She starts to tidy my desk around me, closing books and catalogs as she keeps my place in them.

Hah! We're mostly paperless; I don't need anything on this desk but the computer.

"I obey no laws!" I'm still typing, but a little faster now.

She nudges my arms aside, saves the work and shuts down the computer. Well, that might stop me.

"Taking care of you Guptas is exhausting." Sonia covers the power button on my computer so I can't turn it back on. Which I was planning on doing.

"That's what you get for being born in this family." Computer shut down, my mind goes to other pressing issues. "Oh shit, I don't have anything to wear."

I was going to go home for lunch to get the "eat your heart out" outfit, but then I got distracted by a shipment of art in our storage room I wanted to pick through for my *Female Gaze* show and I kind of lost track of time.

Sonia throws cloth over my head, and I have no idea where she got it from.

"Wait, how do you know this is what I wanted to wear?" I move it off my head and look at it while she finishes collecting things off my desk that need to be signed and delivered.

"It's not. It's better than what you wanted to wear."

"I'll be the judge of that." I hold it up. Oh. It's better than what I was going to wear. It's a tea-length dark green dress that is both comfortable and elegant. It also swirls around me when I move and has pockets.

I can't put anything in the pockets because it would break the line of the dress. But it's good that designers are beginning to realize how amazing pockets are and adding them on more things. And one day I'll actually be able to use the pockets, in a future utopia where donuts don't have calories.

"What shoes do I wear?"

"I'm not your mother. But the ones you have on match, and they're broken in."

Yup, she knows me. I would have gone home and gotten a dress that's uncomfortable and shoes that are new and still hurt like hell.

"I love you," I say to her retreating figure.

"Yeah, yeah. Show me the love in my bonus this year."

"Mercenary." Admiration fills my voice.

I duck into my bathroom to change and I'm sliding my arm through the last sleeve when I hear the door open. "Sonia? Did you forget something?" I walk out of the bathroom, still putting on earrings.

"Not Sonia," Gavin says from his position at the entrance, hands in his pocket, leaning against my doorframe. He's doing that thing where he projects nonchalance, like he's been lounging in my office for hours. Even though I know he must have just walked in.

He's definitely not a small Indian woman. Instead, it's a tall, smirking, white man with a strong jaw line that makes me want to nibble it. He's dressed in another one of his tailored suits, designed specifically to remind me how long it's been since I've had sex.

One year, three months, and two days.

"My blackmailer." I greet him as I turn away to finish putting my earrings in. And to avoid the sight of him in that tux.

I've already accepted that this is a good opportunity to network, and I'm getting off light for the alleged (actual) trespassing I committed. But the petty in me is not ready to give this up without some snark.

"I prefer to think of myself as an opportunity creator."

"Is it part of the blackmail that I have to agree with you?" I ask in a voice so sweet it must be fake.

"I don't think I have enough on you to make that happen."

"You don't. Who's the target anyway?" I ask as I herd him out of the room.

"You know we're not murdering anyone, right?"

"Sure. Yup. Gotcha. But really who is it?"

"Gina Martinez. CEO of a big advertising company. She has an amazing classic car collection, and she wants to trim some of it to make room for new ones. Just like Harrison."

"Wait, am I just here because you're afraid to face the powerful woman alone?"

"No."

The unusually short answer from Gavin makes me look at him sideways.

"You're totally afraid." Now how do I use this information?

"I'm not afraid. I just want to go into battle with every possible weapon at my disposal. And the lady CEO might be more comfortable knowing that I know other strong business ladies."

I feel my stomach flutter at the compliment, and I wish he'd stop doing that. Every time he makes a comment that doesn't revolve around one of us crushing the other, I react like we're on a first date.

Which we most certainly are not doing. "Strong business ladies can see through your sad shenanigans."

"Yes, they can. And she'll know that and see that you're around me anyway, so I still get credit. You're a great judge of character."

I feel moderately bad about the ruse we're playing on

this woman, but I'm comforted by the fact that Carlyle's is a competent auction house that will do a decent job on the sale. They're our main competition at our size and scope, so it physically pains me to admit anything nice about them, even in my head. And Gavin would have to use some medieval torture devices on me before I admit it out loud.

Gavin has a car waiting for us in front of my office building, and I'm impressed the driver was able to hold a spot in the after-work traffic. He gets out as we exit onto the street, and has the door open for us before we reach the vehicle.

"Thank you," I say as I get in.

Once we're settled and on our way, silence permeates the inside of the vehicle. We don't often spend time alone together, in private. I rack my brain, trying to think of when we've had any one-on-one time, but we've always been surrounded by people, either our classmates, then coworkers or the clients we're working with. Well, except for when he came to my office to talk about Stella, and when Gavin caught me in the storeroom.

I've been seeing him alone a lot lately.

"What charity are we supporting anyway?" I say to break up thinking about him.

Gavin purses his lips in thought, as if this was the first time he'd thought about that question. "I think it has to do with animals," he says carefully. "But it could also be related to children. Or a disease."

"Well, that covers almost everything it could possibly be. Real attention to detail there, Gavin."

"Does it matter if I know, as long as someone who needs it gets my money?"

"From their perspective? No. But you should know because it makes you a decent person."

"I go to so many of these, they kind of blur together. This one's at the Plaza, so the food should be decent."

"The Plaza? THE Plaza? Seriously, we're like six blocks away. It would have been quicker to walk there in this traffic."

"But why would we walk, when we can be driven?" He sounds genuinely confused.

"You're such a spoiled brat."

"You grew up in the same place I did. Same schools, similar income, similar addresses. Why aren't you a brat?"

I snort. "Because I had old school Indian parents who made me do things like learn how to cook and gave me a shitty car to learn to drive on, and who didn't send a maid with me when I went to college at Cambridge."

My brother is closer in personality to Gavin than I am. He was never expected to have cooking lessons with Mom, and he stayed closer to home when he went to NYU. So my parents did send their cleaners and cooks over to him at his dorm and then apartment regularly.

Ajay never had to grow up or learn how to do things for himself, since there was always someone there to help him put in minimal effort. That let him spend all his energy on things he liked to do, like painting, instead of things he promised to do, like work at Loot.

Gavin is like that. Well, he does work harder than my brother at his auction house. But I see a lot of the same traits in him that I do in my brother, especially not being able to do basic tasks and only doing what's fun for him.

"I work hard. But if there's something I can do to make my life easier, I'm going to do it. Plus, do you want to put Roger out of work?" Gavin indicates the front of the long vehicle, voice lowering.

"You're a real job creator," I say dryly.

"There're still some things I can do for myself." He extends his arm across the back of my seat and captures my gaze. "I can show you, if you'd like," he offers, voice deep and seductive.

Flirting? Is the man flirting with me? I'm not prepared for this new development, because even though he's asked me out, he hasn't been this playful with me. I wonder if he'll call the police on me if I cover my head and yell "I can't hear you."

Instead of doing that, I scoff. "Not likely." So smooth, Gupta. Smooth like a marble sculpture from the eighteenth century.

The rest of the too-long ride passes in silence, while I try to put him back in the box he was in before. The safe, enemy box where I can imagine dancing over his prostrate form in victory, while he weeps in disappointment.

When the car pulls up in front of the Plaza, Gavin opens the door for me and extends a hand to me.

"Bye, Roger. Thanks for the ride," I say, avoiding Gavin's eyes.

"You're welcome," he says.

As I take Gavin's hand, I brace for the feel of the heat that accompanies his touch. Like clockwork, my hand curls further into his and the tendrils of warmth race up my arm.

I snatch my hand out of his as soon as I get out of the car, not prepared to deal with the emotions he brings up. I compromise by tucking the same hand into the crook of his elbow, with a few layers of cloth between us. I am supposed to be his date, and this is much safer.

Gavin leads us to the ballroom and to our table. Lovely waiters in their spotless uniforms bring me a glass of wine, becoming my favorite people in the whole room.

I sip my drink and take in all the opulence around me. Columns soar to a tall ceiling, and intricate carvings and paintings line the top of the room. Beautiful chandeliers above make the elaborate table settings down in front of us sparkle.

This building has seen so much history since it was built in the 1880s. I wish I could hear what it could tell me about New York.

A voice interrupts me taking mental notes about the beautiful decoration in the room. "Gavin Carlyle. This woman looks too pretty for you. What do you have on her to make her go out with you?"

"He caught me committing what is either a major misdemeanor or a lesser felony. Now he's blackmailing me with the threat of jail to spend time with him. It's this or an orange jumpsuit and group pooping," I say before turning around.

Chapter Nine

The woman laughs. "I like this one."

Gavin gets up, so I do the same. This must be the target. Showtime.

"Gina Rodriguez. It's a surprise to see you here." Gavin smiles and extends his hand.

She accepts the handshake. "Is it? You've been calling and emailing the office about my cars all week."

I turn my head to hide my snicker. She burned him good, and I'm so glad I'm here to watch this in person.

"I'm Priya Gupta. From Loot." I take my turn to offer my hand.

"I know." She shakes my hand. "I've been to your sales. They're always really well put together and entertaining."

"Thank you for saying that. It's nice to hear I'm not the only one enjoying my shows."

"Her shows are great." Gavin slides his arm around me, making me start. When did we get to this level of familiarity? "And we were just discussing the best ways to show your collection in our upcoming car sale by—"

"Do you think Carlyle's can do it?" Gina asks me.

"Oh. Well." This is a weird position to be in. I don't

want Gavin to succeed, but also he has my freedom at stake. Plus honesty.

"Loot could obviously do it better, if we did cars. But if you're wanting an auction house with experience, Carlyle's will do a better job than selling them on eBay, and better than the other houses too."

There. That's all true and I don't have to say really nice things about Gavin. Maybe I should go into politics after I do the President of Loot thing for a while.

"That's a glowing recommendation," Gina says with light sarcasm and a smile. The smart CEO puts her skills on display, picking up on my reticence to compliment the man.

"Gavin here—" I slap his chest "—does have some great ideas that you should hear about for a potential sale."

We all look at him expectantly, me from the vantage point of his arm. I get comfortable in the position and let the man do his work. He outlines the show he wants to put on, talking about the history of cars until my eyes start to glaze over in boredom. But Gina looks happy, so he's saying the right words.

Being this close to him while he works is a unique experience. I can feel every change in his body, like his arm tightening around me as we wait for Gina's response. The hint of vulnerability is unexpected in the usually easygoing man.

I don't think he needs to worry. I might not know cars, but I do know buyers. Whatever he's saying is impressing Gina, and she nods along with his words. Gavin is very good at his job. He wouldn't be a worthy adversary if he wasn't, so I don't have to feel bad admiring him.

Gina makes Gavin sweat, which makes me like her right back. She looks from me to him, and I try to remain as neutral as possible.

She finally responds. "Your ideas are impressive. I'll set up a meeting with your office so we can discuss particulars."

"I look forward to it." Gavin's voice is cool, but I feel him relax. Hard to miss when I'm pressed up against him like a barnacle on the bottom of a ship.

Gavin nudges me back to our seats across the large table from Gina and her date.

"You happy?" I whisper when we settle back into our seats.

"You've done well," Gavin says, but he can't hide his excited little boy smile.

"You really want this sale."

"Yeah."

He doesn't say anything else, so I turn back to the place setting in front of me, where an attentive waiter has dropped off a salad and another glass of wine. This is excellent service.

But then Gavin gets my attention again by continuing. "My dad loves cars. He started restoring vintage cars as a way to de-stress from work and I would watch him. When I got older, he finally let me help. He always says that he likes cars better than paintings or sculptures because they're beautiful, but they still have a functional purpose aside from their beauty."

"That's nice you can do something with him that you both enjoy. Outside of work." Since he shared, it feels natural to share something back. "My mom loves to cook and I join her to spend time with her, but I hate it. So much."

"So you can cook me dinners?" he asks, leaning into me as he delivers the teasing question. As he gets closer, I can smell his aftershave, a citrusy bergamot that reminds me of a nice cup of Earl Grey on a gray, rainy day.

Some of my favorite things. Leftover from living in England, probably.

I snort. "Fat chance. I think you missed the part where I said I hated cooking."

"What do you hate about it?" Gavin leans ever closer to get the butter plate from the other side of me. I stay where I am so he has to brush against me.

"I hated that it was expected of me. I was sent to the kitchen with Mom because I was the girl, while Ajay, the boy, got to go to the office with Dad. I resented that. And all those feelings kind of all come back up when I cook. Which is why I'm on a first name basis with my food delivery guy. Who is a saint."

I don't know why I told him all of that. I don't think there's any way he can use that against me or Loot, but it's still probably too much emotional sharing for rivals.

I just got so caught up when he shared his thing.

"Then I'm glad I could give that guy the night off. He sounds like he works hard." Gavin grabs my own roll and hands it to me. I stick out my tongue at him, but I do take the carbs.

I take another look around the room as we eat our rolls. "This place is nice...like nice enough that the Real Housewives could get in an argument in here."

"Don't tell me you watch that trash?"

"Excuse yourself?" My words and tone give him a warning. "That highly entertaining roller-coaster ride into the highs and lows of human nature?"

"But it's so…" He pauses, maybe searching for a word that won't make me want to punch him. He won't find one; anything he says in that tone will make me want to punch him.

"Amazing?" I say, trying to help him out.

"That's a word." Not one he would use, from his tone of voice.

"Getting up in other people's lives is *the* most deeply ingrained human trait of all of civilization. The French court of Louis XIV hosted a lever and coucher every day so nobles could see the monarchs get up and get ready for bed. Romans have graffiti saying that some guy performed oral sex on ladies against the city wall. People painted scenes from their lives for posterity and they still hang in museums. We make a living selling them. People are nosy. We've always been nosy, and we always will be."

"I can't argue with that."

That's right. Don't trash talk reality TV to me; it won't be a fun time for the trash talker.

Before he even has a chance to talk any more trash, a man who looks like the silver-haired version of Gavin comes to our table. "Gavin, I didn't know you were coming to this," William says, patting Gavin on the shoulder.

"Hi, Dad." He gets up to give his father a handshake. Not wanting to be caught with Gavin, I hunch down more so he doesn't see me.

"Priya, nice to see you too." Busted.

"You as well, William." I get up and shake his hand, putting a smile on my face so he can't see that I'm uncomfortable.

"I saw Gina's here tonight." William turns his attention back to his son without grilling me, despite the questioning look he gave me. Apparently he has other things to worry about.

"Yeah, I was talking to her about the cars. I think we can get it." Gavin has pride in his voice at the prospect.

"It's going to be a high profile sale. I should handle it, with my background in vintage car sales. Let me know when she's coming and I can prepare a mock catalog."

Ooof. This is a weirdly familiar conversation. But I'm usually at the receiving end of it, and the older man stealing my thunder is more tan. I feel a spark of sympathy for Gavin when I would usually enjoy his discomfort; I know the feeling too well to take pleasure in it. Not that I ever thought it would happen to Gavin. He's usually so easygoing it's hard to imagine him not getting what he wants.

Gavin looks less than confident, eyes shifting down and shoulders slumping. "But I already started the process with her. She likes my ideas." His tone is subdued as well.

"I know. But this is for the best. I've done more car sales and you'll be busy with the Richmond Collection as well."

Gavin opens his mouth and then closes it. He opens it again, and I get the sense he drastically changed the content of what he was going to say. "That's fine. I'll let you know when she's free for a meeting."

"Good. Enjoy the night, you two." William walks away, getting to his table across the palatial room before I turn to Gavin.

"Your dad is intense," I say.

"Probably just as intense as yours," he says with a sad smile.

"That's very true. I just didn't... Never mind." His family dynamic is none of my business.

"No, what?"

"I just didn't think you would let it go that easily." The stubborn man doesn't back down from a fight over art with me.

Gavin works his jaw. "It's easier this way. It's fine."

"But you were so excited about it. Why didn't you fight for it?" I can't help digging into the newest facet of Gavin.

"It's no use arguing with Dad. He's stubborn and he'll do a great job with the cars."

I shrug. It's really not my business if he doesn't want to rock the boat with his father. For all the time Dad tries to take shows away from me, I push back. Otherwise I would never get to do any shows. I could probably push more, but I know it's scary to go up against such strong figures. If Gavin doesn't want to because it's too much work, well, that's not entirely surprising from the charming playboy.

The rest of the night is surprisingly enjoyable, considering how it started. When Gavin goes to use the bathroom, I slip over to the other side of the table and slide Gina my card, giving her the elevator pitch about my *Female Gaze* show, and how I think we'll have some pieces she might like.

She agrees to stop by the exhibition, and if she likes it, she'll come to the sale and bring all her richest friends with her. And a few of the other people around the table express interest and take my card too. So the night's not a total bust for me.

After dinner there's a charity auction, led by a very amateur auctioneer.

"He's leaving money on the table! He could get another fifty thousand from that elderly couple in the back, hands down!" I whisper frantically at Gavin, leaning closer so people don't know I'm talking shit at a charity event. They could have at least asked a real auctioneer to donate their time.

"I know," Gavin says in an equally befuddled voice. "And when he called that pop art piece by Richard Hamilton a painting by Andy Warhol, I died inside." He grabs my arm and gives it a shake to emphasize the enormity of the mistake.

We watch for a little longer. Gavin's hand stays where it is, his thumb rubbing slow circles on my arm. My first instinct is to slap his hand away, but the soothing movements combined with the heat I feel whenever we make contact feels kind of nice, so I let it stay there.

"He looks so afraid," I say.

"Public speaking is an acquired skill." Gavin winces in sympathy. We've both suffered through an auctioneer's first time, both our own and the first times of the employees we train and mentor. But it doesn't get easier to watch.

"And he's losing the crowd." The din of side conversations gets louder and louder as the audience decides the entertainment on the stage isn't worth their attention.

"Please make it stop. It's too painful," I say when the auctioneer starts the bidding of an intricate, limited edition Rolex at $250.

"Someone needs to do something." Gavin turns his face away from the stage, hiding it behind my shoulder. I can feel his breath tingle the bare skin of my back and I shudder a little, wondering when we got so comfortable with all the touching.

But not telling him to stop.

"We need to do something," I say.

"What do you mean?" His eyes follow me as I rise from my seat.

"It's for charity." I grab his arm and urge him up. His eyebrows are drawn low over his eyes in confusion, but he follows me without question.

I run into one of the event organizers at the bottom of the stairs leading to the stage.

"What do you guys need?" the harried employee asks me. Her hair is coming down from her bun, and her tie is askew. She's clutching a clipboard and looking morosely at the event unfolding in front of her, knowing it's not going as well as it could.

"The main lady…oh god, I forgot her name. Big personality, slight smell of alcohol wafting around her, great shoes. Anyway, she asked us to help by taking over. We're auctioneers. Professionals." I indicate me and Gavin.

Behind me, Gavin is so close that I can feel him shake in laughter at the lie.

"She never tells us anything," the overworked employee says, but waves us on.

I creep onto the stage and tap the man on the shoulder before he can sell the Rolex for $1,000. I whisper that we're the reinforcements and we're taking over the rest of the show. He throws the microphone at me so fast it almost hits me straight in the face, but I catch it at the last second.

The same rush I always feel before an auction fills me. The intense focus that drowns out anything but the desire to get as much as I can for each piece, and the anticipation of the resulting euphoria of getting a price better than I imagined.

I've felt it since I was a kid, when I would hold auctions in our living room to practice. I could always get Mom to bid higher, but Dad was a tougher sell. Luckily I discovered his weakness: Mom. One sad look from me to her, then one stern look from her to him, and he bid higher.

I keep waiting for the rush to not be there one day when I first raise the gavel, but it hasn't faded in all these years.

I yell into the microphone, "Hello, New York! Let's give a round of applause for your first auctioneer." A weak round of applause goes up in the room and I push through. "We're here to do the second half of the auction, donated from Loot and Carlyle's, your friendly neighborhood auction houses. Now I see some familiar faces in the crowd." I do a slow sweep over the crowd, eyes squinting. "So I know those pockets are deep. And so are those hearts, huh?"

That gets a little bit of a laugh.

"What lot are we doing first?" I exaggerate looking behind me to the podium where the watch is resting. "Ah. This exquisite, limited edition Rolex. Where should we start this?" I ask Gavin, who somehow got a microphone while I was doing introductions.

Gavin considers. "I say you should open the bidding at ten thousand dollars."

I give him a nod of acknowledgement for a very good opening bid for a watch of its name and quality, Gavin once again proving he's just as good as me at this job. I turn back to the crowd.

"The man has spoken. Who'll give me ten thousand? For charity." I raise my arms, inviting the bids.

I see a paddle raised. "The beautiful woman in the front will give me ten. Who'll give me eleven?"

"Eleven. Who will give me twelve?"

A woman with a clipboard marches toward the stage, her pace fast and determined. That must be the organizer trying to figure out why we're on stage. And who we are.

I see a raised paddle and move toward that direction. "Twelve? Who wants to get in on this for such a steal? The dapper man in the back wants in at twelve. Thirteen?"

"Thirteen," a man yells from stage right.

"An excited thirteen. Thank you. Ma'am, do you want to get back in here?"

The original bidder raises her paddle. "Fourteen!" I yell to the crowd.

The organizer slows as the bidding gets higher. She might not know why Gavin and I are on this stage, but we're doing a lot better than the first guy she had up here. It's really not his fault; auctioneering is an art.

I turn back to the other side of the room. "Thank you. Do I have fifteen?"

The crowd is quiet. "Last chance, I'm going to sell it."

"Come on, I can get more than that if I sold this on eBay," Gavin says.

"Ooooo…trash talked by the auctioneer." I shake my head in shame, and see a paddle raised.

"Fifteen thousand. Ah, original bidder's out. It's okay, darling, we'll find you something pretty tonight. Who'll replace her at sixteen?"

Another paddle raised. "Yes! Sixteen. Now we're getting to the good stuff. Now who wants to raise the stakes even higher? Who will give me seventeen?" Silence from the crowd. And the organizer takes a seat. She's happy with the way the numbers are going, since we've already gotten more in one minute than the original auctioneer had for his entire first ten lots.

"I don't know, Gavin. At that price I can take it home." I move back to the podium so I can covet the shiny watch, fingers hovering over the item.

"Not if I outbid you first," Gavin says, walking to the other side of the watch.

We see a paddle raised. "The lady in red has us both beaten at seventeen. Eighteen thousand?"

Another paddle raised. "Eighteen. Does anyone want to end this strong at nineteen?"

"Twenty thousand!" a woman in red yells, jumping up in excitement.

"Twenty thousand it is. I love your enthusiasm and your dress. Do I have twenty-one?" Silence, but I have everyone's attention.

"Sold at twenty thousand dollars!" I slam my hand down on the podium, since they don't have a gavel for me to dramatically end the auction with. "Someone bring me the next lot!"

Chapter Ten

"That was such a rush." I tap on Gavin's leg in the limo at the end of the night, still feeling the high from the sale.

It's been a long time since I've had so much fun at the rostrum, with such low stakes. Not that I didn't want to get a lot of money for the charity, but it's a lot more stressful when I have the future of Loot on my gavel.

The added challenge of making up opening bids on the spot, with no previous research into the items, was exhilarating. And a nice stretch for my skills, to keep them in shape.

"I know, I had to physically move you out of the spotlight so I could get in on it."

Gavin's exaggerating; we seamlessly switched off taking the lead on each lot. We actually made a really good team, since we're both genuinely good at this.

At the end of the sale, the organizer profusely thanked us for taking over. We were both glad that she decided to give us a chance and not call the cops. It would have been extra sad to be arrested while I was going to the dinner so I wouldn't get arrested.

"We could always do that one day, if you wanted?"

Gavin asks, looking out of the window so I can't see his face when he makes the suggestion.

"Throw a charity event?"

"No. Well, if you want, sure. But a joint sale. With both of us at the rostrum. It would bring in a lot of exposure for both of our houses."

I choke out a laugh. "Just because you had one good night doesn't make you on my level," I say, despite the fact that we're definitely peers. "Plus, can you imagine how much our dads would argue? Every commission, every theme, every detail. It would be a disaster."

"Yeah, you're right about that."

I still can't see his face, but his voice sounds strangely blank. It's a change from his usual charm, so I'm about to ask if he's feeling okay when the limo stops in front of my building.

"We're here," he says, getting out of the limo to hold the door open for me.

I step out. "Thanks for not having me arrested. Not that I'm admitting to doing anything arrest-worthy."

"You're welcome. And thanks for helping with Gina."

I nod at him. There's a slight pause while we stand in the busy street, awkwardly not looking at each other. Multiple New Yorkers sigh deeply as they have to go around us on the busy sidewalk, but surprisingly I don't want to leave Gavin.

"It was—" I say.

At the same time, Gavin says, "We should—"

We finally make eye contact. "You go ahead." Gavin waves his hand.

"Anyway, it was a fun night." Now that we're looking at each other, I can't look away from the bright sapphire eyes in front of me.

Gavin moves closer, throwing me into a panic. I tell my feet to move, but they don't listen, snared by those unblinking eyes. He gets closer, stopping when he's so close he could kiss me if he bent his head the last inches that separate us.

I want him to.

No! I don't want his lips on mine. Or anywhere near me.

Without my permission, my body sways toward him, proving me a liar. Like a sunflower, attracted to the energy emanating from the man in front of me.

Attracted to the shiny thing in front of me.

Gavin picks up on the sway and moves even closer, eyes closing as his lips descend.

At the last minute, I turn my head to the side and grab Gavin for a hug. His arms come around me in response, his lips landing somewhere in my hair, and my heart races at the close call.

Or it could be because of how solid Gavin feels against me.

Those are dangerous thoughts. I would lose the little respect I get from Dad if he found out I slept with the enemy. And I'm not going to throw away my future for a fling.

I pull away from the hug, putting distance between Gavin and me. "I'll see you around." I turn away from him without another word and get past my doorman with a quick greeting.

I don't relax until I'm safely alone in my apartment, away from the temptation that he presents.

My mom bursts into my office right before lunchtime.

"Hi, Mom. I didn't think you were coming in to the office today."

"I'm here to take you to lunch," Mom says imperiously. I was afraid of that.

Not that I don't love my mom; she's amazing. She's always supported me, letting me know that I could pursue whatever career I wanted. When I finally got up the courage to tell her I wanted to be more involved in the auction house, she cut the cooking lessons and started taking me to the office, to "have lunch with your father."

More often than not, Dad was too busy for the lunch, so Mom would take me around the different departments, talking to staff so I could learn the business from every angle.

Eventually, she started saying she was too busy doing her charity work for the cooking lessons, telling Dad he better take both of his children to the office. Dad said he didn't have time to babysit, and Mom said she wouldn't be responsible for what she did if he called raising his children babysitting ever again, looking more menacing than I had ever seen her, or have seen her since.

Dad took me to the office after that. And I got to learn auctioneering from the best. I try not to drag Mom into work issues too often, because I want to show her I can do this myself. But I haven't forgotten how much she did for me.

Still, I don't have time for lunch with anyone right now. And Mom's lunches last approximately 82 percent longer than regular lunches.

"I was just going to eat some food at my desk while working today. I have to get the Harrison catalog done this week and I have a sale tonight."

"If you won't eat with your sainted mother, then as your boss, I'm ordering you to a business lunch. To discuss business."

Damn it. Mom is an equal owner in the company, so this is technically an order. "Well played, you crafty woman." I save my progress and grab my jacket and purse from my coat rack.

Mom is as generous as she is crafty, so she doesn't gloat.

We go to a restaurant in the building, so at least we won't waste transportation time. And we've been so often we know the offerings by heart, so no precious minutes wasted on staring blankly at the menu.

"How was your night last night?" Mom asks casually after we put in our usual orders.

Wait a minute...this isn't mother-daughter bonding time; this is an expertly executed ambush. And I fell for it, because I am not worthy to cross swords with this woman.

"It was good," I say carefully. I wish the waiter would come back with a menu I could hide behind. I paste a neutral smile on my face, feeling as wary as Nancy Drew walking into a mysterious old house, not knowing what might be around the corner.

"What did you do?" she asks, eyes pinning me to the seat and daring me to lie. All while having the most benign smile on her face. It's scary. *This* is the content I wished she had taught me. Not how to make her really good dal makhana.

"I went to a charity dinner and ended up helping with the auction itself. You should have seen the amateur they had doing it. Job security for us though, eh?" I'm babbling, but I can't help it.

Maybe I'm not ready to give in yet. I refuse to give her the piece of information she wants the most from my night: that I was with Gavin. Willingly. Sort of.

"And who did you go with?"

"Plenty of people were there." I deliberately misunderstand. "Gina Rodriguez was there. She said she would stop by Loot. And I saw a few other clients."

"But who were you *with*? Who did you go to that widely publicized event with?" Mom's eyes narrow as she goes in for specifics.

Okay, I give in. There's no use fighting; she has the superior intelligence source today. "I went with Gavin Carlyle," I mumble. With about as much dignity as when she caught me staying up late to read auction catalogs in high school.

"With Gavin Carlyle?" Mom's eyes sparkle in excitement. That's not the anger I was expecting.

"Well, yeah. It was a business thing. Sort of." I don't think she knows it was because I trespassed, and I don't think I'll be the one to tell her.

I won't be telling her about the almost kiss either.

Her eyes dull a little. "A business thing? Not a date?"

"Mother!" I look around surreptitiously, trying to see if anyone heard her say that. Employees of the company eat down here all the time. "He is a ruthless man and the competition. I wouldn't betray the company like that."

"So it can be like Romeo and Juliet?" The stars are back in Mom's eyes.

What's going on here? Mom should be a little more concerned about something that could potentially affect Loot's profits. "They died. Both of them. Because of severe miscommunication. That could have been easily cleared up if they had talked to each other."

"Yes, but they enjoyed their time together before all the death. When was the last time you were on a date?"

"Wait, you aren't here to yell at me for spending

time with a rival, you're here to harangue me about dating. J'accuse!" I point my finger at her. Mom has been subtly bugging me to date so I can "settle down" and be happy, but I've been brushing her off because my schedule doesn't really have time for dates right now.

And men get mad when you cancel dates three times in a row because you have to fly to London to wine and dine a newly impoverished, and ready to sell some art, member of the ton.

"Yes, obviously. You'd never let someone use you to take advantage of the company."

The waiter comes to drop off food, cutting into the conversation and giving me a chance to regroup.

"You really aren't dating Gavin? I always thought there was something between you two." Mom sounds so disappointed.

"No! Anger. There's anger between us."

"Anger can sometimes translate into some pretty enjoyable activities."

I toss my fork down on the table and look for a waiter. I'm going to eat this later, because I just lost any appetite I started this lunch with.

"Please stop talking about this," I beg her as I hope for a streaker or a small stampede of pampered, purple-dyed Pomeranians to rush through the restaurant as distraction.

"Well, if you don't have any interest in Gavin, I have a few sons of friends that are single…" Mom abandons her defense of Gavin, moving on to new targets.

"No. I'm fine. I'll make more of an effort to be social… with men." I cringe at the thought of making the effort with my current schedule.

"That's all I ask." That's suspiciously easy agreement. "But I'll just send you some photos and résumés. You can tell me if you want to go out with them, and if you don't, that's fine. But I don't want you to be alone."

That's more like my mother. Oh well, I still got off easier than I thought I would.

I do want what my parents have, eventually. Theirs was an arranged marriage, but they got very lucky and found love with each other after the ceremony. But the thought of looking for a person, and getting all dressed up, and then hiding my quirks long enough to impress the person, all while trying to run my department… It's exhausting just thinking about it.

"Wait, so you really would have been fine if I was on a date with Gavin?"

Mom shrugs, taking a bite of her salmon. "Why not? He's successful, educated, and he looks nice in a suit. You could do worse, beta."

"But what about the enemy business?"

"Enemies? What is this, World War I? We're both successful houses that have survived here for decades. And you shouldn't be talking about work when you're done with work, anyway. Be more like Ajay."

I barely control the violent eye roll that threatens to escape. The man can't even talk about work when he's *at* work.

"Are you going to be at the show tonight?" I change the subject.

Mom gives me the Mom Look. The one that knows what I'm doing. That I'm trying to change the subject because I don't want to talk about something. But she lets it happen. "Of course. I love watching you work."

I rush out of lunch as soon as Mom lets me escape.

Wrangling a group of buyers is a lot easier than going one hour with my mother.

"Sonia, where's the updated buyer list? And the binder with the lots?" I yell into the bid room, where the payment is processed behind our auction space.

The auction is about to start and the familiar rush of adrenaline is buzzing through my veins like it always does. It makes me bounce as I walk, my body expelling the excess energy any way it can.

I hear footsteps running toward me like the stampede scene in *Jumanji*. "Here." The requested folders appear in my line of sight.

"Thank you. Can you get me a samosa too? One of the non-spicy ones please." We try to coordinate snacks at our shows to fit with the theme, and tonight is contemporary Indian, highlighting the artist Raqib Shaw. So I get to have samosas. As long as someone grabs one for me before the gluttonous masses descend on the snack table. And as long as it's one of the mild ones. Spicy food never took with me.

"Will do." Sonia disappears to find me sustenance, for once without judging my low tolerance to spicy food, while I take a last look at the lots. People in suits and black dresses rush around me, getting last-minute tasks done.

A samosa comes into my field of vision.

"Yeeees. You're the best." I grab the food and take a bite into the warm savory pastry. "Remind me to tell you what Mom said about Gavin later," I say, mouth still full and eyes still on the document in front of me.

"What did Mrs. G say about me?"

Chapter Eleven

I choke on the bite and jerk my head up at the deep sound of Gavin's voice, instinctively slamming the books in front of me closed so he doesn't get any trade secrets. "You."

My reaction is half because he's trespassing and half because of the almost kiss we had last time we spent time together. Which I clearly still haven't recovered from.

"Who me?" Gavin looks innocent.

"You can't be back here. Where's security?" I'm glad to slip back into our adversarial relationship from before the charity event. I scan the room to see if there's anyone big enough to physically eject him out of the area.

No one here that I can see.

"I'm a guest. Have to keep up with what the competition is doing." He holds up a paddle to prove his claim.

"Sure, so you can be out there." I point to our salesroom. "Feel free to enjoy all the snacks your incredibly fit belly can handle. But you still can't be in this area." I wave my arm in a circle to indicate the bid room we're in.

"Hmm. I guess I'm trespassing then." The snark is heavy in his tone.

One more reason my impulsive trespassing adventure wasn't the greatest idea; now I've lost the moral high ground.

"Well, you can still get out now." I make shooing motions.

He holds up his hands, either to placate me or ward off my shoos. "I just wanted to wish you luck."

I put a hand on my cocked hip, not responding to that ludicrous statement with words. My eyes have a thing or two to say though.

My suspicions are validated by the fact that his eyes are scanning our room, especially our flyers with buyer information.

"Thanks." I clutch the binders to my chest with my biceps to free my hands so they can turn Gavin around and push him out of the room.

When I make contact with his back, my body melts like a candle during a blackout. He feels so good under my hands, it doesn't take a lot for my mind to imagine us finishing what we started last night in front of my building.

In my fantasy, he'd be a victorious Hercules, naked except a lion skin (which would be fake—I'm not a monster, even in my fantasy), carrying a club.

I'd be wearing something loose and white, in the best Grecian tradition. He would still be pulsing with adrenaline from holding up the world or killing a hydra, and he wouldn't even wait long enough to get me all the way undressed.

"Twenty minutes," a coworker yells, a timely reminder why it wouldn't be a good idea to complete that kiss.

Gavin's giving me a questioning look over his shoulder, which I ignore. Pushing harder with renewed urgency, I get him out of the room.

"Good luck then, Riya." Gavin gives up and leaves me to my last-minute preparations.

After our interactions from the last few days, I'm more nervous than annoyed by seeing Gavin at my sale. I don't know if there was a particular moment when the change happened, but I don't like it, and I'm going to ignore it.

But first, Sonia should be bringing me a samosa as well.

"Now we have our last lot. It's the final opportunity of the night to go home with something, so let's make it count."

I motion to my left side, where our art handlers are bringing out the painting.

"And we couldn't ask for a better piece for our finale: *Self Portrait in the Sculpture Studio at Peckham (After Mocetto) II*, by Raqib Shaw. I like it so much the winner may have to pry it from my sticky little fingers."

I take a long look at the work, not exaggerating about wanting some extra time with the piece before it goes. "Don't worry, our burly art handers are on your side, and they've had years of practice prying things from my sticky little fingers. Let's start at five hundred thousand, shall we?"

"Five hundred..." A paddle goes up and I stumble over the number when I see who it is. Gavin Carlyle. What is he doing?

The thought is enough to do something that hasn't happened in the six years I've been doing real auctions: distract me from the sale. Now the tension in my body is for a completely different reason, one that has nothing to do with getting the highest price.

I clear my throat, hoping no one else noticed the fumble. "Five hundred thousand. Do I have five twenty-five?"

The price gets higher and higher, Gavin responding every time someone beats his bid. I know the piece is important, but I want to ask him why he wants it so badly. It takes everything in me, but I refrain from stopping the sale to have a sidebar where I harangue him for the truth.

And a good thing I don't stop the auction, because the numbers steadily climb higher than what we thought we'd get for it. It's most thrilling for me and the other staff, since no one else in the room knows what our internal estimate, the lowest amount we would have sold for, was. But it's a number we've surpassed a while ago.

I finally slam my gavel down at $1.5 million. Not bad for three minutes of work.

Gavin does win the painting. He better not be faking, planning to not pay. Then we could offer it to the next highest bidder, but they have no obligation to buy. I doubt he would, because it would destroy his reputation. Still, he's never mentioned this love for Shaw to me.

By the end of the night I sell every lot we have, called a white glove sale. Sonia comes up at the end and presents me with the ceremonial white gloves, but all I can think about is food.

I did eat the samosa Gavin brought me. I didn't even consider that he might have done anything to it until after I finished eating. Proving that even an almost kiss with Gavin has dulled my edge, and if I want to stay sharp and run this auction house, I better stay away from him.

I rush to the back and get my stuff. Everyone is buzzing from the amount we took in, making me dodge and duck behind cubicles so I can avoid celebrating people and get food in the least amount of time possible.

Coat and purse in hand, I exit through one of our warehouses on the ground floor. The cool night air inundates me as I open the door, a nice change from the heat of the bright lights and the crowd of the salesroom. I take a moment to lean against the building, closing my eyes and taking in deep breaths of crisp city air.

"Nice job. For a second-rate auction house."

"I can't even take a breath in peace." I keep my eyes closed. The way the last few days were going, I should have expected him to be here. He's been showing up around me like he's trying to serve me a subpoena.

"Is that any way to talk to your biggest buyer of the night?"

"My biggest buyer is a masochist. That's the only reason I can think of that he won't leave me alone." Apparently, I'm not getting rid of him by keeping my eyes closed and wishing him away, so I open my eyes.

He's doing the arrogant, hold-up-a-wall-with-his-shoulder thing again. Someone should tell him the building's been standing for decades; I think it'll be fine without his massive shoulders.

I start walking. His nonsense is not going to keep me from my destination for the evening.

"Where are you going?" he asks, falling into step with me.

"A hot date," I say back before I think better of it. I could have a hot date, if I wanted. My thoughts are depressingly defensive and my mother's voice floats through my head, saying she doesn't want me to end up alone.

Gavin laughs. "Yeah, right."

He doesn't have to sound so disbelieving. I shoot him a dirty look tinged with a bit of hurt I can't hide, and walk faster.

He stops laughing when he realizes I'm ahead of him, and rushes to catch up. "I didn't mean it like that."

"There's a limited amount of ways that can be taken." Up ahead, I see the crosswalk indicator count down. Maybe if I can outrun him past this block, he'll be stuck wandering Midtown until some nice tourist family from Wisconsin takes pity on him and calls him an Uber. Because he's probably too spoiled to find his own way home without a team of support staff.

"So where are we really going?" he asks, having made it past the pedestrian signal with me. Damn Hercules tree trunk thighs.

"Why is it so unbelievable that I could have a date?" I'm not moving past that without an answer.

"No. It's not that you can't have a hot date. It's that I never see you with guys, so I didn't think you were interested in dating." He stumbles over the explanation. He's going to have to put in a lot more effort than that if he wants me to get over this. Effort…his least favorite thing to do. And the one thing he can't ask his employees to do for him.

"Just because I don't parade my partners around like we're at the Westminster Dog Show doesn't mean that I don't date."

"You can date. Every day. Twice a day, if you want."

I wince. Even for the sake of this argument, I can't

pretend that two dates a day isn't exhausting. One date a day is exhausting.

Once a year is still kind of exhausting.

It's too much energy to deal with guys who want me to give all my attention to them when I have deadlines to meet. Too much ego demanding I only focus on them. And Gavin has an ego bigger than most. So he would be doubly exhausting, even if we weren't competitors.

"We've been walking for a while now. Are we walking to New Jersey?" Gavin asks.

"We've been walking for three minutes. And we're going to walk seventeen more because we're getting Shake Shack." Then I process what I just said. "No! *I'm* going to Shake Shack. You're committing a misdemeanor of the stalking variety."

He stays silent for a second while he checks his phone. "We're walking an entire mile?" Someone must have used his Maps App.

"Yes. Because walking is good for you."

"I'm in very expensive shoes." He points down to his feet. "I can't walk in them."

I give him serious side-eye, not believing that he doesn't hear how he sounds sometimes. "We're in the same tax bracket but I would lead the charge to guillotine you."

"Would you give me cake before the big day?"

"That's not how any of that worked."

Despite my blasé statement on the benefits of walking, I'm feeling the effects of the brisk pace I've set. I have to work to keep my heavy breathing quiet and stop myself from clutching the stitch starting in my side. Especially since I just made fun of him for not wanting to do the walk.

And despite his protests about his footwear, he's keeping pace with me. Another perfectly reasonable reason to resent him.

Before I pass out from the exertion, I see the magic sign promising me happiness on a metal tray.

The line is huge, as always, and I gladly get in line if it means I can stop walking. At this point, I've accepted that Gavin is here for the duration of this dinner, and I don't want to waste time arguing with him about it when I could be eating.

"That table just opened up." Gavin points to the back of the room. "Why don't you grab it and I'll get the food?"

I shrug. "ShackBurger, fries and a root beer." I turn on my heel before he can change his mind about getting me dinner. It's payment for letting him eat with me.

I walk to the table before someone else can swoop in and claim it, holding my breath until I'm seated. There's no one more motivated to get a table than a hungry human who wants their Shack Shake.

I sit on the side of the booth facing the line and take the opportunity to stare at Gavin. Even though the art world is small, I haven't seen him this much since we were forced together because the sadists at our school kept putting us in the same class. I don't mind it as much as I thought I would. He's surprisingly entertaining at this stage of my life.

Like a combination Monopoly Man and Chris Hemsworth.

I wonder if there's a way I can watch him be forced to grocery shop for himself. Or do his own laundry.

My own first laundry experience wasn't great, but it

was done in the privacy of another continent, so there's no one here who can mock me for it.

It was the first month at Cambridge, and I realized how much I had relied on our staff up to that point. I called Mom for help in a panic, having run out of all the clothes I brought and the ones I got while I was there. But she hadn't done her own laundry since…ever. She's always had staff too.

The first load was rough. But I had an excuse to buy all new clothes, so it turned into a good thing/expensive learning experience. For the record, those second set of clothes fared much better.

So it would be entertaining to watch spoiled Gavin do an everyday task he's unequipped for.

When my mind puts him in an apron with a burnt Easy Mac in his hand, he interrupts my fantasy by putting non-smoking food in front of me.

"The best for the second-best." He presents the tray with a flourish, and a bow, for some reason.

I pull a burger, the cheese fries, and a drink toward me.

Gavin reaches out to grab one end of the fries. "Wait a minute, you said fries. I got you fries and *me* cheese fries." He jerks his head to the tray, the regular fries sitting rejected on the table.

"I obviously meant the cheese fries. Who doesn't want everything improved by cheese? Sociopaths, Gavin. And the lactose intolerant." I give the tray a light tug in my direction.

"But you didn't say cheese." He stubbornly refuses to give the fries up, tugging them back to him.

"But I meant cheese. Everyone means cheese." This

is my after-auction dinner and, as god as my witness, I shall never eat dry fries again.

"I spent a lot of money tonight."

My eyebrows draw down. "No one asked you to."

Gavin looks around and must realize that we're making a scene. Not that anyone's paying attention. It's New York. And the few people who are paying attention are tourists on vacation, so I'm not going to see them again.

But Gavin might care, because he lets go of the fries.

Victory! I take a nice big bite immediately and contemplate licking a few of the others so he doesn't have second thoughts about giving them up.

"Why did you buy the painting anyway?" I ask, mouth full of cheese and potato.

"It's an amazing piece..."

"Duh. Loot doesn't sell crap."

"And it's going to be a great investment piece. Shaw's prices are just going to go up."

"You helped with that. You paid about $400,000 more than we thought it was going to get." I smile at him smugly, having done my job tonight to get the best price for the painting.

Gavin quirks an eyebrow. "I wasn't bidding against myself. The market wants more Shaw, and they're going to pay very well for it."

"Yeah, that surprised me too." But for every piece that exceeds our wildest dreams, there's one that we want to slap people for not bidding higher on, knowing it's worth more than it got.

"You did a really good job with the auction tonight. I helped, of course." Gavin preens.

I smile and throw a cheese fry at him, which he easily catches and eats. Arrogant man.

Arrogance aside, I kind of like talking to Gavin about work.

"Where are you going to put it?" If he says it's going to art storage, I'm going to revive my master burglar career and steal it from the ungrateful bastard.

"My bedroom. It'll be inspiration when I wake up. You're welcome to come by and see it anytime you want."

He makes me slow down my eating, despite the fact that I'm starving, picturing what his bedroom looks like. Is it a kinky sex dungeon with red silk sheets? Or a tastefully decorated room his interior designer picked out? Maybe it's college frat chic, with empty beer cans and IKEA furniture.

Except now I'm putting myself *in* the bedroom. In lingerie. And I don't even own sexy lingerie.

However it looks, I should stop thinking about it because I'm not going to find out. Not even a little. Unless he has an unfortunate autoerotic asphyxiation accident and the scene gets plastered on the news, I won't be seeing Gavin Carlyle's bedroom.

I think the rest of the night is going to be full of awkward silence, but after our Great Fry Standoff, we fall into easy conversation about the industry. Gossiping about other dealers, the latest sales, and the trends of the market.

He might not know how to change his own tire, but he knows the art market. Okay, I don't even know how to change a tire. Not without calling AAA.

But it's nice to be able to talk to someone about my passion. Dad doesn't take me seriously, Ajay is always focused on his painting, and Mom's uninterested in it all. Sonia and I talk about art about 25 percent of the time, but then we talk about reality TV, food and shirt-less Chris Hemsworth the rest of the time.

But Gavin, he listens to my opinions and debates me where he disagrees. Bringing up good points I didn't consider, even if I don't admit that to him.

By the end of the night, I just had my second civil—no, not just civil, an outright enjoyable—dinner with Gavin Carlyle.

Who knew I would find that with a rival?

Chapter Twelve

Sonia barges into my office the next morning. "Emergency."

"Do I have time to finish this bagel sandwich?" I love Sonia, but everything is an emergency in her opinion. Sometimes it is in fact an emergency. And sometimes she's mad that her favorite show got canceled and she'll never know if Ginny's going to pitch in the MLB again.

Okay, maybe both of us are still bitter about the *Pitch* cliffhanger and cancellation.

"No. You don't," she says.

I take a bite out of said breakfast sandwich, in protest.

"Harrison called."

I drop the bagel and chew faster. Okay, this might be one of the real emergency situations that doesn't come up all that often.

"What did he say?" I ask, dreading the answer. He gave me a week, and calling three days earlier than the week deadline can't be good news.

"He needs the catalog today. He wants to have a meeting with prospective houses by the end of the day, because he's got some country house party this weekend, and he wants to get a head start on it."

I open my mouth and close it, repeating the process until Sonia interrupts the loop by taking my hands and putting them on my keyboard.

"So get to working, because we have until 4:00 p.m. Today."

Well, at least he gave us to the end of the day.

"Okay. Not ideal. But we need to move forward because he might be an inconsiderate ass, but he's a rich inconsiderate ass and we need this deal." I already told Sonia about Dad's ultimatum, so she knows how important this is for me.

"Can you start editing what I've already done in the shared drive and I'll keep working on the rest and maybe get an intern to take the day and pray to all the gods for us? And then another one to feed me this sandwich." I start typing, looking wistfully at the bagel sandwich next to me.

"Sounds like a plan, boss."

"I'll see you at one o'clock to go over final details or have a really big cry if we're not done by then."

"If Harrison doesn't pick us, do you think I can sue him for the carpal *and* cubital tunnel I developed today?" I rub my hands, not kidding about how angry my fingers are over what I put them through this morning. To be fair, this day didn't cause this problem, considering I type on a computer all the time, but it might have exacerbated it.

"Probably not," Sonia says, trying to tidy up all the books I laid open on my floor for the last push of research/inspiration.

At least we managed to get it done. I complained

loudly the entire time, but no one was in the office with me, so I still have my dignity.

Self-talk, or self-complaining, is an important part of my process.

"Is printing going to have the catalog printed by the time I have to leave?" I ask.

"Yes. And they've promised to wrap it up in some fancy box that they said would outshine last year's Christmas sale."

"Oh, that was a good one." I put my feet up on desk and lean back in my ergonomic chair. "I might just need a little nap before I go to the meeting…" My eyes already closing at the sweet, sweet promise of rest.

The universe, however, had other plans. As she often does.

And by universe, I mean my phone. A clip of Wagner's "Ride of the Valkyries" jerks me away from the power nap.

I sigh but like a good business lady reach for my phone, sobbing to myself quietly. Internally. "Hey, it's an email from Mom. With an attachment. I wonder what she— *Oh my god what is this and why is this happening to me?* I donate to charity." I close my eyes again, wondering about the feasibility of pouring bleach directly into them as a cleanse.

"What happened?" Sonia hovers, trying to see what upset me. I want to tell her to stop; this isn't something anyone should see.

But before I can save her, she grabs the phone out of my hand to look at the offending image.

"Is this— Why? Oh god why?" She slams the phone screen down on my desk so neither of us have to see it again. Until I need to use my phone again. Which will be pretty soon thanks to this modern world of gadgets and interwebs. "Who sent you a dick pic?"

I take a few breaths before I answer. "My mom!"

"Chachi?"

"Yes. Should I see why she sent me a dick pic?" I ask Sonia, trying to get out of it even though I should address it or I'll have to get rid of the phone itself. And that's wasteful. "Is this something I can delegate to my right-hand human?"

"No. Hell no. That's sexual harassment."

"Okay, then." I reach for the phone with all the care of a hazardous materials worker in full protective gear approaching an unknown but definitely dangerous specimen.

I back out of the open email through squinted eyes, with one hand spread out in front of the screen to limit my view, getting the offending picture off my screen.

Mom's original email comes back on the screen. "It looks like Mom followed through on her threat to try to set me up with her friends' sons, and she had one of them send me an email introduction. But she didn't screen it before forwarding it." There is some introduction information under the picture, but it's a bit lost in the disgust of the photo.

I get all the facts and then delete the shit out of that email. "I think it was robber baron peen. Or great-grandson of a robber baron peen."

"Then at least there's deep pockets to pay for your therapy and lawyer's fees." Sonia rubs my back in comfort.

"Why are men like this?" I put my phone down again, happy to take a break from it for a little while. Like maybe forever.

"I don't know. But I'm not going to be able to get that image out of my mind anytime soon." Sonia shudders.

Unfortunately, this is not my first dick pic. My first was when I was in charge of the Loot Twitter handle. They slid that shit right into my DMs. And if people can send a dick pic to an auction house, the rest of us have no chance.

I'm not saying anything about consensual dick pics, but this is very much *not* wanted.

"Can I file a workers' compensation claim for stress?" I ask.

"Since that's kind of a work phone, maybe? But you'd have to tell everyone your mom sent you a dick pic."

"How am I supposed to do a seller pitch in this state of mind?"

"Work through it. Or we'll never get to do anything but Indian art for the rest of our careers." Take-no-prisoners Sonia packs my purse for me. "The car is coming in twenty minutes, and you have to stop by printing."

Twenty minutes later on the dot, I'm getting into the company car, catalog box in hand and dick pic ruthlessly pushed to the back of my mind. Harrison's offices are in the financial district, and traffic means it would have been quicker to take public transportation. But I don't want to risk dropping the catalog and I don't want to show up for the meeting all sweaty.

The privacy of the car also gives me a chance to practice the pitch a few more times before the meeting. I need it, because I'm more comfortable in front of a large crowd than working one on one with a prospective client. Maybe because auction crowds are too polite to sass me back on the rostrum, but individuals don't feel as compelled to be nice.

I get to the offices a little early and go to the reception desk to check in.

"Hi, I'm here for a meeting with Harrison at four. I'm Priya Gupta with Loot."

The receptionist scrolls through his computer. "I've got you checked in. Please take a seat in our waiting area and I'll call you when Mr. Richmond is ready."

"Perfect, thanks." I turn to find the area he indicated, and stop, the genuine smile on my face freezing when I see who's already there.

Again?

"Okay, this time I was here first, so can I accuse you of stalking now?" Gavin asks from his seat in the waiting room, his fingers poised over his phone. He's dressed in another sharp suit that costs more than most people's monthly salaries, and he's lounging on the chestnut leather couch.

He has a substantial box next to him as well, and I inch closer to try some corporate espionage. "You wish."

"I very much do, Riya." His voice gets lower, in that sexy, annoying way he has. Annoying because I don't want to find anything he does sexy. But the lust I'm feeling strongly disagrees with my assessment, and my thighs clench together to stop the spread of the sensations I can feel starting down there.

"So, he's seeing us on the same day?" I ignore the battle happening down south, focusing on the meeting at hand.

Gavin nods. "Power move. Having the competition see each other before the meeting."

"He's good at business."

A commotion draws our attention to the front desk,

and I see two nicely dressed men with their own hardcover books. They're arguing with each other and the poor receptionist is trying to get them to calm down.

"More competition," I whisper to Gavin, not taking my eyes off the scene.

"The boys from the Big Two. But they aren't leaving a good first impression on the company."

As much as Gavin and I bicker, we'll always be all smiles and some passive-aggression in public. Because we're professionals.

"Do you think this is going to end in a UFC-style cage match between all the auction house representatives?" I ask, not putting anything past rich investors.

"If it does, can we get on record that I don't feel right punching you in the face."

"That's a bold statement to make when I could kick your butt. When I already kicked your butt in school." I remind him of a recess a long time ago in a private New York City school playground.

When he got his butt kicked for pulling my hair. It was self-defense.

The receptionist calls us over to the front desk. The representatives from the other two auction houses are refusing to make eye contact, and the receptionist is looking like he's reconsidering his career choice so he can go back to wherever he's from to consider a more pleasant career in...manure sales or manual horse insemination, probably.

"Mr. Richmond will see you all in the conference room," he says weakly. "If you'll follow me."

I exchange a look with Gavin. I thought Harrison would meet us all one at a time, but this is a fun change.

I always wanted to compete for the attention of one man with three other men also competing at the same time.

The employee leads us through a long hallway and into a conference room where Harrison is already sitting, reviewing a packet in front of him.

"Hello and thank you for coming to meet me on such short notice." He gets up to shake our hands and indicate that we should sit down. It's cute that he phrases that like any of us had a choice.

If we want this sale, there is no choice.

"I can look at anything you have for me, and then we'll take it from there. Feel free to get some refreshments that we've laid out while I look."

We all hand over our books. It's unexpected, but I've spent so much time this past week on the catalog, it can speak for itself.

Although actually watching Harrison reading our offerings is making my nervous bladder act up, I don't want to leave the room unless it becomes an emergency.

After fifteen awkward and nerve-wrecking minutes of watching Harrison read, I get up to take him up on the offer of snacks. I'm not really hungry, but I'll take the distraction and the opportunity to burn off some nervous energy on the walk to the food.

I'm putting together a plate of mini pastries and fruit when I hear footsteps behind me.

"When I get the sale, what do you want to eat for dinner?" Gavin whispers to me.

"When *I* win, I'm going to eat a victory burger from Shake Shack, and while I'm there, I'm going to research puppies on my phone." I grab a water bottle and return to the table to eat. It's too quiet here, and the sounds of me chewing is like a concert in the room. At least to me.

I feel kind of disappointed that this competition is going to be over. It's always interesting to go up against Gavin directly, firing up my blood and pushing me to come up with better ideas and bigger sales. I don't think I noticed how much he pushes me in a good way until I was working directly against him on this catalog for such a large collection.

But I'm sure there'll be some other art we can fight about in the future.

After an hour of waiting, I've caught up on all the industry news across multiple websites, and also all the entertainment news as well. I'm about to dive into politics, but Harrison saves me from that depressing endeavor by closing the final book.

"Thank you all for the hard work. They're all really good plans. I can't get you all to hold a joint sale, can I?" He looks at us hopefully.

We all look at him without saying anything, not even a fake laugh to put him at ease. Because there's no way that's going to happen. The infighting over every small detail would tear us apart. And nothing would get sold.

Harrison sighs, like he knew he wasn't going to get that but hoped anyway. "No, I guess not. Well, I like the pitches from Carlyle's and Loot best, but I don't have time to get into the details today. So why don't you two come spend this weekend and next week at my house party in Long Island? We can go over details, and I can get to know you both to see who is the better fit?"

Chapter Thirteen

The room erupts in protests. From the losing side of the room because they still want to be in the race. And from the Carlyle/Loot side of the room because we don't know if we can take a week away from work last minute.

"I've made my decision," Harrison says sternly over the din. Then he addresses us exclusively. "I understand it's a lot to ask, but I would appreciate it. And we do have a strong internet connection so you can work from the house if you need to."

"I'd love to." I swallow down any complaints I have with a smile. At this point, it's walk away from the deal or accept it with grace if I want to win. And maybe Gavin will have a doctor's appointment that he can't reschedule.

"I'll be there as well," Gavin says. Well, that was a short five seconds of hope.

"Perfect. I'll send you the address for my house on the North Shore, and I'll expect you there tomorrow. Events start at around noon, so please be there before then. And bring some formal wear for the week. Some casual exercise wear too."

We say our goodbyes and exit his building. The representatives from the big two houses quickly and quietly sulk into the evening, not giving us a goodbye on their way out, but Gavin lingers.

"Are you ready for a Gold Coast week?" he asks.

"I love the Gold Coast. I'm excited to see what I'm sure is an architecturally significant historic mansion. I'm *not* ready to stop working for a week last minute so I can dance whenever a billionaire tells me to."

"And we can't send someone more junior, or he'll freak out thinking we don't value him."

"Takes a billionaire to know a billionaire."

"Not me. Maybe if you combine all the family money," he mumbles. "So when can I pick you up tomorrow?" he asks at a normal volume.

"Excuse me?"

"We can't take two cars to the same place. That's bad for the environment."

"Oh, so you can tell me a time you'll be there, and I can get all ready, get my bags downstairs, wait outside my building for you, and then you can just not show up? So I'm late for the time that Harrison specified and you get the show? Hard pass."

"I wouldn't…" he starts, offended by the suggestion. "Okay, so I might have, in the past, done something similar."

Like the time he sent me an invitation to speak at an auctioning convention, but it was a convention for workers compensation adjusters. I handled it, but it was a terrifying few minutes when I had to figure out what to say.

"Yeah, you did. So I'm not trusting you now, even though you must have realized how old you're getting and are desperate to get at all of this." I move my pointer finger from my head to my toes.

"Oh, Riya, you know only men get better with age." He shakes his head at me in pity.

I scowl at him because it's true according to society, no matter how much I hate the unfair double standard. Which means, as much as I disagree, Mom's right when she says I should start thinking about dating seriously. But I have so much to do at Loot before I can devote the right amount of time to the man endeavor. And while I'm putting it off and getting older and less desirable to the world by the minute, Gavin is getting more distinguished and accomplished in their eyes. The bastard.

"But fine, if you don't trust me, then you can pick me up tomorrow morning," Gavin says.

I open my mouth to tell him to get his own car. "You know what, sure. Send me your address, and I'll text when we're on the way."

I give him an evil smile, thinking of all the possibilities. Leaving him at a random gas station, making him listen to the Spice Girls (who are amazing despite how much he wouldn't like it), or "misplacing" his luggage for the weekend. I'll need to collude with Tom, our driver, before we pick Gavin up.

"That look on your face is a little bit scary."

"If you don't want to come with me, that's your decision."

"No, let's do this."

"But only if you take the train with me right now back to Midtown." I throw the challenge out, because watching the spoiled man try to navigate public transportation will be hilarious. I have a lot to do, reassigning tasks and telling everyone I'll be gone for the next week, but this will be worth the time I lose.

"The train?"

"And I'm going to take pictures." I hold up my phone, evil grin still on my face.

"It's rush hour." He starts to look a little green around the edges.

"Yup."

He sighs. "Okay to all your conditions. Give me your number and I'll text you my address right now." He gets out his phone to do just that.

We walk to the closest station that will take us to Midtown. "Do you need to put money on your Metro-Card?"

"Is that like a Mastercard?"

"Oh god." This might be a bigger undertaking than I originally anticipated. I assumed he hadn't used it in a while but... "Have you never taken the subway? You live in New York City. You've been here your entire life."

"But I always call a car. Remember, I'm a job creator, Riya."

I hope he has to stand next to someone eating tuna on the train. Sure, my nose will be assaulted too, but it will be worth it.

I herd him to the machine to get him a MetroCard and watch (and photodocument) in amusement as he goes through the process on the screen, having to restart his purchase three times.

"Where to now, sadist?" he asks, shiny new Metro-Card in hand.

I think about letting him guide us, but I don't have three hours for him to get used to the subway. It took him long enough to pay. "This way."

I lead him to the right platform and have to grab

him by the belt to stop him from taking the local when we can save time by getting on the express. When the train arrives, I push him into the train with the rush-hour crowd.

"Why aren't they moving to the middle of the train? There're still more people that need to get in, and they're pushing against." He glares at both groups of offending people. Who are probably tourists. Locals would never.

"Soak it all in! All the smells, the scents, and the press of strangers against your body."

"Is that the smell of a medical emergency?" Gavin covers his mouth with his hand.

As the cab gets more crowded, he moves closer to me, one arm sliding around me and the other grasping the bar above us. As the doors close and the train surges forward, I grip him around the waist to keep my own balance.

I feel his body shift to accommodate the movement, a little awkwardly at first but easier with each jerk of the train.

I have no way to give us some distance, with other passengers boxing us in on all sides. And I don't want to. With this much movement, it feels like we're dancing.

Maybe we should have taken the local; then there would have been even more stopping and starting. This is still nice, and it takes more willpower than I would have thought to not rub myself against him intentionally. My downstairs bits are not amused at the restraint.

I close my eyes to block out the din, inhaling the bergamot and cedar of his fancy cologne. If I can't have more rubbing, at least I can use my other senses.

"Do you do this often?" he asks.

"Are you asking me if I come here often?" I raise my head to look at him, laughter in my voice.

He rolls his eyes but otherwise doesn't respond to the question. "You have access to a fleet of company cars. Why go through this?"

"I wasn't lying when I said it can be quicker than getting around by car during rush hour, and it's environmentally friendly. Plus it's interesting to people watch." I shouldn't pretend that I always do the right thing and take the train, but I at least change it up more than this spoiled brat.

"Buy a TV."

"It's good for you to interact with New Yorkers; it'll keep you humble."

"Where's the fun in that?"

The train stays full so I resign myself to (and enjoy) snuggling Gavin in public. When our stop is near, I tug on Gavin's suit jacket, drawing him closer to the doors. "You're almost free of this." I look up at him to savor the misery on his face.

But he isn't looking around in disgust. Instead, he's looking at me, with a half smile on his face.

I get a little lost in the blue of his eyes, as sparkling and vibrant as the Mediterranean Sea on a sunny day, my face softening into a matching smile. Gavin's been pretty surprising this past week...surprising me with how much I enjoy being around him. And he's handling this adventure much better than I thought he would.

I get so lost that I jump when a fellow passenger yells at us angrily. "Can you eye-fuck at home like normal people? Some of us have places to be."

"Yup, that's on us." I grab Gavin's hand and drag him out of the train.

"That's not very ni—" Gavin begins in a stern voice to the stranger.

"Nope, we were being obnoxious."

"He still could have been nicer about it."

I keep Gavin's hand to get him out of the station with minimum fuss. When we get up the stairs, I say, "You didn't even have to meet pizza rat."

We stop outside the station. "What a shame," he says, no disappointment in his voice.

I realize we're still holding hands and snatch mine back like he's one of New York's unique animal residents. "As you did hold up your end of the bargain, we'll be at your place bright and early to pick you up. Be outside on time, or we'll leave without you."

I start walking toward the office. I get out my phone to start taking care of the hundreds of things that need to be done before I can leave.

Gavin falls into step next to me and I give him the stink eye.

He holds up his hands in supplication. "You know this is the way to my office as well. I need to get some stuff there before I can go home to pack."

Great, more awkward moments with Gavin. And I was hoping to have the walk to clear my head.

"And when I do go home, I'm going to take a car." He narrows his eyes at me.

"Baby steps. We'll have you biking to work in no time."

"If he's not outside waiting for us, we can leave," I say to Tom as we drive to the Upper East Side.

"Got it, Priya."

I stifle a yawn, then realize there's no one in the car, so I let it out full force. I lean my head against the soft leather interior and hope we run into traffic so I can get some sleep.

No one is happy that I'm leaving for the week. Sonia and Ajay freaked out at the amount of work I dumped on them, and Dad doesn't understand why I'm going to a "strange man's house in the middle of nowhere."

I tried to explain that we've worked with or around Harrison for years, and that his house near Huntington isn't exactly remote, but Dad doesn't trust any place where you can't see into your neighbor's bedroom window. He's lived in cities too long.

Between telling everyone the same justifications for going and trying to pack for this party where I don't know the dress code/theme/events, I had a very late night.

We stopped to get some coffee, and I hope the magic liquid does its work so I can be up to fighting form by the time Gavin gets in the car.

I think I might need a refund, because when the car stops in front of Gavin's building and I see him, I'm distracted out of the fight by the image of him in the morning, signature tousled hair looking even more just-got-out-of-bed than usual, a T-shirt, jeans and tennis shoes rounding out the outfit. I haven't seen him this casual since elementary school PE. Well, aside from all the bathing suit shots he posts to his socials.

I stare at him, unable to look away or think of anything else besides that bed he just rolled out of. Especially how warm it must be in the chilly New York morning.

When he finishes helping Tom get the luggage put away in the trunk and enters the car, his broad shoulders block out the light for a second. He fills the small space with his effortless energy. It's infectious, making everyone around him feel like they just had a shot of caffeine. It's one of his best weapons, and the reason he's a favorite with clients.

"Did you get that for me?" He points to my coffee, which is resting in one of the car's cup holders.

"No." I pick up the cup in defiance. "But feel free to watch me enjoy it." I add some moans of enjoyment as I take a sip in front of him.

"Excuse me," Gavin calls out to the front seat without taking his eyes of me. "Could we stop at another coffee place?"

"Depends on if you want to get left behind in the wilds of Long Island," I say before Tom can answer.

"Scratch that. I'm good."

I get out my iPad to do some work. I have no idea how much time I'll actually have this week so I need to take advantage of every available moment. Gavin has other plans, if his passive aggressive sighs are anything to go by.

"Is there something I can help you with?" I don't take my eyes off the first draft of the catalog that Ajay's team sent me. It's good stuff. Thank god, because I don't have time to do serious edits on it right now.

"Entertain me?" Gavin asks.

I reach into his inside jacket pocket, fishing out his phone. When the back of my hand brushes his chest, I tell my hormones to cool it and that we aren't going to explore that chest any further.

Treasure obtained, I hold up the phone in front of Gavin, jiggling it a bit when he doesn't take it right away.

"Spoilsport." He finally takes the phone. "So you don't want to play the license plate game?"

I look at him and reach into my Mary Poppins purse to get my headphones and put them on my ears, maintaining eye contact the entire time. Before I turn on my music, I hear him sigh and say, "Cold."

Halfway through the drive, I feel a tap on my shoulder. Since Tom is still in the front seat, it can only be Gavin.

"You're like a toddler," I say, exasperation heavy in my voice.

"But a toddler that can drink."

"Terrifying image." I give in on a sigh. "Why did you interrupt me?"

"What do you think Harrison's going to make us do to get this sale?"

"I try not to think about it beforehand, because if I thought about late nights, elaborate gift baskets, or feeding a millionaire's pet snake with live mice, then I probably wouldn't have gotten into this car today."

Gavin laughs with his head thrown back, and my eyes zero in on the rhythmic way his giant chest moves up and down with the motion.

"The pet snake is a good one, but have you ever had to shuffle a millionaire's mistress out of his hotel room under a catering cart?"

I laugh with him, trying to picture him in that French farce. "But that does make me sad for the wife."

"I did too. Really cut up, actually. But then the next weekend she asked me to send some vintage cufflinks she bought from us to her special friend, so I stopped feeling bad about it after that."

Ah, the people we meet in this job.

We settle into a nice conversation sharing our war stories, and the things we've done to get and keep clients. I don't think about the work I still have to do and the tablet stays unused on my lap, which makes the ride an unexpected but pleasant break.

This makes the second time I've had a civil conversation with Gavin about the industry. An easy, companionable, pleasant conversation. I like talking to people not related to me about my passion. Is this how people with huge friend groups feel?

But does that mean *we're* becoming friends?

"We're almost there, Priya." Tom breaks into my thoughts.

"Thanks, Tom." Oh wow, that went by fast. But now it's time to work. "I hope Harrison decides that dragging us out here is enough to prove how worthy we are, and he just has some simple but well-thought-out questions that I can shine answering. Then I can enjoy a nice dinner and be back in the city before too much goes wrong at home."

"Ditto. Except the part where I get the job. You can still have a nice dinner though."

"So magnanimous of you."

We roll through the elaborate wrought-iron front gate of the property and up the drive. I haven't even seen the house yet, but I can already tell that it's going to be spectacular. The drive is lined with trees, and the flowers on them look so artfully placed that I wouldn't put it past Harrison to have the landscape team go around and arrange each flower for effect.

When I do see the house, I'm not surprised by the way it takes my breath away. I've had that feeling for houses, paintings, sculptures, cabinets, chairs, vases, purses and the odd dress. I haven't felt it for a man though.

That might not be the best sign.

The house is three stories tall, with large windows framed by brick, and vibrant green ivy crawling up the façade, which is so long Harrison probably refers to one side as the East Wing and the other as the West Wing. The front entrance is framed by Ionic columns, with a flickering lantern on each side of the large door.

As we drive up, Harrison's employees come outside, dressed in their finest livery, to greet us and get our bags out of the car. I feel bad for them, because between us we have about four large suitcases and three assorted small bags. I had to pack for every possible situation, which adds up. To fit them all in the car, some traveled in the front seat.

The staff tell us Harrison is waiting in the morning room. I bet there's probably also a drawing room in here, for excess's sake.

I tentatively pass through the entrance, into the foyer. The wood-paneled room is illuminated by the soft glow from the chandelier and fireplace, which flickers over the sculptural elements of the walls. Above the chandelier, a tromp l'oeil painting shows cherubs looking down at us from a painted balcony, curiously watching the lives unfolding beneath them.

A stoic employee with a tray of champagne glasses offers us his goods, and then directs us to the morning room.

Liquid courage in hand, we enter to be greeted by a crowd of about five people in various poses of lounging.

Harrison stands up to greet us. "There you are, now the games can begin."

Chapter Fourteen

I awkwardly laugh at the comment, really regretting my stubbornness, which wouldn't let me walk away from this job.

Maybe Harrison sees the terror on my face, because he laughs too. "Just kidding. This is going to be a relaxing week."

I smile, but he's wrong. Well, for some of us it will be. For two of us in particular, everything we say and do will be under a microscope so Harrison can decide which one of us is worthy enough to sell his art.

"Auctioneers, this is my wife, Pari, and our daughter, Naomi." He points to an older Indian woman and a younger woman who looks a little like them both. "This is my VP, Nate." He indicates a white man who raises his glass at us in greeting. "And these are family friends, Jack and Cindy Chen." An older East Asian man and the white woman next to him nod at us from their couch. "Everyone, this is Priya and Gavin. By the end of this trip, one of them will be selling my art."

"You have a beautiful home here," Gavin says. "It'd be a great spot for a house sale."

Hey! I was thinking of that first, way back at my original lunch with Harrison. "I agree. As I mentioned at our first meeting, this would be the best way to show-case your collection, letting buyers see the enviable life-style they're getting if they buy from us." Ha! Take that.

The easy camaraderie Gavin and I had developed in the car is staying in that car, which is currently driving back to the city.

"I'll give you some time to settle into your rooms, and then I have a light lunch and some activities planned for all of us." Harrison doesn't engage in our vying for his attention.

I take a quick look at the people around me to see what the dress code is, a lot of business casual and rich people lounging wear, which is much more ex-pensive than normal people lounging wear and not as comfortable.

I'm glad I brought lots of dresses. They're so ver-satile, making it look like I put in more effort even though they're only one piece of clothing, so they're half the work.

A smartly dressed man appears out of nowhere to take us up to our rooms.

"Hi," I say as we go up the grand staircase to the sec-ond floor. "I'm Priya. Thank you for taking our bags up."

"Of course, ma'am."

"What's your name?" I ask.

"Jeeves."

"Is it really? Like Jeeves and Wooster?" I love those books and the show. But what are the chances?

Jeeves sighs. "No. My name's Ryan. But Harrison thought Jeeves sounded cooler, probably because of the character, so he started calling me that."

"That's not right," Gavin says.

"Jeeves" keeps a straight face. He's very good at his job. "He pays me extra."

He probably meant that as a defense of his employer, but it just makes it worse.

Jeeves-Ryan probably feels more comfortable with us because we occupy a weird space between the rich clients and people who work for rich clients. We get invited to their house parties and socialize with them at their charity banquets, but at the end of the day, it's a business transaction where we sell their stuff. And to muddy the waters even more, Gavin and I aren't just auctioneers; we're both related to the owners of our respective auction houses.

Jeeves-Ryan, as I will now forever think of him, drops Gavin off first, and then drops me off at the room right next to Gavin's. That's far too close for comfort. And the nefarious wink Gavin throws over his shoulder as he enters his room doesn't make me feel any better about it.

"If you get lost on the way down, just yell and someone will be around to guide you." Jeeves-Ryan gives me a companionable smile as he leaves me to the room.

My guest room is dominated by a majestic curtained four-poster bed with an elaborate headboard. The carved motif on it shows people on a railroad, a shout-out to the source of the Richmonds' vast wealth. The walls are plastered with a blue floral wallpaper, which matches the lush blue sheets on the bed.

I wonder if I can get away with a quick nap because that bed looks enticing, with the duvet looking especially soft. But I work through it because I can't let Carlyle's win.

I start unpacking my stuff so I can see all my armor

options for the upcoming battle. Once everything is out, I choose a sundress and quickly change into it. As I'm finishing up, a knock comes from the door.

"Come in," I call out.

"Hi, ma'am. I wanted to see if you need anything washed, pressed or unpacked for you? Or if there is anything else you need for your stay?"

"I'm almost done but thank you. I'm Priya." I extend my hand.

"I'm Sarah." She shakes my hand.

An idea forms. "Did you offer the same thing to the man next door?"

"Yes. To all our guests. And he requested that we press and hang his clothes."

"I know you don't know us, but the guy next door is arrogant." Honesty makes me add, "He has his moments where he's tolerable. But also he has moments when he never takes anything seriously but everything still goes his way, and also he always looks like he just stepped off of a modeling shoot."

"I understand." She nods along.

I lower my voice. "And if you would be willing—feel free to say no, I don't want you to get in any trouble. But if you could shrink some of his clothes? Nothing major, just enough to make him uncomfortable in his clothes and throw him off his game, that would really help me out."

She lowers her voice conspiratorially. "We get a lot of unique requests. I'll see what I can do."

"Thank you so much."

"It's okay, ma'am. I've run across a few of those, so I'll be happy to help."

Ooh, it sounds like there's a story behind that tone.

If she's been working for Harrison for any length of time, she's seen some interesting stuff. Probably a lot more intense than my wild make-Gavin-slightly-uncomfortable plan.

Before I can dig deeper, I hear another knock on the door. The knocker doesn't wait for me to invite them in, instead barging in a second after the abrupt noise.

"You ready, Riya?" Gavin asks, fresh in a pair of dark slacks, a button-down shirt and a sports coat.

Of course it's him. Who else would barge into any room like he owns it? "No."

"Okay, I can always go down without you." He turns around and heads back out of the door he just entered through.

"I decline." I grab his belt and drag him back into the room and onto the seat next to my vanity. "Sit yourself down here and I'll be right out." I pat him on the shoulder.

Sarah tactfully leaves while we're debating the issue. I flee into the bathroom to touch up my makeup quickly. It's the fastest I've ever done the task, but I don't want to leave Gavin alone in my room too long.

My worries are justified, because when I come out of the bathroom, Gavin is standing across the room, *not* where I left him, peeking through my open suitcase.

I storm over and snap the top down, missing his fingers by inches. Unfortunately.

"I knew you wouldn't be able to help yourself. Which is why I took all my electronics with me into the bathroom." I indicate through the open door my laptop, iPad and phone resting on the counter.

"Maybe I wasn't looking for corporate secrets. Maybe I was looking for your underwear."

I tilt my head at him. "But how would you find something that doesn't exist?"

Pride fills my chest, making it puff out like a balloon inflating, when I see Gavin Carlyle struck dumb. Even if I had to lie to do it. Because with my luck, if I really went commando, I would accidentally flash people constantly.

I saunter out of the room, listening for the sound of his footsteps behind me. I don't hear them, so I'm about to turn around and "help" him out of my room when I finally hear the steps behind me.

"Tell me more about this," he demands, voice rough. He clears his throat.

"How can I tell you about something that doesn't exist?" I tease him even more.

He groans. "Come on, that's not even fair."

"I'm sorry, was there anything in our past interactions that made you think I would ever be fair to you?"

"Professional courtesy?" he asks, voice cracking on the words. And all I had to do was talk about my nether clothes, or lack thereof. If only I had known this earlier.

"Survival of the fittest." I start going back down the stairs.

"So like right now..." he starts, not letting it go.

I stop on the steps, enjoying this surge of power flowing through me and letting it go to my head. "Right now..." I take a step back up so I'm on the step above him and closer to his height. I look him directly in the eyes, unblinking. "Under this fabric..." I clench the dress at my thighs and inch it up, watching his eyes dip down to follow the upward movement of the fabric "...is something you'll never have to worry about, because you'll never get under there."

I drop the dress and walk around him, not-so-gently nudging him in the shoulder on the way down.

"Underestimating your enemy is dangerous," Gavin warns from behind me.

I throw a look over my shoulder, looking him up and down as he follows me. "I think I'll be okay."

We reenter the morning room, everyone in the same position since we left.

"Excellent. Now we can get started with the activities." Harrison indicates that we should all follow him.

"Ten bucks says that his daughter leaves and this becomes a wild sex orgy," Gavin whispers in my ear as we follow Harrison to the back of the house. His voice still sounds rougher than it usually is.

"God I hope not. But I'm also not taking that bet."

Harrison opens a set of French doors into his backyard. I take a deep breath as I walk out, inhaling the fresh air, which carries a salty hint of the nearby sea. The large space isn't fenced in, and the manicured English-style garden (complete with statues) fades to the wild chaos of nature. And we can see it all from the terrace we've walked onto.

We walk down a set of stairs and away from the house, toward a table set up with shooting implements. In front of the table, targets are set up at various distances.

In retrospect, I probably should have known there would be a shooting event at this country house party, if we were keeping with the English house party rules.

I learned to shoot specifically for events like this because it's a great way to network. If I didn't do it I would immediately be excused. Everyone would be nice about it, offering to let me stay inside so I don't have to be around the guns. But then I miss the deals.

I tried staying and not shooting, but not participating seemed to put people off talking business with me.

At least I didn't have to learn how to play golf. I'm glad that making a deal on the golf course is a dying practice. At least with our buyers and sellers it is.

"Let's get some shooting practice in to start the weekend. There's a sink over by the house to wash hands and also some food for lunch over on that table. Enjoy." Harrison encourages us to step up to the table, with a large collection of guns and ammunition. Some of the pieces are antiques, and those I do like shooting, because I start imagining the lives of the people who've shot them before me.

I pick up a Webley Revolver, the weapon that the United Kingdom gave to its military from the late 1800s to the 1960s.

"If you're afraid of the weapon, I'm sure Harrison wouldn't mind if you stayed inside and drank some hot cocoa," Gavin whispers from next to me.

"You know, I think I'll be okay. But your concern is plain adorable."

Harrison has us step back up to the line, two people at a time. Gavin volunteers to go first, along with Harrison's VP, Nate.

Once they start shooting, I take back all the irritated things I thought about this choice of activity, because Gavin is terrible at it. He doesn't even hit the target for five of the ten shots he takes, and the other five are barely on the sheet.

This makes up for taking the week away from work, having to compete with Gavin for the job, and me hav-

ing all these amorous thoughts about Gavin. Watching
him be human, with something he isn't naturally amazing at, is the most fun I've had in a while.

Gavin walks back to where I'm standing when he's
done, head down and shoulders hunched. He's much
more reserved than when he sauntered off. Now I feel
a little bad and I swallow the snarky comment I was
about to make.

"Those antique guns are finicky at the best of times.
Even when they weren't antiques, if we're all honest."
I try to make him feel better. I never thought I'd be
standing here trying to make Gavin feel better after a
failure, but I want him to get back to the arrogant man
I feel comfortable insulting. Otherwise it's kind of like
kicking a hurt puppy. And that takes away from the joy
I felt at his misfortune.

He doesn't take my olive branch for what it is. Instead, he narrows his eyes at me for having witnessed
his failure, sullen in his silence.

"Next round of shooters," Harrison calls out.

"I'll go." I volunteer, along with Harrison's wife.
Anything to get away from the guy who's acting like
Charlie Brown after Lucy pulls the football away.

Nate is still at the table when I step up. "Do you
need any help setting up or shooting?" he asks. Unlike
Gavin, he has a genuine smile on his face and I don't
feel like the offer comes from a place of wanting to
make me look stupid.

But I still don't need the help. "No, thank you. I'm
good."

"Are you sure? The old guns can be a handful."

Okay, the first offer was sweet, the second is moving on to annoying. "I'll manage." I don't know if I'm

baring my teeth at him, but he doesn't ask a third time, so I might be.

I step up to the line and take the gun that Harrison's staff hands me. I check it's loaded and line up my sights. Taking a deep breath to make sure I'm relaxed, I pull the trigger. The shot lands in the center circle on the target, to the right side of it.

I do that a few more times until I'm empty and put down the gun. I nod at my target; I'm not going to win any sharpshooting awards, but it's respectable.

"Good shooting, Priya." Harrison pats me on the back as I turn from the table. Good, he's impressed, making all those hours I spent in that shooting range worth it.

I return to my spot next to Gavin, since he's the only person in this group I really know.

"What's up with that, Jason Bourne?" he asks, his tone still a bit sharp.

I go for honesty, knowing he'll understand better than anyone. "It was this or golf. I made my choice. And I look terrible in khaki pants."

"Ah, I did choose golf." Gavin gives me a small smile. I'm glad he's closer to being back to normal.

Sad Gavin is weird and I don't like it. It's worse than annoying, perfect Gavin. And that surprises me, because I thought nothing could be worse than the Golden Boy.

"Where'd you learn to shoot like that?" Nate approaches us, just as impressed as Harrison had been.

"Loot's head of security taught me when I was a teenager. He's a former super-soldier apparently, so I think he was just happy to be back at the range."

"My compliments to the teacher. And please don't

tell him how I offered to help you when you clearly don't need my help. I'm sorry for that."

I laugh and forgive the man for his earlier statements. I like a man who can admit when he's wrong. "I won't tell him. Scout's honor." I hold up three fingers.

"You weren't a scout." Gavin rats me out.

"Well, I thought about it," I say. "I started going to the meetings but then I ran into scheduling conflicts."

"You had scheduling conflicts in elementary school? That's so sad," Gavin says.

"I think it's charming." Nate smiles at me.

"Oh. Well, then you should have seen my childhood planners. They were filled with Lisa Frank stickers. And not a lot of free time."

"Nate!" Harrison waves him over, and Nate leaves.

"'I think it's charming.'" Gavin puts on his best snooty voice.

"You're such a child."

"Oh come on. You can't believe him. He's a businessman; they lie all the time."

"Because he couldn't just find me charming?" Thanks, buddy.

"No, I didn't mean it like that—" He extends a hand toward me.

"Sure."

Pari's getting some refreshments from the food spread and I see my chance to do some of that networking, and my chance to not hear the terrible things Gavin thinks about me, so I leave without saying bye to Gavin.

Pari is much nicer than Gavin, and I get some finger-size egg salad sandwiches out of the interaction.

The rest of the guests tire themselves out quickly

and Harrison releases us for free time before the formal dinner he planned for tonight.

I need it, because for a whole day I haven't been able to do any work and I've been getting a really irritating itch in the back of my brain, thinking about everything that could go wrong and how unprepared Ajay and Sonia are to handle it.

Sonia is great at her job but doing twice the amount of work is a bit much for everyone. And Ajay...well, Ajay is unprepared to handle his own workload.

I race back to my room, hoping that Harrison wasn't lying to us about the good reception out here.

The internet gods are smiling down on me, because I can see all the panicked emails from today. I set my iPad on the vanity and the wireless keyboard in my lap, getting to work.

Sonia tells me that a seller still needs to give us his pieces, so I tell her to send the head of our contemporary Indian art section; he's intimidating when he wants to be. Iris tells me her brain is melting trying to write the catalog description for a particularly tricky piece, so I do some research and send her a rough one back to get her started.

I see a worrying report on the provenance of a sculpture being considered for an upcoming show. It's an ancient Indian piece, and the dealer who owned it from 1965 to 1982 had a reputation for smuggling pieces out of their country of origin without permission and giving them a fake provenance to sell them.

That kind of looting and smuggling, especially when it's from archaeological sites, destroys context and whatever information an archaeologist could have gotten from that context. And takes items away from the people of the country, who should have access to their own heritage. It's a big problem.

I call Sonia to deal with the issue now.

"Do you need an extraction already?" Sonia asks in place of a hello.

"Ha-ha. You're so funny. I should give you a raise for all the comedy you're bringing to the table."

Silence on the other line. Then, "I mean, I'll take the extra money."

I ignore that; she gets annual raises. "Have you seen the provenance for the large-bosomed woman from the Gupta dynasty?" I also feel a little protective of the statue since she's from the dynasty that shares my name.

Sonia sighs. "Yeah. I noticed."

"We can't sell it."

"I know. I was hoping the name of the dealer was wrong, because it's such a beautiful piece."

"I know," I say, regret filling my voice. Even if there are plenty of people who would take the sale, we're not going there.

"What do we do then?" Sonia sounds so sad I feel like a parent who said their kid can't have ice cream after dinner.

"Call whoever's the local FBI agent for the Art Crime Team. They'll tell you what we do next. And don't tip the seller off until we talk to them. Do we have the piece in possession?"

"No, they just sent us the information sheets to see if we'd be interested in selling it."

"Is it a big seller or buyer?" I cross every part of my body that can cross. We're still going to do the right thing either way, but I can hope it won't be too much of a sacrifice.

"Steady but not huge."

It could have been worse. "'Kay, let me know what Davis says."

"Will do." Sonia hangs up on me.

One problem solved, I keep clearing out my inbox. Mom forwarded another email from a potential suitor. This one contains zero penises but does have a haiku about securities sales. It's somehow impressive and boring at the same time. But I'm still not responding to it.

Sotheby's sent me one of their quarterly emails trying to poach me to their Indian Art Department. It's flattering but I'm not ready to throw over the family business just yet. Plus they're so large everything is clearly separated into departments, meaning I'd be stuck working only in the Indian Art Department. At Loot, at least there's a chance I can one day do shows that are a bit of anything I feel like learning about. Instead of sneaking in other art like in my *Female Gaze* show.

We'll see how much Dad annoys me over Ajay and management positions.

So for now, that email gets a polite rejection, leaving the door open for the future.

Sonia emails me about leads she has on potential sales, and ideas for shows we could do if we get them. I approve the ideas so Sonia can get started with the sellers. Another member of my team, who was formally on Ajay's team until I stole him, sends me a plan for an upcoming exhibition space that requires minimal changes.

I look longingly at the bed for the second time today, but a knock dashes that dream. "Come in."

"Hi, ma'am." Sarah comes in.

"Please call me Priya."

"Maybe Ms. Priya, just in case Harrison is around."

I nod. I don't want to ruffle any feathers.

"I came to see if you need any help getting ready for dinner."

"Harrison's really giving us the whole country house party experience." I can stop wondering what it would be like to live in a Jane Austen novel. Or a regency romance novel. More work than I would have thought, and fewer brooding heroes.

"Yes."

"Well, I don't really need any help, but if you want to hang out here for an hour on your phone, please feel free." I indicate an overstuffed chair.

Sarah looks to the door and then to the chair. She does this a few more times, and then makes her decision. She shrugs, taking the offered seat. "Thank you." She pulls her phone out of a pocket and gets comfortable. "By the way, I was able to do…that thing we discussed."

"You were? Oh, thank you. He's going to be so annoyed, and not able to figure out why." I cackle, clapping my hands and bouncing in my chair.

"It was a pleasure." She goes back to her phone.

We sit in a companionable silence while I get another half hour of work done.

My alarm goes off, which I set to make sure I didn't lose track of time. I stretch the kinks out of my back and wander to the closet to get out some dress options for the night. After throwing them on the bed, I stare at them for a few minutes. I take them one by one to the floor-length mirror and hold them up in front of me.

"I think you look good in the red," Sarah says tentatively from behind me.

"You should be on break—" I hold the red one up to

me. "Oh, yes. You're right, this is much better than the other options. Thank you!"

I rush to the bathroom, looking at my watch and cursing for not giving myself more time to get ready.

After the dress is on, I clear the vanity of my work and return it to its original use. I dump out my makeup bag and fish out the things I need. I slap some eyeliner on and some lipstick and turn to my nearest critic.

"How do I look?" I ask.

"Can I just…" Sarah approaches me, picking at the makeup sprawled on the table and looking at me questioningly.

"If you don't mind, I'd love the help. But I really did just want to give you a break."

"I'm going to school to do makeup, so I don't mind at all."

"Thank you. I never really learned to do all the magic the professionals can do."

"You're in good hands."

She's right; twenty minutes later I look in the mirror and see my face, but fancier. "Have you ever thought about living in the city?"

Yes, I am shamelessly trying to poach Sarah to make me look great all the time. Sonia would love to get in on it too. Mom as well, probably.

Sarah laughs. "My family's out here so I want to stay home till I move out to LA to try to do makeup for movies and TV."

I crinkle my nose. "Ew, LA. If you like no seasons and driving for half of your day I suppose."

"I would only go because of work."

We share another smile. What a loss to the Loot staff.

A loud sound reverberates into the room. I jump and clutch my rapidly beating heart. "What's that?"

"The dinner gong," Sarah says, not missing a beat in cleaning up the makeup on the vanity.

"He has a dinner gong?" Not that it's the craziest thing I've seen. Still. Sarah just nods. "Okay, I'm being summoned to dinner then."

"Enjoy."

"Thank you. And if you want to pretend to clean my room but just hang out here for a bit without cleaning, please feel free."

I go down the stairs and realize I probably should have asked Sarah for directions, because I have no idea how to get to whatever room is being used for dinner tonight.

I peek into a few rooms but don't run into anyone or see any food. The big house is scarily silent, and a bit unnerving.

As I check in the fifth room I come across, I wonder if everyone in this house got kidnapped and they didn't get to me. Which means there's no one around to stop me if I take all this nice art...

"Lost, Riya?" Gavin's voice breaks into my plans for all the crime I was about to commit.

"I live in a two-bedroom condo in Midtown Manhattan, this is a bit much." I turn to face him.

And realize I've made a huge mistake.

Chapter Fifteen

Gavin is in a tight-fitting suit that I stupidly had someone make even tighter. His dinner jacket is pulled tight over his shoulders, making it look like the man is hulking out of his clothes. The shirt is stretched even tighter across his chest, buttons straining to do their job. One deep breath, and they would be defeated.

And then I would see. All. That. Skin.

I want him to breathe deeply.

"Don't you guys have a house in the Hamptons too?"

I swallow and need to remember how to speak English again after the sight in front of me shocked it out of me.

"Um. Yes. Yes, we do." The more I talk, the more English comes back to me. "But lately I try to avoid it since we just throw parties to network and go to parties to network and if I'm going to work on vacation I may as well just stay home and do real work. Ajay has more fun with the Hamptons networking than me anyway." I overshare in my attempt to get back to normal.

Gavin nods and I hold my breath, waiting to see if the buttons will pop, but they don't so I can resume breathing again.

"Yeah, it's exhausting to pretend to be on vacation

with people actually on vacation, while working them for leads," he says.

"I'll have to get a vacation home in Antarctica, somewhere with no art or buyers so I don't have to feel bad about taking a break."

"There must be somewhere closer we can go to get a break." He thinks about it, stealing my hand and tucking it into the crook of his elbow, directing me to the other side of the house.

Silence reigns as both of us legitimately try to think of where else has no art or buyers. "You know, penguins are very charming animals," I say.

"I'll start looking into yachts that can make the trip." He gives up with me, finding no other place that meets the requirements.

"Your bougie ass has to go on one of those scientific research vessels that are made for the trip with the professional crew, who know where all the cutest penguins are."

"How pedestrian." He shakes his head in disappointment and stops in front of a partially open door, the sounds of conversation filtering through. "Ready to get back to work?"

"Back to work destroying you." I immediately smile over my shoulder to take the sting out of my words.

"Back to trying, at any rate."

We're both incapable of not having the last word. Which prompts me to scoff. If I can't get in the last word, at least I'm getting in the last sound.

I ride that victory wave through the doorway and into the next fray.

"Excellent. Now that the last guests are here we can start dinner," Harrison says from the head of the table.

It's a struggle to see him through the decorations—elaborate, sparkling silverware and vases loaded with colorful flowers.

"That's on me, I got lost." I take the first empty seat I see, which happens to be next to Naomi.

"Don't worry," she lets me know. "The first time Nate visited, he got so lost he didn't make it to dinner until dessert was already served."

I send her a warm smile.

"Thanks, squirt," the man of the story says from across the table.

Gavin takes the only other open seat, the one next to Nate and directly across from me. The flames from the candles on the table flicker over his golden hair like it's struggling for every opportunity to throw itself at him but keeps getting pulled back from its goal by the jealous wick.

I get it. He has nice hair.

Harrison calls for the dinner service to start, which gives me a convenient excuse to sublimate my new-found desire for Gavin into something a lot safer: food.

"For our first night, we're doing a nine-course meal," Harrison, all Lord of the Manor, declares from his seat, leaning back into his tall chair and bringing his fingers together in delight as he watches our reaction.

I don't have to fake the excitement plastered on my face. If the food is anything like the house and the decorations, I'm going to leave this table in a snugger dress than the one I sat down in.

My eyes seek out Gavin, my first instinct to share the exciting news with him. I hope it's because he's the only person I really know at this table, but a heavy weight in my stomach tells me I'm lying to myself. I just want to share this moment with him.

Then the heavy weight transforms into a completely different emotion: jealousy. Because Cindy, who's sitting on the other side of Gavin, has realized just how good his muscles look in the shirt I shrank, and her eyes are devouring him like he's the only course she wants tonight.

This is why pranks don't pay.

I try to telepathically tell Jack that his wife is developing wandering eyes, but he's oblivious to the fact, watching the servers bring in canapés for the first course.

Well, fine. I don't care what happens with Jack's marriage, and I don't care what fresh hell Gavin gets himself into. I'll just eat my canapés and drink my wine.

"Harrison, I love the silverware castle centerpiece. Is it late eighteenth century?"

The castle is at the center of the table, surrounded by small figurines of medieval types like knights, ladies and lords around the base. Some are functional, being part of candelabras, salt and pepper holders, or the two knights holding up a butter dish with their swords, while others are purely decorative.

Harrison nods, finishing off his first course. "Excellent eye, and point for Loot. They won't be part of the sale."

"It's a shame, but since I get to see them, it lessens the blow."

"Who can tell me why the centerpieces got so elaborate?" Harrison challenges.

"The fashion changed from service à la française to service à la russe, so instead of all the dishes being brought out at once, servers brought out and served one course at a time. The resulting space on the table led to more elaborate decorations, like your lovely, lovely castle," Gavin interjects before I can, sending me a goofy smile I bet he thinks is charming.

Damn it, I was going to say that too. Servers bring out the second course, a creamy French onion soup, with a brand-new wine pairing, which does lessen the sting of failure. Somewhat.

"Point Carlyle's." Harrison aims his clean spoon at Gavin before dipping it into the soup in front of him.

"Stop being so tacky, Harrison," Pari says, tone stern. "They're guests, not entertainment." They sound like they've had the conversation before.

And the way Harrison looks immediately contrite has me jealous of the affection between the two.

"They know they're the best in the business right now. And this is a difficult decision, Pari." Harrison tries to defend himself.

"If this is about terms…" I try to steer the conversation to the sale. This could be over tonight. "We can promise a large guarantee, and lower seller's commission."

"We can get a better price, and we can waive seller's commission entirely," Gavin counters, not even looking at Harrison as he makes the offer. Instead, his eyes are glued on me.

"Hah," I say, turning my gaze to him. "No one can do it that cheaply without cutting corners."

Gavin quirks his lips at the challenge, his good mood unassailable as ever, and opens his mouth to throw himself into the fight.

But Harrison cuts him off. "All right, maybe I shouldn't

make the first night into a cage match. Why don't you email me the numbers you're offering and other details, and we'll take it from there?"

We both incline our heads as the third course, the salad course, comes. It's a simple Caesar, which is my favorite. And it comes with its own wine too.

Battle over, tension I wasn't even aware of leaves my body, deflating my shoulders. Now I can enjoy the visual and culinary feast in front of me. I finish my third course (and third course wine) just in time for the fish course. I'm not usually a fan of fish, but I do like a succulent misoyaki butterfish.

The rest of the table starts a conversation about securities, and my eyes glaze over. I'd rather own things I can see like a house or a painting, a piece of history, rather than…whatever securities are. I share yet another look with Gavin. At least he's as lost as I am.

We're saved by the fifth course, our first main course. It's a chicken dish with vegetables and potatoes au gratin. And more wine. Yay! I may be getting a bit tipsy, five wine courses in.

Gavin inclines his wineglass to me slightly, an acknowledgment we're taking the rest of the night off from competing and I respond in kind, feeling very charitable with all the wine I've had. Plus, we've been ordered to lay down arms for the time being.

"How do you like working as an auctioneer?" Nate asks me when there's a lull in the conversation.

"I can't imagine doing anything else. I'm surrounded by beautiful things all day and I get to research them and show them off to the world. What made you get into the alternative energy business?"

"I wish I could say it was something noble, but I went

to business school and then got a job at a company that made batteries for phones. Then Harrison poached me."

That is pretty boring. But to each their own. And he must be good at…whatever it is energy executives do to be hired by Harrison.

While Nate is making small talk, Cindy is fawning over Gavin like he invented alternative energy. And he's lapping it up like he's never been complimented before.

Fat chance of that being true.

My bad mood is saved by the sixth course, a literal palate cleanser course of mint sorbet and prosecco. Nothing can be wrong with the world when there's prosecco.

It's swiftly followed by the second main course. It's filet mignon with another side of vegetables and rich garlic mashed potatoes. And seventh course wine.

My stomach isn't quite used to this gastronomic excess, but every dish smells and looks amazing, and I find myself eating more of each than I had anticipated. Reminding myself that this is a marathon and not a sprint just gets me to tell myself to shut up and enjoy each course fully.

Naomi asks me about living in England, and I remind myself to tread lightly, knowing Harrison wants his daughter to come home. I emphasize that visiting Europe is amazing but nothing beats coming home. I share some of my more appropriate stories, leaving out any that ended with me and that hot English man. Or me and that hot Scottish man. Or the fifteen other times with the same hot Scottish man.

Out of the corner of my eye, Harrison nods in satisfaction, so I pat myself on the back and enjoy the cheese boards. I have a very nice eighth wine course buzz going, so when I see the ninth, the dessert course, I let out an excited squeal under my breath. There's crème brûlée and cheesecake. I'm in heaven.

And also, dessert wine.

All of which I gorge on, happily.

After the food is cleared from the table, Harrison offers to take people to the smoking room for cigars.

I want the chance to network as much as the next person, but there's zero chance I'm going to hang out in an enclosed space where people are smoking that nasty smelling business.

I excuse myself as they head to the smoking room. Naomi must feel the same way because she breaks away from the group as well.

"Do you need help getting back to your room?" she asks me.

"No, I've got it now. Thank you." The wine is making me very bold about things that I don't know very much about.

Which I only fully realize when I walk past the dining room for the third time. It's just that all these hallways look the same: dark wood paneling, beautiful lighting fixtures, and portraits of wrinkly older individuals who look unhappy at the general state of things.

I finally do find my room, although I did pass a very nice chaise I contemplated sleeping on if the situation became dire.

As I'm opening the door for my room, movement catches my attention out of the corner of my eye. Gavin walks to his door, his jacket slung over one shoulder and his entire chest is on view in the (unusually) tight shirt he's wearing.

I lean against my door so I can enjoy the view.

"Hey, Riya."

"Hi, Gavin."

Gavin walks past his door and leans his own shoulder on the wall next to where I'm resting. "It's a strange thing. Some of my shirts, this one definitely—" he looks down at himself "—is a little tighter than the last time I wore it." He looks back at me with eyes too astute for my liking. "You wouldn't know anything about that, would you?"

"You just had a nine-course meal. So." My eyes meander over the expanse of his chest, the wine making me not care if he knows I'm enjoying the sight.

"It was like that before dinner though." He takes a step closer.

"Hmm." I'm uninterested in anything but those muscles getting closer to me. "Who knows what science is all about? We both took art history and business classes."

He stops when he's close enough that I either have to jerk my head up to see his face or bury my nose in his chest. I decide to jerk my head up, reasoning if I got my head buried in his chest, it wouldn't be easy to lift it out again.

"I think the shirt had a little help," he says.

I laugh to myself. "Did you freak out when you put it on?"

"I was uncomfortable coming down to dinner. Thought I was imagining things. Then I saw you and your eyes went immediately to my shirt, and I knew. Clever, Riya." He pushes my hair behind my ears on both sides.

"It is. For whoever did it." I will be admitting nothing.

"Stubborn." He shakes his head. "Did you ever won-

der what it would have been like if we weren't constantly in competition?"

Wonder? No. Imagine all the sex we would have?
Constantly.

Like I'm imagining right now.

Chapter Sixteen

When I don't answer, Gavin continues, "I think we could have made a good couple."

I let out another laugh at the thought of being in a relationship with the same man I once used as a target for a game of darts. Lucky for him I'm bad at darts, and it was only his picture.

He uses the movement to slide his arms around me, crossing his arms at my lower back. "We would spend all day taking over the art world and then all night burning off the extra energy," he whispers.

"More like spend *all* of our time arguing over every small, insignificant detail in our lives. Leaving us too exhausted and bitter to do anything at night."

"Or, we'd argue and settle it in bed." He brings his head closer to mine at the second mention of sex.

I don't want to imagine it anymore. He's here, talking about us having sex and smelling amazing and feeling even better.

I close the distance between our mouths. Gavin jerks away from me initially, maybe surprised that I'd gone for it. But then he immediately comes back.

I was the one to initiate our lips touching, but he takes it further, his tongue peeking out to caress my lips, and then delve deeper. I grab him behind the shoulders, trying to get him closer than he currently is. Warmth travels along my veins, settling in the area that wants to get very close to him.

It feels like I'm kissing Michelangelo's *David*. He's just as hard as the marble sculpture. Just as perfectly formed.

I try to pull him even closer, and he gets the message and lifts me up a little to lean me against the wall, putting a hand under my butt. I raise my right leg and give in to the desire to rub against Gavin.

Gavin's mouth leaves mine, and I open mine to complain. He starts sucking on my neck and I moan, mentally withdrawing my complaints.

When his hand slides under my dress, I realize exactly what I'm doing, and who I'm doing it with. So I push him away a little, and take satisfaction with the way he makes a small forward movement to get back to my lips.

I almost give in, but he's still the competition, and pursuing anything with him would still lose any respect I had in Dad's eyes. I've worked too hard for that to happen. Since nothing's changed in my life in the last twenty seconds, I push my hand on his chest to keep him away.

He opens his mouth, and I'm a little afraid of what might come out of it. I don't want to discuss what just happened, so I ward off whatever he's about to say with a quick, "Good night, Gavin."

"Night, Riya."

I turn around and throw myself through my open door, not stopping until I've walked all the way across the room, shedding clothes on the way. I toss on a big shirt and throw myself into the bed. It's very well deserved after the turmoil of the day.

I take out my daily contacts and toss them over the side of the bed in the general direction of the trash. The phone gets a little more care, gently landing on the charger. I reach over and turn off the light.

Unfortunately, my brain can't shut down long enough to give me the rest I deserve, and thoughts of Gavin and this show keep me tossing and turning in the luxurious bed.

"Did you get drunk on a school night?" Sonia asks me on the phone after the lackluster greeting she gets.

"No," I deny vehemently, burying my head back in my pillow. Buzzed is not the same as drunk. And if she wasn't rude enough to call people at the crack of…9:00 a.m., my phone screen tells me, then she'd get a better reception. "But I did stay up way past my bedtime."

"Aren't you practically on vacation?"

"I would be if you didn't keep contacting me to do work."

"Right, actually…"

We discuss work for the next forty-five minutes. By the time Sonia winds down, I have all my electronics on with different information on the screens, and multiple notebooks open. Still in bed though. It's kind of a vacation.

"That's it for now," Sonia says. "Except…"

There's something in her tone that suggests I won't like what she's going to say next. I contemplate hanging up and blaming the cell reception. "What?" I ask cautiously.

"Can you talk to Chachi about calling off Operation: Marry off Priya? She keeps showing me pictures of men and asking me if you'd like them."

"Better you than me." I throw her under the bus. Under the parade of buses coming down the road, driven by Rani Gupta.

"This is a formal HR complaint to my supervisor. Deal with it."

"I don't wanna," I whine.

"Or just get married. Speaking of…how's Gavin?"

"How in the holy name of Michelangelo did you get from marriage to Gavin?"

"Answer the question," she yells.

I jerk my phone away from my ear. "We may have, just possibly, sort of, kissed a little," I say in a rush, hoping she'll be so distracted by the phrasing that she doesn't take in what I said.

"What?" she shrieks. Good thing the phone is already away from my ear. "How was it? Did you guys have sex? Do you want a destination wedding?"

"It was great, damn it. No sex. I'm not getting married." It's easier to just answer her questions than explain why the questions are inherently bad. I've learned that over time.

The phone picks up a voice in the background but not enough for me to find out who it is. Then Sonia comes back and says, "I've got to go. Ajay is trying to foist off more of his work on me. I want more details later." I hear a voice protesting and then the call is cut off.

I look at the clock and contemplate going back to bed for a few more hours but I remind myself I'm not actually on vacation. Instead, I get ready and pack a bag of work.

Time to do some 'sploring and get inspired by my beautiful surroundings.

I don't run into anyone on my way, so people must have stayed up late after dinner. They, unlike me, are on a real vacation, so it might take some time for everyone to wake up.

My terrible sense of direction doesn't stop me from stumbling into the library, which I immediately claim as my own space. The room has floor-to-ceiling wooden bookshelves, with one wall left shelfless for windows looking out over the nature of the estate and the current gray cloudy weather, which makes snuggling in the library seem like a perfect plan.

Despite my best intentions, as soon as I spread out on the soft leather couch with my work on my lap and the calming view in front of me, I fall asleep again.

"Riya, wake up." A voice intrudes on my pleasant dream. I'm running an auction of all the most famous pieces in my art history book, and rich people keep buying them and donating them to museums.

Just when Mindy Kaling is buying a medieval book of hours by a rare female scribe to donate to the Smithsonian, the voice is trying to get me to stop the sale. But I can get a few more hundred thousand out of this auction!

"Riya, come on. I'm bored." It's a shame that the voice is so nice, but also so annoying at the same time.

Bye, Mindy.

I wake up fully and have a mini heart attack when I see Gavin's face right in front of mine.

"Ahh," I yell, jumping up from the couch and almost scattering all the documents I was using for blankets.

"I've got it." Gavin jumps into action, stopping my

iPad from crashing down and collecting paperwork that scattered.

I sit up, and as surreptitiously as I can, straighten my hair and shirt at the same time.

Papers collected, Gavin deposits them in my lap and then lifts my feet to make himself comfortable on the other end of the couch.

"Oh good, you're awake."

I don't dignify that with a response. Not a verbal one, at any rate. I do glare at him like he stole the last slice of cheesecake.

I'm still groggy, so my brain doesn't have the space to be embarrassed that we kissed last night and annoyed that he woke me up at the same time. So it chooses to be annoyed, because of priorities.

"I need some help with a show I'm planning." He starts rubbing my feet. That's not bad, actually.

My eyes close again and my head falls back on the couch arm, this time in contentment. "You can't handle it. Give me all the art and I'll make sure it goes to a good home. And I'm taking the commission for it too."

"Cute. But really, I've got this collector who wants to sell his entire collection, and it's a random selection but he doesn't want to bring any focus on him. So I'm struggling with how to present the show."

"Well, split it up then. No better guarantee of anonymity than the collection being sold at different themed shows."

"I thought of that. But he wants the items sold fast."

"Tell him he can't have everything he wants." I'm much less accommodating when it's not my own clients on the line.

"I would give so much money to be able to tell him that to his face. But I don't want to lose a client…"

"I'm not doing your job for you," I say in disbelief. "But tell me what the pieces are—just because I'm bored and it'll be a good mental exercise."

"They're all over the place. But mostly it boils down to modern to contemporary art and wine."

"Hmm…what's the quality of the pieces?"

"It's all over the place as well."

I'm reminded of an idea. But I'm not going to give it to him just like that. "Why are you asking me for help?"

"Because we're colleagues."

"No, we're competitors."

"Only technically," he says, dismissing my concern. "Now, don't you want to tell me how I should structure this sale? And rub it in that you figured it out when I couldn't?"

"Maybe. Let me ask you something without knowing what it is, and I'll give you the idea." Deals I can work with. Contracts and negotiating for consideration make me comfortable. Whatever is happening with Gavin makes me uncomfortable, but if I can bring us back to the world of mutually beneficial deals, it will make me feel better being around him.

"I don't even get to know what it's about? Just the general theme?"

"Nope."

Gavin looks at me for what seems like a long time. "Okay. Fire away."

"Why don't you stand up to your dad when he takes a sale from you?"

"Wow. Was not expecting that. But a deal's a deal." Gavin falls silent. "When I was growing up, everything came easy. School, athletics, interning at the auction house…"

"You are so unlikeable, Golden Boy."

"And yet you do like me." He winks at me.

I stare at him, not responding to the ridiculous accusation or that ridiculous flirty wink.

"Anyway, it all came easy. Now I work for Carlyle's, and every now and then I disagree with Dad. It's not often, but he's always so adamant, I give in. It's not easy to argue with someone so stubborn." He looks forward out the window to avoid looking at me.

I snort, knowing exactly how it is to argue with a stubborn auctioneer.

Gavin keeps going. "And he does have the most experience—he's probably right. What's the point of debating when he has great ideas?"

"Just because he has good ideas doesn't mean yours aren't too. Gina was really impressed with whatever you said about cars."

I would never have expected Gavin Carlyle to be a little insecure when it came to his father. I guess it makes sense; he's been handed everything on a silver platter and he doesn't know what it's like to fight for the job. I already know he likes the path of least resistance.

That was never an option for me. If I did that, I would be planning a charity event right now instead of fighting for this sale. Another way we're very different people.

"I do have good ideas, sometimes. But not right now, so can you live up to your end of the bargain?" He waves his hand, telling me to get on with it. And that he's done sharing intimate details with me.

Fine. I don't even want to know what goes on in his head.

"Yes, you can have the idea. But I want it noted that I'm only giving it to you because I've already used it and you'll look like you're copying me."

"That seems fair." He starts up the foot massage again on my other foot.

"You should do a wine and artwork pairing. Have a sommelier describe the wine and pair it with the works in the collection and sell them as a pair. But that's all I'm telling you."

"Yes," Gavin says, dropping my foot to get his phone and start making notes. "That's perfect."

"Now let me see some of these pieces." I sit up, putting my feet on the floor, and scoot closer to his side to look at his phone.

"I don't know…we're enemies," he says, a twinkle in those damn eyes as he exaggerates the word *enemies* and shifts to hide his phone screen from me. Clearly, he's not taking this rivalry seriously.

"Only technically," I parrot back at him. "I've earned this, for my help."

He gives in and moves the phone back so I can see the screen. I cuddle closer into his side so I can see better as he flips through photos. Awkwardness from the kiss last night tries to intrude on the office we've made here, but work, being an amazing distraction, keeps it from coming into the space.

An hour later, my declaration to not help is a distant memory and we have papers spread throughout the library floor.

"The Warhol is light and fun…you need a prosecco. Or a rosé."

"The Warhol is bold and elegant…it's a cabernet sauvignon if it's anything."

"You're wrong. More wrong than you've ever been in the history of your life, and let me tell you, you've been wrong a lot." The words don't have any heat despite their intensity, just my natural enjoyment of arguing.

Gavin is about to respond on the merits of an Andy Warhol painting as different wines when the door opens. And I'm glad he was interrupted because he has that furrow in his forehead that lets me know he's going to be a pain in the butt about something.

"Hello, auctioneers," Harrison says as he enters the library. "What are you guys up to?"

"Just some work," I say with a smile.

"You guys are both devoted to your work, I'll give you that."

"What's next on the schedule for the house party?" Gavin asks.

"We're going on a horseback ride to one of the best picnic spots on the estate where we can enjoy a nice lunch."

"That sounds lovely," I say, surprised at how laid back the day's itinerary is.

"I've also got to deal with a last-minute personnel issue."

"I hope everything is okay?" I ask.

"It's fine. But my guy who was going to take us hunting is sick, so we won't be able to go this week."

Oh no. However shall I deal with the disappointment of missing that? *Sarcasm intensifies.*

I'll deal with a big smile; glad I don't have to watch them take down adorable forest animals.

"If you need an event, I would love to plan one," I offer. Any chance to show the man I can throw a great event and make him like me that much better.

"I will take you up on that, actually. For two days from now?" Harrison looks grateful.

"Perfect. I'll have everything ready for then." Once I figure out what I'm going to do.

"Let Sarah know if you need anything. She can get it or will know who can get it for you."

"Let me know if you need me to fill some time as well." Gavin tries to make himself relevant.

"A point to both of your houses. Gavin, you can take the day after. I'm sure what you'll plan is better than what I had scheduled."

I throw a toothy smile over my shoulder at Gavin. Thank god for Harrison reminding me that I'm here to compete with the man, not tell him how to run a show or kiss him.

Chapter Seventeen

After Harrison leaves, Gavin and I go back to our rooms to change for the ride. Despite how much I tried to plan for everything, horseback riding is not something I anticipated. I think I have a blazer somewhere in here, maybe.

I throw on some boots and the blazer over my jeans and a T-shirt, the closest I can get to a horse-appropriate outfit. Or what I think horse-appropriate attire is.

I only take two wrong turns before I get back to the main entrance hall where Harrison said we would meet. Naomi is already waiting on a chaise, looking at her phone.

"Hey. I hope your horses are old and docile," I say.

Naomi shoots me a genuine smile. "We've got an ancient horse that'll treat you right."

"Perfect," I say, gratitude filling my voice. I'm about to ask about where she's living in England when I feel vibration from my butt pocket. I pull out my phone and see Dad flashing on the screen, with a gavel emoji. "Excuse me," I say to Naomi and walk down the hall to take it in privacy.

I take a deep breath, wondering if I'll ever get over the anxiety that comes every time I have to interact with my own father. I love him and I know he loves me too, but I'm constantly on edge about what he'll say or do to hurt me without realizing it.

I answer the call the second before it gets sent to voicemail. "Hi, Dad. What's up?"

"What's up?" he asks with his slight accent. "Is that any way to talk to your father?"

"I'm in the middle of getting this sale," I say, hoping it'll rush him along. It probably won't, but dreaming is free.

"When are you coming back? Ajay can't run a sale tomorrow and I need you to take the rostrum."

"I'm working on something, I can't just drop it because Ajay can't get his shit together." It would be one thing if Ajay had an actual emergency and needed my help, but I'm willing to put money on the fact that the emergency is that he wants more time to paint.

The seller in me is happy that he's productive, because Loot will get to sell his amazing work…hopefully soon. But the coworker in me would like him to pull his own weight.

Ajay probably shouldn't even be doing sales with his position title, but Dad likes it when the family gets on the rostrum. Feels like it gives Loot the small, family business appeal. I have no problem because I love it and would do sales no matter what position I have. Or try to at least.

"Language, Priya."

"Fine. I *respectfully* decline your last-minute request to rearrange my entire schedule to accommodate a coworker who is not fulfilling their duties."

Dad starts lecturing me about helping family when they need it and something about being grateful and I tune him out. I am glad that he's reaching out to me, but I don't have time to take on additional work now because his first choice is busy.

My mind goes into damage control mode. "Okay," I interrupt him, our pending agreement making me on edge, which makes me shorter with Dad than I usually would be. "You do it. The collectors will love seeing you on the rostrum again, and no one else is quicker on their feet." Dad hasn't run a sale in a while, but there's a reason Loot survived opening in the already crowded market of New York. A reason they thrived at it.

It's because my dad is the best auctioneer I know.

Dad pauses, either preparing to yell at me for interrupting him or thinking about the suggestion. "That could work." His words are measured, but there's an undertone of excitement in his voice.

That problem is sorted. And Mom will probably give me a box of chocolates for putting Dad in such a good mood.

"Sonia can help you learn the pieces last minute. Or Diego. He's been working with Ajay's team so he should have some knowledge of the art and he's quick on his feet too."

"Well, it won't be as good as your last-minute charity auction, but I'll manage."

Ah, that's right. Dad hasn't gotten a chance to yell at me for that.

"It's great exposure." I defend myself.

"But did you have to do it with a Carlyle?" Dad snarls.

There it is. Like a modern Romeo and Juliet, or a tanner Hatfield and just as pale McCoy. "He's a talented auctioneer in his own right. And it was for charity."

"That family relies on old connections and cheating to run their business."

I roll my eyes, grateful for the freedom that I don't have during our in-person meetings. And I'm definitely not going to tell him I just spent the morning helping Gavin with a sale. Or that I kissed him.

I don't know which one would make him madder.

"So you've said, Dad. Listen, I better go. I think Harrison just arrived."

"Okay, okay. Did you do the reports for the quarterly meeting?" Dad has an infinite amount of trust for me to do mindless tasks.

"Yes. I did what I could remotely, and I sent the rest to Sonia to finalize. She'll have them on your desk by the end of the week. Well before the meeting."

Dad grunts his thanks. When he's not talking about Loot or his hate for Carlyle's, he's not very loquacious.

"What's an influencer?" he asks before I can hang up.

"Excuse me?"

"Some *influencer* contacted the office to register for our next sale, but I don't know what they do."

I sigh. "They're famous on social media and can encourage people to buy certain products or use certain services."

"Like an advertising company?"

"Sort of? But they can get famous on social media, doing reviews or videos or posts or going viral, and making connections with other influencers, until they're famous themselves. Or they can be already famous themselves already. And then the people who follow them buy the things they tell them to."

There's no response and I take the phone away from

my ear to make sure the call is still connected. It is so I bring it back to my ear. "Dad?"

"No. That can't be a real thing."

"Have Diego take the meeting." He'll be able to suss out whether the influencer is legit and can report back to me. This could help Loot quite a bit, depending on who's calling.

"Fine," Dad says. This is a familiar tone. I most recently heard it when I had to explain what Bitcoin was because a buyer wanted to pay in it. That was a very long day for everyone.

"Love you too, Dad." I try to wrap up this conversation.

"Good luck with Harrison. Tell him I have some new Mughal paintings he might like."

He hangs up before I can respond.

I look at my phone in bemusement, always feeling a bit like a tornado hit me after a phone call with my dad. The in-person meetings are one thing, and I can prepare for them, emotionally and with information. I have no warnings for his phone calls, and they touch down whenever he wants, toss me around for a few minutes, and then spit me back out, leaving as quickly as they came.

But that's one thing I have to give my dad. He makes every other task seem minuscule in comparison, so I'm prepared to get on a large horse now.

I walk back to the entrance, finding a larger crowd than I had left. I nod to Gavin, who looks like Hollywood's version of the cowboy. He's wearing worn jeans (and I would put money on him buying them pre-worn instead of doing any of the work) and a flannel shirt. His hair has the wind-blown effect, but I know that came from product and skill, and not any time spent in the actual wind.

He moves toward me as I join the group. "Are you okay?"

"What? Why would you ask?"

Gavin shrugs. "You look…off. Did someone say something to you? Was it Nate? I knew there was something off with that guy." Gavin looks around, apparently to do who knows what to Nate.

"No, nothing with Nate. I'm fine." I'm not freaked out that Gavin Carlyle can read me like I'm a book at a first-grade reading level with more pictures than words. Not freaked out in the slightest.

But before he can follow up on my lie and before I can plan an escape, probably involving a cleverly fashioned shiv made out of a filed-down eighteenth-century porcelain bowl, our host comes down the stairs.

"Is everyone ready for some time with nature?" Harrison says.

God no. The sun can give you an illness, and nature has ticks that can make you allergic to delicious meat and there are wolves.

"Do you think there's Wi-Fi in nature?" Gavin asks me under his breath, still watching me a little too closely. I start a little, because I didn't realize how close he had gotten to me.

"Probably not," I murmur back. "Is it too late to genetically modify a horse to make it a hotspot?"

"Probably too late for us. But a great idea for a niche business in the future."

"Don't steal the idea. I know that's how you usually operate but control yourself."

But threatening Gavin won't get me a sale, so I smile

it off when Harrison looks our way and hope I don't crack my head open falling off this horse.

"Follow me." Harrison leads us out of the front of the house and along the side until we get to stables. And I say they're stables only because of the smell, because the exterior looks like it's a miniature version of the house, with the same elegant column and brick design.

And by miniature version, I mean miniature for this crowd, but a regular-size house for a normal human.

When we enter the building, my eyes are immediately drawn to the rows of stalls along the sides, all containing large horses.

Maybe unnaturally large? How big are these things supposed to be anyway? These seem *too* large.

My heart starts pounding, and fight or flight kicks in, making me want to run far away from the potential threat.

Harrison starts assigning the horses to us one by one and I cross my fingers that Harrison gives me that old pony Naomi mentioned.

"Priya, you can have my favorite mount, Daisy. She's been with me the longest, so she's not the most energetic, but she'll get you where you need to go. Gavin, you can have Mister Ed, who's been with me almost as long."

I throw a grateful look at Naomi, who must have put a good word in. "That sounds perfect." My only other horseback riding experiences are a birthday party with a pony in fifth grade and a handful of rides with clients since then. Each one stressful since it happens so infrequently.

I get up on Daisy with help from the stable staff, and then direct my horse slowly to the others.

"Everyone who wants to trot can leave first, and if you don't feel comfortable with that, you can follow Jim at a slower pace," Harrison says while pacing back and forth on his horse, like staying still is too much for him and the horse.

"Jim? Where's Jim?" I ask, looking around for my savior.

A grizzled older man raises his hand and I direct my horse carefully over to him. Gavin comes up behind me, and I give him a suspicious look over my shoulder. Knowing him, he'll do something that makes Daisy lose it and throw me. Embarrassing me in front of the entire party, and especially Harrison.

He does look good on a horse though. Like he's in an ad for expensive cologne. I can't believe I kissed all of that last night…half because he's so model attractive, and half because I don't want to find him attractive or his kisses enjoyable.

But enjoyable as it was, it won't be happening again.

"You're hanging with the slowpokes?" I look around, hoping someone joins us so it's not a romantic horse ride with Gavin and Jim, but the universe doesn't want to help me out here.

"Yeah. It's been a while so I shouldn't push it. I'm going to have a big show to put on soon." He indicates the house behind him, leaving no doubt as to who he thinks will be winning this sale.

"I agree. You should be healthy to come see *me* do this show. Spoiler alert: I'm going to be amazing," I say, half my mind on not agitating this horse and the other half on sassing Gavin. Luckily, it's second nature to me, so I only really need half my brain to do the task.

The rest of the riders race ahead and Jim holds us

back until they get out of range. Then we slowly make our way to the picnic site, while Jim keeps an eagle eye on us.

"How long have you been in this area?" I ask Jim to distract myself from the fact that my life is in the hoofs of a majestic animal that may or may not resent humans. I don't know how well Harrison treats his horses.

"Born and raised here. My dad is part of the historic society of Huntington."

"Oh?" I perk up at the thought of history. "Do they have a museum or exhibition space?"

"They do, in town. I can tell you a little about the area, if you'd like?"

"I'd love that." Because I always say yes to history, and because it'll be a great distraction from my fears of riding.

Jim explains that in the 1890s, robber barons and other rich types built mansions and fake castles in the area, sometimes bringing entire rooms and structures from Europe so they could pretend to be aristocrats of old, but geographically in America. They used any style that appealed to them, making a unique mix of Roman, Mediterranean, English Tudor, French, Gothic, Georgian and Spanish homes on Long Island.

After World War II, three hundred of the five hundred mansions were destroyed or turned into suburbs as people lost fortunes or decided the upkeep was too expensive. But the Richmonds were lucky, or smart, or a little of both, and they managed to hold on to their fortunes and their property.

When Jim is done giving us the tour, Gavin pulls up next to me. His horse nudges mine in the shoulder and I glare at Gavin.

"My horse doesn't want to be touched by your horse." And if Daisy rears up and knocks me off as a result, I'm going to be mad. And get revenge, when I'm out of the hospital and the cast(s) comes off.

"Are you sure that's what Daisy wants?" he says, looking at my horse with amusement.

Daisy is nuzzling Mister Ed and whinnying softly. "Girl, control yourself. Don't let him know you're that into him," I whisper at her. She blatantly ignores me, moving closer and closer to Mister Ed. The move makes my leg brush against Gavin's.

"I think they like us, Ed. Keep sending out those pheromones." Gavin pats his horse on the neck. "And, Daisy, thank you for not playing games with my friend here and being honest with your feelings." The last part may be addressed to my horse, but he's looking at me.

I change tactics. "Well thank *you*, Mister Ed, for not trying to steal Daisy's sugar cubes when her back is turned."

"Thank *you,* Daisy, for knowing that there's enough sugar cubes to go around and appreciating when Mister Ed uses his skills and talents to get some sugar cubes for himself."

"Well, thank *you*, Mister Ed, for not using under-handed techniques to take any sugar cubes from Daisy."

"Well thank *you,* Daisy, for having a great ass."

That gets a pause out of me. "Wait, are you still talking about the horse?" Or is this still an elaborate metaphor for me? And my ass?

"It's what Mister Ed is thinking." Gavin keeps a straight face through that bit of nonsense.

"You're out of control, Carlyle. But I'll let you know

when we get a painting with primo horse ass. If that's what you're into."

"*Mister Ed* will appreciate it."

"We're here. The picnic is just ahead." Jim sounds relieved to be getting rid of us and this uncomfortably equine-themed conversation.

As promised, a few minutes later we ride into a verdant clearing. The horses are already tied up to one side and there are blue-and-white gingham blankets set up on the grass. Each blanket has multiple picnic baskets on it, some containing real china, while others have containers of food.

This is possibly the classiest picnic I've ever been to. And I would expect nothing less from Harrison.

The fast group has already claimed their blankets, leaving only one for me and Gavin.

Jim takes the horses to the side as we settle in. Without discussing it, Gavin starts getting out the china and I take out and open the containers. We can occasionally work together, apparently.

"This is beautiful." I start scooping potato salad onto the plates he's holding up.

The clearing is surrounded by magnolia trees dripping in pink flowers for their early spring bloom. Some flowers are already on the ground, dotting the grass with their spots of color. Spanish moss hangs from the trees, making a curtain that further secludes the peaceful clearing. Birds hover near the circle of blankets, indignant we're invading their space but still curious about the newcomers, and our food. And being very vocal about not getting any of it.

"I don't even miss the Wi-Fi." Gavin picks a sandwich out of the container I just opened.

Let's not go that far.

We're sitting close to Naomi and Nate on their blanket. "Have you guys been here long?" I ask them in an attempt to ignore my own blanket mate.

"I'm on my second sandwich," Nate responds.

Harrison comes to our blanket and sits down with us. "Priya, I have something for you."

"A gift for me?" I say in surprise.

"Yes. Gavin said you love spicy food, so I had my staff find some extra spicy hot sauce for you to put on the sandwiches." Harrison takes a small bottle out from behind his back and presents it to me like a kid presenting a really ugly drawing of their mom that their mom has to pretend to love.

Because I hate spicy food, which Gavin knows from our long acquaintance. And I can't tell Harrison I don't want the gift he went to any trouble to get. It's too awkward for someone I'm wooing in a business capacity.

I don't look at the little liar next to me, but I can feel his glee at the situation I'm in, waiting to see how I'll respond.

Chapter Eighteen

"Thank you so much. This is so thoughtful of both of you." I do the only thing I can, taking the bottle from Harrison and hoping he'll go back to his other guests.

When he doesn't leave, I know I'm not getting out of this without eating some of the spicy stuff. I open the bottle and shake out a small dollop on my sandwich.

"Don't be shy on our account. I know how much you love the stuff and how much effort Harrison went through to get this for you," Gavin says, smug as he can be next me.

I shake another small dollop on my sandwich, ruining the food. At least I had a few bites of savory goodness before it was desecrated.

This is some cold shit. It was well known in our school growing up how much this Indian couldn't handle spicy food. My classmates made fun of me, led by the man of the hour, Gavin.

Everyone's still looking at me expectantly, so I take a bite of the tainted sandwich. The smallest bite I can possibly take while still consuming some of the food. "Mmm…this is so good. Thank you again, Harrison, for doing this for me." I salute him with the sandwich, mouth very much on fire.

Just smile through it. Breathe, and smile through it.

"Good. I want my guests to be as happy as they can be." Satisfied that he did his duty as a host, he *finally* walks away from our blanket.

Once his back is turned, I frantically look through the baskets for some water, because my mouth hasn't stopped burning. Tears are forming.

"Are you looking for this?" Gavin, who's enjoying himself more than anyone has a right to at the suffering of another human being, is holding all of the bottles of water that were in the baskets.

"Give it," I snap as I reach for a bottle. I throw a quick look at Nate and Naomi, relieved to see they're focusing on a conversation with Cindy on their other side.

"But you love the spice so much, I wouldn't want you to dilute it." He raises the bottles even higher. The heartless giant.

I shove at Gavin repeatedly, who laughs the entire time as I push him to the ground. I snatch a bottle from him and quickly bounce back up, focusing on the burning in my mouth over the burning desire I felt when I was pressed against him.

"You must be so proud of yourself right now," I say after I drink the entire bottle of water.

"Exceptionally. And you deserved it after making me so uncomfortable I wanted to tear through my clothes all last night." He gives me an arch look.

I glare at him in response and then look longingly at my sandwich. My stomach rumbles, protesting the fact that food is so close but I can't eat it.

A very deep sigh comes from next to me. Gavin's hand comes into my view and takes the plate away from me, and replaces it with his own, unspicy plate.

My head snaps to his direction, and he takes a big bite of the sandwich. "This is a really good hot sauce. Artisanal. Harrison probably spent a lot of money getting this for you."

I take a bite of the regular sandwich, groaning in relief when my mouth isn't assaulted by any new heat. It'll probably take longer for the burning to go away entirely, but a plain ham and cheese is a good start. "Why are you eating it?"

"Because unlike you, I actually like spicy food."

"Weirdo," I say, without any heat. I'm too busy enjoying the plain sandwich. "Here, knock yourself out. But literally, please." I shove the bottle of hot sauce at him.

Gavin looks at me, not breaking eye contact while he opens the bottle and puts even more hot sauce on the sandwich. And some over his potato salad for good measure.

Whatever, it's his taste buds.

By my second sandwich, the burning in my mouth has gone away enough that I can enjoy the expensive food laid out for us. Digging deeper into the basket reveals brownies. I toss one at Gavin and start devouring mine.

"Are you going to tell me what made you so upset today?" Gavin asks when my guard is lowered with chocolate.

He's still on that? Why does he care? It's unnerving that he's digging into my emotions. "Why do you care? Looking for ways to find out my weaknesses?"

"No. I just care." He sounds frustrated.

"Why?"

"You've been in my life since we were in kindergarten. That's a long time to know someone and not care about them a little. And despite wanting to beat you at work, I don't want anything bad to happen to you in general."

What is this new Gavin? Has he been hit on the head lately? Did he have a loss of oxygen to the brain recently? He's deviating from our roles and I'm not entirely comfortable with it. And where's all this assertiveness when it's time to stand up to his dad? "It's just work stuff," I mumble.

"Work stuff or family stuff?" Gavin asks, remembering our conversation about our fathers.

I shrug. "Maybe a bit of both. But nothing I can't handle." I'm used to it, after working for Loot for so long. And because of the strange conversations we had at the dinner, I know he's used to family and business drama as well.

"I'm sure you can handle anything that gets thrown at you, Riya. But it doesn't mean you should have to. You can always find another job. You're smart."

I look at him, my mouth slightly open. No one has really been…protective of me because of Dad. Sonia, Ajay and Mom all assume I can handle it and don't need any interference.

Because I can.

I finally say, "I'm doing just fine. And I don't want to talk about it anymore. What about you and your dad? Has Gina called?"

Gavin shrugs and eats the rest of his brownie. "I think so. They're probably scheduling the meeting soon."

This is better. I would much rather talk about his

stuff. "Are you going to tell him your ideas about it? How you want to do it?"

Gavin's smile fades. "Probably not."

I leave it at that, having only brought it up to deflect from talking about my own father. And if I press more, he might take that as permission for him to press me more.

Despite the heavy conversation, we enjoy the rest of the picnic, playing lawn games until it's time to go back to the house. I firmly trounce Gavin at bocce ball and he dominates at croquet. I restrain from hitting his head with the croquet mallet when he brags about winning, so I call that an extra win for me.

Sooner than I'm ready, it's time to return to the house. That means I have to get back on the horse, who to be fair is a lot calmer than I thought she was going to be. Daisy stays calm on the ride back, even if she gets closer to Mister Ed and his rider than I'm happy with.

Back at the house Harrison tells us that dinner will be served buffet style between six and seven, or we can go to the kitchen and help ourselves to anything in there anytime we would like. He also tells us what time to meet if we want to go to his planned event tomorrow and come with tennis shoes.

The second I'm off the horse, I escape Gavin's easy smile and run to my room. I haven't done any work on the financial proposal for Harrison, and it's time to remember I'm not a guest invited to a friend's house for a vacation; I'm here to work.

I open up my laptop and start typing our offer. Dad isn't going to like some of the terms, but this sale could do so much for our name and my ability to sell what I want, there's no option but to be cutthroat to get this art.

Plus, Mom won't let Dad disown me or fire me, so I'd rather deal with the fallout of an angry Dad than no art.

After I've made the offer the best I can, I edit it six times. When I get to the point that I can't see the words on the screen anymore, I hit send and breathe a sigh of relief.

I finish up a few more work tasks, and by the time Sarah comes in to check on me, I let her in on my offer to plan an event. She tells me Harrison gave her the heads-up, and I ask her for the things I need to make the day a reality. She stays to brainstorm some great ideas with me for the event and leaves me to more work when we're done.

After my eyes start to blur a second time on the laptop screen, I close the computer. I stretch out the kinks in my back, wincing when I acknowledge a vanity's stool might not be the best place to work for hours on end.

That makes me look at the clock, and I swear. I've blown right past dinner, and it's now 9:30 p.m.

My stomach growls, yelling at me for missing the meal.

I make my way down the stairs and try to remember where the kitchen is. I must be getting used to the house, because it only takes me a few wrong turns before I find the right room. I turn the light on and open the fridge, trying to see what I can whip up.

"Late night?" asks an even-more-relaxed-than-I-thought-possible Gavin from the entrance to the room.

He's wearing the same worn jeans from earlier and a faded T-shirt, and he's barefoot, looking even better than when he's dressed in a suit.

I would give anything for him to not be so attractive right now. He's hell on my concentration.

I'm glad I didn't change straight into my pj's, instead opting for a short sundress in case I ran into anyone on my way to the kitchen.

"Yes. And worth it. I just sent Harrison the proposal that's going to win this sale." I turn my attention back to the fridge and the pressing issue of dinner. Now that work is done, my stomach is making its needs known. And it doesn't care how much my libido wants to keep staring at Gavin.

"That's funny, how'd you get my proposal off my computer? But thanks for sending it in."

"I'll let you have your delusion. You won't have anything else when I get the sale."

"What are you cooking for us?" Gavin changes the subject before we can get in this argument again.

"Uh, for you? Tonight's menu is some poison with a side of arsenic."

"As delicious as that sounds, I was hoping for some steak, or maybe chicken…"

"Then you can cook it yourself." I fill my arms with ingredients, moving everything to the kitchen island so I can get the pan that I need.

"You wouldn't let me starve, would you?" He turns on his puppy-dog eyes.

"I'd watch that with pleasure. Maybe with some popcorn."

"But then you wouldn't get the satisfaction of watching me cry when you beat me."

I turn on the oven. "You make a very sad but very compelling argument. You can have some of these tacos. But you can't enjoy them."

"Understood. I'm sure they'll be the worst tacos I've ever had," he promises with a salute.

"All right. Dial it down on the commitment to my orders. But make yourself useful and chop these tomatoes, onions, and avocado." I start grilling the steak. "You're making guacamole."

"So how exactly do I…" Gavin looks at the assembled ingredients.

"Okay, this may be too advanced." I take the avocado away from him. "Let's just cut the tomato and onion. Take this knife and start cutting into these. And then grate this cheese." I pantomime the movements.

"I will get right on that, once I find…" Gavin roots around the cabinets. "Eureka." He stands up with a bottle of whiskey in his hand and a boyish smile on his face. He pours us both a glass.

"And entertain me while I do this." Damn that's a smooth whiskey. Rich people perks.

"Did you hear the rumors for the upcoming Sotheby's sale?" Gavin asks, starting on his assigned tasks.

We cook the rest of the meal in amiable conversation, discussing the most recent rumors of our competitors.

We've got so many thoughts on the subject; we keep talking about it through the dinner itself. I was worried that without any distractions my mind wouldn't be able to stop thinking about our kiss last night, but it's not awkward, despite the change in our relationship.

We clean up after we're done, helping ourselves to more of the whiskey during the process.

"Thanks for cooking. I know you don't like doing it, but your tacos were amazing. And you saved me from having to eat cereal for dinner."

He remembered our discussion about cooking. I

change the subject to cover how charmed that makes me. "Cereal for dinner is amazing, you monster."

We leave the kitchen, well-fed and content after a day of fresh air in nature, and then a productive evening in front of our computers.

Usually I love the constant busyness of the city. It makes me feel like I'm never alone, since someone is always doing something at all hours, moving from activity to activity and creating the city's heartbeat. But every now and then the quiet of nature can be pleasant. For a visit.

A short one.

"Hey, Riya, check this out." Gavin opens the door to a room and beckons me over.

"Why are you breaking into our host's rooms?" I ask, but curiosity drives me over to the door.

"I stumbled across this room getting lost earlier. And if he wanted to keep us out, he could have locked the door." He opens the door wider to let me go in first.

I enter but I can't see anything in the darkness beyond the outlines of furniture. Gavin enters and closes the door behind him, leaving us in the dark, with only the soft light of the moon coming in through the window.

"Is this where you off me because you know I'm going to win?" I ask Gavin.

In response, he turns on the light and I'm shocked out of my usual sassiness.

Because I've never seen this many penises and breasts in one place.

Chapter Nineteen

The walls of the room are a deep, seductive red velvet damask, and they complement the contents of the room well.

Because most of the flat surfaces are covered in naked flesh. Paintings of naked men and women, sculptures of naked people, naked people going to war, naked people having a picnic, naked people having sex, and some satyrs thrown in for fun.

"Wow." There are some red velvet damask sofas to match the walls, and I plop down on one to take in the room.

"Harrison has a sex room." Gavin sits across from me on his own sofa, looking around the room as well.

"At least there's no actual sex toys or ropes hanging in this sex room. That would be kind of awkward to know about a client." I like to think I'm not a prude, since there's a lot of nakedness and sex in the art world. We even have an annual erotic art sale for Valentine's Day that Ajay and I take turns leading. But seeing the depth of this collection, waiting to be discovered in a random room in a house, is…unexpected.

"He has a room of porn." Gavin's head is on a swivel to take it all in.

"Most art is just porn plus time. Except modern art-work I guess," I say without looking at him.

"Abstract boobies are still boobies."

I snort. "Can you jerk off to abstract boobies?"

"I can try." Figures.

We keep looking at the works around us. It's a truly impressive collection, in quantity and quality.

"I think a lot about what would happen if we weren't heirs of competing houses," Gavin says, bringing up the subject he began last night. "Maybe if we were co-workers who worked at the same Big Two House, we would go out to a happy hour on a Friday after work."

Do I think about if we weren't trapped in these positions? Only when he does something to make me horny. Which is almost every time I see the bastard, lately.

"You would probably ignore me for the prettier, better-at-flirting lady standing next to me."

"No, I wouldn't. I would have approached you at the bar and asked to buy you a drink."

"I would have told you that I could buy my own drinks."

"Or you could buy me one; I'm easy."

"All of New York City knows," I murmur to myself. Louder, I say, "I wouldn't have bought you a drink either, moocher."

"And then, after we each bought our own drinks, I would have tried to impress you by telling you how much art I can move in one night."

"Then I would have pointed out that I can move more." Competitive till the very end, even if we were on the same team.

"I would have given in, because I'm trying to seduce you. And the play to your ego would have worked." His voice gets deeper and I feel it reverberating throughout my whole body, reaching places that I'm not comfortable he can access.

"Maybe," I say, as honest as I am competitive. "But what would you have done with that victory?" I ask, curious about where he's going with this.

"I would have taken you on a date to Paulie Gee's for pizza and ice cream in Greenpoint, getting you there by the East River Ferry for the best views of Manhattan. Then I'd call in some favors to show you to a private exhibition at our auction house that I curated for you of your favorite artworks we had in the warehouse at the time." I open my mouth to ask what that would be, but Gavin answers before I can ask. "You like Neoclassical art best, even though you tell your dad your favorite is ancient Indian art."

Wow. He's thought about this.

I nod begrudgingly. "I think it's interesting the way they try to visually tie their culture to antiquity. It's so political and manipulative and pretty. How did you know that?"

"You did a high school presentation on Napoleon's furniture, and your eyes lit up even though you put most people to sleep. And you've tried really hard to sell Neoclassical art at Loot."

"You've paid a lot of attention to me over the years."

He shrugs. "You could tell me what my favorite art is too."

"Ancient Rome. Imperial Rome specifically because it was all about the grandeur of the young, dynastic ruler and flashy military campaigns and subsequent victory parades, instead of the public sacrifice of old wise statesmen in the Roman Republic."

Gavin smiles at me, one of his more genuine ones instead of the ones he deploys to charm. "That's right."

"That would be a pretty good date," I say, conceding the point. "What would you have done after the private show?" Our voices are both low, forcing us to lean in to be heard.

"I would hope, and pray, and sacrifice the biggest goat I can find to Venus, hoping you'd consider kissing me goodnight."

It's beginning to get very warm in this sex room. And my libido isn't helped by that fact that all I can see is naked flesh out of my peripherals while I'm having this conversation with the man I can acknowledge that I want but can't have.

But even if I can't have him fully, there is something I can have. "Okay, I took pity on you and kissed you." I slowly raise my hand to the top of my dress and start unbuttoning the long row of buttons that goes down the front. "What would you do next?" I raise my eyebrows in challenge.

Gavin doesn't answer, eyes laser-focused on tracking the movement of my hand as it undoes each button. "What?" he asks when I stop unbuttoning at the front clasp of my bra, and caress the soft, round cleavage that's exposed.

"I'm kissing you," I remind him. "What are you going to do next?"

Gavin gets up off his chair and moves toward me. I shake my head and extend my hand to tell him to stop. I don't want him to actually touch me. There's too much between us and it would open a can of very angry paternal worms.

But I can have this. As long as we don't touch, it won't get that complicated. I hope.

I warn myself that he could laugh at me, or use this to blackmail me. But after Gavin planned that surprisingly thoughtful date in his head, I want to take this little chance.

Gavin freezes at the extended hand and then sits back down on an exhale. "Right. In that case, while I'm kissing you, I would slide my hands under that dress, cupping your fantastic ass."

"Hmm." I stand up and turn around, getting back on the couch on my knees and looking over my right shoulder. "Like this?" I slide both hands under my dress, one up each leg, dragging up material as I go. I stop when I reach my own ass, feeling the curves.

"Yes," Gavin hisses out through clenched teeth. "Like that."

"While your hands were on my ass, mine would be on your abs," I whisper, giving him an expectant look. This is the moment of truth, to see if he'll play along with me.

Gavin grabs the bottom of his shirt, pulls it over his head, tosses it over his shoulder and narrowly misses hitting a painting in the process. I'm so far gone to lust I don't care about the potential damage, because my attention is dragged to ridges of his ab muscles. He starts rubbing his hand up and down the surface, just like I said I was going to do.

I feel my clit tingling, crying out for attention by those same hands.

Gavin breaks into my concentration. "Then I'd unbutton all of those buttons down that dress that've been teasing me all night with the thought of what they're hiding."

I turn back around and my hands accomplish the deed. I pull on the sides of my dress, showing Gavin my matching lacy black underwear, and shift on the couch to put my feet up. I feel a moment of nervousness that I'm curvier than his usual type, but then I remember that I've got the same body type as the curvy naked women I'm surrounded by.

Thank god for the tastes of perverts past.

"And then I'd take off that bra. Not all the way off, since I'm too impatient touching what I revealed to get your clothes all the way off."

I match reality to what he's saying, unclasping the bra but keeping it hanging down from my shoulders, and palm my own breasts, playing with my own nipples.

"I'd think it was really unfair that you still had so many clothes on." I bite my lips at the thought of his hands replacing mine on my breasts.

Gavin takes the hint and stands to take off his shoes and socks, then his jeans and underwear, leaving them in a pile under his feet. His erection juts out toward me as he sits back down, running his hands back up and down on his chest, slowly.

"And then I'd grab your dick, making it even harder with each stroke."

He moves his hands all the way down his chest until he reaches his penis, firmly grasping it while he strokes it.

Gavin's voice is even rougher when he responds. "I'm a gentleman, so I wouldn't leave your clit alone while you're being so generous."

I push my underwear out of the way, sliding my finger through the wet folds of my vulva and finding my clit. I throw my head back to the couch with the movement, sensation radiating from my clit.

"Jesus, you're as fucking hot as Titian's *Venus of Urbino*."

And he's the *Farnese Hercules*, leaning on his club, muscular body at rest, but ready to explode into action at the slightest provocation.

I moan, half in pleasure at what I'm doing, and half in frustration, because I wish it was his hands on me right now, not my own. I imagine how his rougher hands would feel on me, and I get wetter.

We both touch ourselves faster, moaning as we increase the speed.

"I would be touching your tits right now," Gavin growls at me, voice so low now it rumbles through me and sends even more fire to my clit. My head snaps upright again, his voice reminding me that I shouldn't miss the show while he's in front of me.

His abdominal muscles are clenched as he strains toward an orgasm. His eyes are locked on me through eyelids drawn low.

I follow his direction, and my other hand rises to caress the closest breast. I can feel the pressure build inside me, but I don't want to come before he does. Because I want to make him wilder than he makes me. As revenge, because I don't want to feel this way toward him.

Eyes locked with mine, Gavin comes. A few seconds later, I come too. I ride the waves of my orgasm for the next few moments and close my eyes as if I could hide from what happened.

When I catch my breath, I cautiously open one eye

and see Gavin sprawled out on the couch in rest like the *Barberini Fawn*, his own head thrown back and his eyes closed. Hand still on his softening cock.

That's when I feel it. The same way that my breath gets taken away when I look at beautiful art, I feel it right now looking at Gavin.

I need to leave.

I channel my inner ninja and start putting my clothes back on, slowly and quietly. I may need to practice my ninja skills, because Gavin opens his eyes and watches me work.

"So…" Gavin's voice is still breathless from the exertion of what he just did.

"Nope." I want to talk to him as much as I want Harrison to choose him for the sale.

"Okay." He doesn't try to press the issue as he cleans himself up with his underwear and puts the rest of his clothes back on.

We finish getting dressed in a silence that gets heavier the longer we don't speak. We make it all the way back to our rooms without breaking the no-talking rule. The walk seems longer than it was on the way out, but that's probably an effect of the awkwardness.

Note to self: next time I masturbate in front of someone I'm not sure I like, I'm going to plan to not walk with him after it's all over.

"Goodnight," Gavin says as he opens his door.

"Night." I open my own door as fast as I can and close it firmly behind me. "Oh my god," I whisper to myself, crossing the room and throwing myself on the bed. Now that the post-orgasmic glow is gone and the awkward walk to the rooms is over, it hits me that I just masturbated in front of Gavin.

I grab my phone from the side table. "Siri, call Sonia so she can judge my life choices."

"I'm sorry, I didn't understand that," my phone says to me, a lot of sass for an AI.

"Call Sonia, please." I add the please so when the robots take over, Siri will remember I'm a good human.

"Calling Sonia."

The phone rings and right before it can go to voicemail, she answers.

"Are you on fire?" she asks, sleep in her voice.

"What? No. Why?"

"That is the only acceptable reason to call me on a Sunday night after I've gone to sleep, when I have to be up at the crack of dawn tomorrow to do my job and yours."

"Well, fine. I was gonna tell you about some casual mutual masturbation that occurred tonight, but if you want to get your beauty sleep in, then I can respect that."

"What?" she screeches, now fully awake.

"Shit." I turn the volume down, regretting putting it on speakerphone since Gavin is in the room next to me. I explain what happened between us, not leaving anything out. She would know.

"So, did you guys have sex after all that?" Any trace of sleep is gone from Sonia's voice after my explanation, leaving a focused businesswoman who has information she wants to extract from me.

"No. And we won't," I say, firm.

"Why not?" She doesn't sound judgmental, just curious.

"I've been competing with Gavin my entire life. I can't just suddenly forget that and fuck him."

"Seems like you've already gotten over it."

Damn smart witch lady. "But I have shit to do. Shit that becomes so much harder if I start something with Gavin Carlyle. Like getting Dad's respect."

"Forget his name. Forget your dad. Just live your life. And from now on do shocking sex stuff earlier in the day so you don't wake me up during prime sleep hours."

Easy for Sonia to say. A lot harder for me to throw aside decades of feeling inadequate and constantly trying to make Dad proud as a result. "Sure, I'll rearrange my sexual escapades for you in the future."

"That's all I ask," she says, not picking up on the sarcasm. Or not caring.

"He's been different lately." I can't stop myself from offering the information. "There's still the competition and pranks, but there's moments when he's really sweet." Like first making me eat spicy food then giving me regular food or having fun with me at the charity event. I sigh. "Anyway, night. And thank you again for helping out at the office."

"Yeah, remember that when you see what Ajay is doing to your shows."

"Wait, what?" I ask, but she's already hung up.

I can't do anything about my shows or Gavin tonight, so I might as well push that to tomorrow to worry about.

Chapter Twenty

"Come in," I yell at the knock on my door. I've been awake for a half hour, but I have no motivation to get out of bed and deal with reality, or Gavin. Not just yet. So instead I grabbed my phone and made a wonderful cocoon of my blankets to block out the real world.

Sarah sticks her head in the door. "Is this a good time?"

"Please, yes. Come in. I'm trying to build up the will to get out of bed."

"You're a guest here," she says, bringing new towels. "Sleep in and enjoy."

"I think I'm somewhere in between." I smile. "I can reuse my towels. The environment and all that."

"Sounds good." She stops on her way to the bathroom. "And just so you know, we're all set to have everything for tomorrow."

"Thank you! You really are my hero."

She gives me a smile and a nod as she leaves the room.

I finally get out of bed and trip over piles of shoes and clothes to get ready. Harrison said to wear tennis shoes, so I assume we're doing something athletic. I dress in the workout clothes that I brought on the off chance I could convince myself to go on a run while I'm here.

I'm grateful for my delusion, since it means I can be appropriately dressed for this event. Whatever it is.

Gavin is already waiting in the foyer when I come down the stairs, and I take an involuntary step back, my end goal to hide under the covers in my room. He looks better than anyone has a right to in his tight, spandex-y shirt and loose shorts that hit above his knees. Even the sight of his hairy legs is making me horny again.

I'm in so much trouble.

Fleeing, not just to my guest room but back to the city, is looking more and more appealing every second.

But then Harrison comes into the foyer. I can't let Gavin get more time with him than me.

Sometimes it's really inconvenient to want to be good at my job.

And Gavin has already realized I'm here because he smiles in my direction. I nod and quickly look away before I have to interact with him. I can still feel his eyes boring into me from behind, but if I don't acknowledge it, then it isn't happening. Right? That's how that works?

I head straight for Harrison.

"Harrison, I emailed you Loot's proposal last night. After you get a chance to look at it please let me know if there's anything else you want to discuss."

"I glanced through it this morning. It's impressive and I'll let you know when I've gone through the whole thing. Both of yours." He directs the last part over my shoulder. I turn to come face to sexy shoulder with Gavin. Sometime when I was talking to Harrison, he snuck up behind me.

"Great," I say to Harrison as he walks away. That

means I'll be back to real life soon, and away from the temptation that is Gavin Carlyle.

"Morning. How'd you sleep?" the object of my annoyance says from behind me.

"Good, good, good." *Oh god, please stop saying good.*

"Good." He flashes me a smile, not adding anything about the night before.

Okay, this I can handle. As long as we don't talk about what happened last night, I'll be fine. I'll still obsess over it, but I can pretend.

"I wonder if Harrison decided to ignore Pari and have us cage fight to the death?" I ask, indicating our workout clothes.

"If he does, then I'm not going to go easy on you because you're a hot girl."

"Oh." I giggle awkwardly. My hand raises without my permission to tuck my hair behind my ear. Shit, I even look away *coyly*.

Jesus, I'm in *so* much trouble.

I clear my throat. "I wouldn't expect anything less." I try to get back to the adversarial relationship we had over twelve hours ago, hardening my voice after the giggle.

But it's hard. He must have given me sexually transmitted stupidity. And we didn't even do the deed.

What'll happen if we do have sex? Will I show up the next day in a pastel swing skirt and matching cardigan, offering him a glass of whiskey in one hand and the Richmond sale in the other, candidate for Stepford wife of the year? Would I lose my edge, the drive to compete?

Either way, Dad would lose all respect for me and not trust me to do the shows I want.

Harrison saves me from that future by calling for our attention.

"Good morning, everyone. I hope you all brought your athletic skills, because today's event is a tennis tournament in my court."

"Yay." I feign enthusiasm, luckily drowned out by the genuine enthusiasm from everyone else.

"We're really going for a perfect week of patrician shit this week," a voice whispers from my side.

I twist my head and jump away from the source of the voice, putting my hands up to defend myself if needed. I was so busy trying to avoid Gavin by stepping away from him that I didn't realize he'd gotten even closer. And that's a sad metaphor for my life right now.

"Whoa, there." He puts his hands up. "The cage fight isn't till later."

"You can never be too prepared for a cage fight," I say weakly.

"But everyone expects the fight, since it happens at a scheduled time. It's not the Spanish Inquisition."

Because no one expects the Spanish Inquisition, just like that Monty Python skit. Nice.

"Did Sir Stuck-Up just make a Monty Python reference…*and* say this week was too patrician for him? The shock. Very unexpected."

"My dad loves them." He sounds sheepish, like he does every time he gets vulnerable or personal.

"Mine too," I admit.

"Hey, the hated enemies have something in common," Gavin says as we start following Harrison to his private tennis court. "Maybe we should get them together and force them to have a cordial night watching Monty Python together."

"You really want to see a fight to the death, don't you?"

"Fight to the death?" Gavin snorts. "More like two old men getting winded slap fighting."

I laugh, and then immediately feel bad for laughing at Dad's expense.

Harrison gets to the courts before I can further betray my family honor. He's becoming really helpful at interrupting awkward moments for me. Sure, he was nowhere to be seen yesterday. Although that ended… happily for me.

Pun very much intended.

"I thought I'd put some friendly competition into this weekend." He gives the auctioneers a wink to single us out. "So we'll play tournament style and the winner gets a very nice, very old bottle of Dom Perignon."

"I hope you aren't as good at tennis as you are at shooting," Nate says to me as Harrison separates us into groups on the two courts. Because only having one would have been so plebeian, apparently.

"I'm firmly mediocre. And very sad that the champagne wasn't a prize for the shooting part of this week."

"I don't think alcohol and guns mixing would have been a good idea," Gavin says from my other side. The words are directed at me, but he's looking at Nate with an unsmiling look on his face, arms crossed like he's a bouncer at the hottest club of the moment.

What crawled up his butt?

"I wouldn't have drunk it while we were shooting." My eyes travel from Nate to Gavin, who look like two big silverback gorillas mad they're in the same enclosure. Not enough space for the ego of two successful men at the height of their careers.

"Who wants to play first?" Harrison's at a chalk-board, ready to organize our day.

"I'll go." Anything to get this over with.

Harrison writes my name on the board and I pick up a racket and tennis balls. Cindy volunteers to play against me, and it ends up being a short and decisive victory for her. I breathe a sigh of relief that I don't have to play another game, taking a seat on the short bleachers next to the courts.

Tennis was another thing Dad thought I should learn because all the young ladies at my school were doing it. It was one more thing I had to do that meant I spent less time at the office, guaranteeing that I was going to hate it forever.

Just like cooking. Except I don't even get delicious food out of it, so I tried even less at it.

Nate and Gavin are playing on the opposite court, and their game looks a lot more intense than mine. I watch as Nate gets to forty and Gavin is still at love. Gavin looks like he wants to repeatedly beat the racket into the court until he makes a dent. I hope he does... that would have to give me an advantage.

I root for him a little bit. To myself, of course. I'm not at the place where I'm admitting that out loud.

They furiously smack tennis balls back and forth, each staying neck and neck until Gavin finally catches up and then wins.

I clap along with the other spectators, appreciating the show they put on. It's the second time I've seen him look anything but effortless, and it's a good look to see him have to try at something.

His hair is even out of place, and some beads of sweat gleam on his brow.

The games keep going while Harrison's staff serves the spectators/losers food and wine. Nate joins me and Naomi in the bleachers, to make a growing group of losers.

Losers happily chowing down on expensive food and wine.

"So you work at an auction house?" Nate asks, picking at his plate of finger sandwiches.

"Yup. It's my family's auction house and I organize and run sales there."

"I don't know too much about art or history. It's impressive to have learned all that."

"I really enjoy it. But you don't need to know too much history if you're a buyer, you can just get whatever makes you happy. And if I've done my job, you'll have learned about the context and meaning through the exhibition."

"Maybe I'll come check out a sale."

See. Always working even when everyone else is on vacation.

"We'd love to have you. I've got cards upstairs and I'll give you one. You can always contact me if you have any questions about buying, or to tell me what you like and I can recommend particular sales that you might be interested in." Just bring that energy industry wallet.

"What do you think I would like?" he asks.

Naomi snorts behind us. "To appreciate art, you'd have to tear yourself away from work long enough to look at it."

"Hey, squirt. I'm not that bad." Nate looks over his shoulder.

"You really are, Executive Jr.," she says.

"I could be worse… I could work like your father."

"Saying you're not as bad as the worst isn't a great victory. The bar is higher than the ground."

"On the off chance I get a minute, what art do you think I should get?" The words are directed at me, but he's still looking at Naomi.

I answer anyway, even though I don't think anyone particularly wants me in this conversation, sparking off each other like they are. Especially since I would have to back Nate, workaholics sticking together and all that. "Well, newbies can go either way really. Some like the modern aesthetic with abstract art because they don't need a lot of historical knowledge, but some people like the pieces that reference mythology or biblical stories they know, something they can connect to."

"I think I would like something modern."

I start listing the best works that I think would fit his tastes. Naomi chimes in with her expertise, already on her way to becoming a discerning collector. Probably from learning from her father.

We're still discussing art when I hear yelling. A yellow ball comes flying toward the bleachers, and would have hit Nate right in the chest if he hadn't dodged out of the way, dropping his plate and wineglass in the process.

"Sorry," Gavin yells from the court, lifting his racket in apology.

"Watch it," I yell back. He shouldn't be pranking me…he had the last prank. It's my turn—we have a system, damn it.

My heart takes some time to get back to beating at a normal pace from the excitement, and I use the moment to take in how good Gavin looks when he exercises. He took his outer shirt off so he's playing in a tank top, and he's glistening like the Roman soldiers in Jacques-Louis David's painting the *Oath of the Horatii*. Which is very glisteny.

I remind myself he just hit a ball at me so lusting after him is not a good look. So instead of looking at him, I help Nate pick up his discarded eating utensils.

Gavin makes it all the way to the finals before he loses to Harrison. He gives me a wink when we gather for the small winner's circle, and I know he let Harrison win. I mean, Harrison is a good player, but Gavin is playing significantly slower than when he played his other opponents.

Touché, rival, touché.

"Age might have won over beauty, but I'm a good sport and I'm not keeping my own champagne." He gives the box to Gavin, who accepts it with a cloying smile. "Dinner tonight, everyone, then we're going to have some after-dinner drinks and dancing for whoever wants it."

"Harrison, if I could make an announcement about tomorrow?" I say before everyone can disperse.

"Of course. Our hunting trip got canceled and Priya kindly offered to plan us an event in its place," Harrison says to the crowd of expectant guests.

"Tomorrow if everyone can wear exercise clothes they don't mind getting dirty, we'll meet on the back terrace at 11:00 a.m. White shirts are recommended but I'll have some extras if you don't have anything," I say.

"I'm intrigued. What are we doing?" Pari asks.

"It's a surprise. Hopefully a fun one." And one that Pari will know better than anyone, once she realizes what it is.

"We're going to get dirty?" Cindy wrinkles her face

like I asked her to climb in a crawl space and remove whatever is causing a house to smell so bad.

"Nothing permanent. And if you don't want to participate, watching will be fun too." Like she couldn't just buy a new…whatever gets ruined. Like she can't just buy a million new whatevers get ruined.

"I'm looking forward to what you have for us. Now I have to get some work done." Harrison walks back to the house.

He's not the only one. Dismissed by the teacher, I head back to do my own work. Gavin must have the same idea, because he walks back with me.

"Do you think this is going to be Lizzo dancing or *Pride and Prejudice* dancing tonight?" I ask to make conversation.

Mostly because in the silence, alone with just the two of us, my mind keeps going back to the sex room. And what we did in that sex room, which raises the temperature in the hallway significantly.

"I don't know what either of those would mean, so I hope it's just some calm swaying. Maybe a gentle two-step." We stop in front of our doors and he starts moving his shoulders back and forth with his feet, with no participation from his hips.

"Oh no, please stop that. You should sit out the dancing, whatever it ends up being." I laugh.

"You don't want to see these sweet moves?" He starts alternating between doing the Sprinkler and slowly backing up toward me. And then both of those things at once.

"Please stop," I beg, getting breathless with laughter. "I'll give you five dollars if you stop." I found yet another thing he can't manage effortlessly. So many imperfections in this man...making him human.

"And deprive you of all of this." He gets so close his butt is rubbing up against me. But awkwardly.

He's adorable. An adorable, human man.

I look around quickly, making sure no one else is here to see the failure. I'm protective over those bad dance moves now.

I'm surprised how much fun I'm having with him. I'm not surprised how fun he is; he's built his whole brand around it. But I didn't think we would get to the point where we would have fun *together*.

But here we are.

"You work on that. You work on that until dinner, and don't bother doing any other work."

"You wish, Riya." He straightens and walks to his own door, opening it. "See you at dinner."

"See you."

Safe in my room, I can pretend that I'm not affected by Gavin. It's not true, but in these four walls, with no judgmental, mind-reading cousins around, I can pretend whatever I want.

I might as well make myself a princess of England while I'm at it. Very nice houses. And very nice art collection.

I work through the emails and voicemails I've been blissfully ignoring for most of the day.

Anything on fire yet? I text Sonia.

It's been a fire free day...except for the fire in your loins!

This is what I get for trying to be a good supervisor. I ignore her shenanigans so I can review the intelligence that our client development team found.

I call them my Gossip Squad, because they're on the lookout for any collectors who've said they want to sell their art, or a big collector experiencing one of the big three Ds that lead to art sales: divorce, debt or death. They compile them into nice gossip reports that *Page Six* would kill for. Making them my favorite people.

I start setting up meetings to schmooze. But subtly, so the clients don't think they're little guppies being stalked by shark me.

Do sharks eat guppies? I'm not up on my oceanography.

And I'm not looking it up, because I have guppies to hunt here.

Chapter Twenty-One

Dinner tonight isn't as elaborate as the nine-course dinner we were graced with the first day, and my stomach is thankful I won't gorge myself as much again.

The reasonable amount of food we're offered is amazing and the conversation is an enjoyable side dish.

Nate brings up the tips we talked about to get his first collection going, and everyone jumps in to contribute their opinions. Harrison, Pari and Jack, as well as Gavin of course, are knowledgeable in the field, making a lively debate over what Nate's first piece should be.

Nate picks mine, of course. I mentally brush dirt off my shoulder.

But it's hot to see Gavin in his element, talking about art with so much competence. Even debating me about art with points that are just as good as mine, if I'm honest, he's still hot. About as attractive as he was when we did the auction together or when we were in the sex room and he compared me to artworks.

And he's wearing another one of his shrunken shirts. I know he wore it on purpose because he caught my eyes from across the table when he sat down and flexed, with a devilish wink. I almost missed the wink because I got a little distracted by the way his chest looked when he flexed it, which he also noticed.

After the deconstructed ice cream sundae dessert (which is just a dessert that I have to assemble…dessert with homework), Harrison gets our attention.

"If you would all follow me to the evening drawing room, we can start the after-dinner entertainment."

He leads us through the labyrinth of hallways to a room we haven't seen yet. Which is an impressive feat since I've poked my head in a lot of these rooms while getting lost. This one has dark purple damask walls, with matching purple-and-gold damask couches.

There are giant mirrors on top of golden peacocks on each side of the room, like the birds are holding the mirrors up. And there's a giant clock on the mantel with Athena surrounded by a temple made of golden columns, sitting on a couch with an intricate and tiny battle scene on the side. All the tables and couches are moved to the sides of the room.

The furniture pieces are so beautiful that I wish I could spend more time studying them. Is that on the schedule? I hope so. Maybe instead of the dancing.

"Since a lot of you might not be up on your nineteenth-century quadrille, we have teachers here to help everyone out," Harrison says.

Thank god. Because that's one thing that isn't on the private school curriculum anymore. But I think they replaced it with science, so I can't complain.

Harrison hired two teachers for us and they're dressed in full Regency costume. Now I really feel underdressed in a dark blue tea-length dress.

And I contemplate twisting my ankle as a defense against participating in this.

The teachers take over, dividing us into groups to take us through the dance, which apparently has five parts to it, involves a lot of partner switching, and looks better when you have a large skirt to swoosh around in.

Harrison's staff are good at their jobs, so they make sure the alcohol is flowing while we dance. I don't think I've drunk this many days in a row since college. Back then I didn't have to worry about Loot's employees, revenue or the market.

When the teachers feel they've taught us all they can in forty-five minutes, they let us loose on each other, promising to be around in case anyone needs help.

Gavin strides toward me, eyes capturing mine and not letting me avoid him. "Can I profane your holy shrine with my unworthiest hand?" He bows in front of me and offers his hand, in the most Shakespearean way possible.

I laugh, not doing well on my resolution to not be affected by Gavin. "Sure. But if you see me napping later and I appear to be dead, please don't stab yourself. Until a reputable doctor confirms the death and a week passes just in case, then, do what you feel is necessary." I take his hand.

"Good policy. Kind of you to care about me." Gavin tucks my hand into his elbow, resting his hand on top of mine so my hand is sandwiched between his forearm and palm.

"On second thought, do stab yourself but not fatally." I don't want to feel guilty over his death, but I'll take the advantage of him stopping work long enough to heal.

"There's my Riya," Gavin says affectionately, patting me on the hand that's on his arm.

The first strains of music fill the room and I immediately regret my decision not to twist my ankle earlier.

"Did you take in anything that they taught us?" I ask as we stand opposite Jack and Cindy. Harrison and Pari and Nate and Naomi are to the left of our group.

"Not a thing. I plan to twirl you whenever I get lost."

"Thanks for the heads-up," I say as people start moving.

The first step isn't so bad. Gavin and I bow to each other. Then it immediately gets more complicated, with turns and constant partner switches. Twice I go to the wrong partner and a few times I grab the wrong hands.

But I'm not the only one struggling; a few times I come out of a turn and I have two partners waiting for me. Or none.

This looks a lot cooler in the *Pride and Prejudice* movies.

No one crashes into each other hard enough to cause injury, so I think we can call it a mild success. Or at least not an abject failure.

When the dance is over, Harrison, Pari, Naomi and Nate stay in the center of the room to do a smaller quadrille. They're much better at it, and it looks a lot more like the movies.

"I think they've done this before," Gavin whispers at me, snagging two wineglasses from a passing server.

"I doubt Harrison would have us do something he wasn't already amazing at," I whisper back, taking the glass offered.

"Oh no, do you think he'll want to do a dance as part of his show?" His breath tickles the hair near my ear as he leans down to make sure the person we're wooing doesn't hear us talking shit.

"If there is, you can have him. And enjoy."

Gavin snorts. "No, I'll make Dad do it at that point."

After a few more dances, the teachers spring back into action. "That was great, everyone. Now we're going to move on to something a little different and do a waltz. This was a scandalous dance for the time because it let couples dance in each other's arms. People thought it was going to lead to licentious consequences."

Well, it's not grinding but okay. Not that there's anything wrong with licentious consequences. Or grinding.

Nate walks to me and extends his hand. "Can I have this waltz?"

"Of course." I take his hand and hear a small, unhappy grunt from next to me. I whip my head around and look at Gavin with brows drawn low over my eyes, but he's sipping on wine and looking innocent. So I know he's suspicious.

But I've got a young VP in front of me who has expressed interest in building an art collection. He's going to be a very, very rich executive one day, so I need to get him hooked on art and Loot in the early stages.

We get our hands in position and try to move our feet like the dance teachers are telling us to. Nate knows what he's doing, but I keep stomping all over his feet. He's a good sport about it, and we end up laughing more than actual dancing.

In the corner of my eye, I see Gavin trying the dance with the Naomi, and my good mood dissipates.

I don't like that at all.

Only for her, because he's way too old to be creeping on her innocent, college self. I'm basically a selfless superhero, looking out for the youth of America.

And I don't like seeing him and Cindy getting along

so well because of the sanctity of marriage. Just me being a selfless superhero again.

We go through the same dances for the rest of the night, the teachers cutting in and helping those who need it most (me and Gavin).

At 10:00 p.m., Harrison offers to take people to the smoking room again for cigars. I contemplate going for the extra time with Harrison but imagining being around the strong smell makes my stomach turn a little. So I decide to take my chance with Gavin getting the extra time.

I say my good nights as everyone disperses from the evening drawing room. To my surprise, Gavin follows me up the stairs.

"You didn't want a smoke with the lads?" I ask in a terrible accent, feeling very English after the night we've had.

Gavin shudders. "No. Cigars smell horrible. And they taste worse."

"Cigars aside, Harrison really knows how to throw a good house party," I say when we get to our doors.

We're at our rooms, so technically, the night should end. But I don't want it to.

"I get the feeling this isn't his first rodeo." He leans against the wood-paneled wall, apparently as eager as me to go to our rooms alone.

"Like that man's ever been to a rodeo."

"Rodeo Drive in Beverly Hills probably."

"Most definitely." I laugh with him. "It's nice to be here, whatever the reason is."

"I agree, especially after last night." Gavin lowers his voice, causing goose bumps on my skin like it was a physical touch.

I clear my throat. "I thought we agreed not to talk about that." Good thing no one is around to hear that piece of news.

"Nope. Because we would have had to talk about it to *decide* not to talk about it."

"Well, that's a bad system," I say, uncomfortable that we're still talking about it, because every time we do, I'm reminded how much I want him.

"I really enjoyed it." Gavin directs us back to the topic I don't want to discuss.

"Yeah, it wasn't the worst. I guess." It's hard for me to be this honest with anything outside of work. Mostly because I haven't had the practice, since I'm always so focused on work.

"It was great, and we didn't even touch." Gavin moves close enough that we could easily be touching right now, but stays just far enough that I find myself leaning closer to him, like a magnet that's powerless to stop the move. "I wonder how much better it would have been if we had been touching."

I wish he would stop talking about how much he wants to touch me and just do it. I'm done being driven to levels of unknown frustration with the unfulfilled desire. I'm done with getting turned on by him and only having my own hand to get me off.

I'm done feeling guilty because I'm feeling all of that for someone unsuitable.

"Why don't you come in my room and find out?" I ask, going after what I want in my personal life for once.

Chapter Twenty-Two

Gavin's eyes get big as he looks at me in disbelief. I don't think I have the strength to say the words out loud again, so I turn away and hold my door open.

Gavin doesn't say anything, and I start to get worried. This could still be an elaborate prank on me. And this is his payoff, now that I bent enough to invite him in.

"If you want. Or not. Whatever." I make one last effort.

The words galvanize him into action. "Yes, Riya. I really do want." He sends me a steamy look as he enters the room before me.

"Oh, boy." Watching that fine butt walk into my room is making me wonder if this is the best idea. It sounded great in the hall, but now I can see the bed behind him and it's getting a lot more real.

But then the butt stops. "Wait," he says as he turns around.

"What? Yeah. No, I was just kidding," I say in a rush to save face.

"Let's go to my room. I have condoms," he says at the same time.

"Do you not want to do this?" he asks after he takes

in what I said. "I can leave if you've changed your mind."

"Ignore that. Let's do your suggestion." I march out of the room and open his door, not waiting for him to go in.

Gavin follows behind, closing the door after he comes in. He walks directly to me and reaches both hands out to frame my face. "I've been wanting to do this for so long."

My brows furrow, but before I can ask just how long he's been wanting to do this, he kisses me.

His lips touch mine, and the desire to ask him anything flies out of the window, replaced by the desire to get in the bed behind him.

Gavin angles his head and deepens the kiss by adding tongue. His hands move urgently to my hips to pull me flush against his hard body, taking their time after I'm where he wants me. I'm perfectly happy to be there, especially when I can feel his hard dick press against my soft stomach.

My body takes the initiative and rubs against the parts of Gavin it has access to. Gavin pushes me gently back toward the bed, stopping when the back of my legs hit it. Then he sweeps me high on his chest with his arms under my ass.

He tumbles me onto the bed, following me down immediately. His lips move from my lips to kiss a path to my ear. "You're more beautiful than *The Rokeby Venus*." He kisses lower, down to my neck. "And *The Nude Maja*." He kisses my breasts through my dress. "And all the Renaissance Venuses I can think of."

I make a sound of frustration because of the layer of cloth between my skin and his mouth. This is so close to perfection, if he would just get my dress off. The words are really doing this for me, same as his kisses, and I want more of it all.

"I don't think I'll be able to go slow this time." Gavin sends me the warning from against my stomach, where he's moved down to.

"Who asked you to?" I say, arching my pelvis further into him. I get wetter and wetter at the thought that I'm going to finally be having sex with Gavin. Well, if he can stop talking about it and get to business.

Permission granted; he explodes into action. He scrambles to push up my dress, moving his head up to my face and taking my lips again as his hands get my underwear down. My own hands jump into action, undoing his belt.

I unzip his pants before he takes over and moves back to shove the pants down. My hands reach for his retreating back as he walks across the room, unbuttoning his shirt on the way, and reaches into his bag. He holds up a condom, excitement in his smile as he comes back to bed, putting the condom on.

I get on my knees and kiss every part of him I can reach, kissing his chest and giving his neck a light bite before Gavin pushes me down until my back is against the sheets.

I shove my hands through his hair, watching it stand up in different directions. I take perverse pleasure in being the one to genuinely ruffle the always artfully careless man, so I run my hands though it a few more times.

Gavin reaches down to swipe his fingers through my wet folds, zeroing in on my clit. Meanwhile his dick is impatient, rhythmically thrusting against my hip.

After a few rubs, he stops the movement. I start to groan in disappointment, but then change it to a moan of pleasure when he guides his cock to my entrance and rubs the tip against my clit a few times before he pushes in.

Despite his warning that he wouldn't be slow, he carefully slides into me, taking the time to stop and rub my clit when he feels resistance. With each stroke of his hand my body pulls him in deeper, getting slicker.

Finally, he's completely in, with my dress gathered around my waist and Gavin with his shirt still hanging on his back, all the buttons undone.

There's something arousing about the fact that Gavin wants me so much he can't wait for the time it would take for us to undress fully.

Gavin begins thrusting into me, picking up speed with each thrust. His fingers keep rubbing my clit as he thrusts, making sure that I'm racing toward orgasm just like he is. His other hand, not to be outdone, pushes my dress down at the collar, reaching for my breast.

I feel my muscles get tighter around Gavin's penis as I get closer to coming. He groans and increases his pace again in response.

I break apart in orgasm at the dual sensations of his cock filling me and the pressure of his hands on my clit. Gavin follows close behind, face twisted in pleasure as he does. After, he collapses beside me, still breathing heavily.

I turn my head and my lips curve into a small smile. Gavin's eyes are closed and his chest is heaving as he gulps in huge mouthfuls of air.

Wait, aren't I supposed to be the one with the heaving bosom?

For the sake of honesty, my bosom is exhibiting its own amount of up and down movement.

He's covered in a thin layer of sweat, and I mentally pat myself on the back. Rapid heartbeat, sweat, wild hair, and heavy breathing. I've flapped the unflappable Gavin Carlyle.

Once Gavin catches his breath a little, he takes off the condom and tosses it to the trashcan by the bed.

"I should go," I say, my voice still affected by what we just did. I half-heartedly pull my dress down and move to slide off the bed.

Gavin turns to me and reaches out to touch my elbow. "You can stay if you want."

"Okay. For a little bit. I'll just go to the bathroom."

I leave the bed and walk to his bathroom. I'm too lazy to go back to my room for pajamas, so I snag one of Gavin's button-down shirts on my way.

After I use the facilities, I look at myself in the mirror.

I look as flapped as Gavin is. My hair is a tangled mess and I have red marks where Gavin's five-o'clock shadow rubbed against me.

I smile as I finish washing my hands and go back to bed. Gavin took his shirt off while I was gone and got comfortable in the bed so I slide in next to him.

Gavin turns the light off and then pulls me into his side, head buried in my hair and limbs extended to cover me.

I fall asleep surrounded by Gavin's smell, touch and heat.

The next morning, I wake up to light shining directly in my face. My heart starts to pound when I feel a heavy weight on my side pushing me into the bed, and I don't recognize the room I'm in.

Then information starts slowly filtering through my sleep-addled brain and I remember I'm in the enemy's room. And we had sex last night.

I slowly slide away from Gavin, trying not to wake him. I want to get back in my room so I can process the events without being distracted by Gavin's perfect hair and perfect body and perfect peen.

I thrust a leg off the bed first and the momentum has the rest of me sliding off like a less flexible slinky. I land on the floor with a muted thump. Thankfully for my knees, Harrison has all his rooms carpeted in a thick, soft carpet, both for its sound dampening and its cushioning properties.

I peek my head back up and release a breath of relief that Gavin didn't wake up. I tiptoe to the couch to get my clothes and debate with myself if I should take the time to get dressed or take the chance of running into someone only in Gavin's shirt.

There's rustling from the bed as Gavin turns around to his other side, facing away from me. But the movement still causes me to freeze in fear.

Nope, the embarrassment of getting caught sneaking out of Gavin's room in the shirt is better than having to face Gavin.

Sneaking out of Gavin's room, I pull the door closed softly behind me. There's no one in the hallways and I rush to my room next door. I open that door with much less care and heave a sigh of relief when I'm safely back in my own room.

Now I just need some distractions so I don't have to think closely about Gavin.

My phone is still on my bedside table. Perfect. There has to be something on there that needs my attention, and I do have an event to plan today. I see a text from Sarah that everything is being set up on the grounds.

One thing going to plan today, at least. I change quickly, pack a bag of things I'll need and run down the stairs, only going the wrong way down the right hallway once this time.

I'm practically a resident here.

"Sarah," I yell and wave when I get closer to one of the tents beyond the terrace. "Everything looks perfect!"

They set up the tent beautifully. They somehow found an actual rickshaw to put in the corner and the top of the tent has colorful fabric hanging from the ceiling. Each side has freestanding columns and Indian style arches.

Colorful mason jars decorated with gold-painted henna designs on the outside and tea light candles inside sit atop the tables, along with elephant-shaped cookies with matching henna patterns on them for when the guests want to take a break.

On one side are large baskets, each with a different color powder. The long table next to them contains filled water balloons and water guns.

"Can I hug you?" I look at her with gratitude.

Sarah laughs. "Yes."

Permission granted, I give her that hug. "This must have cost so much."

"Mr. Harrison said to spare no expense," Jeeves/ Ryan, putting up the finishing touches of some hanging lanterns, says from a ladder behind me.

"Seriously, how did you do this on such short notice?" I ask Sarah, convinced the answer is going to involve some sort of evil magic involving blood sacrifice.

"They were all your ideas. Mrs. Harrison has some amazing decorations already, and we have an Indian couple down the road who host a lot of great events too. And one of their maids owed me a favor."

"Thank you so much for calling it in for me." I take another long look around the tent. This is going to get me the show for sure.

"Oh, were you able to get the white shirts and fanny packs?" I ask.

"Yup." Sarah points to the items sitting on the table next to the powders.

"Oh, let's get them out of the packaging so they don't know we're trying to give them stuff from Target."

We work on arranging the shirts to hide their common origins. We finish the task just before people start arriving.

"This is amazing!" Naomi says.

"Thanks, but it's all Sarah and your employees," I say.

A man in black workout pants and a white shirt appears from behind me to offer Naomi a cocktail glass.

I send a questioning look at Sarah over my shoulder and she mouths, "Themed cocktails."

Seriously. Amazing.

"This is interesting," Jack says.

"What are you having us do?" Cindy asks as she takes her drink.

"I'll tell everyone when we're all here," I say, hopefully mysterious in a fun way.

"I think I know where this event is going...and I'm

very excited for it!" Pari says, winking at me. "And impressed you got the Shaws' rickshaw!"

"It was all Sarah," I say.

Gavin gets to the tent second to last. He's in the same shorts from the tennis day, and he has a tight white shirt on. Another one I can blame on myself for the shrinking prank.

He tries to make eye contact with me, but I avoid him and take a sharp left turn to help Sarah arrange the appetizers on the tables instead. Then Harrison comes and I turn back to the crowd.

"Hi, everyone. Harrison was kind enough to let me plan an event, and loan me the best employees in the universe to make it happen." I send a grateful look to Sarah. "And since it's March and the beginning of spring, we're going to celebrate Holi!"

Chapter Twenty-Three

"Yes!" The Richmonds all cheer.

"We haven't done a proper Holi in too long," Pari adds.

In everyone else, I see a lot of blank faces. I rush to explain. "It's the Indian festival of colors to celebrate the harvest, and spring, and good triumphing over evil and forgiveness and play and new love..." I clear my throat when I list that last one. New lovers, apparently, in this Indian's case. "And well, a lot of things. To celebrate, everyone throws colored powder at each other. And there's music and food."

Still with the blank faces.

"Like a color run with less running."

A chorus of "Ohhh" comes from my audience. That figures.

"If anyone needs a white shirt they can get colorful, we have a selection on the table, as well as some fanny packs and plastic pouches for storage. For the powder."

Everyone still looks a little unsure about the activities, so I take the lead and head to the powder baskets to start filling baggies. People start drifting over and picking their own colors.

"And don't forget to get some water balloons and

water guns pre-filled with water and more powder," I remind everyone. "When you're all loaded up, I'll meet you all in the center of that field right here." I point to an area to the side of the house, past a path dotted with sculptures, stone benches, and hedges with vibrantly colorful flowers poking out in their spring awakening.

"Is this going to destroy my grass?" Harrison asks teasingly while overfilling his powder bags.

"It's organic," I say, hoping that's true. This is a bit last minute.

I carry my cache to the center of the lawn, water gun slung over my back and my fanny pack stuffed with powder baggies and water balloons, which are all earmarked for a very specific person.

The same person, unaware of the powder storm waiting for them, approaches me with a smile, loaded down with his own weapons.

"Hi," Gavin says when he stops a respectable distance away from me. But it doesn't matter that he's not touching me, because I can feel his eyes on me, retracing the same path his hands and mouth took last night.

"Hello," I say, a little breathless despite reminding myself he's the competition.

He takes a furtive look around, and then returns those tactile eyes to me again. I hunch down and a little back at the look, trying to create a little space and prevent myself from throwing myself at him and recreating the night before. Right here in the open.

"You snuck out early this morning. I was hoping we'd have a chance to go another round, maybe slower. Maybe we get all our clothes off this time." His voice is low, seductive.

"Oh, dear," I whisper. Everyone else is still busy

getting their equipment for the event, so I don't have to worry about them seeing the temptation that's being presented here. "Let's not take out a full-page advertisement about that."

Gavin physically pulls back. "Don't you want to do it again?"

"It was just a one-off."

"I'm not proposing, Priya. But I told you when you stole Stella that I wanted to go out with you."

"But I didn't think you were serious," I say, throwing my arms out and shrugging. "Like maybe it was a way to get me to lower my guard and take away my edge."

"Wow. Your terrible opinion of me aside, I thought we would be good together, and nothing that's happened since then has changed my mind. If anything, it's made me believe it more." The nice words contrast sharply with the cool tone he says them in.

And he's back to calling me Priya. I should be happy, since I hate when he uses the nickname, but I'm strangely disappointed to see it go. I feel like I've just lost something that I didn't know I had in the first place.

So now I'm bereft and confused.

"I…" I start, but I don't know what I'm going to say. But then I'm saved by the crowd of people heading our way. "Talk later?" I ask instead, taking the coward's way out.

He nods curtly. He might have been taking this a lot more seriously than I originally thought.

I don't want him to. It makes everything even more complicated. Having lustful feelings for Gavin is one thing, acting on them is another. But to go in on this 100 percent…for a relationship? That would be chaos. He'd eventually get sick of his girlfriend beating him, or I would change how I worked so I wouldn't hurt his feelings.

Then I'd lose a part of me that I've carried since elementary school when I vowed to take over Loot.

And that's if Dad would even let me be in charge. Which would be doubtful if he thought I was making bad decisions, like dating a Carlyle.

I shake off the thoughts and turn my attention back to the faces circled around me, which are a lot more eager than they were five minutes ago. Back to the work.

I think they've had time to get used to the idea of throwing things at their closest friends. My hypothesis is confirmed when I catch a few of them sending sneaking glances at each other when they think no one's looking.

"All right, everyone, spread out a little so everyone starts with their own bubble. Give everyone a sporting chance." I spread my arms out and turn in a circle, showing everyone how much space they should give. "And everyone has to participate. It's good luck." I wave Sarah and the other helpful staff over.

The crowd falls in line without too much fuss, but Harrison and Naomi are inching closer to poor Pari, who doesn't see them because she's looking at Cindy with unholy glee in her eyes.

I may be positioned a little close to Gavin as well. I've got a lot to work out here, through this powder battle.

I raise my hand up to get everyone's attention. It works pretty well since everyone is raring to go.

"On your mark…" I draw out the big moment. "Get set…" I get some impatient looks. "Throw!"

In the next few minutes, a haze descends on the

world as clouds of color fill my vision. The guests are laughing nonstop and I mentally pat myself on the back.

The event is already a success.

I turn in a circle, throwing powder at whoever is in front of me. Luckily, everyone takes the hits in good spirits and returns a throw to me.

I'm looking for Gavin when I feel a balloon pop on the back of my right shoulder. This water is freezing!

Shoulders hunched and slightly shivering, I turn and see a smirking Gavin, water gun pointed right at me.

Ha. Wait until he finds out that his water gun isn't filled with water.

I take a handful of bright yellow powder but don't throw it right away. And I'm glad I don't, so I get to see the look of confusion in Gavin's eyes as he furiously pumps his toy gun, but every time he pulls on the plastic trigger nothing happens.

"Problem, Gavin?" I ask in a voice so sugary it belongs in a candy shop.

"Riya…what did you do?" he growls. He's trying so hard to be stern, but it's a hard image to solidify in my mind since he's covered in colored powder and holding an obnoxiously bright plastic weapon.

A weapon I jammed, and enlisted Sarah's help in making sure Gavin got the right one.

In lieu of answering, I throw the powder at his face. Still trying to get the gun working, he doesn't have time to block the throw, so the powder hits him directly. He does close his eyes, at least.

Gavin isn't shocked for long, and he drops the gun, abandoning it to grab a bag of bright green powder. By the look in his eyes, I'm going to be covered in that pretty soon.

Good thing it's my favorite color.

I'm not retreating, I'm just advancing in another direction, I comfort myself, channeling General Oliver P. Smith, as I turn tail and run away from Gavin. I jerk my head backward and forward, making sure I'm not going to crash into anything in front of me and then back to see where Gavin is and throw another handful of powder at him.

We keep going, circling the large lawn a few times.

I'm laughing as I run, making me a lot more winded a lot faster than normal. Which is fast, because who has time for the gym?

Honestly, I'm going to look into that membership tomorrow.

I make it to a nearby stone fountain with green moss charmingly crawling up a merman spitting water through a shell, and use it as cover to get away from Gavin. I use the momentary gap in pursuit to clutch my side and try to catch my breath.

"Are you okay, Riya?" Gavin asks, concerned.

Hmm. So I'm officially back to Riya again, am I?

"I'm fine," I say, presenting the opposite image as I take a seat on the fountain and put my head between my knees. Is that supposed to help? Or is that for panic? Or nausea, maybe?

I'll look it up when my lungs aren't burning quite so angrily.

"You don't look fine." He takes a seat next to me. I feel gentle but firm hands on my shoulder. "It'll help your lungs more if you sit up tall."

"This is a perfectly natural reaction to the inhalation of powder," I force out. I may be hacking up a lung but I will always use my last breath to contradict Gavin Carlyle.

Gavin takes a look around at all the other people who aren't heaving in gulps of air. "Is it though?"

Oh, and now we're back to teasing? Not all the way back, if the semi-cold tone is anything to go by, but closer to normal.

My breathing calms a little at the thought that he's less mad at me. And the rest I've had probably isn't hurting anything. "I ran a lot more than they did."

Their laughter floats over from the center of the lawn. They're also beginning to slow down, standing in place and throwing powder to anyone they can reach without too much effort.

Some of the crowd is already back at the baskets, refilling their bags.

"The event's a success," Gavin says, drawing my attention back to him.

"Thank you. I'm sure yours will be as well." I try the gracious route. It's a bit overgrown from lack of use with this particular man, but I like the view.

"That looked physically painful."

Okay, maybe a lot overgrown.

"Yeah, okay. I hope it's terrible and mine looks even better in contrast and you lose all your clients and the creditors have to take all your art and you're left staring at empty walls," I say in a rush.

Gavin laughs. "That's better."

I shake my head at him, his bad mood apparently a distant memory. "Are you a masochist, Carlyle?"

He gives me a considering look. "I didn't think I was. I like easy. Maybe that's a little bit of a flaw. School, navigating the art market, and auctioneering all come naturally. It's even easy to give in to Dad, most times. But you…"

"Well? What about me? Don't stop there." I throw some more powder at his chest, hoping to get my answer from him. I'm not a patient person. That's my flaw. Probably not my only one.

"You're difficult," he concludes, a smile still on his face from previously laughing at me.

"Oh." My face falls in disappointment and I pick at my bag of powder. That's not a compliment.

"But I think you might be worth it."

"Oh." The words take my breath like the running previously did. Even though Gavin has been honest about pursuing me, I never thought he'd get this emotionally honest with me. Or that there were any emotions to get honest about.

I have no idea how to respond to that, because I don't know what I want.

Which is a lie. I suspect I do know what I want, but I don't know how I can get it without everything else I've worked for crashing down.

But he's been so honest with me; I feel the need to reciprocate. "I don't know how to do work and a relationship. And I especially don't know how to do it with you."

"So you like things easy too then," he says.

"I do not," I say hotly, reflexively denying the ludicrous claim. I work more hours than anyone at the damn auction house, and my team brings in more money than any other department. All while Dad tries to take my work away from me. None of that is easy.

"You work hard at the job, I'll give you that. But adding a relationship into that makes it hard. And, yeah, a relationship with me would be even harder. Hardest probably," he mutters the last part under his breath, like he doesn't want to give me any more ammunition, but he wants to be honest. "So you're running. Even though it would be good."

I slam my hand down in my lap, hitting the bag and causing a small cloud of powder to drift up. I cough, ruining the gravity of the moment but not letting it distract me from the conversation. "It's easy to sit here and say we'd be good, but it's a little different when you'll have to take me to Sunday night dinner with the Carlyles. Your dad is not my biggest fan."

"Because you keep beating him. And your dad hates me, because I can beat him too. I get that. But our moms are reasonable women. And it'd be worth it."

"This is a ridiculous conversation." I get up and start pacing in front of Gavin.

Gavin might be right; I do think work and a relationship would be too much. When I first started at the auction house, I'd meet guys, but I was so busy they got annoyed and moved on. And I didn't exactly care that they were going. More like a weak "No, please don't go," while not looking up from my phone, answering emails.

And it never really got less busy. In fact, the work always increased. There was always another collection to get, another sale to put on, another record to break. And no one could hold my attention better than the job.

The more time I spent at the job, the fewer people I met, until I was surrounded by art world folks. And I couldn't date anyone in the industry; everyone was either a client, or competition or they worked for me. Or were related to me.

Awkward.

"Let's not call it dating then." Gavin shrugs, back to his no-worries attitude. "Let's just enjoy hanging out together. And having sex with each other, I hope. And we'll just see what happens. Handle each challenge as it comes up, while hoping none come up at all."

He sounds so reasonable. Or maybe I just want him to be right so it's easier to seduce me with his path of least resistance attitude. To make me believe we can do this, and it won't affect my professional and family relationships. I want it so much, laughing with Gavin, playing with Gavin, and having really hot sex with Gavin.

I want it almost as much as I've wanted to succeed at work. Almost. So why not give it a try?

"I guess I can try that. But if this is another one of your pranks…or so you can throw me off my game—" I make my voice as threatening as it can get "—I'll disembowel you with the best-preserved medieval torture instruments that I find with the weight of all my antique dealer connections."

The threat isn't carrying much weight, since Gavin is already smiling. But it's easier to fall back into banter with Gavin instead of the vulnerability of the emotional heart-to-heart we just had.

Gavin's eyebrows go up in incredulity. "I'm not the one who gave me a jammed gun." He points back to the yard where the plastic toy lies useless.

"Your face when you tried to pull the trigger." I clutch my stomach as I laugh, filing that away in my mind to remember the moment when I have to deal with Dad in the future, or a stubborn seller.

"Oh god, you're never going to stop with the pranks,

are you?" Gavin asks, speaking to the heavens for the answer.

I answer even though that feels rhetorical. "Why would I do that?" But they have been getting a lot gentler lately. Maybe I've subconsciously wanted to be with him for a while. Or maybe it was that damn perfect-hair, perfect-smile, perfect-body, perfect-brain combination making me weak with lust.

Gavin grabs my hands, now that the relationship conversation and the threats of mayhem are over.

"Come here and seal it with a kiss." He tugs me down to his level.

I resist. "There are people around," I say with all the shocked offense of a Victorian chaperone.

He drops my hands, accepting the fact that I'm not ready for others to know about…whatever this is.

"If that's what you want, Riya." He gives me a hot look. "But if you really want to make sure no one knows we're involved, then…" He draws closer. I get closer as well, curious as to what he's going to suggest. "Then we should keep up the enemy ruse."

It takes me too long to catch on to what he means. When I do, I try to scramble back, but it's too late and all I can do is close my eyes and mouth before Gavin throws a handful of powder at me.

In deference to our new involvement, he gets most of it on my chest. But he's still laughing like a loon. And running away from me. How can he laugh and run at the same time? Not fair.

Taking chase, I dig into my own fanny pack.

I have to make it look believable.

Chapter Twenty-Four

After a few hours of attacking each other with powder and taking chai and samosa breaks, everyone is slumped in their chairs, exhausted.

"Hi, everyone." I stand to get everyone's attention. "I hope you enjoyed the event today."

I get a chorus of cheers that make me as proud as when I get more than the upper estimate during a sale.

And now Harrison has seen firsthand how well I can put on an event.

"Thank you for celebrating Holi with me. Harrison, thank you for giving me the day. And, Sarah, thank you again for putting all this together for us." I clap in everyone's direction.

"And Sarah asked the staff to make some Indian dishes for dinner tonight, so we'll be enjoying chaat, butter chicken, tandoori chicken, garlic naan and kaali daal. And some kulfi to round out the night." All my favorites, coincidently. It's no crime to enjoy my work.

And with the smiles I'm getting, everyone else will enjoy my work too.

"But first, showers. There're hoses set up with towels near the house so we don't track too much powder into Harrison's beautiful home."

That gets even more smiles. Wait till they discover that they're going to be finding powder in weird places for weeks.

After hosing down, Gavin and I fall back behind Cindy and Pari, making the last of the group to walk into the house.

Gavin extends his arm out, the crook of his elbow waiting for me to tuck my hand in. There's no one watching us, and I can already feel the heat radiating from him, so I take him up on the offer. The hose water was cold, and it's still early spring.

Don't people on estates have heated hoses for their exotic, delicate flowers?

"So you get to do that every year?" Gavin asks.

"We actually didn't do it when I was young. Mom and Dad were too busy and there was no one else to celebrate with. Would have just been me, Ajay and Sonia throwing powder in a local public park. But I'm trying to get an annual Loot sponsored event started. It'll be great publicity."

"You really do always think about business."

"You already knew that."

"Yes, but not the scope of it. Monetizing a cultural festival." He exaggerates a scandalized tone, but the corners of his mouth are tilted up, telling me it's more banter than real judgment.

"If color runs can make money off of Holi, so can I. At least I'm Indian. If anyone should profit off of this cultural event, it's me."

"That's mercenary. It's a wonder I ever win against you."

"Don't be ashamed that you don't have the killer instinct. Some people just don't have the temperament for this type of work." I bump into him so he knows I'm joking.

I snatch my hand back when we enter the house. Gavin flashes me a look I can only interpret as disappointed. I shrug, not able to move at light speed to get comfortable with this just yet.

His face reverts to his usual good-humored expression. "I'll see you at dinner."

"Oh, you don't want to…" I indicate my door, hoping he gets the message about the shower, or the bed, or the floor…wherever. "I thought maybe we could do some of that hanging out plus you were talking about?"

Gavin groans and jerks forward for a quick kiss on my lips. More of a peck, really. A disappointing one.

"You're killing me, Smalls. I want to." And he does sound regretful, rubbing balm on the sting his words cause with another quick kiss. "But I've got to get some work done for my event tomorrow. And some other work to finish up as well." He looks at his door and then back to me. "When you were accusing me of sleeping with you only for the edge it would give me, I didn't know it was because that's what you were doing to me."

He's gone from regretful to desperate now. That is a good development.

"Go work. I get it." I push him away lightly.

"This isn't a trick? Or a test?"

"No. I've been on the other end of that enough times to never do it to you." I'm probably one of the few people who can understand the work obsession, and genuinely won't mind when he has to work. Because I'll be doing my own work. Like I should be now. "I mean, I don't get it, if you wanted me to stay with you, why didn't you just say that? I can't with the mind reading."

"Ditto." Gavin makes up his mind. "We can do hanging out plus after dinner, if you want. And a lot slower this time. I promise."

Hmm. Something to look forward to.

Dinner is taking forever.

My shower took forever. Checking my email took forever. Calling Mom and listening to her talking about some Astor who just became single took forever.

I couldn't even fall asleep during the nap I allowed myself earlier. Which means I'm tired and horny and maybe I have a little heat stroke from all that running in the sun.

It's a lot more exercise than I've gotten for a while. And a lot more sun, probably.

But all I want is to get to Gavin's promise of after dinner hanging out plus, and it's making me antsy.

One thing I have going for me is that Harrison's amazing staff are cooking all of my comfort foods, so as soon as they come out, I'll start feeling better.

One thing *not* going for me is that they're on Indian Standard Time, so dinner is running a little late. So is Gavin, actually.

I wasn't expecting everyone to get *that* into the theme today.

At least the wine is on time.

Gavin comes into the dining room after the chaat appetizers are served, hair still wet from his shower.

"I'm sorry I'm late, Harrison. I was getting some last-minute details ready for tomorrow."

"Of course. I can't put you to work then get mad at you when you do it."

"Did I miss anything?" Gavin asks me.

"No. I drank your wine so they wouldn't notice you weren't here." I point to his glass, the last few drops of wine I didn't get still at the bottom.

"Kind of you. But what would you have done when they didn't see anyone, you know, in the seat?"

"Say you had diarrhea and stepped out? I don't know, Gavin. I can't take care of everything. I was on wine duty."

"And you delivered." Gavin starts looking around for someone to refill his glass.

"Darn tootin'."

"Excuse me?" That stops him from his search. "Did you just say 'Darn tootin'?"

"I said it."

I'm saved from further inquiry into my word choice by the server bringing out the dishes. They bring everything out family style, so the center of the table is soon covered in warm, delicious-smelling food.

"I was so happy you asked the staff to make butter chicken." Gavin heaps a large portion onto his plate.

"Obviously. Everyone loves butter chicken." I take a bite to prove my point. "What was so important that you had to miss the chaat?"

"You'll see tomorrow. And I see you have one right there on your plate." He inches his right hand closer to my plate.

I slap my hand over his. "I don't mind using the same knife for two different courses, which means I will use the spare one on you."

He crinkles his nose. "One knife, two courses? You heathen."

"We're having Indian food. I won't even need one knife tonight."

"Are you going to use both of them on me then?" He's amused at the exchange, proving my earlier assessment that he's a masochist.

"I'm just saying I *could*, that's all."

Gavin retracts his hand, and I cave. I pick up the chaat and put it on his plate. There's butter chicken and garlic naan in front of me, so I won't be wasting any stomach room on anything that isn't the magic orange sauce and the warm buttery garlic carbs anyway.

Gavin winks at me as he pops it in his mouth whole. I watch his strong jaw work on the food, and then he swallows.

"This food is not very spicy." He casts accusatory eyes my way.

"Obviously. I asked the staff to go easy. I told them that your delicate pale taste buds couldn't handle all that flavor all at once." I rub his arm in comfort.

"Bold accusation coming from you."

"All's fair in food and war."

"And auctioning."

"And auctioning," I say.

Nate gets my attention from across the table. "Priya, I've been looking through some of those recommendations you gave me and they're amazing."

"I bet it's not the art he thinks is amazing," Gavin murmurs under his breath, in my direction.

I kick him under the table without looking away from Nate. "I hope we can get you in the auction room one day soon. There's nothing like the energy of a live sale."

"I think I will. As long as you're there to help me get my bearings."

"Of course."

"Of course," Gavin mocks under his breath.

"Harrison, please let me know if you have any questions about the proposal I sent you," I say. The vacation is almost over—only two more days—and Harrison seems like he wants to draw this out until the last minute.

"Or if you have any questions for me," Gavin gets out after swallowing his bite of chicken.

"I'm still reviewing both of them. You're both very talented."

That's nice, but not any indication of which way he's leaning.

Cindy starts talking about a vacation she and Jack went on last year, and the rest of them start debating the pros and cons of the various vacation spots.

"What's your favorite places to visit? You two are the experts," Harrison asks, knowing how much travel goes into our jobs.

"Oh, for me it's England. The English collected on a massive scale publicly and privately, and the major worldwide auction houses started there, so there's a lot to see. It's also comforting to know we now have rules and regulations in place now to prevent the sort of large-scale theft they used to create those huge collections."

"You sound conflicted," Naomi says.

Smart girl. "I am. They're stunning collections, housed in lavish country estates or museums that take up multiple city blocks. And especially in the country houses, seeing an Indian sculpture in front of an English landscape painting next to a Chinese jade Buddha next to a narwhal tusk, with a Louis XIV chair in front of it, is a trip." I take a breath. "But I can't ignore that most of those pieces were outright stolen, or were bought with money made by treating people terribly under colonialism. It's why my nana, my maternal grandfather, started Loot, to be in control of the sale of Indian art. And why he called it Loot, a sassy reference to the history of the art market."

Hopefully we've done a better job only selling pieces we can legally sell, and compensating everyone well.

"What about you, Gavin?" Cindy asks from his other side. She leans in and I resent her immediately, and maybe irrationally.

This newfound jealously is not a good feeling and I want to return to the time before it, please and thank you. I don't need all of the emotions that Gavin inspires distracting me from work.

"I love Roman art, so for me it has to be anywhere in Italy, especially Rome, or along the stretch of the Mediterranean that was part of the Roman Empire."

Travel talk takes us through the rest of dinner and dessert. It's not a hardship; I do genuinely love traveling, even though I end up working. I love seeing the places that my pieces come from, giving me context I wouldn't otherwise have.

As the talk winds down after dessert, Gavin tells us when we're meeting for his event the next day.

When we get up to go back to our doors, Gavin touches me on my elbow. "Which room do you want to be in tonight? I've got to talk to Harrison about logistics for tomorrow and then I'll come meet you."

"*Just* talking about the event tomorrow?" I ask reflexively, not able to restrain myself from accusing him, despite how far we've come.

Gavin gives me an exasperated look but humors me. "Yes, just the event. I don't need to cheat, Riya."

I shrug. "My room then." I don't want to sneak out again the next morning.

"I'll get there as fast as I can." Gavin gives me a quick peck on the lips before running back down the stairs.

He's going back to our host. Did he walk upstairs just to drop me off at my room?

I could get used to the sweet side of Gavin.

Standing outside my room, I'm so wrapped up in imagining all the wonderful things I'm going to do to him, and that he's going to do to me, that I don't realize there's anyone near me.

So I jump out of my own skin when I hear a voice behind me.

"That's quite the chemistry you two have there."

Chapter Twenty-Five

"Pari, you scared me." A slight understatement. Everything in this house seems more dramatic because of its grand scale and all the shadows it creates, and people jumping out from behind furniture seems a lot scarier than it normally would.

Then again, I doubt someone as classy as Pari would jump out from behind a large vase, so she was probably just standing there the whole time and I didn't see her. I was so distracted there could have been a herd of stampeding hippos coming down this hallway and I wouldn't have noticed.

Until they trampled me, probably.

"The words scared you?" She regally arches just one eyebrow in question and tilts her head, her high, neat bun of black and gray hair giving her quite the imposing silhouette while she regards me.

The words too, I guess. "We're not dating or anything. Just business peers. More business rivals, really."

"Are you attracted to all of your business peers?"

"Ew, no," I reflexively respond.

Pari sends me a knowing look. The look of an Indian mother who knows she's right and isn't afraid to point it out to me. I see it often enough. "See," she says, probably in case I don't decipher the look.

"It doesn't matter. I want a lot of things I can't have. I want to develop abs right now, without doing anything. I want to be a famous singer but I can't carry a tune. I want to get your husband's sale." I wince as I let out the pitch even after I accused Gavin of working his pitch behind my back.

It's very hard to turn it off. Maybe I should book that trip to Antarctica.

"I can't help with any of those things. Especially the last one, since the works are Harrison's babies that predate me. But I can see there's something between you and Gavin. Something like young love."

Her words hit me like a cannon blast, and I do my best to mentally scramble away from the projectile, by denying her words.

I don't love Gavin. I *can't* love him. We're just supposed to be having *fun*. There's nothing fun about feelings; they're *complicated*.

"I think you may be mistaking all our anger for… that other emotion. And I think it's against an HR regulation, probably. And Gavin dates models," I say, rambling despite my efforts not to.

Great, in my effort to deny this relationship, I'm now worried I don't stack up to his previous lovers.

Or I would be, if I cared. Which I don't.

Pari inclines her head. "Maybe. There's supposed to be a thin line between love and hate."

"No. With all due respect," I hasten to add, remembering this is a client's wife, and the woman whose house I'm staying in. "I think I would know."

"Would you?"

I nod vigorously, squashing the logical part of me that says I would be the last one to know because I would deny it to the end.

"I don't mean to intrude. Just to tell you what a good couple you two make. I'll see you tomorrow."

"See you," I say weakly. I feel just as drained as I do after a conversation with my mom. It must be a skill all Indian mothers have. Scary women.

I get into my room and flop on the bed. Half a day into Gavin's and my very casual, hanging out with sexy times *whatever*, and he's already making me crazy.

This is the opposite of fun and casual.

I could call it off. But then I'd miss…him. Having sex with him, sure. But also talking about art with him. And about our crazy fathers. And vacations in Antarctica. So even if he has me tied up in more knots than a mall food-court pretzel, I want to enjoy this. For a little longer at least.

Decision made, I ransack my suitcase for the sexiest thing I can find. I wasn't planning on anyone seeing my underwear this trip, so it's slim pickings, but I grab the smallest and laciest things I can find. Dressed, I get back on the bed and look at the door. Enticingly.

That loses its allure in about five minutes, and I get my iPad out, doing some writing on an upcoming exhibition catalog.

I get so wrapped up in what I'm doing, I don't know how much time passes until my door bounds open.

After my brain is done processing the fact that Gavin is not a murderer or here to steal my work product, I try to shift my terrified look into one I hope is seductive.

"You should knock." Wait, that's not seductive. I am so bad at this with him.

But he didn't even knock.

"I already had an invitation to come in." He walks
farther into the room, kicking the door closed behind
him.

"You look amazing." His eyes wander from my feet,
up my legs, over my hips, butt, back, breasts and ending
at my face. And then it goes to the item on the bed in
front of me, set up in the least ergonomic way possible.

"Am I interrupting?"

"Yes." I smile at him to take the bite out of the word.
"But I'll allow it." I move my work stuff off the bed and
saunter over to him.

"Did you get everything settled that you needed to?"
I slide my hands into his sport coat and slip it off his
shoulders. His hands go to the curve of my waist, pulling me slightly closer, but mostly digging in where they
touch.

"Yup, all set for tomorrow." His voice is distracted,
and his eyes had long left my face for my breasts.

I unbutton his shirt and slide it off his shoulders to
land on top of his sports coat. His eyes don't move from
my breasts the entire time, and I'm flattered.

I put my hands to his back and hear his hiss at the
same time I feel his exhale.

He pulls me even closer, but I resist. I want to actually see him this time. It was hot that the first time was
so frenzied that we didn't even get our clothes off, but
I want to take it slower this time.

He takes the nonverbal direction, settling me back
at the distance I was before he interfered.

Satisfied that he's not going to interrupt me again,
I focus on his chest. That chest that I had seen in the

dark sex room is even better in the light of a less sexually charged room.

And if I had thought he was Hercules then, I'm sure of it now.

I slide my hands down the ridges of his muscles, sure that this body could help Atlas hold up the world on his broad shoulders.

"I think taking my time was a stupid idea," Gavin says through clenched teeth. The fingers at my hip haven't moved, and they've dug in a little tighter. Digging into me like we're carved by a master Renaissance sculptor making flesh out of marble. Like they're going to stay there as long as any marble sculpture would last.

"No, I think it is a great idea."

"We're already more naked than last time. Next time we'll get all the way naked. But not now."

"But I want it slow." I slowly undo his belt and slide it through the loops.

"Then you'll get it slow," he says, resigned. But the way his body is straining to get closer to mine, muscles clenched, I don't know how much he'll be able to deliver on that.

I speed up the process, hooking my fingers in his boxer briefs and pants to let them fall to the ground together. His erection bobs out of its constraints to point toward me.

Now that he's completely naked in front of me, I entwine my arms around his neck and pull him down for a kiss. The movement releases whatever hold I had on Gavin, and he thrusts his hands in my underwear, pushing them down until he lets gravity take over.

He does my bra next, unclasping it and letting it get stuck between us since I refuse to lower my arms and let go of him. He pulls me in closer, and I rub against him where I can reach, liking the friction very much.

Without breaking the kiss, he sweeps me up and away from the small mountain of clothes we made. He puts me on the bed, and the bra falls away. He replaces it with himself, giving my breasts the same friction the rest of me got.

His hand takes a trip down my body, making a stop at my breasts and following the twists and turns of my curves down to my clit.

I arch against him, getting wetter with each move.

I want to drive him as wild as he drives me, so I hook my leg over his and use the momentum to flip us over.

Gavin doesn't care about his new position, but he does crunch up to capture my lips again, making his abs deliciously hard. From my position straddling him, I duck the kiss and now I get some complaints.

"Come back."

"One second, I want to do something."

"Do it later."

"I want to suck your dick."

He lies back down, quiet and compliant now. "Okay, you can do it now."

"That was an easy negotiation," I murmur, multitasking the sass and the blowjob.

Without any further interruption from the blow-ee, I take his cock in my hands and give it a few swipes, watching as it gets harder.

I lower my mouth, darting my tongue out to lick the crown gently.

"Give me more."

Silly man. He should know better than anyone how contrary I can be when ordered to do something. In retaliation I move my head up and kiss his lower abdomen while stroking his penis with my hands.

"Wait, no." Gavin sounds so forlorn.

Feeling like he's learned his lesson, I move my mouth back down, taking his whole dick in my mouth without warning and sucking.

"Yes." Gavin clutches the sheets by his hips, twisting them in his fists.

Mouth and hands working in tandem, I stroke his shaft, feeling him writhe more and more as I work.

"I'm about to come," Gavin says.

I immediately pull my mouth away; I don't want it to end that soon.

Before he can complain about the loss, I crawl back up his body. I position his penis at my clit and move my hips back and forth on it, rubbing the head of his penis on my clit. I groan as the movement starts the build-up to orgasm.

"Condom," Gavin manages to get out even though his head is thrown back on my pillows.

Damn, I almost forgot. Good thing I'm on the pill as well.

I get off Gavin, intending to get the condom for him, but he rushes off the bed first and grabs it out of his pants pocket. He has the condom on before he gets back to the bed.

He grabs me by the hips and pulls me onto my back, then flips me over onto my stomach. He pulls me back and positions me on my knees at the edge of the bed, leaving him the perfect height to enter me from behind.

I think Gavin's tired of not being in charge. I'm about to tease him for it when he slowly pushes into me from behind. He reaches his hand around to play with my clit while he's thrusting.

He makes a sound of frustration when he can't reach my clit because of the physics of our position. He taps on my hip, the only warning I get before he flips me back over, still standing in front of me. He enters me again, this time with much easier access to my clit.

He keeps thrusting, and I feel myself getting closer to orgasm. When I do break, Gavin comes right after me.

He gets rid of the condom while I crawl under my covers.

"Lights," I yell.

Gavin sighs, but for once, decides it would take longer to argue with me about who should do it than just doing it. And he knows he's going to lose because he's the one standing.

The lights turn off and a few seconds later the other side of the bed dips.

"You're staying?" I ask.

Gavin scoots over until he's snuggling my back. "You wouldn't be tacky enough to kick me out of your bed after the pleasure I gave you."

"I faked it," I say into the pillow. "But you can stay anyway."

Gavin laughs, making me and the bed shake with the action. "It's a good thing I have healthy self-confidence."

"Arrogance," I say on a yawn.

Gavin kisses my shoulder. "If you say so, Riya."

Chapter Twenty-Six

There's nowhere to flee when someone sleeps over in your bed. Especially when they have a hold of one of your boobs.

I could very easily wake Gavin up and tell him to get out, but then I have to talk to him. And he'll charm me despite my best intentions and I'll give him anything he wants. Because of all that damn charm.

I slowly reach out to the bedside table for my phone, wondering what time it is. Before I can get to it, Gavin tightens his arm around me, dragging me back in by my boob, and kissing me on the head.

"Morning, Riya."

"Hi." Caught. But I'm at least facing away, so his presence is dulled somewhat.

"Are you ready for the excellent event that's going to win the sale today?" The voice is no less confident even though it's roughened by sleep.

"Ha! Did you see how happy Harrison was to throw some powder at his daughter? Or at his wife? Or his friend? Like a kid in a candy shop."

Thank god Gavin's making the awkward morning-after easy on me. I don't know if he's the Priya whisperer and he did it on purpose, or if he's just that focused on the job. As focused as me, actually.

Either way, it's attractive.

"What time is it?" Gavin reaches over me for my phone and flattens me between him and the bed in the process. It makes me laugh.

He yawns, getting a look at my screen. "Oh damn, it's later than I thought. Did we set an alarm last night?"

"No, we didn't." My voice is muffled by my pillow.

"We were a bit busy." He pushes himself up, and turns me around to face him. "We could be busy again." His eyebrows wag up and down in invitation.

"Sure, if you want to give me an orgasm and be late to your own event, I won't argue with you." I reach up and kiss Gavin, one of my legs rubbing the back of his. He returns the kiss, and then pulls away when I try to deepen it.

"You're right. I should get going." At least he sounds regretful.

"Whatever." I turn back to my side and close my eyes.

"See you later." He gives me another kiss on the head as he gets out of bed.

I wave in his direction and hear the rustling sound of him putting on his clothes. He slips out the door and leaves me alone in the room.

I sigh and sit up. I'm not getting back to sleep again after that wakeup. I'm dissatisfied and I want him to come back and have sex with me and also not remind me of his name or our jobs. What's in a name, anyway?

Course, they died at the end of that…so maybe the name was important, after all.

I'm going to do work to distract myself from the tragedy that is my life. I set up my remote workstation on the vintage vanity. I'm getting used to being surrounded by all the Gilded Age beauty…a redecoration might be in order for my office when I get back.

Maybe a redecoration will occupy my time when I get home and there's no more Gavin. Because even though he sounds optimistic about wanting something with me now, here in this secluded, luxurious mansion paradise, I can't believe he would still be excited about being with me once reality, and our dads, set in.

I'm seven internet tabs into doing some research for a piece from 800 C.E. India when my phone rings.

It's Dad again.

I seriously contemplate not answering this time. I'm still on a high from all the sex with Gavin and how much fun I've been having this week, and I really don't want him to interfere with that.

But unlike most children across the world, he's also my boss, and it's during business hours. So I slide across the screen to answer the call.

"Priya, you need to come home." His voice is urgent, and I jump up in response.

I start rushing around the room, throwing my things in a suitcase. "What's wrong?"

"You're out there for this maybe sale of something we don't even do, but we have other real sales you need to be focusing on. Smaller, sure things. If you haven't gotten it by now, you aren't going to get it."

"Harrison is still reviewing our proposal." I stop panicking, confident that everyone I love, and all the art I love, is safe and there's no emergency.

"This has gone on too long. You don't have the experience to pull in this sale, because we don't work in this field."

I mute the phone quickly so I can scream into my pillow. It's getting harder and harder to deal with the casual ways that Dad dismisses my abilities and accomplishments. And those Big Two Houses' job offers look better and better.

Scream over, I unmute the phone and try to catch up with what Dad is saying. He's going on about something related to a smaller show he wants my department to put on.

I don't want that sale. It's a perfectly respectable sale, but it's not that exciting, and it's not going to bring in all that much money. Or much notice from the art market. It's peanuts compared to what I can get for the Harrison sale.

I interrupt whatever he was trying to say. "It's happening. I'm here. I've put in a lot of time for this show, and I'm going to stay until I get an answer. You agreed to let me do this," I say firmly, standing up to my dad for the first time in a really long time.

I don't think I can keep going on like this. Gavin is my enemy and he still gives me more respect as an auctioneer than my own father does.

It might be time to have a talk with Dad when I get back. Or make Mom do it.

And if I can get this sale before I have that conversation, it'll go that much smoother.

As I go downstairs, I try to recapture the good feelings of the morning, but I don't have high hopes for getting it back.

"What's wrong?" Gavin asks me first thing when

he sees me. This again? What, does he have my phone bugged? A chip in my brain that lets him read all my thoughts?

"Nothing. I'm fine."

Gavin gets that look on his face that he gets when he's about to dig in. A look I've only seen him get with me because everyone else gets laid-back Gavin. But then Harrison comes to my rescue and calls Gavin away before he can make good on his look.

I turn and notice Naomi is right behind me. "Hey, Naomi. Were you given any details for today?" I ask with a smile.

"Nope. They've kept the details quieter than if they were holding state secrets," Naomi says. "At least we're going to find out sooner rather than later."

"And Gavin didn't even tell us what to wear."

"It's the most annoying part of all of this."

After that commiseration we stand in a comfortable silence for a few minutes.

Naomi breaks the silence. "How long have you and Gavin been dating?"

"Whoa. No. We're not dating. We're just work peers from different companies." Why does everyone in this family think we're a thing? We are clearly sworn enemies and no one is picking up on our subtext correctly. Which is just rude, frankly.

"You guys have more chemistry than Meg Ryan and Tom Hanks in the nineties."

I laugh awkwardly. Need to get out of this conversation. It's time to deflect, deflect, deflect. I rack my brain to find another topic, any topic. I'm debating between puppies dressed up for Halloween and the new fashion lines when Gavin interrupts. "Good morning, Harrison's house party."

Thank god, my savior.

"I know you've been anxiously waiting for this day," Gavin says.

Okay, my savior is a little more pompous than I anticipated.

"And I'm going to make sure it's amazing."

A *lot* more pompous than I anticipated. But I'm being rescued from talking to this lovely infant so I'll be grateful.

"I rented a yacht for the day to cruise along the North Shore!"

My hopes fall. Damn it, that's a good day. Maybe just as good as Holi. Maybe more, if the cheers from this group is any indication.

I knew his solution to the problem would be to throw even more money at it than me.

Gavin leads us out the front door to a luxurious minibus parked in the circular driveway. We take our seats, and a man in a suit brings us mimosas. He even hired staff for the bus ride.

This is going to be spectacular. I hate it.

"Hey, Riya," Gavin says as he sits down next to me.

I flag down the man with the alcohol and snag a glass, taking a healthy swig. "That nickname never gets old."

"Where's my affectionate nickname?"

"Oh. Hmm. I should get right on that. How about Super Annoying Entitled Man Who Lives to Annoy Me?"

"I mean, that doesn't really roll off the tongue." He purses his lips. "How about Light of My Life?"

"No, we should go with honesty. Makes Me Ill?"

"More like Makes Me Come, amiright?" He holds his hand up for a high five.

"Did you really think I was going to high-five that?" I point to his hand with my glass.

"How about Not as Good an Auctioneer as Me?" he asks, putting his hand down, un-fived. "Since we're going with honesty."

"I think we're not being realistic about nicknames. They should really be one or two words long. Jackass? Moron? Spoiled Brat? Richie Rich? Any striking your interest?"

"I like your initiative, but I feel like we can keep workshopping this until we find one we all like."

The words of the exchange are just as biting as the ones we'd had before this trip, but the tone has gotten a lot lighter than it was before, the same way that the pranks have gotten more harmless since then.

When I think back on it, the tone had started getting lighter ever since Gavin barged into my room and accused me of stealing his girlfriend. The back and forth has been just as quick, but more…teasing, now.

"Hercules." Because he reminds me of the confident, muscular demigod that swaggers around with us mere mortals.

"Because I'm so strong?" He flexes his biceps and kisses each one in turn.

"Because you're going to have to accomplish more than twelve labors to get with this." I wave my finger, encompassing all of me.

Gavin stops the man with the champagne and gets two more glasses of the bubbly. "Then I should have some more sustenance before you ask me to slay a lion or a Minotaur."

After the annoyingly perfect beautiful ride to the harbor, in the annoyingly perfect spring weather, we get to an annoyingly large yacht.

"Ah, I was wondering whether to upgrade my yacht to the newest model. It'll be nice to see it in action before I commit," Harrison says when he gets out of the van.

This perfect day keeps getting worse. For me.

We board the yacht, where there're appetizers already set up on a table outside overlooking the water.

"If everyone wants to make a plate of food and grab some drinks, there's a surprise inside the boat as well."

The way this day is going for me, it'll probably be a bedazzle-your-watchband-with-diamonds station.

And Harrison's Rolex band will have just gotten scuffed.

We all make a plate, and then follow Gavin into the ship's interior. And I immediately get overwhelmed by a red cloud of rage.

Chapter Twenty-Seven

Because this is perfection. Canvasses and sculptures are set up in the lounge, turning the boat into a floating art gallery.

"I have a friend who's a gallery owner out here, and he loaned me some pieces so we can be outside seeing the scenery or inside seeing the hottest pieces of the Long Island art scene."

"Well played, Hercules. Well played," I whisper-growl through clenched teeth to Gavin as he walks toward the door to get his own plate.

"A compliment? From the prickly Ms. Gupta. As I live and breathe," Gavin says, his best Southern accent on full display.

"Is Southern belle really how you want to play this?"

"Please immediately forget I said that."

"Nope. You're Scarlett now. You should get some food, Scarlett. You should never be hungry again." And I haven't seen him eat since last night.

"I'll get something in a second."

Gavin puts his hand on my lower back. The touch is light but I still shiver. "There are a few pieces I want your opinion on."

"You've put this together. I don't think you need my opinion."

"Of course I don't need your opinion. But I want it. You've got great taste."

That hand is still on my lower back and he's giving me compliments. I feel proud. And giddy. Like an unfamiliar lightness is bubbling up in me and nothing else can be that bad because that hand and those compliments are here to get me through it. Is this what relationships feel like?

Maybe this is why people go out of their way to get changed after work and find bars with like-minded people. Why they download apps, taking up precious space on limited cell phones that could be used to take pictures of art and dogs and contract provisions.

I think this is worth coming home at 5:00 p.m. for. To chase that feeling.

I mean, I'll still have to put in some work after I go home. Five is way too early to stop working when there's so much to do. But it would be nice to do it with someone else on the other side of the couch. And not just Sonia.

Could we really do it? Or would the hundred annoying little things keeping us apart get in the way over time?

Is holding on to this feeling worth the fights?

And will the feeling even stay? Will it fade? Or will it get even deeper, maybe becoming love?

"Riya, the painting I want you to see is over here." Gavin pulls me toward it.

I don't know how long he's been trying to get me where he wants me, but considering the impatience in his pulling, it might have been a while.

"Do you think it's going to jump off the wall and run away?"

"Maybe someone here has slippery fingers," he whispers in my ear.

"They're all richer than Croesus and you and Bill Gates combined."

"You know they'd just do it for the thrill."

Well, I can't argue with that.

"What do you think?" Gavin asks me when he stops in front of some art.

"Hmm. I think you shouldn't ask me about contemporary art. Except for a few artists Loot sells that I love, I tap out of the contemporary world."

"But you still know what sells."

"Fine. It shows promise because it feels very Banksy, and it's charming. But I think the edgier collectors won't find it new and unique enough. Sell it quick before the entire market catches up with the edgier collectors."

"Now this one."

I turn to the next painting he indicates. "Oh, I like this series." It references classic paintings and sculptures in the style of thirst trap Instagram posts, complete with sassy comments. "I'd put this in my room and make a show about it." I consider. "Actually..." I get my phone out of my clutch and take a quick picture, then zoom in and get a picture of the signature. Or what could be the signature. It's a bit squiggly.

"Seriously?" Gavin asks me.

"What, Hercules? There's no sign saying I can't." I'll respect a sign, but without it, I'm photo-documenting everything.

"I knew I forgot something." Gavin snaps his fingers.

"Who's the artist?" I ask nonchalantly.

"No way, Riya. You aren't getting this artist."

"We'll see." I send the photo to Sonia so she can get the research team tracking the artist down based on the work and ambiguous signature.

We walk around the room, checking out the rest of the new talent. There's nothing as good as thirst trap art history, so the rest of Gavin's art is safe.

"Sonia told me we're putting Stella in an upcoming sale," I say, half because he should know and half because I want to provoke him.

Gavin laughs, which is exactly the reaction I knew he'd have. Or at least the one I hoped he'd have. To show that we can steal each other's art and still like each other. "You're a piece of work."

"A piece of *art*, you mean. Now, come get some food. If you faint in front of me, I'm letting you fall and stealing your phone to get all your sellers' and buyers' contact information." I grab him by the arm and haul him outside to the nice spread he had set up for us. Once he has a full plate in hand and I've seen him take a bite, I wander off and take a seat at the bow of the ship.

I'd like to think I went out there for the sun and the gorgeous views, but that isn't it. A small crowd, with Harrison, has formed at the bow.

"You guys throw the best house parties," Harrison says as I sit down.

"Just imagine the sale I'd throw."

"I like you, Priya. You never turn off. You're like me."

I don't know if I should be offended or complimented. I'll put off deciding until I find out if I get the sale.

"You really won't do a joint sale?" he asks again, tone in the manner of a toddler asking to go to Disneyland.

"Alas, we can't. There'd be too much to argue over, too many creative decisions that we would never be able to agree on. Your sale would be us arguing on a dais that's not completely built, prices we couldn't agree on, with no catalog because we couldn't agree on an artistic vision. And not selling anything for you."

Harrison laughs at the image. "I doubt you two would ever let it get to that. But I've met your fathers, so I could see there would be arguments."

"The arguments might draw some attention because people love to watch drama, but I think the focus should be on your stunning art."

"Maybe so. But you two would do great things together."

I laugh, but cringe inside. Is everyone trying to set me up with Gavin? Don't they know it's hard enough to avoid the delicious man with my own weak will?

Help comes from an unexpected corner, Pari distracting Harrison with some questions about an upcoming charity banquet. I send a smile back in thanks.

I'm grateful she changed the subject, even though I know she shares her husband's opinion. So does his daughter. I need to get away from the whole matchmaking family.

I don't have to be strong for too long. Just two more days left for this working vacation. Then back to my domain, and Gavin back to his.

No more seeing him. No more stumbling on to sex rooms with him. No more sleeping with him. He says we could try to keep this going, but life will get in the way. I know it, even though I wish it was different.

And then there'll be no more Gavin and Priya time. Just work.

That makes me feel empty. A physical ache in my stomach that isn't going away.

Sitting on an expensive yacht with a beautiful view of Long Island, eating delicious food and sipping on expensive wine. But I feel empty.

This is ridiculous. I've been fine without him for over two decades.

But now that I know what I'd be missing, it feels different. *I* feel different.

And I don't know what to do with that.

I smile and nod through the rest of the conversation, hoping no one notices the change in my mood.

Gavin comes to the bow of the ship fifteen minutes later, joining the conversation. "The captain says he'll take us wherever you want. Well, anywhere we can get to and back by the end of the day, at least," he tells Harrison.

"I'll go talk to him about the route. And see that show you've put on for me in the lounge."

With Harrison leaving, the rest of the group disbands soon. Cindy and Jack say they're going to see the art, and Pari says she should help Harrison before he buys the boat from the owner or steals it in a fit of piracy.

But she winks at me on the way out, so I doubt her motives.

Gavin turns to me with an eyebrow quirked. "What's that about?"

"Just Pari being Pari." I hope he drops it.

"About what?" Of course he's not going to drop it. "Is it about the show? Should I be worried?" he asks with an exaggerated eyebrow wag.

"Yes, you should be worried. Because I'm better than you. But no, that was unrelated to the show." I try to hide how little I want to answer the question.

"Then what was it?"

I must not be hiding my discomfort well, because the humor is gone from Gavin's voice now. Stubborn Gavin is making an appearance. It's not a side of him I see very often, especially not after we graduated high school. It's so rare I thought it went away to be entirely replaced by his carefree playboy routine. But here it is again, playboy Gavin dropped for a focused Gavin trying hard to get what he wants.

This Gavin worries me. Because it means he's using all of his effort, making himself a formidable opponent. Even more so than usual.

Fine, if he wants honesty so bad, he can have it.

"Pari, and Naomi actually, and maybe Harrison, all think we'd be a great couple." I laugh at that outrageous suggestion.

Gavin smiles, good humor restored. He leans back and takes a long drink, eyes watching me over the wineglass. Letting me stew about what his response will be.

Not that I know what response I want. If he agrees, then it'll be more awkward conversations about how we wouldn't work out. And if he laughs it off, I'll be crushed. I have no right to be crushed, but I'll be crushed all the same.

So I kind of want to snatch the wine he's so calmly drinking and toss it overboard.

Before I can act on the impulse, he sets the glass back down. "They're pretty smart people, the Richmonds. The best, most expensive educations for the three of them."

Great, he doesn't agree or laugh it off. Contrary Gavin.

"Just because they're smart, it doesn't mean they're right about this."

"And they don't even know we've slept together. Under their roof. Two and a half times."

"A half?" I ask, distracted by those memories.

"The bit in the sex room." He gives me a rakish smile.

"Shh." I surreptitiously look around to see if any of the Richmonds are around to hear what we've done in their home.

Gavin pantomimes zipping his mouth shut. Fat chance that'll stick.

He proves it by opening his mouth again. "I'm just saying they must know human nature pretty well."

"You're incorrigible."

Gavin takes pity on me. "All right. We won't talk about how everyone around us can see we'd make an unstoppable couple, taking over the art world and having great sex."

"I somehow don't think any of the Richmonds are thinking about us…being intimate." I try to say with as much dignity as possible.

"They have a sex room, Priya." Gavin sounds so scandalized; I can picture him clutching pearls as he says that.

I roll my eyes and turn my head to look out over the sea.

Nothing has changed in my present or future, but I feel a little less empty looking at the view now.

For whatever reason.

Yes, Brain. I know the reason. No, Brain. I'm not

acknowledging that it's the person sitting next to me who's making me feel less lonely. "Tell me something about you I don't know."

"I like broccoli."

"First of all, ew. Second of all, something better than that." I slap him lightly with the back of my hand.

"Okay. But you asked for this, Riya." He takes a deep breath and I get more curious about what he's about to say. He draws it out even more by not answering, instead taking a deep sip of that wine again.

"Out with it!"

Chapter Twenty-Eight

"Your sixteenth birthday." He pauses, probably for even more dramatic effect, the jerk.

But I lean closer to him, interested in where this is going.

"Or yours and Ajay's, I suppose."

"I know I have a twin, get on with it." I make a circular motion with my right hand, encouraging him to get going with this story.

"You didn't invite me." He casts an accusatory look my way.

"Of course I didn't. Me and the team had just won first place at Academic Decathlon and you stole our gold trophy from Mrs. Jacobs's room and spray-painted it bright pink. We worked hard for that, you know."

"I did it because you got a higher grade than me on the history essay and I wasn't happy about it."

"You were such a little shit. Still are, most of the time," I say with affection.

"That's your opinion. Anyway, you were having that party at the Met. And I was jealous that I wasn't invited. So I snuck in."

"You snuck in to my sixteenth birthday?"

"That's not the part I'm telling you about. So I snuck in, and you were all having a great time."

"It was a good party." Or at least until it wasn't. But I've recovered from that now. Time. Wounds. Healing. And all that jazz.

"Yeah, but then there was this guy, Blake."

Wait, what does this have to do with Blake?

"And he had been talking about how he was going to bag the most chicks that year. Don't give me that look, it wasn't my phrasing," he says when he sees my reaction. "And then he was all over you," Gavin continues, accusatorially.

"I don't know that you can call getting me some punch and holding my hand 'all over' me, but okay."

"He was fawning."

"He was being nice."

"He was trying to get in your pants. Trust me, I was a teenage boy and I can recognize the signs."

"Kindness?" I ask in disbelief.

"It's all a ruse."

"That sad bit of social commentary aside, what did you do?"

Blake had been exceptionally nice to me that night. So nice that by the end of the party, we had snuck out of the main party hall and he gave me my first kiss in the Temple of Dendur room.

I had been so focused on excelling in school, I hadn't made time for the dating thing. But having Blake give me that much attention, and that kiss, made me want to try all of that out.

We were going to leave the party (and my parents' watchful eyes) and maybe knock out some more firsts for me, but he left me waiting on the Met steps while he got our coats. Some friends found me twenty minutes later and I went back inside with them instead of explaining who I was waiting for and why.

I was too embarrassed to ask Blake later where he had been, and he didn't try to talk to me at school either. So the entire incident got filed away in my mind as an awkward childhood story I tried to avoid thinking about.

"I snuck into your party. And when I was sneaking, I saw him kiss you," Gavin growled through clenched teeth.

"O...kay."

"And when he told you to meet him on the steps so you guys could leave and continue what you were doing, I had to stop myself from punching him. I had just heard him talking about all the girls he had slept with that year and didn't want him to say that about you."

"What did you do?"

"Nothing illegal. I just found Blake getting the coats and told him that if he kept his date with you, I was going to make sure it got out that his father's second family was living in the Berkshires."

"What?"

"Blackmail," Gavin summarizes clearly.

"But why?" Why would teenaged, entitled, hates-to-work Gavin put himself out for me?

"The noble reason or the real reason?"

"Both." Why not? I've got time. I'm on a boat and my tablet's at home.

"I was noble and wanted to protect any and all women from a slimeball."

"And the real reason?" I press when he pauses for too long.

"I was jealous of him and the attention you were giving him."

"Come again?" I'm going to need him to repeat that before I even begin to believe it. We've always had such an adversarial relationship. And now to find out he's been lusting after me as long as I've been lusting after him? It's a lot to take, that truths I thought I knew since I was a kid were wrong.

"I told you I've been thinking about you for a while. No one else has captured my attention for as long as you. Plus you were mine to annoy…have been since kindergarten."

"That's a really long while," I say instead of processing the ramifications of that statement.

"I don't think I realized what it really was then. Or anytime since. I just wanted to be around you. I told myself it was just competition and I wanted to rub in my successes because you get this cute scrunch in your forehead when I win." He suits action to words and pantomimes the alleged scrunch. "But then you stole my girlfriend and I felt things deeper than competition. Things I want to pursue."

"Nope. Still not ready for any of this." I cover my ears with both hands and tuck my chin into my chest.

I'm not ready for him to be serious, a marked change from the Gavin I know. Because if he's serious, I would really have to think about seriously accepting or denying him. Instead of this "hanging out plus" we've settled on.

And with his newest admission, he's making me reexamine a lot of feelings I've had about this man since I've known him. And making me think I think I could maybe love him.

"All right, Riya. I'll stop." He tugs my arms down and gives my hand a squeeze when it's back at my side. The affectionate move sends goose bumps up my arm, and I feel a little shiver.

I look around to see if anyone is watching us and savor the contact while I can.

Gavin sees my discomfort and drops the hand.

I've never had such conflicting emotions: I'm glad he let go without a fuss *and* I want to jump him to get that hand back where it belongs—in mine.

He's making me lose my mind. I've always been so sure about everything—what I want (to run Loot) and how to get it (make so much money Dad can't ignore me). But this conflict is a new feeling I don't like.

"Tell me something I don't know about you," Gavin demands.

"Dad doesn't respect me as an auctioneer." I shouldn't have told him that. That's a lot of ammunition to give someone I shouldn't trust; someone I'm perpetually competing with. But it came out without me giving myself time to censor it.

"What? I knew you guys argued about the direction of Loot, but how can he not see how good you are?"

I can't stop the flow of words now that the dam's burst. "Dad wants Ajay to follow in his footsteps. He wants his son to run the company as the male heir and he wants me to be happy getting profits from the company while staying out of the way, I assume while running charity boards like Mom does."

"But you're a better auctioneer than your brother."

"Yes, I know."

"Better by a lot."

"That has not escaped my attention."

"Oh." Gavin looks uncomfortable, like only the privileged can when confronted with injustice they can't do anything about. "Well, that's stupid then."

"Yeah." Now that I put it out there, I want to collect all the words back and hide them under my shirt. It's not something that I've vocalized with anyone else besides Sonia and Ajay, and I don't like the resulting vulnerability.

"It's not right. You're amazing at this. And any boss that can't see that isn't using his resources accurately. And any *father* that doesn't see that…" Gavin shakes his head in disapproval.

That's a nice reaction. I'm getting more comfortable with my split-second decision to tell him.

"Yeah." I start getting worked up on my own behalf. "It's really messed up!"

"What are you going to do about it?"

I deflate. Someone should tell him that I need to vent, and this isn't a problem with a solution.

"If I knew that, I would have done it already," I say in my best *duh* voice. "And my current front runner for ideas is to wait Dad out and then steal the company from Ajay. Depositing his cut into his bank account at regular intervals. As long as he stays away from my decisions," I hurry to add in case he thinks I'm heartless.

"That seems like the best outcome," Gavin says carefully, trying to give the diplomatic answer. "But that seems like a long time from now?" He makes the statement into a question, pointing out the one flaw in my master plan.

"A very long time from now, probably. But in the meantime, there's still work to be done." I incline my head toward Harrison.

"Yeah, when I get Harrison's collection, you'll have so much time for all that work."

My mood immediately lightens with Gavin's words. He's surprisingly astute when he wants to be, knowing I don't want to talk about the subject anymore and making me comfortable with our old dynamic in the same sentence.

"I wouldn't worry too much about my schedule. But when I get the Harrison sale, you can focus on going to the French Riviera, or watching lacrosse, or the art of making your hair look effortless, with effort. Whatever you do in your spare time."

Gavin lies down next to me, his feet by my head and his head by my feet, doodling on my leg with his finger. The sensations his languid motions cause work their way up my body, making me shiver at the teasing touch. That combined with the gentle sway of the boat help me relax fully for the first time in a while.

"Seriously, how much time do you spend on your hair?" I ask, a question I've been wondering about only whenever I see him.

"You like it?" He preens, craning his neck toward me so I get the best view.

"So nice…" I sit up and lean forward, ostensibly to take a closer look. "Especially this part." I reach up to his head and then violently run my hands through his hair, making it stick up on its end. "Ew. How much product do you put in your hair?"

"A lot. Looking this good doesn't come easy." Gavin laughs as he closes his eyes to the sway of the boat, leaving his hair in all its wild glory.

"It doesn't even look like you have anything in there." I look closer at the mess on the top of his head, inspecting it like I'm a scientist or a particularly thorough detective.

"That's because they're expensive products." He continues drawing the lazy pattern on my leg.

"Apparently." I wipe my hands on his shorts, not caring if it ruins them. He deserves it for getting all that shit on my hands.

We spend the rest of the trip watching the coast go by. We talk a little about the art market, but mostly fall into a comfortable silence. The others don't come back to the bow, leaving us in our own little world at the head of the ship. I forget they were even there, to be honest. And forget I have to worry about them judging us.

Since Harrison's blocked all talk of the sale until he reads the proposals, and I didn't bring my laptop with me on the boat, I can enjoy the closest thing I've had to a real break in a long time.

Maybe I can convince Dad to buy the company a boat. But then he'd just expect me and Mom to host parties on it for potential clients.

Maybe not, then.

Instead I'll have to enjoy this one quiet moment of rest I get, with a man who is still as wrong as he can be for me.

I'll soak it all up while I can, knowing that it won't be around for very long.

Chapter Twenty-Nine

That evening we're all a little bit subdued at dinner, even though the food is perfection. Everyone else is probably a little tired from all the time in the sun.

I'm subdued because of that, sure, and because this is the second to last dinner I'm going to have at the house. And although it's a nice house, that won't be what I miss the most.

It's the second to last dinner I have with Gavin, in the little bubble we've made out here on the shores of Long Island.

"I've read your proposals." Harrison breaks the silence as we all start on our main course.

"You have?" I look up from my chicken at Gavin, stomach dropping as I wait for the response.

Harrison nods and takes a sip of his wine. "They're both very good."

"Have you made a decision on them?" Gavin asks.

My heart rate increases and I want to fly over the table and cover Harrison's mouth with my hands, anything to stop the words coming out of his mouth. If Harrison has decided, then there's no reason to stay. It'll be back to the city.

"No."

My entire body sags in relief. One more day. Two more nights. I've got a little more time before I have to stop this with Gavin.

"You're both very talented. I'll be taking my allotted last day before I make a decision."

"Take your time," I say with feeling. Take another month, please. Or a year. Maybe ten. Whatever.

"Either way, you can't go wrong with either of us," Gavin says.

I send him a small smile. I think this is his way of flirting with me, complimenting me in front of a potential client. It means a lot more than any other flirting I've gotten in the past.

I was worried that sleeping with Gavin and competing with him would turn out to be awkward at best and wildly damaging professionally at worst, decreasing my standing as an auctioneer. But it hasn't been either of those things so far.

Of course, we haven't gotten to the real test though: how the loser handles it when Harrison chooses only one of us.

I've lost to Gavin in the past, and he's lost to me. But we weren't involved then, and my ability to do non-Indian art shows wasn't on the line. I try to imagine how I'd feel losing to him this time, but my mind doesn't make the trip into the hypothetical with me.

Which makes me think it's because I won't be able to handle it. Not winning is always hard for me, and my brain especially doesn't think I'll be able to deal with it in this scenario.

Then the real question is, should I continue something I know will cause me pain? It's a little too late to be considering the question, since we've left "just colleagues" behind either way. But maybe if I get out now, the pain will be less?

Or maybe just till the end of this trip. I'm already involved; I might as well enjoy it for a few more days.

"But of course, there is one less right option." I wink at Gavin and smile at Harrison. He'll just have to deal with my own version of flirting back, which is mostly threats to beat him professionally.

After dinner, Harrison takes everyone who wants to smoke to the smoking room again. I decline the invitation and feel a thrill shoot through me when Gavin refuses as well, sending me a hot look instead.

He follows me up the stairs, and without talking about it, follows me to my room. I open the door and go in, expecting him to keep following behind me.

When I turn around and see him still standing in the hallway, I tip my head and give him a questioning look.

"I didn't want to assume…" He looks at me expectantly.

"I mean, I guess I should rest up for whatever Harrison has planned for us. It'll probably be peacock wrangling, and I'll need my strength."

"Those peacocks can be pretty feisty. I get it." He doesn't come any farther, committed to this consent business.

But if he wants to come in, he can ask. It'll do him good to have to ask for what he wants. To work for what he wants. For once.

"I can show you my best peacock-wrangling moves, if you want," he offers, resting his shoulder on his door when he realizes I won't be giving in all that easily.

I grab him by the shirt and pull him into my room with a roll of my eyes. It's as close to an ask as I'm get-

ting. "You can come if you promise not to tell me anything about peacock wrangling."

"I can do that too." He kicks the door closed on his
way in, hands already reaching for me. The determined
look on his face makes me feel a bit like prey, like I'm
the peacock and he's going to use some of those wrangling moves on me.

And I'm going to enjoy it.

I wake up feeling like I'm in the Sahara. Having gone
to bed in chilly Long Island, it takes me a few minutes
to realize the cause.

The light snoring next to me helps me remember
that I just spent the *third* night in a row with Gavin
Carlyle. This time there's no event to run off to, and I
don't even want to.

Okay. So I do think about fleeing my own bed for
about thirty seconds, but then I realize how comfortable I am with Gavin's arms around me, and give in.

This is what I want, and I'm going to savor it until
that feeling goes away.

I snuggle deeper into the cocoon created by the blankets and Gavin.

"I don't think you can get any closer than you already are, Riya," he says, amusement coming from
above my head.

I sniff disdainfully. "It's rude to point that out."

Gavin stretches and then settles his arms even more
firmly around me, pulling me closer.

"Can we ditch the events today and sleep in all day? I
haven't done that for years," I say, really warming up to
the idea of doing nothing all day but lying in bed with

Gavin. And having more sex with Gavin. And ordering delivery so I don't have to leave this room.

"We might as well. Harrison isn't asking us anything about our proposals and he shuts us down whenever we try to talk about it."

"I think it would be frowned upon to come on this business trip and stay in bed having sex the entire time." But I don't get up.

"I think I've heard some business trips end up being just that."

I turn around in the tight circle of his arms and bury my nose in the crook of his neck.

"Well, if you insist." Gavin starts kissing me, hands leisurely meandering down my back.

The alarm on my phone interrupts us before we get to the good part, and I groan in frustration as I turn to switch it off.

Not one to miss an opportunity, Gavin moves on to kissing my shoulders and back.

"We should be responsible." I sigh resentfully as I turn off the noise.

"You be responsible. I'm going to make you come."

The words stop me in my attempt to get out of bed. "I suppose I can shower later..."

Gavin disappears under the covers and reappears at the vee of my thighs.

One orgasm later, I decide this is an exceptional way to wake up every morning.

After getting ready (with no time for a shower—but worth it), we make our way downstairs for whatever event is today. With no clothing direction, I put on a dress that I hope will fit any situation.

Gavin and I come down together, not caring if anyone guesses what's going on. They've already assumed we're having sex anyway. Pari and Naomi give identical, and kind of scary, knowing looks when we join the group. The genetics are strong in this family.

I give them a bland smile and refuse to engage with the speculation.

Harrison comes down after us, talking to Jeeves/ Ryan as he comes down. The poor guy looks harassed, so there must be a lot of last-minute tasks to do before the event.

"Morning, all. For the last day of our week together, I've planned a polo match for you to watch on the south lawn."

"At least we don't have to play," Gavin mumbles to me out of the corner of his mouth.

"It could be worse."

"Gavin. Priya." Harrison nods at us but doesn't meet our eyes when he passes, and I wonder what caused the change in his demeanor toward us.

I don't have time to find out since he leads us out to the south lawn, which has been transformed into a polo field for the day. Tents with chairs and refreshments are set up on a raised dais on one side of a rectangular area roped off for the game play.

The horses are warming up, running back and forth on the field, and causing a tiny earthquake every time they pass. From their perches on the horses, the players, dressed in immaculate uniforms, are swinging large mallets at small balls.

Rich people sports are weird.

Gavin disappears to find me a drink and I get comfortable for my last day of peace. I feel a slight twinge of guilt when I remember that I haven't even spoken to Sonia for a few days, and I haven't got much work done at all since I started having sex with Gavin.

I knew he'd be terrible for my productivity.

Like saying *Bloody Mary* three times in a mirror, thoughts of work summons work, and my phone vibrates with a call from Dad.

Gavin is approaching and I make a split-second decision to blow off the real world for one more day. I've got more than enough unused vacation days due to me, if nothing else.

I ignore the call from Dad, a first from me. I feel intense guilt until the phone stops ringing, then I only feel a low-level guilt muffled with the thrill of rebellion.

Gavin hands me a mint julep, and my phone vibrates some more. The second time ignoring it is much easier, and I feel only the low-level guilt and the thrill of rebellion.

I turn off the vibration and take a sip of the drink. I nod at Gavin in thanks and settle in to watch the game. Match? Whatever it's called.

"Someone desperately needs you?" Gavin takes his own seat and points to my phone on the table, where *Dad* is flashing on my phone. Again.

"He probably misplaced his favorite coffee cup and wants to know where it is." I turn the phone over so I can't see the screen.

This is getting easier, once I've committed to taking a day off. Maybe I should have started doing this earlier.

Gavin raises his eyebrow. "It seems like there are other people who are closer who could help him with that. Like at the office."

"Probably. But then he would miss out on an oppor-

tunity to make my day harder, and he never does that."
I put the phone in my clutch, even farther out of sight
so it doesn't keep reminding me of my responsibilities
on my impromptu day off.

"I have to admit another deep, dark secret," I whisper as I lean in and motion Gavin closer. I want to get
back to where we were this morning, the pleasant peace
that was threatened by this phone call.

Gavin leans his head closer to mine. "Yes? Go on."

"I've never been to a polo match," I admit, then lean
back to accept the fallout of my stunning revelation.

"You peasant." He sounds mock shocked, crinkling
his nose like I assume the queen does when she catches
a whiff of the unwashed masses she's waving at from
the comfort of her open-air horse-drawn carriage.

"Don't let Harrison know or he'll probably have me
thrown off the estate," I say in a British accent, the fan-
ciest of accents.

"Never," he replies in one as well.

Gavin looks around and moves to the chair on the
other side of me. I follow him with my eyes, wondering what he's up to now. He sits down and angles his
chair away from the open front of the tent. I'm about to
break down and ask what he's doing when he slides his
hand on top of mine, entwining our fingers.

Clever, sweet man. Now we're out of sight from anyone outside the tent and we can enjoy a semi-public display of affection.

Just like normal people on a date.

His thumb strokes my knuckles and I sip my mint
julep, enjoying the spring day outside. Usually when
I plan to have a day out, even just in the city nature of
Manhattan parks, I don't make it further than getting

my shoes on before I remember some bit of work I need to do, derailing any attempt at fresh air.

Nate and Cindy come over to our table and sit down. I try to tug my hand away from Gavin but he doesn't let it go, instead gripping it even tighter.

He's lucky I like his hand where it is. And that the tablecloth covers it from the newcomers.

"Who are we rooting for today?" I ask the newcomers.

"Harrison owns the team that supplied all the players and horses for today, so I think we're safe whatever we do," Nate says.

"Excellent. I'm going green then. They have the best choice in uniform color," I say, firmly behind a team I didn't know existed until ten minutes ago.

"I'm going purple. They have the best-looking players," Cindy announces to the group, undressing multiple players at once with her eyes.

I fix a smile on my face, hoping she can't see the grimace. Cindy's as old as my mom, and although I wish her and her downstairs parts the best, it's disconcerting to witness any part of it.

"I'm rooting green, too," Gavin says. "Their horses have the prettiest hair."

Nate gives Gavin a worried look. I get it; Gavin and his "refuse to take anything seriously" attitude annoyed me a lot before this trip too.

I feel a little different about it now. Now it reminds me it's nice to play every now and then.

Chapter Thirty

The game is a lot more…watching horse butt than I anticipated it would be. And being concerned for the horses.

"What if one of the mallets hits the horses?" I say. "I would be. So. Mad."

I reclaimed my hand from Gavin two chukkers ago so I could watch the action through my fingers, same way I watch horror or suspense movies. Much more comforting that way.

"I think they've all trained well enough that we don't need to worry about that," Nate tries to reassure me.

"But why are the horses doing all the work? This seems unfair." I've switched from the green team to team all the horses about a minute after the play started.

"Yeah. Think about the horses, Nate." Gavin eggs me on.

"They still have to ride the horses and swing a mallet, without hitting any horses." Nate tries to defend the sport of kings, one that started as a war game for military practice and evolved to be played while bored rich people in big hats sipped alcohol.

I sip my mint julep and comfort myself with the fact that I'm not a stereotype. I'm not bored, and I have no hat.

"Go horse, go!" I yell encouragement at a pretty brown horse that has green socks to match his rider's shirt. Gavin seconds my horse cheer, brushing against me to do it.

I file this game away in my memory. I only have one more day until reality intrudes and I don't know if we'll last. I need to start hoarding the memories like a squirrel hiding nuts for winter. For when the cold comes.

Harrison wanders over to our table as part of his mingling duties. "How is everyone enjoying the game?"

"It's a lot of fun to watch," I say, surprised at how true it is.

Harrison gives me a curt nod, with the same uncomfortable look he gave me when he came downstairs this morning. I really want to know what's put that look on his face. Did he pick Gavin? He has to know there'd be no hard feelings if he did. Well, not against him. Gavin and my father, on the other hand, would not fare so well.

Harrison sits down at our table and watches the game with us for a little, talking shop with Nate and about Cindy's new house with her. And he loosens up during the conversations, making me wonder if I'd imagined the initial awkwardness.

"This has been such an amazing week. Thank you for having us out." Gavin sucks up to Harrison a little more before the final decision.

"It's going to be rough getting back to the real world after this." Well, hard not only because I'm leaving a beautiful mansion, but also because I'm afraid work might interfere with what Gavin and I have. That I won't be strong enough to juggle Gavin and the competition, and I'll have to make a choice about one or the other.

"But I'll be redirecting all my energy into planning your show." I send Harrison a charming smile.

"Oh, but I thought… Priya, don't you know?" Confused is a strange look on a billionaire businessperson.

"Um, know about what?"

"Have you talked to your dad today?" Now he's back to looking uncomfortable, eyeing the open front of the tent like he wants to escape.

"No, he called earlier but I wasn't able to answer at the time."

"You should call him back." Harrison gets up. "And please remember, I appreciate your work. You're a good auctioneer and I look forward to working with you in the future."

I share another look with Gavin and get my phone out of my clutch. "Excuse me. I should make a call real quick."

Everyone looks relieved to not be in the conversation anymore, and I wake up my phone screen as I walk out of the tent and away from the game. Both so no one can overhear and so I can hear the phone over the match.

Five more missed calls from my dad, making eight total in the span of a half hour. Now I feel guilty, hoping everything is okay.

I call him back, eyes still on Gavin sitting in the tent, joking with our tablemates.

"Finally, you check your phone," Dad answers without a hello, sounding a lot annoyed with me.

If he's annoyed, everyone should be safe. So this is about work, and my worry decreases. "I'm talking to you now. What's going on? Is everyone okay?" Just to make sure.

"No. I have important business to talk to you about and I don't need my employees ignoring my calls."

I sigh. He frames this as a business discussion, but I hear the dad in his lecture. "Dad, I'm still working, despite what you think, and I need to get back to that. So, if you could let me know what's going on…"

"It's about work. I've pulled Loot from the competition for this sale, so come home."

The world freezes around me. The frantic sounds of hooves on the ground, the cheers of the crowd, and the sound of conversations from spectators all fade around me, leaving me with a buzzing sound in my ear.

I think it's rage. Not the hot rage sparked over an instant, but a cold rage that has been festering inside me for a while now, spreading inch by inch every time I get ignored or overlooked, and now I think I'm more rage than person.

But I didn't even notice it was growing. Until now. Now I'm all too aware of it.

"What?" I ask in disbelief, hoping I heard all of that wrong. Giving him one last chance to reverse the tide of anger. Or at least stop it from spilling out.

"I negotiated with Carlyle to drop this sale, in exchange for another one we've both been going after. Big ancient Indian art collection. You know how hard it is to get a legal collection that big, of Indian art that old. You need to get back to the office to start cataloging and…"

I drown out the rest of what Dad's saying. The rage, the one that had been steadily simmering since Dad told me, explodes at the continued proof that my own father doesn't respect me. And to hear he negotiated with Gavin? After all we've been through?

I'm sitting here thinking I might love this man, and he's negotiating behind my back?

I need fewer men in my life.

"You negotiated with Gavin behind my back?" I ask through clenched teeth, needing and fearing the confirmation all at once.

"What, the son? No. With his father, William Carlyle."

At least there's something in this shit day.

Dad starts to talk about the work I need to do when I get back, and I cut him off. "No," I say, so quietly that I don't know if he will even hear me. He couldn't have done this. He wouldn't interfere like that. We had a deal. However little he respects me, I thought he respected a deal.

Dad stops talking immediately. "What do you mean no?" He sounds wary, like he's unsure how to respond to a word I've never used to him in a work context.

"You're kidding." I frame it as a command, hoping that I can will this all into a cruel joke. A cruel joke I can recover from. Eventually. This would be a lot harder.

"No. It's done. I know we had the deal, but we can move it to another collection. This is too important."

More silence as I process what just happened.

"How could you? This was mine." I turn away from the field and tents, feeling very different than I did when I left that area a few minutes ago.

"It's my decision. I'm the CEO and president. I'm within my rights to do what I want with my company. And this is the best for the company."

"I was working on this show. I was so close to getting it. And unless you tell me that the *Mona Lisa* is in that collection you got, I sincerely doubt whatever you got was worth a fraction of what I could have brought in. And the sales that would have followed..." I growl in frustration.

"It's my decision," Dad reiterates. "It's not a guarantee we would have gotten the sale. But the pieces I got will remind everyone why Loot is the best at what we do: Indian art. And maybe it'll get Ajay excited about work too."

"You cannot be this dense."

"I'm your boss. And your father. You can't talk to me that way," Dad says sharply. But he doesn't sound so sure.

"I'm your best employee. And if you don't want to acknowledge that, it's your loss. But if you don't fucking acknowledge that you need to branch out into a wider market in order to stay relevant, that's a bad business decision. And if you think Ajay is going to be excited about any of it, you're blind."

"Language," Dad barks. "You and I are going to have a long talk when you get home."

"No, we aren't. Because I quit."

"You can't quit. You're my daughter!"

I hang up the phone before I have to respond to that. I stare at the phone for a few seconds, until my phone lights up again indicating another call from Dad.

I throw the technology on the ground in a fit of temper. Then I feel stupid about it, since now I have to fish it out of the grass. And hope I don't have a cracked screen to deal with. The distraction helps me feel a little less angry.

I squat down and find my phone, noting neutrally it's not cracked. That's one less thing to worry about, I suppose. I sink fully down to the ground after I get the phone, needing a minute with all of this.

I still can't believe Dad would do this to me. I know he doesn't respect my opinions, but it's a sound decision to branch out. I can't believe he refuses to see that.

And to just take away any chance I had of building my dream...

The tears come, falling freely.

After any makeup I had is completely ruined, I try to wipe my face. My hands come back with streaks of black, so I can't go back through the polo fields.

But the game should be ending soon. I need to move fast.

I skirt the edge of the field, avoiding everyone as they focus on the game. I grab a napkin from a passing waiter to wipe my face. He gives me a worrying look, but he's too well trained to comment on my Halloween-mask face.

Hoping I got all the makeup off my face, I enter the house. I'm halfway to the stairs when the door opens behind me. I look back, reflexive curiosity overriding the need to flee.

"Priya, can I talk to you?" the host of this weekend asks.

"Harrison. Thank you again for all your hospitality."

I will be professional and pleasant to him if it kills me. This isn't the only art he's ever going to sell, and he's a buyer as well. I need to maintain this relationship. Even if it kills me.

"I want to thank you for all your work on this. It was very well done and I'm sorry if it was for nothing."

I shake my head, wanting this conversation over so

I can cry in peace and wipe this too-wide smile off my face. It's beginning to hurt my cheeks.

"It's my job. I look forward to working with you on another project." I take a step backwards to the stairs, hoping that will help end the conversation.

"Honestly, I didn't even know who I was going to pick. You guys both gave me such great options. Maybe I should thank your dad for taking the decision out of my hand." He tries a tentative smile, wanting to lighten the mood.

"I'll be sure to tell him Loot could help." Fat chance. I'm not talking to the CEO of Loot.

Harrison's face falls. "But I have a feeling you were the last to know about the new development. And that's not right."

"It's business. One adapts. You know." I don't know if I can form longer sentences without breaking into tears again, so I need to get out of this conversation. I keep looking back and forth to the stairs, wanting to go up them, now.

"I'll be in contact for some buying I want to do. As you know, my art collection is going to get smaller and I'll need to replace some blank spaces on the wall."

"Give me a call or email and we can set up an appointment to go over some items I have in mind for you specifically." If I still even work at the company. Which seems unlikely since I just cussed at my boss and told him I quit.

Maybe I can get Harrison to come wherever I end up. When I stop being sad.

"Sounds good." Harrison looks uncomfortable again.

I take that as my cue to leave and turn around. Then

I stop and look back at him. "Actually, if I could impose on you one more time?"

"Anything." He sounds relieved to be able to help.

"Would it be possible to give me a ride to the closest Long Island Rail station so I can get back into the city? Have to get back quickly." It would take way too long to get a company car out here when I feel this shitty.

"I'm not going to make you do all those train changes with luggage. I'll have Sarah drive you straight to your apartment."

"Thank you," I say in relief. That does make it a lot easier to get back home. And quicker.

I rush up the stairs to pack everything up and run out of the house before I have to see anyone else.

Especially Gavin.

I hear a knock on my door and freeze in the process of shoving my toiletries into their small bag with one hand and wiping up my snot with the other. "Who is it?"

"Sarah." A voice calls out.

I rush to the door to let her in. "Hi. Thank you for saving me one more time."

"Oh my." Sarah, being a consummate professional, takes one look at me with my stuffed toiletries bag and then behind, seeing open suitcases haphazardly filled with stuff. She efficiently and gently pushes me back into the room. "Harrison says you're leaving a day early."

"Yeah." Even I can hear how pathetic I sound.

"Okay then. Why don't you sit and I'll finish packing everything?"

"I don't think I can sit still," I whisper.

Not entirely true. I can sit still, but then I'll just want

to ugly cry a bunch and I would like to avoid that until I'm in the comfort and privacy of my own home.

She changes course from directing me to the bed, to directing me to the vanity. "Why don't you finish up with the stuff on the vanity, and I'll get the clothes?"

"Yeah. Sounds good."

With Sarah's efficient calm, I'm able to go through the motions of getting all my stuff together. Some tears leak out, but Sarah doesn't comment on them, which I'm very grateful for.

"Let's get you home," she says once we get all my luggage collected at my room's door.

"Thank you."

She hands me a tissue and takes some of my luggage for me. "We'll go through the elevator with all of this."

"There's an elevator?" I shouldn't be surprised but it does help distract me a little from my sadness.

I step out the door with my own load of luggage and hear someone shout my name from behind me.

I was so close.

Chapter Thirty-One

Of course I can't slip away without seeing Gavin one last time. Because nothing can go my way today. If I made bets, I'd put money on Sarah's tires being flat or the freeway being closed as well.

"Hi, Gavin. I have to leave a little earlier than anticipated, but congratulations on your upcoming sale." I try to avoid looking him in the eyes and keep moving after Sarah to the elevator.

"Wait." He touches me lightly on the elbow. "What's going on? Is everything okay?" He moves to stand in front of me. "You've been crying." He sends an accusatory look to Sarah, who responds with wide eyes, unsure what to do.

I make eye contact with Gavin and immediately regret it. His is the face of me losing, in a spectacular fashion, and I resent him for it. I guess that answers the question of what happens when lovers compete—it doesn't end well.

"It's nothing." Why won't he drop this?

"Please tell me what's wrong. I can't fix it if I don't know what's wrong." He looks pleading and ready to punch someone at the same time.

"You have the show. There's no reason for me to stick around."

"I have the show? What show?" He does a convincing job of looking confused.

"Dad just told me. He negotiated with your dad to get Harrison's collection, in exchange for some other Indian art collection they were both competing for."

"What? That can't be worth it."

I send him a dirty look through swollen eyes. *Yeah, I know.*

Gavin catches my look. "But that's also mean and fucked up to do to his daughter."

Again, he's not telling me anything I don't know.

"If the sale's decided, then let me come back with you. I can get my stuff together in a few minutes. You don't look like you should be alone."

"No. Don't bother." I hold out my hand to stop him. I look back at Sarah, who is studiously looking at a wall sconce to give me some privacy. Not even one of the more interesting light sconces in the house. "You've got to talk through the details with Harrison, and I have to deal with work issues. We both knew we had to leave this fantasy sometime." I indicate the opulence around me, which has witnessed two low points in my life in one day. Lucky lamps. "So it's just ending a day earlier."

I'm surprised at how badly I wanted that extra day.

"But we could still see each other when we're back in the city." Gavin tries on a bit of my stubborn, another departure from his usual laid-back attitude. I'm a bad influence on him, I guess. "I'll call you when I'm back."

I shake my head. "I need some time." Too much is happening all at once.

"Riya, I know you're hurt, but I didn't do anything. I want to be here for you now."

"This isn't about what you want," I whisper furiously. "I know it's not your fault. But I can't look at you without thinking about how much you get just for being you. And how hard I have to fight to get half of it. And then there are the days I don't get anything no matter how hard I try. You won today and I lost. I'm tired and angry and my dad's a jerk. I just want to be alone."

"Okay." He gets out of my way, looking around like those wall sconces can help him out of this. "But I… I love you." Now his eyes are laser focused on me.

"What?" He can't be telling me this right now. I just had my heart broken by my own father and he's here trying to make a relationship. I can't handle this.

Especially since I might be falling in love with him right back. From the loud moments with him—hosting an auction, arguing with him about art—to the quiet ones—watching the coast go by on the bow of a boat—I want them all on repeat for the rest of my life.

But I can't deal with this many emotions at one time. And it's just like him to force it on me on *his* timeline, not caring about what I might be feeling or what I might need.

"This isn't about you! Like I don't have enough to deal with coping with the fact that I'm never going to be good enough for my own father, one of the people who is supposed to love me unconditionally? Or the fact that he favors Ajay over me? Instead I've felt like I'm constantly competing with a brother I love for attention that our father never wants to give me? You think *now* is the right time to put me through your shit?"

"I… No. I didn't think." He has the grace to look subdued, head bowed down to the plush carpet.

"You don't think. That's the point. And now, I'm going home to deal with the shitstorm that is my life and career."

I turn and walk down the hallway, Sarah walking next to me. I hope she didn't hear what just happened, but the laws of physics state that's improbable.

She is, however, nice enough to not mention it on the walk down the hall, or the elevator ride, or the walk to her car. We make it all the way to the freeway before I start crying again, tears silently streaming down my face.

"I'm sorry. I was doing so well."

"It's okay. Do you want me to stop at a White Castle?"

I sniff. "Yes, please." She's perfect. I need to poach her for the company. But then I remember I don't work for that company.

This has been a terrible day. I was expecting to have to say goodbye to Gavin at some point, never believing a relationship would be as easy as he thought, but to lose him and work at once is a big blow. Work is supposed to be the thing I'm going to throw myself into to get over Gavin. The thing that was going to be my constant and give me strength and purpose.

What am I supposed to do now?

When we get back to my building, Sarah offers to come up and help me with my luggage, but I let her head back to Harrison's house. I need some time to be alone.

I get upstairs with my luggage and drop it all just inside the door. I head straight to the bedroom and collapse on the bed, curling up in the fetal position and dragging a spare blanket from the foot of the bed over me.

I'll deal with everything tomorrow.

The next morning, I wake up without having set an alarm. I slowly roll over and see the sun peeking through my blinds.

I get my phone from the bed next to me where I left it last night and turn it on, dread pooling in my stomach at finally having to face what happened.

I immediately regret the decision when the phone dings with voicemails, texts and emails.

I contemplate turning the phone back off and pulling the covers back over my head, but I suppose I should at least listen to everything in case there's an actual emergency on my phone. I tally the missed calls up before I dig in to the messages: nine from Mom, five from Sonia, three from Ajay and none from Dad or Gavin.

Mom's worried. She said Dad told her something was wrong but wouldn't give her any details so she demands I call back and let her know who she should be mad at. The message catches her saying that it's probably going to be Kabir under her breath before it cuts out.

Sonia's confused. She said Dad told her I'm coming back but there's a lot of tension in the office and she wants me to let her know how much longer she has to be the supervisor, and also to let her know if I'm okay.

Ajay's contrite. Dad must have told him what he did, and Ajay's deeply sorry that he indirectly interfered with my sale. He also wants to show me the painting he did when I was gone, hoping it'll cheer me up when I get back to the office.

Apparently Dad didn't tell him everything then.

I ignore everyone, not having the energy to respond. I do find just enough energy to drag myself to the couch, where I stay the rest of the day wrapped in a blanket, my streaming service asking me multiple times if I'm still watching. Yes, but thanks for the reminder.

Finally, when the sun goes down and I know Sonia's day should be over, I call her back.

"Oh thank god," she says before I can say anything. "Please take your job back. I hate this much responsibility. I just want to look at pretty art and have a life."

The normalcy of the request makes me laugh, but the events of the last few days catch up with me and the laugh cuts off abruptly.

"Priya, are you okay?" Sonia gets serious.

"Not really."

"Where are you?" I can already hear her packing up her purse, rustling paperwork around her desk.

"Home."

"Okay, I'm coming. Have you eaten? Doesn't matter, I'm bringing food."

"You don't need to come…"

Sonia scoffs. "Right. I'm coming."

I drag myself to the bathroom to do the bare minimum in personal hygiene, and then curl back into a ball of athleisure on the couch.

Even thinking about explaining it all to Sonia makes me want to throw something.

Before I start destroying my home, I hear a knock on my door. I psych myself up to get up, but then the lock turns.

It's a good thing that I gave Sonia a key for emergencies. This has to qualify.

"I have pizza and gyro and cheesecake and pad thai."

Sonia bursts in, bumping the door closed behind her, a lot of smells coming from all of my favorite take-out comfort foods. She sets all the bags on the table in front of me, goes to my kitchen, and comes back with plates, utensils and wine bottles. No glasses, just the bottles. "What do you want first?"

"None of it."

"Okay, I'll make you a plate with a little of everything then."

How Indian of her.

She opens one of the wine bottles first and hands it to me. When I don't do anything with it, she pushes at the end until I take a sip. Satisfied, she fixes me that plate.

After I attempt a few bites, Sonia stops being patient. "So. What's happening?"

I put the plate down, not able to eat and go through everything again. I focus on the plate while I tell her what happened so I don't have to look at Sonia and lose it.

I'm gratified by the sounds of outrage that come from her at the exact perfect moments.

"I'm quitting too then," she says.

"You can't quit. Your parents will throw a fit if you quit after you spent most of your life in another country away from them *for* this job."

Sonia shrugs. "They made that choice, thinking it would be a good opportunity for me. They can't get mad that I'm taking whatever opportunities I want."

Sonia still sounds a little bitter about that, which is fair. I can relate to her a little on the subject of withholding parents. Well, withholding parent; Mom's great.

Sonia puts more food on my plate, despite me not having finished the amount she initially gave me. "I still can't believe Chacha would do that. I know he's stubborn, but I'm genuinely shocked that he doesn't listen to you more. You're his best employee."

"It doesn't matter anymore," I say, despite it clearly mattering very much. Mattering so much it's the reason I spent all day watching TV instead of at work.

"So. Are we going to Sotheby's or Christie's? Let me know so I can get a head start hating the other side. And getting the swag made."

"Don't do anything yet. And don't give up anything for me. I might decide to give it all up and go back to school for something else. Maybe I'll be an accountant this go-around."

Sonia looks at me in silence for two beats. She's remembering how much I hated math growing up.

I cave. "Okay. Maybe not that. But there're plenty of other jobs between accountant and auctioneer."

"Actor, if we're working alphabetically."

I lift my plate back up, picking at the food. I can't imagine doing anything else but working at an auction house. The ache in my stomach that developed after Dad's revelations and ending things with Gavin gets deeper at the thought of not doing what I love.

"Now that work is out of the way, should we talk about what else has been happening to you?" Sonia asks.

I know exactly what she wants to know. "There's nothing to tell. I had a fling. A weeklong fling. And it's over, which I knew was going to happen from the beginning."

"That sounds really, really reasonable. But you're sad about it," Sonia points out gently. "So I'm not one hundred percent sure that's accurate."

"You're not supposed to bring it up."

"I'm here for you." She indicates the food. Which I didn't even want, it should be noted. "But I'm not going to lie to you. Now why can't we have the funny, charming, sexy man who is smart and into us?"

"Ew. Royal we."

"Answer the question, avoiding April."

"I don't want to talk about it."

Sonia stares me down for a solid minute. I don't know what she's looking for, but I squirm under the intense gaze.

"Fine. I'll table it. *For now.*" The emphasis warns me she isn't going to let it go forever.

We eat in front of the glow of the TV for a bit. But I can still feel her thinking about how much she wants to interfere.

"It wouldn't work because we're enemies," I say to get ahead of her not being able to control herself.

"Right. But—"

"I know what you're going to say," I interrupt her. *"But you quit, Priya. You're just an unemployed person with no auction house to fight for."* I imitate her voice. Not flatteringly, if her scowl is anything to go by.

"That's a good response I came up with," the real Sonia says.

"Sure. But it's really annoying the way everything just works for him, and he skates through life collecting accolades he doesn't have to struggle for. Doesn't even work for! Really annoying. Especially when some of us put in eighty-hour weeks."

"Yes, but—"

"All right. I know he works hard! Harder than Ajay, that's for sure. And I guess I can't blame him that he has family support and connections. Oh, and sometimes his dad is very Kabir Gupta about things, too. So I guess he knows a small fraction of what I deal with."

"Yes. I was going to say that," Sonia says dryly.

"And he never takes anything seriously!"

"Okay. But—"

"I mean, sometimes he takes things seriously, I suppose," I admit. "He put on this really good event for the house party. I was impressed. And it is nice to laugh with him."

"But…" Sonia trails off.

"Well? Out with it!"

"Oh, you're going to let me finish this time?" She waits for me to interrupt and I don't give her the satisfaction.

"*But* I think you can get over *annoying* when he's making you come on the regular."

I should stop sharing things with Sonia if she's just going to use them against me in this aggressive manner. "Well, who told you to make sense?" I ask belligerently.

It's just hard to let go of a lifetime of seeing someone in one box—the enemy—and have to readjust to seeing them in another box—a lover and maybe even a partner.

Sonia rolls her eyes at me. "He matches you intellectually, he makes you laugh and the sex is good. You're even arguing in favor of him against *yourself*."

"Yeah. But he chose a shit time to try to have an emotional conversation with me when I was already going through the wringer."

Sonia looks at me, waiting for what we both know is coming. I don't disappoint.

"*Fine*. When I put it like that, having bad timing isn't the worst characteristic for him to possess," I say. "But you should be backing me up completely and ready to burn down Gavin's Upper East Side town house, not making sense against me." She might need to be demoted from best friend. Cousin I can't change much.

"Am *I* the one making sense against you?" she asks incredulously.

I ignore that. "Plus, I stormed off when I found out what Dad did and Gavin said he loved me. Maybe he'll give up on me now and decide I'm too much trouble." Just as I decide that I want something more with him.

Typical, aggravating Gavin.

She shrugs. "You had a bad day after some rough news. I think that's something he can get over. And if he can't, you'll actually have a compelling reason to not be with him. One I'm sure you'll still debate yourself out of, but it'll be stronger than the other points." She reaches for my phone. "Now, do you want me to call him, or should I send him a text from your phone?"

I slap her hand down before she can steal the prize. "I'll call him, eventually." When the embarrassment dies down and I can control my emotions.

"I'll hold you to that." The words are harsh, but she puts the blanket over me, tucking it into my sides as I bring my plate closer to me so we can have a TV marathon. I bump her back up to best friend for letting this go and taking care of me.

Which is good because without her, the winner for my best friend title is my Postmates delivery person.

Chapter Thirty-Two

"Didi, are you home?" Ajay barges through my front door. "I have your favorite cheesecake from the bodega around the corner. The cashier asked if you were dead since she hasn't seen you. How much time do you spend at that place, anyway?"

I raise my head over the back of the couch and see a masculine version of me breaking into my home. With the key I stupidly gave him when I was handing them out like candy on Halloween to Sonia and Mom as well.

"What are you doing here?" I quickly close the box I was eating from. Which happens to contain the cheesecake Sonia brought me yesterday.

"I felt a disturbance in the twin bond…"

"Not a thing."

"And you haven't been at work since you got back. Sonia wouldn't tell me what's wrong." He sounds hurt that Sonia knows and he doesn't. I feel a twinge at being a bad sister, but how do I tell him I'm sad about something that involves him but he doesn't have control over?

That's not protecting my baby brother.

Ajay detours to my kitchen for some forks, and only judges me silently when he sees what I'm eating. He pulls it out of my hand and replaces it with the superior product. He claims the second-best cheesecake that Sonia mistakenly thinks is the best, for himself.

"I quit." I don't ease him into the news.

"Wait, *you* quit *work*? What happened in Long Island?"

I roll my eyes and give him a very brief summary. I didn't mean to tell him about Gavin and me, but it all comes out with the rest of it. Damn twin bond that might exist.

"Yeah," he says after I finish. "I guess that makes sense then. Dad and I have not been making your life any easier."

"It's okay. I love you. I don't mind helping you." Most days.

"You shouldn't have to." Ajay sighs, head dropping down to focus on his dessert. "I know that; I'm sorry. And I'll talk to Dad about my work. It's just so hard to talk to him."

"I get that." Better than anyone, probably. "You don't have to do it now if you aren't ready."

"I've actually started the conversation a few times. Told him I wanted to paint more and maybe just focus on client relations."

That would be a great idea, actually. Ajay is the best at that since it's mostly schmoozing rich people, something that comes naturally to him.

"Dad thought I was joking. He kept laughing and saying it was the best joke he'd heard in a while and then he assigned me a new show."

"I didn't know you'd tried."

"Nothing came from it, so I didn't want to advertise."

"Dad has a…unique view of the world." An understatement because I still want to comfort Ajay. "Well,

I won't be involved with Loot anymore, so take all the time you need."

"I'm going to tell him," Ajay says, maybe more to himself than to me.

"Eat your cheesecake, Ajay." I turn the TV back on, spending some time with my baby brother.

"Wait, so you and Carlyle? After all the protests? Sitting in a tree? K-I-S-S-I-N-G?"

"Eat your cheesecake, Ajay."

I'm bored.

It's only been three days since I got back from Long Island, and without work, I have nothing to do.

I love TV, but I'm so used to watching it while working that I'm a little restless watching it without something else to do.

I try to be on my phone while I'm watching, but Mom keeps calling and I keep ignoring her, which makes me feel guilty. I try to text every now and then so she knows I'm safe and doesn't call the National Guard (which she's threatened to do), but that just makes her call even more right after the text, assuming I'm free if I can text.

Gavin starts calling too, but I'm not ready to talk to him yet either. I do feel a deep relief when I see his name flash on my screen, but it's followed by a paralyzing fear of having to talk to him about feelings that I'm not sure I can acknowledge to him, and the call goes to voicemail.

When I get too restless, I start cleaning with the TV on, then cooking. I have enough food to feed a soccer team.

Apartment spotless and belly (and fridge) full, I leave the apartment and go to my local bodega, where the owner always keeps some art market periodicals in stock since she's so close to the major auction houses.

Just because I'm not working doesn't mean I can't keep up to date on the market. Who knows where I'll end up?

The owner is relieved to know I'm not dead, not having believed Ajay. And throws in free cheesecake.

I'm going through a great article on some potential upcoming trends, and eating cheesecake, when my door opens. "Sonia?" I ask, peeking up over the back of the couch.

"That's funny. You don't look like you're incapable of talking. So you should be able to talk to me on the phone that's right next to you there." Mom sweeps into the room, eyes taking in my condo and then landing on me, in sweats on the couch. She's carrying a bag of what smells like butter chicken and garlic naan that she drops off on my kitchen counter.

I sigh; I still have Sonia's leftovers in my fridge and the food that I made too.

But I'm not surprised.

"I told you I was fine," I mumble. But I'm busted, and now I can't avoid Mom. I could probably create a diversion by telling her Shah Rukh Khan is here and run out the front door while she's looking for him. But I would never be able to return.

I should probably just deal with this now.

"No. You texted me you were fine. Which is exactly what a kidnapper would text me if they had taken you."

I pause to let her hear what she just said. When she doesn't, I ask, "Do you hear you?"

"Yes. But *you* can't hear me when you ignore my calls."

"Mom, I quit. Which means you can't bug me during the business day anymore."

"You can't quit being my daughter, beta," Mom says gently.

She comes to the couch and sits down next to me. She takes stock of the table in front of me with spread-out industry magazines and a bottle of wine, and restrains herself from commenting on what's in front of her.

But I can hear her think the judgment. Just like I can hear Sonia think sassy things at me.

"I heard what your dad did."

The pity in her voice makes me lose the grip I have on my emotions, and I take a page out of my old playbook and crawl directly into my mom's lap.

Or as far into her lap as I can get. I'm a bit bigger than the last time I attempted it.

"I know, beta. I'm sorry your father did that to you. He was wrong."

"It's not fair. I worked so hard so he would be proud." I swallow the lump in the back of my throat, managing to keep the tears from leaking out.

Just barely.

"I know how hard you worked. And I know it's not as exciting, but *I'm* so proud of you." She runs her hands down my hair in comfort, snagging on some tangles on the way. I know she feels bad for me because she doesn't nag me to brush my hair right now.

"I know *you're* proud. You always told me. Dad never did."

"Sorry I wasn't more withholding," Mom says in what she must think is under her breath. "I let your father have it," she says louder. "I told him he's completely wrong to treat you like he does."

"It doesn't matter. He's never going to change. And I don't even care."

"Yes. I see that you don't care at all."

Ouch. Sarcasm from my mother. This is not what I needed today.

"People want me, Mom. I have Sotheby's and Christie's banging down my electronic door, begging me to say yes to them."

"Of course you do. You're my daughter."

"And I quit. I'm not putting up with this anymore."

"You can quit if you want," Mom says carefully. "Or you can *not* quit."

"I'm not going be treated like this anymore. I won't stand for it." The words are confident but the quivering tone belies the confidence.

"No. You shouldn't have to. But you and your father forget that Loot is mine. My father started it."

"So?" I'm confused as to what she's trying to say. Of course I know Nana started the company.

"So he left it to me and only me. Your father, and all you kids, work for me."

That's a weird dynamic I never would have guessed. "But no one ever said anything." Dad certainly walks around like he's the boss.

Mom shrugs. "I don't like business. I was more than happy to let your father handle the company while I got to spend my time giving back through charity work. It's what I enjoy."

"But… Wait… What?"

"Everything worked. Your father was happy where he was, I was happy with him doing the work. And I got to spend more time with you, Ajay and Sonia, as well as my causes. We never got around to making anything official."

"So…what are you saying?"

"I'm saying I get the earnings reports just like any owner. And I've seen the sales your department brings in. It's a smart business decision to promote you and demote your father. You're the future of Loot."

I pull back from my mother and look at her with equal parts fear and admiration. "Mom. You're savage."

"I'm a good businessperson. If you don't want to be your father's boss, then it may be time for him to retire and travel with me for my charity work. And for fun." Mom loves giving back, but she loves having a good time too.

"I don't want my mom to just give me a company."

Mom snorts. "You were always going to get this company because of who your parents are. You and Ajay and Sonia. But you're going to run it because you're better at this than almost anyone else on the planet."

"You're biased." I feel emotional at getting some validation from one parent.

"I'm not biased; you're just perfect. I'm not going to argue with facts." Mom gives me an exaggerated kiss on the cheek.

She gets a laugh out of me, and I move to sit on the other side of the couch, taking a drink of wine. I'm dehydrated and I think there's some sort of hydration in this wine. Or there was at one point.

"I don't want to win like that. I don't know. I think it'll be good to work somewhere else. At least for a while. Get away from Loot and all its emotional baggage. Just work."

"Think about it. Will you come to dinner tomorrow?" Mom gets up and walks to the kitchen.

"Depends. Who else will be at dinner?"

"Has Sonia visited?" Mom starts making plates from the food she brought.

"You know she's been here. And you didn't answer."

"You have to forgive your father eventually. Why not tomorrow?"

Now I get mad all over again. "He hasn't even said sorry. How am I supposed to forgive someone when they don't even ask for my forgiveness?"

"Because you're the bigger person?"

"I'm the kid!" I say indignantly.

"Because you're the less stubborn person, then."

"I'm really not though." She should know this about me.

"Well, it's always been close. I'll work on him next." She brings the plate to me.

"I don't want you to," I continue over her when she starts to protest. "Seriously. I've put so much effort into this. I want him to put in the effort for once. Or I'm done."

"Oh, beta. You're never going to be done with family who loves you. And he does love you. Despite how bad he is at showing it. And I know that's not an excuse, but it's true." She puts the plate in front of me. "Now eat."

"I'm not hungry," I protest weakly.

"Did I ask if you were hungry? No. Eat."

I tear some naan and dip it in the butter chicken sauce but send her sad eyes while I do to let her know this is being done under protest.

"And while you're doing that you can tell me about Gavin Carlyle."

"Mom! Have you been talking to Sonia? She's such a tattletale."

"She is not. She's simply taking what you told her and telling your mother so I can be in the loop."

"That's literally the definition of a tattletale."

Mom shrugs. "So she's a tattletale. And what's so wrong with that?"

As I look at her in disbelief, I hope she's forgotten what she was originally talking about.

"So, Gavin." No luck for me. "I hear he's courting you."

Please let that be the exact way that Sonia phrased it when she told Mom. Shared dick pic aside, I don't want Mom to know I'm doing the nasty with anyone.

Or that courting in the modern age apparently means mutual masturbation in an opulent sex room.

"So? Even if he wants to…court me, it doesn't mean I'm interested in him."

"But are you?"

Clever woman, my mom. She realizes when I haven't actually answered the question yet. "No. As if."

"Yes, it's very convincing when you say no and then use slang from the nineties."

"I guess it wouldn't matter now. It's not like I can disappoint Dad by fraternizing with the enemy."

"The Carlyles aren't enemies, beta. We're competitors. But also peers."

"That's not what Dad thinks."

"Oh really? I've had a standing weekly lunch date with Laura Carlyle since we moved here."

"What?" She never mentioned this before.

She shrugs like it's not a big deal, destroying my entire worldview developed in childhood with one elegant shoulder movement. "We met when we were planning a charity event for literacy. Who else in the world knows what I'm going through? We don't talk specifics, but it's comforting to get advice and talk through problems with someone who's in the same position as me."

"What do you tell Dad?"

"Excuse me? I don't owe him an accounting of my time. I tell him I'm going to lunch with a friend, and then I leave."

"But…"

"They're nice. The Carlyles. You could do worse."

"You're just grandbaby mad."

"You two would make the most adorable babies."

"Whoa." I physically recoil at the responsibility. "Even if we get together, I'm not giving you grandbabies anytime soon."

"One step at a time." She pats my knee.

"I don't know," I wail, Mom catching me at a weak moment. Made weaker by everything I just learned. I need time to process all this. "I don't have any real complaints other than I'm scared at how hard it would be to coexist with someone I've always competed with."

"It might be hard, but not impossible."

The word *hard* makes something click in my brain. Since when am I afraid of hard work? I thrive in hard situations. "You're right. Sonia's right. I'm right. And I'm not afraid of hard work." I stand, mind made up. "I have to go do something. Can you put the food away?"

"Yes, I can," Mom says, giant smile on her face. Then she looks me up and down. "But maybe you should change first. And run a brush through your hair."

Chapter Thirty-Three

I ring the doorbell of the elegant Upper East Side town house in front of me, wishing the owner would hurry up and answer. When the owner isn't forthcoming, I knock on the door urgently. I had an epiphany and would like to act on it, please and thank you. I hear barking on the other side, making me pause in the frantic knocking.

I didn't think Gavin had a dog. But this is the address he gave me to pick him up at before Harrison's party. Did he give me the wrong address initially?

"Calm down, you little brat," Gavin says from behind the door as he starts the unlocking process. Thank god. But also who is he talking to?

"Gavin," I say to the man in front of me when he *finally* opens the door. "Oh, hello to you too," I say to the adorable white-and-brown bulldog puppy in Gavin's arms, distracting me from why I'm here.

I move forward to scratch the puppy under the chin, and it puts its tiny perfect paws on my hands and chews on my fingers with sharp baby teeth.

Is this heaven? This feels like heaven.

Until the puppy launches himself into my arms and I extend my arms to take him from Gavin, hugging the slight weight to me as he tries to eat my hair. *This* is heaven.

"Gavin, look. He likes my hair."

"I can see that."

I finally lift my head from the bundle in my arms, only to be shocked at the sight that awaits me. Gavin's hair is unusually mussed and he's got bags under his eyes. His shirt has suspicious stains on it, and his right sock has a hole in it. A puppy-teeth-size hole.

This is good. This makes him more approachable. So much so that I can get through what I came for, helped by the comforting weight in my arms.

"Gavin Carlyle," I say without any other preamble, needing to get it out fast before I can get too nervous. "I like you and I miss you and I'm sorry I snapped at you back in Long Island." I pause for a half second before continuing. "Nope, actually I just lied when I said I like you, because I love you but I didn't want to put it out there if you had changed your mind. Because that gives you something on me. But I'm trying to be more honest with my feelings regardless of how vulnerable that makes me. And to trust you." I bury my head in the puppy's neck, inhaling puppy smell so I can avoid his reaction to my admission.

"Wow."

"Is that a good wow or a bad wow?" My voice is muffled by the wiggling puppy I'm using as a shield, and by the sound of my own heartbeat in my ears.

"It's a come-in wow." Gavin steps back from his front door.

"Okay, but can you tell me if you want me, too, before I come in? I'd rather just leave if you don't want to give this a try anymore."

"Come in, Riya."

That's not an answer, but I did just say I was trying to trust Gavin more, so I come in. He leads me through his impeccably decorated temple to excess and expensive interior design. Dark wood paneling competes with damask wallpaper and antique furniture. Paintings and sculptures complete the look. It's nice, and I hope this isn't the last time I get to see it, because I could spend some time here studying his furniture. And being with the man who owns it.

Gavin leads me to a living room, but this building is so historic it was probably originally called a drawing room. I sit down on one of his couches and focus on petting the puppy in my arms, since Gavin still hasn't said anything in response to my declaration.

"Priya Gupta. I miss you too. I'm sorry I wasn't more supportive back at Harrison's. I get now why it was wrong of me to have put my feelings first when you were going through so much, and why you reacted like you did. I love you and I want to give us a try, too." Gavin smiles softly at me as he mimics what I just said to him.

"Well, that's good then," I say, not sure how to be relaxed with Gavin just yet.

He doesn't have that problem, because he sits down next to me and kisses me. I melt into the couch, so relieved to have his lips when I thought I'd never feel them again that I could kiss him forever.

Or I would have if a little puppy wasn't trying his hardest to get involved in this kiss. And his puppy kisses are getting a little too close to our human one.

I break away from Gavin, laughing. "Who is this?

And how long have you had a puppy?" It can't be that long; he's so tiny.

"He's not mine. I was going to deliver him to you tomorrow. Since neither of us really won the bet, I thought it only fair that I live up to half of my part of the bet and provide you with a puppy. Riya, meet Leo. Short for Leonardo Dog Vinci because I know you love puns. But you can rename him if you think that's stupid. Leo, this is your new momma, and she isn't going to like you chewing on her art."

I laugh in delight at the puppy and the name. "Hi, Leo. Do you love art like me?"

"He's already tried to eat about four expensive paintings and pee on one statue."

"I hope you didn't eat any priceless art, Leonardo Dog Vinci." I raise him up to look him in the eyes as I give the stern warning. The puppy tilts his face at me and I don't care anymore. Maybe he can chew on some art that I don't like as much.

"I stopped him in time," Gavin says.

"You weren't supposed to get me a puppy though, you were supposed to potty train my puppy…"

"No one won the bet, so this is more a gesture than payment."

"I'll take it." Like I would let him take Leo away from me now that I've met him and fallen in love with him.

"Speaking about our competition, it's not right that we didn't get a fair go at it," Gavin says.

That's an understatement about what occurred.

"So I wanted to give you the show."

I shake my head. "I don't want it like this." I wanted to earn it, not get it out of pity.

"I don't want it like this either. But I had a feeling you'd say that. So I spoke to Harrison and asked him to give you any pieces you wanted for your *Female Gaze* show. We could cross-promote and it would be a great opportunity for him to get the extra exposure."

I open my mouth to protest the charity, but Gavin cuts me off.

"Harrison already agreed to it as well. And he's happy to resolve it like this with both of us getting something after how awkwardly it ended in Long Island, so if you turn him down it won't be good for your future professional relationship with him."

"If you're gonna twist my arm." I give in to the thing I wanted in the first place. "Have you guys decided the pieces or do I get to pick?" Maybe I can stay at Loot for one more show.

"You get to pick. Whatever you want, however many you want. You can come to Carlyle's when Harrison sends everything over and we'll ship you everything you pick."

That's a nice gesture. A thoughtful and selfless one too that gives us both something out of this. I knew I wasn't wrong to compliment his intelligence.

"I actually kind of quit Loot." I drop the fact into the conversation without any segue.

"What? You love that place. A lot."

I shrug. "It was kind of a last straw situation. It's not a good environment for me, and I think I need a break from it. Break length to be determined."

"Come work for Carlyle's," Gavin says impulsively.

I wasn't expecting that.

My eyebrows snap down and I open my mouth to protest but he interrupts.

"As my boss. I know you think I'm a privileged shit, and I've been known to not take things as seriously as I should. But I want to show you how much I respect you and show you how hard I can work. I talked to Dad about Gina's cars, because you were right, I need to fight harder for the things I want, and he's going to let me put on the show. This is the kind of manager I could use."

He digs into his pocket to pull out a metro card, holding it like it's a gold medal at the Olympics. "I've even been taking the subway more. Not all the time. Or most of the time. But some of the time. It can really save time during rush hour."

I laugh at his proud look. "You were really going to come for me?"

"Of course. I wasn't going to let you go that easy. I just had to wait for the puppy. I was also going to bring this to give you." He gets up from the couch and retrieves a big package wrapped in brown paper from his hall.

"What's that?" I ask.

"Why don't you give me the puppy and open it?" He reaches for Leo and I pull back, giving him a dark look.

He pulls his hands up, rightly afraid of what I'll do if he tries to take this precious cargo from me. "Or I can open it while you hold Leo."

He unwraps the package to reveal the Raqib Shaw painting he bought from me at my last auction.

Now I'm even more confused, but at least not about my feelings this time. "Is there a problem with it? Because we have a whole department that handles customer complaints. Or at least Loot does." I have to keep reminding myself that's not me as of a few days ago.

"No, nothing like that. It's for you. It was always for you."

"I…" am speechless.

I rub my forehead with one hand, the one not currently juggling a wiggly puppy. This is too much to take at one time. He got it for me? But that happened before we hooked up.

But it could be true. He isn't a huge contemporary art fan, so I was surprised when he even bid on it, much less kept bidding on it until he won.

This is all so sweet. Gavin being more observant and thoughtful than I give him credit for. And working hard to make me happy, even after I told him to get lost. This puppy couldn't have been easy to watch, as shown by Gavin's current appearance.

"Thank you for the painting. And the puppy. And the job offer. I don't know what I want to do, but I'm not going to rush into something new. I've still got a lot to work through with Loot and my dad."

That thought makes me sober up again after the happiness of the last few minutes, but I move on to happier thoughts.

"But whatever I do, I want to do it with you," I say, ready to take the plunge with him. He's knocked down every concern I had.

He started to lightly erode my concerns since I stole his girlfriend, all through the country house party, and now he's flooded past my worries, saying all the right things. Over time showing me he can take things seriously…or at least that he can take me seriously.

Even if he didn't have the best reaction to my news before, he's not afraid to own up to it and apologize for his bad timing. And bad timing's not really that severe a sin anyway.

Or maybe he's just learned that I'll forgive anything if it comes with a puppy. Either way he's learning.

Gavin's eyes light up.

"You're aggravatingly perfect without trying, and you make me happy and I love you," I say again.

"I love you too." Gavin smiles at me, making my stomach warm in happiness. Not only because of everything he's said, but because that smile is devastating.

Maybe I should have let him help me that day in Long Island, if I would have gotten this feeling of comfort to help me through all the turmoil over the last few days.

I pull back. "By the way, I said I love you first."

He looks too indignant for someone who was just kissing me. "No, you didn't. I did, in Harrison's mansion. We can call Sarah if you need a third-party witness."

I wave him away. "I think we can all agree you said it at the worst time and that shouldn't be counted."

"Is that the technicality you want to start our lives on?"

"If it means starting out life with me winning, then yeah."

"Riya, I'm going to let this one slide since you've had a few days. But don't get used to this easy agreement."

"I would never." I love arguing with this man too much for that.

Chapter Thirty-Four

"Mom." I walk into the apartment holding Gavin's hand. "I have a puppy!"

"And a Gavin," Gavin adds about himself.

After I texted Mom and Sonia that everything was good with Gavin...even perfect with Gavin, she said that she was still at my apartment, cooking even more for me. She ordered me to come back and bring Gavin over so she could meet him formally. I don't want to fight with both parents at once, so I complied.

Plus I have very good food at my home.

"I'm sure my daughter didn't mean that to reflect her priorities. Hi, Gavin." She hugs the wary man. "Have you eaten?"

"I have, Mrs. Gupta. Thank you."

"Call me Rani. I'll just make you a small plate then." She walks into my little-used kitchen, which is getting a workout lately.

I shake my head at Gavin behind Mom's back, pantomiming to him that he's getting a plate with a huge pile of food on it. Mom makes my prediction a reality when she turns back with a plate containing a small model of Mount Everest.

I give him a knowing look as she hands the plate to Gavin, who looks unsure of what just happened.

Super-effective Indian mothering is what just happened. He's going to need to get used to that if he wants to stick around.

"This is a small plate?"

"Of course," Mom says as she cleans up the counter. "Priya has larger plates if you want more?"

"I'm good. Thank you for this. It smells wonderful." He raises the plate at Mom in thanks.

He's gonna put on so much weight. He should always offer to make his own plate. Amateur.

"Now that both of you are happy and fed, I've got a charity board meeting to attend. Gavin, give my love to your mother and tell her I'll see her next week for our brunch."

Gavin gives me a questioning look as Mom leaves.

I shrug. "Apparently they've been having a secret friendship all these years."

Gavin's eyes get bigger. "And no one noticed." He nods. "Impressive."

Gavin takes his plate to my living room, making himself at home on my couch. I take a moment to bask in the sight of Gavin in my apartment, new puppy jumping up his shin to get to his plate of food.

"When you're done with that food… I think you have some puppy responsibilities to attend to." I jerk my head to the messes Leo made in the corner of my living room in the few minutes he's been here.

"Since you're such a big fan of technicalities, I feel obliged to point out again that neither of us won the bet."

I stare at him, internally acknowledging I don't have

a leg to stand on but not wanting to deal with the mess. It's smelly.

I look back at the puppy, who gave up trying to jump on Gavin and instead is chewing on my coffee table leg. How can something so precious make such a terrible smell?

"Since no one won the bet, this ankle biter is a present." He nudges the puppy with his foot. Leo ignores him, doubling down on the table leg. "So you should pick that up."

I keep up the stare. He makes sense, but I don't want to do it. Gavin keeps eating, so I sigh deep and take the high road to clean up Leo's surprises.

But Gavin gets to clean up the next one. Since he's so determined to stick around.

The thought makes me smile while I do the smelly work.

Halfway through my midmorning lounge, I hear a knock on my door.

My midmorning lounge is different than my morning lounging, because by midmorning, I manage to open my iPad and check out the news while I watch Netflix.

It's also separated from my morning lounge by a midmorning snack and taking Leo out for his second potty time.

It's been a few days since Gavin and I told each other we love each other. We've settled into a nice routine where, after work, he comes over, or makes me (and Leo) go all the way to the Upper East Side (which I don't argue against because he has a backyard so when I need to take Leo out I don't have to take a long elevator ride). Then we eat together, work out together or watch some TV, discussing the market throughout, and enjoy some sexy times before bed.

Before he gets done with work, I spend the day learning to watch TV without doing anything else and reading all the books I've been too busy to read until now.

It's been kind of nice since I pushed through the initial boredom.

I wonder if the knock is Gavin leaving work early. Or Mom and/or Sonia coming to check up on me again. I swoop up Leo who started yapping at the knock like the best little guard dog, and get up to open the door, ready to tease Gavin about being away from work in the middle of the day.

I wasn't expecting my dad.

But here he is, Kabir Gupta in the flesh, looking uncomfortable. This is why people look through the peephole. Well, this situation and murderers.

I still feel hurt when I see him, but the anger is mostly gone. I'm tired of being angry over this situation and that anger not doing anything productive.

But it is time to have this conversation, as much as I wish I could push it off and close the door on his face. Best to get it over with and not have it hanging over my head.

"Hi," I say when he doesn't say anything to me.

"Hello. Can I come in?"

The usually confident man looks awkward and unsure, tone subdued and feet shuffling restlessly.

"Um…sure. Yeah." I back up a few feet and let Dad in.

He enters the condo and takes in the scene. My housekeeper comes once a month, and usually that's enough since I spend most of my time at work anyway.

It looks a little different when I'm home all the time. A little messier.

We sit down at the table and stare at each other. I'm not offering him some chai and Parle-G biscuits after what he's done to me.

Leo squirms in my arms and I let him down to investigate the new person. "Who's this?" Dad reaches down to pat the curious bulldog on the head, and then starts in surprise when Leo sneezes on him.

"Leonardo Dog Vinci. He was a present."

"How long have you had him?"

"Just a few days." But it could have been longer and he wouldn't have known. I don't remember the last time we talked about anything other than work.

This relationship wasn't great before he threw me under the bus.

"I thought you quit. Why are you reading art world magazines?" He indicates the magazines and newspapers spread out on my coffee table.

"I quit Loot, not the industry," I reply flatly. "I've been offered jobs at a few different houses, so I just need to choose one and then I'll be back in the auction world saddle."

I decide not to tell him one of the offers is from Gavin.

Dad winces. "This is ridiculous. Come back to Loot. Your work is piling up."

"I don't have any work to pile up, since I quit."

Dad sighs. "Sonia's been helping, but it's too much on top of her regular work, so we have three late deliveries, and two clients are thinking of backing out of sales because they haven't heard from you. I sent Ajay to talk to them and then I dealt with complaints for days after. And I don't know where any of the contracts are."

"That sounds like an inconvenience. But you're the CEO, I'm sure you'll figure it out."

"But you can do it better. You've created quite the department at Loot, and your influence extends beyond it. We all need you."

He's never said that before. And they're the words I've wanted to hear from him for a long time, but I think they might be too late because they don't cause any of the relief or happiness that I expected they would.

"Thanks, but we both know you prefer Ajay, so now you can focus on him." The anger might be gone, but apparently the bitterness is still there, if my tone is anything to go by.

"Your mom told me that you think I prefer Ajay, but it's not true," he says gruffly, looking out of the window like it's a valid method of escape from this conversation.

I'm sixty-five floors up…so that's not going to happen.

I raise my eyebrows. "I've lived my life so I think I know how you feel about me."

"It's not true." He sees the disbelief on my face and rushes to elaborate. "Yes, I did spend more time with Ajay when you were younger. I was taught that men worked and earned, and women took care of the home. So I brought Ajay to the company and left you at home. And… I didn't know how to relate to a daughter like I did a son."

"Thanks for continuing tens of thousands of years of misogyny." I feel the twisting in my stomach at the verbal reminder that he doesn't want me anywhere near the company, when that's where I want to be.

"But I'm glad you showed me I was wrong. I'm glad you came to the office and kept coming. You are better at this than Ajay and I'm so proud over everything you do." Dad still looks deeply uncomfortable, which makes sense, considering I haven't seen him discuss his emotions in…ever.

"But you always gave Ajay the best of everything. Job positions, shows, contacts. Everything." I say what's been bothering me for years, needing an answer even if it's one I don't think I'll like. I need him to say it and maybe I can move on.

Dad looks down to Leo, petting the puppy again, probably to avoid looking at me. "Your mother told me that was how you saw it. Yelled at me, more like." He mumbles the last part under his breath, and I can imagine Mom tearing into him about the subject. She was pretty fired up when she came to see me the first time. "I thought I was helping Ajay. I don't know if you've noticed, but he's not the most dedicated worker."

As someone who Ajay shoves his work at every time he gets hit by painting inspiration, I give Dad an incredulous look. He doesn't see because he's still avoiding meeting my eyes.

"I wanted to help him, encourage him to work harder. And I hoped he'd rise to the occasion. You never needed my help. I gave you a position with flexibility so you could do whatever you wanted. And you've succeeded beyond anything I thought possible." He looks up then, slight smile on his face. And I do think I might see pride in his eyes.

"But why Harrison then? Why did you take that collection away from me? Why don't you let me do more diverse shows?" A few tears leak out, despite me trying to keep them in, as I remember how dismissed and insignificant I felt when I found out, from *Harrison* no less, what was happening with my work.

"It was wrong and I'm sorry. I'm scared." Dad works his jaw after he says that, the words physically paining him. "I've never sold anything other than Indian art. Wouldn't even know where to start. I went to business school and picked up enough about Indian art history to carve out a career in it. But I can't do it for all the art in the world; I'm too old to do it. And I guess I thought if I couldn't do it, no one else possibly could." He looks up at me now, meeting my teary gaze. "But you can. You *do*. So you can sell whatever you want and I won't stop you anymore."

I don't think I've ever heard Dad apologize for anything. And he looks earnest. I'm no psychologist or master interrogator, but his eyes look sad.

"Do you forgive me?" he asks when I don't say anything.

I think back on all the times I cried in my room because I didn't feel good enough, of the times I worked hard to spite the man in front of me. I don't know if I would have worked quite as hard if it wasn't for him, which I guess means he's at least partly responsible for making me a beast of an auctioneer.

Still. "Are you just doing this because Mom threatened to give me your job?"

"No! I want you to take my job. Well, preferably not now," he admits when he sees my look of disbelief. "But all I've ever wanted is for you, Ajay and Sonia to run Loot. I was hoping as equals, but maybe it would be better if you and Sonia managed the company."

"I *provisionally* forgive you. But I don't want you to

ever ignore me in favor of Ajay again. You don't have to treat me better, just equal."

"I won't," he promises, sniffling like he's getting choked up himself. "I love you, beta."

"I love you too, Dad." I get off the couch to give him a hug. Leo, not sure what's happening but already not wanting to be left out, yelps a little puppy bark to let us know he wants attention too.

"Can I tell your mom you forgive me?" Dad jokes. He's done with the emotional moment between us now, and to be honest, so am I. This is a lot more honest and deeper than we usually get and I need a break to process it.

"I'll tell her you're *provisionally* forgiven."

"That should be enough to stop her from withholding her gulab jamun from me."

I ease Dad into another topic. "Speaking of food, Mom wants to have a dinner party on Saturday. That you're probably now reinvited to."

"I always love your mother's dinner parties." He pats his stomach in preparation for the large amount of food she always makes for her parties.

"Right. About the guest list though…"

Chapter Thirty-Five

"This is a disaster," I whisper to Gavin as my eyes dart to the closed door. We're hiding out in a bathroom of my parents' town house, while everyone else is in the dining room at the world's most awkward dinner party.

Mom insisted on the party to make sure everyone in the families (the dads) were going to play nice once Gavin and I announce the relationship.

Thus far, they have not proven they can play nice. Aggravating when both men can do business with soulless millionaires regularly, but they can't fake being cordial to each other for one night.

It started out innocuously enough, just some not-good-natured banter like "My auction house is better than yours" and "No, mine is."

There was some "My gross profits are bigger than yours," to which the response was "Well, my net profits are bigger than yours."

At one point William said he had been working at auctioning longer, and Dad said he was over the hill and the industry needed some new blood.

Not surprisingly, we haven't told the dads we're dating yet. When we walked in, Mom and Laura were going to do it for us, but the dads started passive-aggressive arguing the second they saw each other, so I said we were all here to learn how to be civil to each other, for professionalism.

Spoiler: no one has learned anything. Except me learning this isn't going to work.

"Hey, Riya." Gavin grabs my cheeks and makes me focus on his beautiful blue eyes. "You're the fiercest debater I know. You can convince those two old men about anything."

"No. An important marker of maturity is realizing your limitations, and those two crazy men who gave us DNA are mine." The best thing we can do now is leave and date in secret for the rest of our lives.

It's the only logical path.

"You have some of that DNA. You're an upgraded model," Gavin says, sounding a little desperate in response to what I can see in the mirror is a terrified look in my eyes.

"I'm not upgraded. I have Mom's reason, which tempers Dad's irrationality. But that means I'm no match for his unbridled irrationalness."

"What are our options at this point?" Gavin looks around like the answer is hiding in the cabinet under the sink, behind the extra toilet paper.

"Jump out the window? We're on the first floor, so no worry about injuries. And then we're going to have to flee the country, but I think we can really grow to love the aggressive politeness of Canada. Ooh and maple syrup."

A knock on the door breaks into our planning, and we freeze in fear.

"Guys, are one or both of you in there?" Mom asks.

"If you are both in there, don't let us know," Laura says from the other side of the door.

"Just me," I lie. Sometimes, a lie is best for everyone involved.

"Okay, well get back out here. Your dads are arguing about the Christmas sales last year, and they can only sustain themselves on the certainty they're right so long before they realize both of you are gone. Tell Gavin too…wherever he is," Mom dryly says.

Yeah, not fooling the combined powers of the moms at all.

"Okay, I'll get right on that. You go back to the table first." Casual, I can do casual. I'm just a normal human, using a bathroom, for its intended purpose. Alone. Nothing to see here.

Mom sighs her patented Rani Gutpa sigh as she walks away. "Children," she whispers to Laura, forgetting that her doors aren't soundproof.

"This is a bandage," I say after we hear the moms' footsteps fade.

"Hiding in the bathroom? Well, yeah. It's not solving the problem."

I shake my head. "No, let's tear off this bandage. Quick."

Gavin's eyes widen as he realizes what I'm about to do. He reaches for me as I slip out of the door but jerks back when he realizes he has to let me go or make a scene.

I march through the house with all the determination of Hannibal crossing the Alps. I wonder if Hannibal was as hopped up on moscato as I am. Probably, he did take elephants up the Alps; that man must have been wine drunk.

I wonder if his heart was beating this fast as well.

"I have an announcement." Four score and seven years… No! That's the wrong speech.

"What is it, beta?" Dad asks me, looking mildly concerned at my clenched fists and increased respiration.

"I'm dating him." I turn dramatically to indicate Gavin, only to draw everyone's attention to the very confused waiter bringing in the main course.

Hey. Where's my coward of a boyfriend?

"Okay. Hello, son. Why don't you sit down with us?" Dad asks, not missing a beat.

The mom gallery at the side of the table bursts into laughter… *Not helping, moms.* I send them a glare to let them know they're getting cheesy necklaces that say Mom for Christmas that they'll have to wear because they love us, but they'll hate them, because they're going to be so very tacky.

And now I have to do this again. "No, not Peter." Then I turn to him. "Not that you're not great and some person would be so lucky…"

"I'm going to leave this here." Peter drops his serving tray on the table and rushes back to the kitchen.

Take me with you, Peter; anything to save me from how awkward this is.

"If you need more of a break, you don't have to come back to work on Monday. Take another week, or as long as you need," Dad says, his concern not helping me right now.

"No, I'm dating the coward Gavin." Or maybe not anymore now that I see what he's made of when the going gets tough.

He runs. Like he's in the Olympics after recovering from an injury and he has something to prove.

"What?" Dad gets up, his face a mix of confused and angry. Confangry?

"What?" William gets up as well, the look on his face twins with the confrangry on Dad's. I don't think they would appreciate that being pointed out by me right now.

"It's true," Gavin says from behind me.

There he is. He must have taken the ferry around the Statue of Liberty to get from the bathroom to the dining room, but he's here.

I grab his arm and pull him closer to me, throwing my arm around him and angling our bodies so he has to deal with the brunt of the questions the dads are throwing at us.

At least their reactions are predictable.

"When did this happen?" William asks.

"How could you betray the family like this?" my drama king dad asks.

"How would this work?" William follows up.

"Are you sure you don't want to take another look at Peter? Anyone else? I can try to call Chris Hemsworth's people if you want?" Dad offers.

"Wait, hold on now." I move away from Gavin. "Do you have Chris Hemsworth's number?"

Gavin pinches me in the side.

"Just asking for science," I mumble to him.

"I doubt that there's anything academic about your interest in Hemsworth," he whispers back.

"Hello, when can Chris come out to New York?" Dad says into his phone.

"Dad, stop it right now." I lunge across the table and snatch the phone out of his hand.

"Hi, sorry. Kabir dialed the wrong number. Have a good day," I say into the phone before I end the call.

"I'm keeping this." I put the phone in my pocket. "Mom, can you help?" I want her to order the dads to get over it so we can all move on with our lives.

"You look like you have everything in hand," she says, taking a sip of wine and enjoying the show.

"Okay then. Dad, this is happening. You aren't going to do anything to stop it, or I'll make Mom fire you. William, I look forward to getting to know you better the longer I date your son."

"Seriously, Dad, I love Priya so we all need to get used to Sunday dinners together. And holidays. We aren't asking your permission."

"You love her?" Both dads say in unison. They look at each other in horror, probably imagining all the times they're going to have to get along for the rest of our lives. Or however long this lasts.

"That's right. Christmases, birthdays, Easters, Diwalis… We'll probably do our own thing on New Years', but Thanksgivings are going to be family oriented," Gavin says.

They look more and more concerned.

"And your opinions aren't requested or welcome. Unless they're positive," I say.

We hold our breaths as the dads process the new information. The moment lasts so long I have to fight the desire to take it all back, but then Dad turns to William.

"You know, if our companies merge because of these two, we'll be in a much stronger position to compete with Christie's and Sotheby's."

Now William turns calculating. "This could work well for everyone."

Agape, I turn to Gavin. Are they trying to profit from our relationship? We should be the only ones to benefit from this relationship.

Laura gets up from the table and gives us a hug. "I for one am happy for you two regardless of how much you'll contribute to our profits for the next year."

"Imagine if we did a combined Christmas show? High profile. A lot of people in the city already." William starts brainstorming.

"Yes." Dad pulls out an iPad mini from his jacket pocket that I didn't even notice was there and starts typing. "We can do it in the outdoor plaza at 30 Rock… right in front of Christie's." He laughs like a toddler in delight at sticking it to the monolith.

"I like sticking it to Christie's, but I think our clients will complain about the weather…we can find a Golden Age mansion to rent for the event," William says, getting out his phone.

"Yes. I'll call a real estate agent tomorrow who specializes in old mansions like that and he can make a list of places we can tour at the end of the week."

"Excellent. I'll get another real estate agent on it, so we have variety. And I'll start making lists of caterers. We need a traditional Christmas dinner: ham, fruitcake, the works."

I take a page out of the Indian soap operas and check out everyone for their reaction. Gavin looks just as shocked as I am. But the moms are calmly sipping their drinks. They've had a lot more practice with the dads.

The meltdown at the beginning was expected, and I knew they'd eventually get over it. But I was not expecting the speed at which Dad pivoted from "Aiiii the world is ending!" to "How do I monetize this relationship?"

But…yay for us?

"Mom, I'm scared. So we're going away from this." I indicate the corporate synergy happening at our dining table.

"Good call. Both of you be here for dinner next Sunday. I'm making Ajay and Sonia come as well."

Good. More people to witness and buffer all of this.

"Or we could host it?" Laura says. "We could switch off so you don't have to do all the work."

"I'll take you up on that." The moms clink wineglasses as we leave the house.

We walk to the subway station in a daze.

"That was really weird," he finally says halfway home. He wraps his arms around me and sways with the train. He's really getting the hang of this public transportation thing. "Do you think they're going to hold an auction at our wedding?" he asks.

"Probably." I lean into his chest, and then jerk back up. "Wait, what?"

We aren't getting married. No one said anything about weddings. I just got over looking at him like an enemy and admitted I loved him, and he's trying to get hitched?

"Oh look, our stop." Gavin drags me out of the train when it comes to a stop.

It's a stop too soon, but I don't mind the walk if it means I don't have to think about what Gavin just said.

Because there is no way we're getting married anytime soon.

Chapter Thirty-Six

Eleven Months Later

"I don't have much time, so we need to do this fast," I whisper, hunching down lower and looking over my shoulder to make sure Gavin hasn't found me.

I already had to sneak away too many times for comfort, and I suspect he's starting to doubt my claim that my bladder is really that tiny.

"Are you sure we should do this?" I ask Sonia, biting my lip.

"Yes, we need to switch the shows around, because some of the sellers for the show that was supposed to be first aren't delivering their stuff and show two is being very compliant."

I sigh into the phone. "Fine."

"And you should listen to Gavin and stop calling me on your honeymoon!"

"Don't tell me what to do, woman!" I whisper-yell at her through the phone.

"I have everything under control, and I will call you if I need your micromanaging. And now I'm going to hang up so you can spend time with your new husband."

She matches her actions with her words and hangs up on me.

"Rude, insubordinate..." I mutter to myself, looking at the satellite phone.

"Caught," Gavin says to me, making me jump up from where I'm hidden behind a box of supplies in the cargo hold of a ship.

Unfortunately for me, ships have tight spaces and I hit my head on some random and probably unnecessary (completely necessary) piping.

"We agreed not to work on our honeymoon." Gavin has the nerve to use my own words against me, while he leans on the boxes I'm still crouched behind.

"Entire shows are being moved around. Don't you think I should be involved in that?" I rub my head and try to look pitiful and injured.

Gavin steps around the boxes and wraps his arms around me. "No. Because it's our honeymoon and Sonia is very competent."

He kisses me, warming me more effectively than the six layers of clothing I'm wearing. His hands start their laborious trip under all those layers when we hear the loudspeaker interrupt us. "Anyone who wants to go to the day trip to kayak to penguins, meet us at the deck in twenty minutes."

"Ooh, penguins." I remove his hands from their journey and use the freed hands to drag a groaning Gavin up to our stateroom.

Gavin remembered that the only way we were going to get a vacation was to go where there's no art. So during the chaos that was our multiple event, multicultural Indian and Western wedding extravaganza a week ago,

Gavin slipped tickets for a cruise to Antarctica under the door of my suite.

On a very legitimate, very serious, scientific vessel. Who knows where all the best penguins are.

It turned out to be a needed gift, and I focused on it when the wedding got tough.

The ceremony itself was beautiful and stress free. We had a Hindu ceremony, followed by a Christian one right after. I wore a white gown, with my bangles, full bridal henna and a red veil with dark red roses embroidered on the edges. Harrison even let us use the ballroom at his Long Island house because he still felt bad. I took it because it's a gorgeous house, and I have very fond memories of the place.

After the ceremony, however, it was a free-for-all.

Dad kept trying to poach Carlyle's clients, trotting me around from person to person. And William wasn't any better, doing the same with Gavin and our clients.

It did keep them from arguing.

But it was exhausting. When I got overwhelmed and started planning some light patricide, Gavin stole me and we had a very pleasant interlude in the sex room.

This time, there *was* touching.

That helped carry me through the rest of the reception with a genuine smile on my face.

Back in our honeymoon stateroom, Gavin pulls on all his layers, while putting another layer on me. We go up to the top deck to meet for our penguin excursion.

I'm still vaguely impressed that he got me to marry him so soon. Don't get me wrong, I love him. And we've known each other since we were infants, so I wasn't worried about going all-in with him so soon.

But we had so much going on, I kept trying to put off

the actual wedding part. Gavin was persistent though, and he won by basically planning the wedding for me, with the help of the moms.

And now I get a small thrill every time I look at my ring finger, a physical reminder that there's a person out there who promised to argue about art with me, have sex with me, and take Antarctic vacations with me for the rest of my life.

That might be even better than work. But I'm not telling Gavin that.

* * * * *

Acknowledgments

Phew, it's been such a long journey to get here, and so many people have helped along the way!

Thank you to Mom and Dad for the love and support you've given me since I was born, with just enough strife to make me funny. Dad, I love you more and I win because it's in writing.

Thank you to my husband, not only for your love and support, but also for always taking my writing seriously, even when all you could see of me from across the couch was the back of my laptop. One day I'll get enough book money to make you a househusband! And when I do, please remember I like my margaritas blended, not shaken.

Thank you to Oliver James, even though you can't read this (Daddy will read it to you), for snoring by my side through almost every word. You fail spectacularly at being my combination security, HR and editor, but I'll still pay you in treats like you did any of your jobs.

Thank you to Pitch Wars but especially Farah Heron. Thank you for picking my manuscript when I didn't have faith in me, for loving it, and for making it better.

Thank you to Jana Hanson, my agent, for your belief

in me and your relentless championing of this book, and for finding it the perfect home.

Thank you to everyone at Carina, but especially Deborah Nemeth and Stephanie Doig. Thank you for choosing *Two Houses* and for making it the book it is today. Deb, thank you for making me a better writer. Sorry for my…creative approach to the English language. And for all the ellipses.

Thank you to all my family and friends, from grade school, college, law school, adulthood and of the writing variety, for all your friendship and support. I love you all.

About the Author

Suleena Bibra has read romance in one form or another since she could pick her own books. She occasionally branches out to other genres, but really, what's the point if there's no kissing? She also loves to laugh, which probably has to do with her dad putting *Monty Python* on whenever her mom wasn't looking.

Possessing a "madness to gaze at trifles," Suleena studied art history in college and loves to travel every opportunity she gets. A bit indecisive, she has worked as a museum intern, lawyer, workers' compensation adjuster, and private investigator. Author is best, though, so she can continue living out a bunch of other careers without changing out of her pajamas.

Suleena writes romcoms heavy on shenanigans, chicanery, and banter. She spends the rest of her time annoying her stubborn but adorable bulldog (who also doubles as her particularly lazy writing assistant) with her love.

For more on Suleena, you can follow her on Twitter @suleenabibra, Instagram @suleenabibra, and on the website she occasionally remembers how to update, www.suleenabibra.com.

**Snowbound at Christmas
leads to holiday sparks...**

Casting director Perla Sambrano knows Gael
Montez is the *perfect* actor for her new film project. As long as she forgets his oh-so-tempting allure and keeps her heart out of it.

Because their chemistry's no act and she needs
to be careful...

The Montez men hurt the women they love.
Or so Gael believes. Keeping things professional
with Perla is the only way to protect her. Until a
snowstorm strands them together, leading to an
unplanned Christmas fling that lands them both
on the naughty list!

Read on for a sneak preview of
Just for the Holidays... *by Adriana Herrera.*

Available now from Harlequin Desire!

One

"I'm bored of playing the same character," Gael Montez muttered as he flipped through the pages of the script Manolo, his manager—and uncle—had asked him to review. "Is there nothing else I can do other than play the ambiguously ethnic guy in superhero ensembles?"

"*Ambiguously ethnic guy* parts in billion-dollar franchises make for a very good living," his uncle responded in that lecturing tone that put Gael's teeth on edge. "Space Squadron money is nothing to lift your nose at, *mijo*," Manolo continued in that soothing, fatherly voice of his. "And this role has you as the lead, plus you'd get a producer credit. You're just in a mood this time of the year." The older man lifted his champagne flute, signaling to the private jet's flight attendant. Gael glanced away, annoyed that his uncle was right on both counts. His current gig as part of the cast of one of the most popular movie franchises ever was a dream job for anyone, *and* he hated Christmas.

Well, he didn't hate it exactly; it just brought back memories he'd rather forget. And he'd have to put his most cheerful face on by the time they landed because there was no way he was going to put a damper on his mother's favorite holiday. Not after the year she'd had.

"I'm not in a mood."

That got him a scoff from his sister Gabi. "You're always in a funk in December, Señor Grinch."

Gael bared his teeth at his sister, who loved to comment about his less than festive disposition around the holidays and every other attitude of Gael's she found lacking. Gabi lived to bust his balls. "I'm just tired," he said, and he felt it. Bone tired and depleted in a way that was starting to worry him. It was like in the past year he'd become completely numb. He did his work, and he did it well—Gael had high standards for himself and he never gave anything less than one hundred percent to any of his performances. He just couldn't get excited about *anything* lately. Maybe he was burnt out. Since his breakout role in an acclaimed cable series five years ago, he'd been working constantly. Offers just started coming in, and they never stopped. And his immigrant kid mentality wouldn't let him turn anything down. He couldn't even remember the last time he'd taken more than a few days off to just do nothing. Maybe he needed a break.

He had the next ten days, at least.

The production schedule for the most recent installment of the Space Squadron—in which Gael played the brown guy with superpowers—allowed for time off from the press tours for the holidays. Which was why Gael, Gabi and his uncle were on their way from LA to his house in the Hamptons, where his mother and the rest of their family would be spending Christmas. He was looking forward to not having to be on for the cameras 24/7.

He wasn't an ungrateful ass. He knew how lucky he was to have made it as far as he had. You didn't have to be in Hollywood too long as a Latinx actor to notice there weren't many others around. Never mind being cast for one of the most profitable movie franchises in history. On paper, he was living the dream. His profile was growing with every one of the movies he was in, and what's more, he was able to provide for his entire family. Hell, it seemed he employed half of them.

But five years into what seemed like movie after movie where his culture had no bearing—where his roots were some muddled inconsequential footnote—he yearned to take on a project that would show a different side to him. He had a couple of friends from Squadron— Tanusha, a Malaysian actress who was his love interest in the movies, and Kwaw, a Ghanaian actor who was his friend off and on screen—who had warned Gael about that, to not let himself get pigeonholed as the hot ethnic guy in all his projects. Kwaw already had indie projects lined up before filming for the next Squadron and Tanusha was directing a documentary about the effects of climate change in her country.

Meanwhile Gael was reading scripts for more movies that only required him to flex his muscles and look pretty. He tossed the script on the table and took a swig of his champagne. "I'm not interested in this, Manolo."

"Did you even read what the starting offer is? It's more than what you're making with the Space Squadron movies and you would have *the leading role and an executive producer credit.* That's a great opportunity."

"I've never heard of this production company, anyone in this writer's room or the director. Looks like it's a bunch of frat bros trying to make a buck off the popularity of the Marvel franchises." That came from Gabi, who for the past three years had been working as Gael's publicist. It was a bit of Latinx cliché to have his family working for him, but his sister was excellent at what she did, and had a keen eye for what was a good use of his time and what wasn't.

"Gabi, I appreciate your opinion, but I've been doing this a bit longer than you have. I've been with your brother from the time that no one gave him an audition."

Gael scowled at Manolo's harsh tone. He loved his uncle and he was grateful for the support he'd given him over the years. It was true that he'd helped him get to where he was. That he'd been there every step of the way. But sometimes Manolo acted like Gael's abilities and talents were incidental. Like it hadn't been Gael busting his ass working two jobs while going to drama school. Or it wasn't Gael who ran from audition to audition from the time he was eighteen until he finally caught a break that last year of college. And he didn't owe that break to Manolo; that had been because of… well, that wasn't anything Gael would be rehashing, not if he wanted to show up at his mother's in a better frame of mind. None of it mattered anymore. What did matter was Manolo's high-handedness.

Gael turned to his sister, ignoring the glares she and Manolo were directing at each other and pointed to the stack of screenplays he was supposed to look over. "What project do you think I should do next?"

"Nothing in that pile," Gabi replied, clearly ready for the question. "Gael, you're in a good place in your career. Money and work wise. You *can* afford to take on a passion project, bro." That earned her a sneer from Manolo, which Gabi roundly ignored.

She was in more casual attire today, her usual designer power suits replaced by Gucci sneakers and a track suit—*a Prada track suit*, but nonetheless it was dressing down for her. They may have been twins, but Gabi took more after their mother. She was short and very curvy, while Gael was tall and brawny. He'd inherited his father's bronze skin and green eyes, as well as his height. Gael was well over six feet tall and made sure he stayed in Hollywood Heartthrob shape. It was part of his job to look the part, after all. Like his mother said, if the acting gig hadn't worked out he could've been right at home in an NFL defensive line.

What Gabi lacked in stature, she made up by being a total hardass, and his sister was rarely wrong when it came to the choices that would make his career move in the right direction. Whether Manolo liked it or not, Gabi had an instinct for this stuff.

In the family, they'd always joked that Gabi had been born clutching her planner and with her iPhone to her ear. His little sister worked hard and kept her finger on the pulse of what was happening in the industry. Manolo was more focused on the money side, on the moves that kept the family financially secure. They both loved their jobs, and frankly, their jobs depended on Gael staying employed.

That meant that when it came down to it, he always made the choice that guaranteed him—and all of them—security. That particular approach had cost him dearly through the years, but he was a realist, and when you had people depending on you like he did, you didn't always get what you want. Gael thought he'd made peace with that, but in the last year he'd started losing his drive. Taking every lucrative offer that came along was killing his passion for the craft. He needed something to rekindle the fire he'd always felt for acting. In theory he had everything any Latinx actor at this stage in their career could ask for, and still he felt... dissatisfied.

And yet. There had been a time not too long ago when nothing and no one felt more important than career success. A time where he'd made choices that might've seemed heartless to some in order to stay on the path he'd set for himself.

"Did you hear me, Gael?" His sister's voice snatched him back from his thoughts.

"Sorry, what did you say?"

She sucked her teeth at him for daring to ignore her, but soon was talking excitedly. "Word is Violeta Torrejos just signed on to direct a period series about Francisco Rios and his wife. It's about their time at Harvard."

Gael perked up immediately at the mention of the Puerto Rican freedom fighter who was one of his heroes.

"They're still looking for an actor to play the lead." Gabi smiled knowingly as he sat up in his chair. That last morsel of information jolting him out of the ennui he'd been steeped in a second ago.

"No eso, no. I already told them this part's not right for you and—" Manolo protested, but Gael held his hand up, annoyed that Manolo has passed on a project like that without running it by him first.

"Tio, esperate," he interrupted and turned to his little sister. "Tell me."

Gabi grinned icily at their uncle, then bent her head to scroll on her phone, presumably looking for the information she had on the project. "It's called *The Liberator and His Love.* The showrunner is Pedro Galvañes."

That was a good sign. Galvañes's name attached to a project usually meant there would be a lot of buzz for the show. "They've cast Jasmin Lin Rodriguez as Claudia Mieses," Gabi informed him, eyes still on her phone screen.

Also a good sign, Gael thought—excitement already coursing through him. He knew Jasmin and she didn't sign on to just any project.

Gael leaned back, considering the information his sister had just given him. It was exciting to think about. A series about Francisco Rios, the leader of the Puerto Rican independence movement, was a dream project. The man had led an extraordinary life. He'd graduated from Harvard Law School in 1921—the first Puerto Rican to do so. While studying there he'd met Claudia Mieses, a Peruvian biochemist—and the first Latina to be accepted to Radcliffe College—who was remarkable in her own right. Gael had always thought their love story was a romance for the ages. And that Rios's life story deserved to be told. Being a part of bringing something like *this* to the big screen was more than a dream; it was the kind of opportunity that had drawn him to be an actor in the first place.

"I want it," he said with finality, feeling a buzz of excitement he hadn't felt in months. "Who do we talk to?" he asked. Hell, he'd probably be willing to do the part for free. But his sister frowned at his question, her expression almost reluctant. When he looked at Manolo, Gael noticed the man looked smug. Clearly the other shoe was about to drop.

"The studio producing the series is Sambrano," Gabi

blurted out, as if trying to quiet their uncle before he could get the first word in. No wonder the older man was smiling. What felt like a ball of lead sank through Gael. The skin on his face felt hot. He shouldn't be surprised that the mention of Sambrano still had this effect on him after all these years, but it did.

"Tell him who's in charge of casting, Gabriela." His uncle sounded a little bit too pleased with himself for that nugget to be anything other than the person Gael suspected it was.

Gabi fidgeted, her eyes everywhere but on Gael. "Perla Sambrano's doing the casting."

Unsurprisingly, he felt the blood at his temples at the mere mention of his ex-girlfriend. Perla Sambrano was someone he took pains not to think about.

"She's working for the studios now," Gabi added, pulling him from his thoughts. "She's their new VP of Casting and Talent Acquisitions." His sister's tone was sharp, laced with recrimination. Perla Sambrano had been the reason for the one and only time his twin had stopped speaking to him.

"I don't know if this is the right project," he said, ruthlessly tamping down the pang of discomfort that flashed in his chest. He stared at his sister, expecting her to rehash old arguments. But she just stared at him, disappointment written all over her face, and he knew enough not to take the bait. That conversation was over and done with. He would not apologize for making the choices that had them all sitting in a private jet heading to the ten-million-dollar mansion his money had bought.

"This is not going to work, Gabi," he told his sister, before turning away from her withering glare. He looked at his uncle and felt a surge of irritation at the pleased little smirk on his face. He was not some damn toy for Manolo and Gabi to compete over. "These aren't going to work either," Gael quickly added, gesturing to his uncle's pile of scripts. "Let's keep looking." That made Manolo's smile flag, but he wasn't here to save anyone's feelings. This was his career, and family or not, they worked for him.

Gabi nodded tersely. She opened her mouth as if to say something, but then seemed to let it go. Gael focused on the book he'd been reading on his phone and tried very hard not to think about Perla or the project.

Dwelling on ancient history was not a habit he indulged in.

"You really don't mind doing this?" Perla's older sister asked. Esmeralda's warm smile always seemed to calm her even when she could only see it through the screen of her monitor.

"Of course, I don't mind," Perla said, honestly. She couldn't exactly blame Esmeralda for looking a little doubtful. A year ago, no one, Perla included, would've believed that she'd be ready for a conference call at 7:00 a.m. on a Saturday two days before Christmas, but here she was.

To be fair, a lot had happened in the last twelve months. First, her half sister, Esmeralda, had taken up the helm as president of Sambrano Studios, the television empire their father, Patricio Sambrano, had built. The same television empire everyone expected to be passed to Perla and her brother—Patricio's legitimate children. Instead, the Sambrano patriarch had surprised everyone by expressing his last wish was to see Esmeralda, the child he'd fathered out of wedlock, lead the billion-dollar studios into the future. In the aftermath, Perla had gained a relationship with Esmeralda after years of estrangement.

Unlike her mother and brother, Perla didn't begrudge her sister the position. She'd never wanted that kind of responsibility. In truth, until ten months ago when Esmeralda had reached out to her hoping to mend their relationship, Perla thought she would never set foot in the company's offices again. She'd even sold her shares to make sure she never had to sit in a board meeting for the rest of her life. But Esmeralda's warmth and passion for keeping their family legacy alive had lit a fire under Perla. And now here she was, the new VP of Global Casting and Talent Acquisitions for Sambrano Studios. As her sister said, putting to good use all that fancy schooling their father had paid for.

"Perlita?" Her sister's soothing voice pulled Perla out of her musings, and when she looked at the screen, she saw that Esmeralda's fiancé and the CEO of Sambrano Studios, Rodrigo Almanzar, had joined her. They sat side by side, shoulders and arms pressed together. Completely comfortable with each other. They made quite the power couple, but their chemistry was not reserved just for the boardroom. Esmeralda and Rodrigo were the very definition of soulmates. You only had to see them together to know they were perfect for each other. Even when they had been at each other's throats competing for the top spot at Sambrano, they could not stay away from each other. And even if Perla would never be jealous of what her sister had, she did feel a pang of longing for that kind of connection.

"I'm ready," Perla assured her sister.

"And after this, no more working," Esme chastised, making Perla smile. "We've all been working nonstop."

Perla would never admit it to anyone, but it felt good to finally have this, family who cared about her without making her feel like a child. Family that didn't make her feel expendable.

Her mother, Carmelina, had always been overbearing and the worst kind of helicopter mom. She constantly made Perla feel like she was useless. But Esmeralda treated her like an adult. Like a competent, trustworthy adult capable of taking on responsibilities. And more than that, Esmeralda made Perla feel like her presence mattered, like she valued her opinion.

"Let's get on with this meeting, then." Perla nodded, getting herself in order. They would be doing a virtual conference call with the producer and director of an upcoming series project.

The conversation with the show producers started well, and before she knew it, it was Perla's turn to ask some questions about casting. "Pedro, I know you have such deep connections with some of the best Latinx actors." Perla spoke truthfully. Pedro Galvañes was a legend, and was also infamously vain, which was confirmed when he smiled widely at her compliment.

"We know who we want," Galvañes confirmed. "Violeta has pretty much confirmed Jasmine Lin Rodriguez to play the part of Claudia Mieses."

Perla, Esmeralda and Rodrigo all nodded enthusiastically at that. The Puerto Rican actress was a rising star, especially coming out of her huge success with the Carmen in Charge series.

"That's wonderful. She's perfect for that role." Perla grinned, not even trying to hold back her excitement.

"Yes, she is," Violeta chimed in. "And we need someone who can really hold his own with her. Francisco Rios was such a presence, larger than life. We need an actor that exudes that charisma and power, but who can also play the part of romantic heartthrob. This is a romance after all." She winked, eliciting a smile from Perla and the other faces on the screen.

"Yes, we need a powerhouse to play Mr. Rios," Perla agreed. She'd been reading up on Francisco Rios since Esmeralda announced Sambrano would be making *The Liberator and His Love*. The man was a legend, and they needed an actor with a lot of depth to do him justice.

"Who did you have in mind?" Rodrigo asked, not one to beat around the bush.

"We want Gael Montez," Violeta announced, and Perla's heart skittered in her chest like a caged bird. As if the very mention of the man aggrieved the organ he had so badly battered.

"Montez," Esmeralda said, and Perla could hear her sister's effort to sound neutral. One night after one too many glasses of champagne, Perla had confessed the entire sordid story about her college boyfriend and her first—only, if she was honest—love.

A story she tried extremely hard to never think about, and now it seemed she would be tasked with securing him for a role.

"He's perfect for the part. Strapping like Rios was, and compelling on screen," Pedro said, before Esme could finish what she was about to say. "But we have not been able to get so much as a call back from his people. The man's manager is a real piece of work. He flat-out refused to pass on the script to Montez."

Over the thumping of her heart and rushing of blood

between her temples, Perla was able to process the mention of Manolo Montez, Gael's uncle and manager. She'd never liked Manolo and had always suspected he'd had a hand in how things had ended between her and Gael six years earlier. She wasn't at all surprised to hear he was still running interference. Manolo was never shy about the intensely specific vision he had for Gael's career. And the plan seemed to be very much about keeping Gael's status as the family's golden goose by encouraging him to take whatever role paid the most money.

He was ruthless, too. If Manolo thought this wasn't the right kind of project for Gael, he'd do whatever it took to keep it off his nephew's radar. And the truth was this was a passion project for everyone involved. The hope was that the expected accolades and critical acclaim would be an incentive for the bigger Hollywood names they were attempting to bring on. Manolo would never see it that way.

And Perla should be glad for Manolo's shitty ways because that meant she wouldn't have to deal with Gael. Except the more she thought about it, the more she agreed with Pedro and Violeta's assessment that he was the right actor for the part. What's more, she knew this was the kind of project Gael would've loved to be a part of. In college when he'd been the darling of their college's drama school, this would've been a dream for Gael. Being Puerto Rican, he longed to play the kinds of roles that allowed him to represent his roots, even if he'd decidedly strayed from that as his career took off.

And like the fool she had always been when it came to that man, the words were out of her mouth before she could stop them. "Gael's a friend. I bet I can talk him into taking the part. I'll give him a call."

Esmeralda and Rodrigo's stunned silence was somehow louder than the delighted cheers coming from Pedro and Violeta.

Once the call was done, Perla's pulse was still racing as she reckoned with what she'd done. She'd practically assured them she could secure Gael. She hadn't seen or talked to the man in six years. Since he'd come to her apartment on Christmas Eve and told her he'd finish the last semester of school online because he'd gotten a role in a new show. Then he'd dumped her with the excuse of needing to focus on his career. Even after all this time, she could barely recall the details of what he'd said. The pain of his betrayal still fogged her recollection of that horrible night. She sometimes wished the same fog would blur the two years before that. That she could forget how happy she'd been with him. But the memories of what she'd lost were still intact, and just as insidious as the pain of losing Gael had been.

"You don't have to do this, *hermana*." Esmeralda's uncertain tone shook Perla out of her thoughts. "I'll call Violeta and Pedro myself and tell them they need to go with someone else."

Perla felt queasy and furious at herself for still letting the mere thought of him get to her like that.

God, she could not believe she'd put herself in this situation. But this was just like her, to try to please people, even if it came at the cost of her own peace of mind. Still, this was her job. She oversaw the casting of this project, a show she knew could be the talk of the awards season next year if they cast it well. She wanted them to have the best possible actors, not just for the sake of popularity, but because Francisco Rios deserved to have someone in that role who understood the man they were playing. Who got the size of the shoes they were attempting to fill.

Perla smiled at her sister through the tightness in her throat, trying to express as much gratitude as she could for Esmeralda wanting to make this easier. "It's okay, Esme. I can do this. I shouldn't have said I could talk Gael into taking the role," she admitted. "But I can give him a call." *Or give someone in his camp a call, because I don't know if I can handle hearing his voice. Or maybe I'll just dial up my old college roommate, who I iced out without explanation after her twin brother broke up with me.*

"If you're sure," Esme said, the concern coming through in her voice.

"I am." Perla attempted to infuse her voice with confidence, trying to reassure her sister and herself. "Honestly, it's not a big deal. Gael and I are not super close anymore, but we're not enemies." Friends didn't exactly go six years without speaking a word to each other, but Perla hoped her sister didn't know her well enough to tell she was lying through her teeth.

"Okay," Esme relented, but Perla clearly saw the concern on her sister's face. "But if you change your mind call me." She waved a hand then, her eyes widening as if remembering something important. "Or better yet, you can tell me in person when you're here."

Perla's mouth tugged up at that. Last year had been the worst Christmas of her life—well, the second worst. Her mother and brother had shunned her after she'd gone against them by selling her shares to the studio. The decision had thwarted their plans to destroy her father's legacy, and they'd stopped speaking to her after that. She'd ended up spending the holidays completely alone—in a

Swiss chalet in the Alps, but still, alone. But this year, she was going to Punta Cana with Rodrigo and Esmeralda. Esme's mother and aunties would be there too. Perla had been looking forward to it for months. The idea of being around people who actually wanted her there, with people who liked being around *each other*, made her chest radiate with warmth.

"By the time you wake up tomorrow, I'll be there. I'm taking the jet out of Westchester. We leave at 11:00 p.m." She couldn't wait to be on the beach even though she'd miss the snow. She was a New York girl, after all, and loved seeing a White Christmas morning. But this year the blanket of white would have to come from the sandy beaches of Dominican Republic.

She said her goodbyes and sat there for another minute, considering her options. She didn't know what prospect would be worst, to call and have Manolo send some lackey to rebuff her, or actually get a response from Gael. Just the possibility of hearing his voice made her nauseated. She breathed through the jittery energy that was threatening to overwhelm her. There were no two ways about it, and the more she delayed it the worse she would look when she had to break it to the production team that she had not in fact been able to secure Gael Montez for the project. She grabbed her phone and stared at it for a long moment, considering what to say on the off chance she got ahold of Gael himself. Maybe it wouldn't be that bad? It was business after all. Gael could not begrudge her trying to woo him to the project. It *was* her job. Yeah…it would be fine. She'd call, put forth the offer and hope they accepted.

Maybe if she kept telling herself that, she'd start believing the lie.

She tapped on her phone and the screen came to life with an image of Perla and Esmeralda with their arms around each other at the studio's holiday party just a week earlier. She had to do this. For her sister, and for herself. This was her job now. And dammit, she would do it. Gael would understand that better than anyone; how could *he* judge *her* for putting her job ahead of personal feelings after the way he'd treated her? Still, she couldn't help but send a prayer up asking for a Christmas miracle.

Just as she was about to search in her contacts for Gael's old number, the screen of her phone lit up with a phone number she never thought she would see again.